Also available from JN Welsh and Carina Press

In Tune
In Harmony

Also available from JN Welsh

Before We Say Goodbye
Gigolo All the Way
The Letter—an erotic romance novella
Bittersweet

In Rhythm deals with topics some readers may find difficult, including descriptions of drug use, abuse and recovery.

IN RHYTHM

JN WELSH

Recycling programs for this product may not exist in your area.

ISBN-13: 978-1-335-89589-9

In Rhythm

First published in 2019. This edition published in 2024.

Carina Press
22 Adelaide St. West, 41st Floor
Toronto, Ontario M5H 4E3, Canada
www.CarinaPress.com

Printed in U.S.A.

To all the women on the one and twos showing
up and showing out, pursuing your dreams,
and making music for the niches and the masses.
I see you. You are my inspiration. And to disco,
for without it there would be no dance music.

Chapter One

"Where there is no Temptation there is no victory." Asha "Velvet" Kendall repeated the Italian proverb to herself as she climbed the stairs to the Temptation Festival's minor stage. She scanned the crowd, undulating like a loose-stitched quilt to the electric sounds of Bedazzled Beats. Their sound played through the speakers at one of the Temptation Festival's small stages. The sun beat down on Velvet's brown skin, but this was par for the course. She and her bestie Bonnie "Candy" Fairchild powered through, playing their music with smiles and energy that rivaled Ritalin for every attendee.

Velvet rotated a dial on the controller, layering an echo effect on the song. As the music approached its crescendo, the crowd thickened until the dense group popped like beans on a beating drum. This was what happened when they played. The participants swayed and waved, frantically waiting for the beat to drop. With her hand on her bedazzled headphones, Velvet continued to tease the crowd, and all the while the melody of Candy's song haunted in the background. Just as the anticipation became almost painful, Velvet picked up the mic.

"You ready, LA? Let's go!"

Both she and Candy released their faders and graced

the place with bass. When the heavy beat trembled and the bass covered the crowd, the fans went wild.

Velvet loved these moments. Seeing people enjoy her music encouraged her to grind harder toward her goals. She wouldn't be satisfied until Bedazzled Beats played the main stage as headliners at this festival. The fans had voted them here, like they'd done for every other act. She would do whatever she had to do to get them to vote her and Candy to one of the most coveted spots in their industry.

"Thanks, guys, you've been awesome! We'll see you soon." Velvet whirled and bopped around on the stage, pointing at individual attendees, shooting out hand-formed hearts and mouthing to them. *I see you.*

Candy closed out their set with a remix version of "Be You," their hottest song. The excited cries of the fans echoed through the festival. The words were easy, positive and catchy, and the crowd sang along. If there was anyone there who didn't know who Bedazzled Beats were? They did now.

Velvet gyrated over to Candy, who was entranced by her own set. Velvet draped her arm around her friend's shoulders and couldn't think of a better person to DJ with. Their music styles complemented each other and they both wanted to be the best for the Temptation crowd.

Both she and Candy repeated their farewells into their mics before they unplugged their computers and hurried down the stairs.

Bernard "LED" Royal clapped his hands and pumped his fists. "You were fantastic, babe." He reached for Candy, and puckered for a kiss.

LED turned to Velvet. "Killed it."

Someone handed her and Candy towels and bottled water. "Thanks."

"The crowd was amazing." Backstage, Velvet weaved through festival staff, and passed artists on their way to or decompressing from the stage, and their entourages who hung around.

"Hell, yeah," LED said.

"This chick was fire. I love you, girl." Candy raised her hand and Velvet slapped her high five.

"The way you closed out was epic. I had to hug you to make sure you were real." Velvet laughed.

"The Candy and Velvet love fest is in full swing," LED said and others around them laughed.

"Don't be jelly." Velvet pretended to kiss and make out with Candy.

"You guys are cray." LED had been witness to her and Candy's foolery since they'd been introduced two years ago.

"You know it." Candy patted LED's chest.

Velvet listened as the crowd cheered for the next performer. "I want the main stage. Headlining here would be everything."

"Tall order, but I can see it happening one day. One stage at a time." LED had always been supportive of her and Candy, but Velvet glimpsed a tinge of doubt. She'd gotten versions of that same line every time she announced her aspirations. Though LED's version lacked the level of flat-out amusement and condescending notes as others, it still bugged her.

Velvet didn't have much time to think about it before they glided down the conveyor belt of the festival assembly line. Hired handlers helped them secure their equipment. They stopped for photographers and videographers who snapped photos of their every move. Most of the cameras angled at Candy whose pixie appeal matched the festival standard. They were ushered to press for comments where she and Candy posed for additional pictures as well as ones in their signature face-to-face pose.

"How was your first Temptation experience?" a reporter asked.

"Absolutely awesome," Candy exclaimed. "The crowd gave us pure love."

"We hope the fans vote us back next year. We'd love to play the main stage." Velvet made her campaign for next year official.

"Those are coveted spots. Do you think you have a chance with the famous DJ lineups out there?"

Velvet smiled over her gnashing teeth. "The power is in the hands of the fans. Anything is possible." She raised her hands to the sky and jumped up, her showmanship unwavering. If no one had faith in Bedazzled Beats making it to the main stage, she'd just have to carry the mother lode until they did.

Another reporter jumped in with his question and almost blocked her. "You ladies have been a rocket on the rise. What's next for Bedazzled Beats?"

"Velveteen?" Candy lobbed it over to her.

From the beginning of their career many of the media folks had defaulted to Candy. Her friend's uncontested beauty, posh style and fair-skinned currency gave them what they needed. Access. They played the game when it was in session. Candy lined it up and Velvet hit it out the park. As women they still hit ceilings and walls but since the day they decided to pursue their music career there was no stopping them.

"We'll be doing more festivals and clubs and hope to get started on our album soon," Velvet spoke into the microphone.

"Yeah. We have a lot of great music coming for our fans so stay tuned." Candy pointed into the lens the reporter's camera guy had fixed on them.

"Very cool. If your album is anything like your performance tonight the entire scene will be after your tracks. Any label announcements?"

The reporter highlighted yet another gaping hole in her and Candy's plans. Tommy Boombox, their agent, had lined up a few label meetings but Bedazzled Beats were still label-less.

Candy deferred to her to answer. "We'll have news on that soon so make sure to connect with us on social."

"And sign up to our fan club via our website for Bedazzled Beats merch," Candy added.

They answered more questions and posed for more pictures until the press found another DJ to cover.

They really needed to find a manager and soon. Boombox had gotten them some really great gigs since they'd opened for Luke "The Musical Prophet" Anderson in Los Angeles almost a year ago. They couldn't have dreamed up that type of exposure. Her and Candy's hustle had paid off and now Tommy hustled for them, too. However, with their sights set on the Temptation Festival main stage, they were going to need a lot more help.

They reconnected with LED, and as they made their way backstage to the artist lounge, a member of the press stopped LED.

"I'd love to cover your Egyptian performance tomorrow. Any official press welcomed?"

"I'm sure my manager would love to help you out."

LED communicated his manager's name, all while being a one-man bodyguard clearing the path for her and Candy.

Velvet fanned post-performance heat from her neck, in addition to the bit of envy hovering over her. She and Candy handled the aspects of their career not handled by Boombox and Velvet wished the manager volley that LED had just pulled was part of her repertoire. She reminded herself of the moving train she rode, and that eventually more things would fall into place for her and Candy. *You'll get there.*

"You're going to bring the house down tomorrow at the Egyptian." Velvet nudged LED.

Both Bedazzled Beats and LED were playing the nightclub after the festival closed tomorrow night. Velvet's fingers itched to play again and she had just finished her set with Candy.

"By the way, I have a special guest that's going to blow the roof clear off the spot." LED wrapped his arm around Candy's waist, despite the oval sweat mark on her lower back.

"Yeah? Who?" The cool breeze from the air-conditioning backstage blew against Velvet's scalp of her half Mohawk.

LED pressed his index finger against his lips. "He's going to come through after he does a little press."

"Oh. A secret DJ? Is he performing tonight?" Velvet inquired.

"He performs tomorrow night and then will do the Egyptian with us," LED responded.

"Main stage?"

"Yup."

"Closing out the festival? Wow. Those are all big

guns on the main stage. That can only be Tekko, The Musical Prophet or Tres Armadas."

"I'm excited to see all those guys," Candy cheered.

Joe "Tekko" Kim and Luke were their friends and wouldn't be in town until tomorrow. Velvet looked forward to seeing them play. She hadn't officially met the members of Tres Armadas but she had seen them perform a few years ago. Back then, Velvet played underground clubs spinning vinyl and she and Candy attended festivals as fans researching their future career.

"Guess we'll just have to see who shows up." Velvet strode toward the snack bar, gulped an energy drink, and fed her face with a granola and fruit yogurt cup. Candy participated, as well.

"If you ladies want something more just let them know, but the festival food is tight. Performers eat free," LED informed them.

"We know," Candy mumbled through a cheek full of chips.

"Post-performance hunger is no joke." LED laughed at them as they finished up their snacks. "Well, our performances are done for the day. Now it's all about networking and enjoying the festival."

Music from the ongoing performances played in the club-lit lounge backstage. Neon bars and signs provided shelter from the sun as well as an evening feel. Candy danced around her, yanking Velvet back to the moment. Velvet marched in place and in time to the music. *Damn, I love music.* "I Love Music," by the O'Jays played in her head, engulfed in one of Candy's sexy, groovy house beats. She grabbed Candy's hand, twirling her bestie.

Velvet shared her O'Jays remix and Candy lit up at

the idea to add to their future DJ set. "Let's do it with some underground groove house."

"Now you're talkin'." Velvet's familiarity with those lifted brows and dimpled cheeks spanned back to nights, after college classes, and weekends under the "turntablism" tutelage of their mentor DJ Reynard "FeNom" West. They later became never-ending students of dance music history and culture. The bittersweet memory of their time with the DJ made her pulse flare and Velvet tried to shake it off. They owed it to themselves and their teacher to blow the scene up.

"That's my cue to get you ladies some drinks."

"Thanks, Bernard," Velvet said. She was glad Candy had chosen a less possessive and more fun boyfriend than the last nightmare she'd gone out with. Though pansexual, Candy settled into LED like she'd finally found her emotional and romantic match. LED treated Velvet like a sister and she liked it when they all hung out together.

"Stop calling out my government name, *Asha.* There's beauty in anonymity."

"All right, all right." Velvet pulled a Charms Blow Pop out of a clip she used to attach it to her hair. She unwrapped the lollipop. "Let me just grab Nuts so we can take her with us."

"You and that scooter are inseparable," LED ragged on her.

"You're just upset because you don't have your own wheels to push." Velvet popped the lollipop in her mouth. She enjoyed riding her through the festivals ever since she was an attendee, whether festival policy allowed it or not. Nuts and Blow Pops, her must-haves, went with her wherever she traveled. She left to reclaim her scooter. "Don't do shots without me."

Velvet walked a fair distance to a secure area to retrieve Nuts from one of the attendants backstage. She glided back to her friends and navigated through makeshift corridors, false partitions and moving bodies.

"Great show, Velvet," someone called to her, and she returned the greeting with a wave.

When she returned her eyes forward, she found herself a split second from crashing into some dude walking ahead. His neon rainbow tie-dyed shirt and black and yellow hat blared like a stop sign on a city street. She swerved Nuts to a halt and tapped the ass of her victim with one of her handlebars.

"Ow." He regarded her and her scooter over his shoulder.

"Oh, man. My bad, I wasn't looking." She hopped off and walked Nuts past the wayward fan. The smell of cherries, maybe almonds, or both awakened her senses. She glanced at the shadowed face and more words followed.

"What?" The tone of his question rested between bass and baritone.

Velvet sounded perfectly clear in her head, but forgot she had a big, red ball of hard candy in her mouth. She pulled at the white stick and stepped back. "Sorry. That was negligent driving on my part. You all right?"

"Yes." His response carried an accent she couldn't quite place due to his economy of words. But as far as accents went, he definitely had one.

"Cool." Her shoulders sagged back down to a normal level.

"Be careful with that." Many of her fellow DJs hailed

from the Netherlands and based on the *d* pronunciation of *th* he used, Velvet identified him as Dutch.

She shrugged. "Okay, byeeee." She didn't need a lecture on scooter safety. She pushed off her strong leg, balanced on Nuts and glided to LED and Candy, who were gathered around a high table glowing with blue light. A centerpiece tray of too many shots decorated the middle. Velvet braked and rested Nuts against a chair.

"What is it?" Velvet asked over the thudding music.

"Fireball," LED said and clinked shot glasses with them.

"Blessed be." Candy readied the glass to her lips.

"Ah! He's here. Come here, man. Have this shot with us," LED called to someone behind her and Candy.

Velvet aimed her attention in the direction of LED's head movements. A man emerged from the shadows in a rainbow tie-dyed shirt. He took off his black and yellow hat and raked his fingers through his hair. Velvet's heart stilled. Isaak "Zazzle" Van Sandt of Tres Armadas, the most famous DJ trio in dance music, headed to their table.

Chapter Two

His swag enveloped every step, snaring Velvet in a trance. Her body swayed as Candy wiggled her arm, bumping her out of his spell. Velvet blinked and widened her eyes to regain her bearings.

"Hey, man." Zazzle came over and took a shot glass from LED.

Zazzle's gaze lingered long enough for Velvet to notice and the heat from her center shot up and traveled throughout her entire body.

What the hell? This is the same guy I nearly ran over?

Her novel reaction to him was more than she could endure. Candy again touched her arm. Pulling her attention away from Zazzle's honey brown eyes required a level of difficulty that made Velvet's pits sweat. She fixed her gaze on Candy's brimming smile, which informed her that any poker face she thought she had was a false facade.

"Zaz man, meet Candy and Velvet, the powerhouse ladies murdering the scene right now. Ladies, meet Zazzle from Tres Armadas."

"Pleasure to meet you," Zazzle said to Candy.

Candy waved so fast her hand blurred. "Nice to meet you, too."

Zazzle then turned to Velvet. "You grabbed my ass." He flashed her a smile that somehow discovered a new erogenous zone she didn't even know she had.

"What?" Candy asked.

"I didn't." Velvet's face flamed. "It was an accident—"

"Way to go, Velvet," LED teased her, then addressed Zazzle. "What are you wearing, man?"

"I don't get recognized if I'm not wearing black." Zazzle and the men of Tres Armadas always wore a uniform of signature black in photos and when they performed. Another reason, perhaps, why she hadn't recognized him when she nearly ran him over.

"Where are the rest of the guys?" LED asked.

"They're doing their thing." Zazzle seemed to lack interest in the whereabouts of his bandmates but Velvet had only just met him. Maybe that was his version of *resting bitch face*. "I saw your set earlier on the Sugar Plum stage. It was great," he said.

"*You* saw our set?" Candy's eyes bulged.

"Yeah. I like to scope out the new DJ/producers joining the party." Zazzle's melodic voice lulled her like a magical harpsichord.

"We love your stuff. Right, Velvet?" Candy tried to help her recover.

Velvet still worked to resist getting drawn into the magnetic pull of Zazzle's vibe. *Am I dreaming this up? Did he feel it, too?* "Yeah."

Candy stifled a laugh.

"Since when are you a woman of so few words?" LED frowned at Velvet. "I bet if he asked you about the origins of dance music, you'd have something to say."

Candy elbowed LED in the ribs before raising her brows.

"I'll keep that in mind." Zazzle tipped his hat at her. "Just don't run me over if I disagree with you."

"That would be a mistake." Velvet rejoiced at the return of her voice.

Zazzle raised an eyebrow. "Would it, now?"

"She's like Obi-Wan Kenobi with the history," LED said. "Fuck that. Yoda."

"I study, as well. I'm sure the conversation would be lively." Zazzle cocked his head.

"You have no idea," Candy mumbled.

"And here, I thought we were friends." Velvet shook her head. "I'm not that bad. I mean, I'm good with the history but I think they're exaggerating a bit."

Both Candy and LED burst out laughing.

"Whatever." Velvet waved her hand to dismiss the cackling couple. "I'm high-pitch offended right now."

"Don't be. I'm sure it's a compliment," Zazzle suggested, which only sent Candy and LED into more fits of laughter.

"All right." LED wiped tears from his eyes and collected himself. He passed the shots around. "These shots aren't gonna drink themselves. On three… One. Two. Three."

They all swung back the shots. The alcoholic version of a red fireball jawbreaker candy, that always took forever to suck down to a chewable form, slid down her throat.

"Ow. Hot." Candy stuck out her tongue and fanned her mouth.

With her visual connection to her new heartthrob still intact, Velvet licked her thumb and index finger. "Yum." She coughed a bit from the burning sensation trailing down her esophagus.

Zazzle's eyes followed her like deer tracks. She plugged into every inch of him. He was taller than he appeared in any image she had seen of him. His Oxford blue jeans formed to every inch of his lower body. His dark brown hair was cut to perfection and long enough that he needed to push it out of his face every once in a while for an "I'm so cool" effect. As far as cool was concerned, he had that down pat.

They grabbed some road beers and headed out onto the green grass of the festival grounds. "Time for festival shenanigans." Candy rubbed her hands together. "Are you going to hang out with us for a bit, Zazzle?"

"Sure." Zazzle fixed his hat back on his head. "You guys taking anything?"

Candy twirled her arms above her head. "I'm a high off my performance kinda gal."

"Only once in a blue for me, man. I'm good," LED added.

"That's a no for me." Velvet appreciated that he asked the group instead of assuming that popping or smoking something was required for them to enjoy the festival. "You?"

Zazzle hesitated a moment. "Just thought I'd ask."

LED slapped a too-large straw hat on his head, even though the sun was low. Velvet would normally be yards ahead by now but she walked her scooter slightly behind LED and Candy. Zazzle had her drunk with all sorts of possibilities she couldn't explain. If a few seconds alone was all she had, she'd use the time to catch up.

"C'mon, guys. Troy G is up." LED led them to a viewing spot among a less dense group of dancing fans.

Velvet couldn't help herself and moved her body as she straddled her scooter.

The lights from the massive main stage twinkled with its fairy-tale theme. Gigantic mermaids and coral reefs spanned acres of land with purples and sea blues. Neon colors illuminated various parts of the structure and huge screens highlighted images that either supported the theme or gave attendees in the distance visuals of their favorite artists.

"It's so beautiful," Candy awed when they found a spot to watch the DJ play.

"He's on fire," Velvet said of Troy G who jumped around the stage.

Zazzle stepped in line with her. His warmth penetrated the cooling temperatures left in the wake of the setting sun and caused the hair on her arms to rise. He hadn't touched her yet, a problem soon rectified when his arm rested against hers. She melted.

"Velvet? What do your loved ones call you?" Cinnamon from the Fireball emanated from his breath as he spoke close to her ear.

Her breathing became heavier with each passing second. "Asha."

"Isaak." He pressed his palm against his chest. "You and Candy are really talented. And you seem close."

"We're best friends. There is no one in the world I'd rather be doing this with. You must feel that way about Tres Armadas. You guys are world known."

"Yeah." His tone didn't match his words and her muscles reacted to the change in his body.

"I must sound like a fan." She turned to face him.

"That's not entirely a bad thing." He cleared her five feet five inches, hair included, by about half a foot. Though he wore a hat, the light from the stage and the yellow, orange and red hues of the sky accentuated his strong jaw. His amber gems entranced her and his lips curled. The seductive way his lids lowered to her lips made her lick them in response. She forced herself to study how LED clapped his hands above his head and how Candy pumped her fist in the air.

Lord help me.

Zazzle touched her chin, bringing her gaze back to his. "I have a secret."

Had any buster she just met ever attempted such a bold gesture, he would have been laid out on the ground after she decked him. Such misfortune did not find Zazzle.

"Oh, yeah? What's that?" she asked.

His lower lip disappeared behind his teeth. He released the glistening flesh and Velvet restrained her impulse to press her mouth against his. "I like you."

She'd heard the Dutch were direct. Noted. "I have a secret, too."

"Do tell."

She curled her index finger to draw him near. "I know." *Whew! Thank goodness it wasn't just me.*

He chuckled. "And confident. I like that."

She allowed him to continue to think she had it all together because inside she bloomed like a lily. Though she put on a good face, she all but crapped her black psychedelic pants. Maybe some distance would help.

"I'm glad I can entertain you. Come on, let's watch Troy G." Velvet pulled him with one hand and dragged Nuts with the other. She laid her scooter down and then danced with her friends.

Zazzle joined in close beside her as they circled up and grooved to the electro house beats that pumped through the speakers.

"Hey…" Troy yelled through the microphone.

"Ho!" the crowd yelled back.

"Hip Hop Hooray" by Naughty by Nature rang in her ears. Everything about the scene from its house origins to the call and response between the DJ and the fans dated back to the 1970s. Velvet had learned that during her years of education with DJ FeNom. He belonged up there on the Temptation stage but Velvet knew that would only ever be a dream for her mentor, whose struggles with substance dependency had forced him to make a choice between the scene and sobriety.

Velvet shook it off and focused on the vibrant energy of her friends. They did comedic moves with serious faces and rocked out like springs lined their footwear instead of soles. Zazzle's initial steps were modest but when he let loose he moved with rhythm that rivaled her own, and she'd minored in dance at the College of New York City Nightclubs. He raised his arms and his body bopped like it did when he performed. She couldn't take her eyes off him.

She'd once read an article that compared dancing to language. It explained the movements as the words and rhythm as grammar. Zazzle's communication needed no translation. Whether he knew it or not, he was a performer to his core. She admired that quality. As a DJ, she walked a dual path—one where showmanship entertained large crowds, and the other one that respected the art form and its evolutionary roots. In the end, all she wanted to do was make people happy with her music and move the crowd.

LED and Candy egged Zazzle on, but Velvet saw the hundreds of fans in their vicinity who might recognize the wildest member of Tres Armadas. Velvet yanked his hands down to his sides and pulled him close. Her plan to conceal him came with unexpected side effects as the length of his torso pressed against hers. Zazzle's hands gripped her waist and he danced with her.

"You can't move like that." Velvet tried to focus on his smiling face.

"Like what?" The heat from his mouth grazed her lips and her pulse beat faster than Usain Bolt's hundred-meter sprint.

"Like you're onstage. They're gonna recognize you."

"Then maybe you should do a better job of hiding me." His teeth caught his lower lip again and this time obliterated her resistance.

"I can try." She drew his head toward hers by the brim of his hat until his lips pressed against hers. The music swirled around them and the brightness from the flashing lights sparkled through her closed lids. Their mouths joined in a kiss too tender to be real. Her arms wrapped around his shoulders and his arms tightened around her waist. His rough jeans imprinted against her pelvis. The pressure against her belly forced the air out of her and she opened her mouth to breathe. Zazzle's tongue slipped inside, his taste sweeter than the liquor they shared earlier. He inhaled sharply through his nose and their kiss exploded into wet and wild lips smacking.

Velvet cupped his shoulders. "W-wh…wait. Just give me a sec."

"Too fast?"

"Yes… I mean…no. I don't know." Velvet's senses returned, and her eyes located Candy's beaming face. Velvet stifled her giddiness. She'd just kissed Zazzle from Tres Armadas in public.

"Be right back." Candy dragged Velvet a few feet

away. "Thought you could use a little breather there. I could tell you two liked each other from back at that lounge but damn." Candy wiped imaginary sweat off her brow.

"I don't know. I just… I can't help it. That's crazy, right?"

"Well, Bernard and I hooked up pretty quick."

"It was a couple days, not an hour." Velvet doubted that fact would slow her down.

"Only you can determine if the speed is too fast or just right. Which do you feel?"

"Both." Velvet covered her face.

Candy giggled. "Oh, boy."

"I just met him, but I feel…"

"What?" Candy asked.

Velvet looked at Zazzle, who chatted with LED. "It feels good. Right." When Zazzle kissed her, she never wanted it to end and when he stood close to her, she always wanted him there. Those desires petrified. Feelings with such a potent arrival normally came with a speedy expiration date.

"Fuck it." Candy pumped herself up like she readied to jump out of an airplane and skydive. Velvet's bestie occasionally did this when she feared an outcome but needed a pep talk to get her out of her comfort zone. "Just go. Have fun and get to know him. Don't second-guess it."

"Yeah?" Velvet didn't need to do too much to excite herself. The situation with Zazzle already had her body sizzling with anticipation.

"Live! No regrets." Candy held Velvet by the wrists.

"Yeah," Velvet repeated, this time with more certainty.

Candy yanked her into a side hug and they trudged back to LED and Zazzle.

They continued to enjoy the music and the splendor around them until Troy G's set neared the end.

"We're going to grab something to eat before the next set, you guys want to come?" LED asked.

"I had an early dinner with the guys. I don't mind hanging back or checking out the rest of the festival." Zazzle rested his hand on her lower back.

Velvet fiddled with the beads lining the waistband on her pants. She didn't want to separate from her friends but she didn't want to leave Zazzle either.

"You hungry, Velveteen?" Candy winked.

"Umm…not really—"

"Then why don't you chill with Zazzle, we'll go eat, and bring you back something for later." Candy's suggestion was more a decree.

"Is that cool?" Zazzle tugged her waist.

"Yeah," Velvet said.

"Just text us when you're ready and we'll meet up." LED's mischievous smile accompanied an arched brow.

Velvet stared after LED and Candy's departing figures, their bodies eaten up quickly by the swarm of fans on the grass.

"I don't think they're coming back." Zazzle held a hand out to her. "Want to see what else is going on?"

Velvet peered up at him. Mischief stamped across his forehead in bold caps. She grasped his hand and they jumped from professional acquaintances to festival couple in one gesture.

They perused the festival vending area and investigated the yoga and meditation tents. They received a quickie massage that the masseuse assured them would invigorate and give them longevity.

"Wanna get your face painted? It might help people not recognize you," she teased.

"Pass, but you should go for it," he said.

She side-eyed him. "Just testing your boundaries."

Their hand connection began to sweat and Zazzle transferred her to his opposite side. "There are other ways to test."

Velvet choked on air. "I set myself up for that one, didn't I?"

"If you're lucky, I'll show you." Seductive humor danced at the corners of his mouth.

She scoffed. "You mean if *you're* lucky."

His contagious laughter traveled all the way down to their joined hands. "So what's the story with you and dance music origins? LED and Candy have me interested."

Her shoulders tensed. "Well, let me ask you a question. Where do you think dance music originates?"

"The UK of course, then LA," he answered.

She drew brakes and stared at him. "No, you didn't just say that. I like you, Zazzle, so I'm going to give you a chance to redeem yourself, here. When was dance music born and DJs started to rock parties?"

Zazzle frowned as if he concentrated on retrieving the answer. "The '90s. I'm sure of it."

Velvet let his hand go and crossed her arms. "You're a DJ and you don't know the origins of your craft? Let me take you on a little journey. Dance music started in the form of disco in New York nightclubs in the '70s."

"I disagree. Chicago is where dance music started." His confidence puffed his chest.

"But you just said the UK and LA." Her eyes lowered to slits.

"I was kidding."

"And now?"

"Not kidding."

She swiped her arm through the air between them. "Eh-hem. Still wrong."

He stretched his arms out and his shoulders climbed to his ears. "How am I wrong? House music is clearly dance music."

"That is correct. House music origins start in Chicago but let's be clear, it's one hundred percent linked to New York disco."

"Is it now?"

"Yes! The alienation of disco started with its ties to drug culture, and then was literally trampled on a baseball field when it became obvious that it was created by black and brown gay youth who found a hub of acceptance in nightclubs. July 12, 1979, aka 'The Night Disco Died' at Comiskey Park in Chicago, ring a bell?"

"I heard it in a song once."

She smacked her forehead so hard with her palm she swore she'd see a bruise later.

"But the music today brings people together, no?" he questioned.

"So did disco. That PLUR lifestyle of Peace, Love, Unity and Respect is yet another borrowed and repackaged element of '70s dance culture."

"You can't deny Europe's role in dance music popularity. London and Manchester techno? Acid? Come on."

"Not at all. The UK, in particular, helped dance music grow. People in the US who listened to the sounds coming out of the UK were awed by the music. But where was it coming from?" Velvet gave him an opportunity to respond.

"The US. Chicago and Detroit."

That he knew those details turned her on. "Exactly. DJs like Frankie Knuckles from Chicago, and techno/house DJs like Jeff Mills and Kevin Saunderson from Detroit. Go figure, right? We needed other countries to make our own shit popular again before we embraced it."

"You're an educator. You should do a course on this."

"It's not like you can't look this shit up. It's a matter of interest, not accessibility." Velvet eyed him. "I'm going to give you one more chance to redeem yourself."

"I didn't realize I needed redemption."

She ignored him. "It's an out of genre music question."

"Music is my genre." Zazzle rolled his neck and shoulders like he readied for the fighting ring, and her shoulders bounced mirthfully.

"A real DJ knows this answer." She clapped her hands together. "Ready?"

"Wow. Not harsh at all. Candy and LED did not overexaggerate your…uh…passion."

"They did try to warn you." She shrugged. "Don't let me down, okay?"

He stroked her arm. "I'll try not to."

"Are you trying to distract me?"

A mouthful of teeth sparkled at her. "Is it working?"

"No." She feigned dismissiveness but his touch still haunted. "This is serious."

"Yes, this is serious." He stifled a smile, making him too adorable for his own good.

She rolled her eyes. “You know New York City boroughs, right?”

“Yes. Brooklyn, the Bronx, Queens, Staten Island and Manhattan,” he rattled off. She loved that he used *the* in front of Bronx. It was a New York native move that she appreciated.

“In what New York City borough was hip-hop created?”

“Hmm… Queens?”

She gasped and her lungs stopped functioning altogether.

Zazzle grabbed her by the shoulder. “I’m kidding, I’m kidding. The Bronx.” He jiggled her shoulders and she started breathing again.

Her neck muscles thawed and she pointed up at him. “You almost lost me forever.”

“Then I’m even happier I answered correctly.” His hands slid down her arms to her wrists and he placed her hands around his waist. The action magnetized their bodies. “The last thing I want to do is lose you.”

He captured her lips and her, and her heart pattered. Their tongues touched and she doubted her panties could withstand another kiss from him. He sucked her lower lip and his hand slid to her ass, the motion pressed her against the hardness forming below his pelvis.

“Zazzle.” She mumbled against his lips. “We’re in the middle of the festival.”

“I can’t explain this, Velvet.”

“Me either.”

“And… I’m not sure I need to. I just don’t want to miss it.” His amber orbs shined like the sun hitting a jar of honey.

She pulled away and tried to think of the right words to say.

"Not so fast." He hauled her back to him. "What are you doing later?"

"Unless it's performance-related, we don't plan that far ahead," she teased.

"Come back to my place."

If he thought she was that easy, he was absolutely right. At least this time. She wasn't in the habit of banging dudes she just met but she struggled to summon the morals required for the present situation.

"I don't sleep around."

"I'm not asking you to sleep around. Just with me."

His suggestion tempted her to shimmy out of her iridescent rhinestone chainmail halter top but she opted to stick with option number one: keep clothes on.

"And you? Am I just another addition to your playlist?"

"I don't have a playlist except the one I want to make with you, tonight." He tapped her lips with a brief kiss. "Come with me."

"But Candy—"

"She'll understand. Plus I'm sure she and LED could use some alone time. Don't you think?"

"The festival has some great performers—"

"No one, I'm sure, you haven't seen play before. Plus you have a full lineup tomorrow including us." He pecked her chin. "Say you'll come."

Her fear had her creating obstacles and excuses that couldn't hold up against what she truly wanted.

"Yes. I'll go with you."

Chapter Three

Zazzle's mussed hair and Velvet's disheveled clothes indicated they had a problem keeping their hands to themselves. His scent stuck to her like the glitter from the design the face paint lady had drawn on her shoulder. Velvet huffed air like she had done cardio by the time the car stopped on the short ride to his place. Time jetted past them and she wanted to savor every second with him.

Zazzle's accommodations reaffirmed to Velvet how big-time he was and just how low-time Bedazzled Beats were in comparison. The three-floor rental complete with viewing deck conflicted with their carefree time at the festival.

"Are you kidding me?" She rested her scooter at the entrance and spun through the open floor plan with its luxury, contemporary furnishings. Her head tilted back as she stared up at the glass skylight that appeared to replace the roof. The bright lights in the house blinded.

The place came with amenities like the three-foot-tall gift basket that lay on an asymmetrical glass coffee table in the middle of the living area, untouched.

He zoomed around the island and through the open kitchen. "Can I get you something to drink? Beer?

Wine? I'm pretty sure they have everything. I can make you a cocktail."

Velvet stilled her movements for them both. "Beer's fine." Whether she kissed him like she'd never stop or needed a breather from the quantum speed their relationship leapt, he adjusted to whatever pace she threw at him.

Spending time with Zazzle had allowed her to get lost in him to the point where she forgot what being Zazzle from Tres Armadas meant for him beyond the festival grounds. She'd seen fans lose their minds and their shirts when he danced onstage. That Tres Armadas not only played one of Temptation's most coveted time slots, but would also close out the festival tomorrow night, stamped the trio with approval from the fans who'd voted them there. The regal digs surrounding her, and Tres Armadas's popularity, certified his celebrity.

Velvet dreamed of one day holding that spot. One goal at a time, she reminded herself. *I'm going to get there.* "Are you psyched to play tomorrow?"

He rummaged through a refrigerator and produced two bottles of beer. "We've played the festival for several years now and you would think it's no longer fun. That there's no magic, no thrill, but it's still amazing to close out the event."

"I'd give my left eyeball to play the main stage." Her internal declaration made it past her lips.

His eyebrows knitted.

"Too much?"

He pinched his index finger and thumb together. "You don't have to give up an eyeball. You just have to work hard. I've been at this for a while and all the fans want is good music. They want to see you give it your all and know that you love the music as much as they do. I've seen you perform and your vinyl set was fucking phenomenal. I'm sure that's why the fans voted you here."

Her eyes bulged. "You've seen my vinyl set? When?"

"When you were getting a massage in the yoga tent." He casually handed her a beer.

"Oh." Her cheeks warmed. She loved playing records with all their perfect imperfections. She could rock a party the new-fashioned way and the old-fashioned way, but still cherished and nurtured her vinyl skills, even in the technological realm of the current dance music scene.

"Just keep doing what you're doing..." He swigged his beer. "Times ten."

Her forehead wrinkled. "Times ten?"

"More if you can handle it. A good manager can help you push, but you have to go for it. Leave the crowd wanting more. Make them call for encores so they remember your name. They'll chant it later and the effect will multiply. The more fans who see Bedazzled Beats perform, the more fans who have the power to vote for you."

Velvet mentally jotted down everything he said, some of which she and Candy were already working on. "Thanks for the tips."

"Anytime." He guzzled his beer, finishing it in one shot.

Did he have nerves like she did? She guzzled her own beer and held the sweating bottle so tightly she thought it might slip through her fingers. She positioned herself at the window and saw him approach in the reflection of the glass.

"This is nice." She faced him and her head referenced the house.

"I only arrived this morning so I haven't been here much with press and other engagements or it might not be so nice," he admitted.

"Wild parties, huh?"

"Sometimes."

"You're hot and famous. Of course you'd party." She omitted "with women" from her inquiry.

"You think I'm hot?" He grinned.

"I didn't say—"

"Yes, you said." He placed one hand on her hip.

Velvet grabbed his hand. "Come on." They ran up the stairs until they reached the top. Her contracting lungs craved air. It wasn't her house but she found the glass partition that led outdoors. She unlocked it and stepped onto the viewing deck with Zazzle close behind her.

The other houses were further away than she realized, and from the height of the viewing deck she could see the festival lights. A cream-colored patio daybed with retractable canopy and complete with throw pillows rested in the corner.

Velvet sat down on it and tested the stability of the elastic rattan and steel frame. She grinned. "Convenient."

He scratched his head. "I didn't put it there. I promise."

"Too bad."

"In that case, it was my idea," he cheesed.

She strolled over to the railing and looked out at the expanse of land around them. A large dimly lit concrete circle sat a fair distance away from the house but remained part of the property's lawn. Symmetrical lines formed an *H* in the middle. "Is that a helipad?" She pointed to it and looked to him for confirmation.

"Yes."

"You have a helicopter?"

The breeze fluttered his hair. "No, but one will take us to the Egyptian tomorrow night after our festival set, and then to my house in the LA area."

"We're flying after the festival, too, but we're sharing a ride with LED and all our stuff." Velvet thought the convenience of his life must be nice but again his celebrity infiltrated their regular moments. "If your house in LA accommodates a helicopter, like this one, then you can officially call it property. It must be massive."

"If taking you to my place tonight by helicopter will impress you, I can arrange it."

"Umm, no thanks." Not that she didn't have the capacity to enjoy the lifestyle perks of the rich and famous, but she much preferred their no-frills vibe. She squinted to make out the San Gabriel Mountains against the towns adjacent to San Bernardino. The lights from the giant Ferris wheel and light show from the main stage electrified against the darkened landscapes.

"You can see it all from here. Amazing," she awed. His arms circled her from behind. She closed her eyes and sank into Zazzle's heat.

"You're amazing." He planted a kiss on her neck and turned her to him. "I've only known you for a little bit but I've never met anyone like you, Asha."

"You're just saying that. There are billions of women in the world. I can name dozens of truly amazing ones."

He jiggled her chin. "Woman, I'm complimenting you. Let me."

Nervous laughter escaped her lips. "Sorry. Try it again."

He smiled. "You're so vibrant. Like the music you play. Like your passion for dance music. It's life itself. I feel it."

She stroked his cheek. "I feel the same way about you, Isaak."

"I want you, Asha. Is that all right with you?"

She put her arms around his neck and pulled him to her. "That's more than all right with me, Zazzle." She locked lips with him, and welcomed the taste of him again.

"I'm not Zazzle. Here with you, I'm Isaak." His mouth mushed her lips. His hand glided up and over her belly to massage her breasts.

"Isaak," she moaned.

"Yes." He undid the tie on her halter top and as his eyes roved over her exposed body, she shivered.

He yanked her pants down and she wiggled out of them, her black polka-dot underwear the only barrier to nudity. She tugged his shirt up until she freed him from the rainbow-colored garment. His inkless skin was lighter than the kisses the sun left on his face and her palms smoothed the soft muscle definition of his chest and abs.

His staccato breath mimicked hers. "Here?" His eyes searched the grounds.

She kissed over his chest and up to his lips. "Yes. Here." Her hands found his neck and played with his hair as she tugged him to the patio daybed. She released him to scoot onto the cushion, watching him as he unbuttoned his jeans and pushed them down and off with his underwear. The dark deck shadowed his erection, yet it still commanded her attention. She slid her panties off and flung them aside while he retrieved a condom from his jeans. The Temptation Festival logo glowed on the black wrapper.

"I didn't know they glowed." She plucked the condom from him.

He chuckled and his hardening cock bounced. "I wanted to keep this one for my collection, but right now, all I want is you."

"Collection?"

"Yes, I collect condoms. The cooler the better. Like this one," he said.

"Sorry, but we need you," she said to the condom. Zazzle's melodic laughter made her swoon. She tore open the wrapper and passed the rolled rubber to him. She used her inner calves to caress up the length of his leg while he sheathed himself.

His body descended over her figure and he moved with her like he'd done in various ways since she met him. Their rhythm had been in sync and their connection unbroken even when they disagreed. Now as he captured her mouth, and his skilled tongue explored with familiarity, she wanted to steep out every drop of goodness from what blossomed between them.

"Isaak?" She sank back into the cushions and his upper body blanketed her while the lower half of his body nestled between her limbs.

"Yeah, baby."

"Is this real?"

He nodded. "Yes, *schatje.* This is real." He consumed her mouth.

The word he used felt good. She didn't know what the word meant and she didn't care to ask. All she knew was that Isaak injected himself into her bloodstream and she was infected with him to her core.

He kissed her deep and for long torturous minutes. Steadying himself on his forearm, he slid one hand between their legs. His fingers glided over her skin until he cleared a path to her clit. Her back arched and when she moaned, his tongue plunged deeper into her mouth. She swallowed the taste of him and pawed his shoulders.

"Shit! You're so wet for me, baby." He stayed there, stroking her, watching her. If he didn't stop, she'd explode.

She pulled his hand away. "I don't want to come yet. I want to come with you inside me."

Desire splayed on his features. "I should do more."

Damn, he is fucking adorable. "This is more, Isaak. Having you inside me, fucking me, *is* more." She squeezed him closer.

"I want you this way, too, Asha." Devouring her mouth again, he maneuvered his cock to her center and the pressure of his tip rubbing against her clit made her hips lift to meet the touch. Her hands grasped at the pillows behind her and she dug her nails into the fluff.

"Hold me," he rasped. "I want to feel you all over me."

She did as he commanded with enthusiasm. He positioned his cock at her entrance and filled her to capacity.

"Isaak. Fuck," she moaned. "Fuck, you feel…" She lost herself in pleasure with him.

"So good, baby." He groaned as he moved within her. His hips lunged with determination and she received each thrust with force of her own. Her insides cried for more and tingled as he plunged deeper and in rhythm with her. Their eyes locked as the growing storm that swelled inside her grew inside him, too. She tipped her hips up to help him reach her G-spot and his increased momentum delivered sensations that continued to balloon within her. She caressed the sides of his torso and her nails raked over his now-perspiring back. Not even the cool night breeze, kissing them both, tempered the passion building between them. She gripped his pounding hips and jerked him to her.

"Isaak," she called and locked her arms around him like shark jaws. Every inch of her trembled and exploded at her orgasm's brilliant arrival.

She blinked at the stars dazzling her vision. *Don't black out. Hold him. Stay with him.* She panted into the crook of his neck and her iron legs clamped around him in a full-body grip. His short pumps sent shock waves through her. His pelvis moved down tempo and an image of him dancing flashed in her mind. The rhythmic lunges continued until he erupted. The heat of his arrival scorched her internal walls through the latex like hot syrup. Her muscles contracted around his shaft.

He rolled them onto their sides and wrapped his arms and legs around her, keeping them connected like two puzzle pieces. He kissed her hair, her temple, her cheek and one eyelid until she lifted her face so he could kiss her lips.

"That was fucking unbelievable," he mumbled.

She smacked her mouth against his and then cuddled into him. She could feel his pounding heart against her breasts. "Mmm-hmm."

"Are you cold?" he asked when her body quivered.

"That's all you," she giggled.

That drew a laugh from him that vibrated down her form. "I should get you inside to a warm bed."

"No." She whined and held him tighter. "The sun will come up in a little bit. Let's stay up and watch it."

Her stomach growled.

"You're hungry."

"Then feed me." She bit his arm. "Before I eat you."

"You have to let me go, baby."

She did with reluctance. He held on to his condom-covered cock and slowly withdrew. A vacancy sign hung on her pussy in neon lights.

He pulled a throw that rested on the side of the day-bed and draped it over her. "I shall return."

She stared at the stars. Since the moment they met, whether right or wrong, she'd known she would end up in his bed. Collecting her feelings felt like catching dandelion seeds blowing in the wind. That didn't stop reality from descending on her. What did all this mean? Had they gone too fast? She knew him on another level but what did she really know about him? How did he feel? Was she just his festival bang?

"You okay?" Zazzle's soft question interrupted her downward spiral. He brought a tray of snacks on a dark wood tray and a six-pack of bottled beer in the other.

"Just thinking."

He sat down and placed the tray between them. "About me?"

She nodded. "About all of this." She examined the cheese crackers and fruit that were on the tray. "You're so European."

"You're funny, you know that?"

"So I've been told. It normally takes a while but I guess..." She stuffed her mouth to temper her response. "I'm comfortable with you."

He stroked her cheek. "I'm comfortable with you, too."

"Doesn't that scare you?" Obviously, she hadn't stuffed her mouth enough.

"Yes and no. I try not to attempt to explain what I can't. I like being with you. It's enough for now."

"I should try to adopt your philosophy. It's mad healthy."

He laughed again. She liked that she could make him laugh so easily. He snuggled under the blanket with her and put his arm around her shoulder. They ate in silence for a bit.

Zazzle adjusted the retractable canopy to cover them. "Do you think we'll make it till the sun comes up?" A DJ's biggest commodity was time. Between creating, traveling, press and performing, they got little sleep, him less than her as part of a high-in-demand trio. That either of them lasted this long, after a few hours of festival romping, was a testament to how much they liked each other and valued this time together.

She yawned. "Of course," she lied.

He leaned his head against hers and a soft moan escaped her lips. She focused on this present moment, enveloped in his warm body, and committed it to memory. She was exactly where she wanted to be. With him.

Chapter Four

Velvet leaned against the glass doorframe, peering at Zazzle's sleeping figure. The blanket covered his pelvis but his sprawled-out limbs covered the daybed. She longed to be under him again and licked her lower lip as she watched him. She didn't want to leave but she needed to create some space between them. From the moment she'd tapped his ass with Nuts he'd become her only focus. Last night at the festival, and here at his rental house, had been out of this world but she had press appointments and the other half of Bedazzled Beats to consider before they performed tonight at the Egyptian with LED. Her stomach flipped as she squatted down next to the daybed and shook him awake.

"*Goedemorgen.*" Zazzle stretched, and his eyes gave her dressed figure the up and down. He sat up. "You're leaving?"

"My car will be here in—" she checked her phone "—three minutes."

He reached for her. "Stay."

"I really want to, but I can't. Candy's been blowing up my phone since last night. We have to work. You do, too. You're performing twice tonight, remember?" Her weak explanation insulted their festival night together.

He groaned.

"I had the best time with you, Isaak, but I really do have to go." She ran her hand through his silky, messy hair.

He pulled her to him and held her like he never wanted to let her go. "I don't want this to end. I'm myself here with you...without..."

His tone awakened concern in the middle of her chest. She pulled away enough to study his face. "What's up?"

He caressed her cheek with his thumb. "It's nothing." His weak smile synched her heart.

"You sure?" She didn't believe him but they'd known each other for less than twenty-four hours. Maybe she overreacted given their speedy romance.

"Yes." He stood and tugged on his jeans. "I'll walk you out."

They jogged down the stairs hand in hand. He dragged Nuts for her and put her and her scooter in the waiting car.

"I'll see you later." She offered him a smile but it wavered.

"Yes, later." He held on to her a moment longer. His parting kiss bruised her lips and sadness welled in her throat. He closed the door and her car pulled off, leaving Zazzle and their magical night together in her rearview.

"Velveteen, I said go for it, not ghost me and LED for the rest of the night," Candy complained as she packed to make their late checkout time.

"I know. It just kind of happened," Velvet said. At least Candy had allowed her to wash the sex off with a quick shower before she really went after her. A lot had happened and Velvet worked to keep it in perspective while her emotions were ready to race ahead.

They had to drop their bags off at the concierge desk and then jet over to meet with music bloggers, journalists and vloggers, so they dressed in day-to-night outfits.

"Now, tell me everything."

Velvet told Candy most everything that happened, but kept some of the events of the night to herself.

"It's so unlike you to have a one-night stand, but he *is* the most popular member of Tres Armadas." Candy eyed her. "Unless, you don't think it will end up being a one-night stand, after all."

"I don't know. It's different with him. Yeah, everything happened fast but I wanted it to. I think he might feel the same." The events of the night swirled in Velvet's head, the last image of him saying goodbye. "I know he does. Leaving this morning…it was like leaving a piece of molten chocolate cake on a plate and you know how much I love those things."

"Yeah, I do. You almost forked my hand one time when you weren't in a sharing mood." Candy frowned as if feeling a fork stab her skin. "Love, huh?" Candy fluttered her eyebrows.

"You know what I mean." Velvet rolled her eyes as she yanked up her black patent-leather leggings and wrestled into a black-and-white-checkered halter. She worked on her hair next. "I just… I don't know him. We talked and stuff, but can you really know someone in such a short time?"

"Maybe not one hundred percent, but I think you can know whether or not you want to spend more time getting to know him. Sometimes that's a couple months, sometimes it's a lifetime."

"Look at you, all guru and shit." Velvet finished making up her face and then hugged her friend's shoulders.

"I'm serious. Bernard and I are pretty inseparable and have been since the day we met."

Velvet had a front-row seat to the LED and Candy romance fest. Ever since they met a year ago they made a long-distance romance work.

"I think you two are a special case," Velvet said. "Anyway, did you guys have fun last night?"

"Yeah. We always do." Candy smiled and Velvet only imagined what brought on that spread across Candy's face. "I missed you, though."

"Aww." Velvet kissed her cheek. "Well, you'll be with me all day. We have interviews and need to work on some songs before we catch Tekko, Luke and Tres Armadas tonight. Then we have to fly to the Egyptian for our club performance with LED. This is super cute, by the way." Velvet motioned to Candy's white '60s two-piece dress with the face of her favorite hip-hop artist dotted all over the garment. She wore black knee-high socks and white high-top platform sneakers.

"Thanks." Candy modeled her outfit. "You, too."

"I know." Velvet winked.

"Loser." Candy formed an *L* with her hand and placed it on her forehead. "I'm so excited. Sucks that we won't get a chance to hang out with Tekko or really meet Luke."

"They're bigger than us, babe. Tekko's off to Manila after he performs and Luke goes to Singapore. They have to fly out right after their performances. We'll see them again soon," Velvet assured her friend. Bedazzled Beats still had a few months of gigs left before they'd take some time off to work on their album, even if they didn't have a manager or hadn't settled on a label yet. They needed to focus on their own shit so they could be in high demand like the DJs they admired.

"It's still going to be a great night." Candy clapped her hands.

"Hell yeah." Velvet had left Zazzle only an hour ago, and she brimmed with excitement for the end of the festival just so she could see him and Tres Armadas close out the show. "The best night," Velvet confirmed.

"The trio is back together again." LED slapped his hands to Velvet's in a VIP viewing section close to the stage. "You ready for Tres Armadas?"

"Where have you been all day?"

"I have my own career shit to do. I'm not just here to pal around, Miss Kendall."

"That's true." She tapped her chin. "We owe your management a big thanks for the 'copter ride, later."

"We're both performing so it's nothing." LED, the master of shrugs, shrugged and then hooked his arm around Candy to kiss the top of her head. "Right, babe?"

"Yeah, yeah."

"They're on," LED said, and the light show began. The darkness of midnight and its twinkling stars were the perfect backdrop for the fairy-tale theme and laser light show that scattered over acres of land. Attendees on the packed field waved flags from their countries, cheered and reached their hands for the stage. The screams swelled like one voice.

Velvet could see the members of Tres Armadas congregating at the bottom of the staircase that led up to the stage as their intro played, and the electricity of the performance spanned miles. She identified Zazzle and her stomach dropped like she rode a roller coaster. The men were dressed in signature black short-sleeved shirts and black jeans.

Velvet cheered like a fan. As her lungs filled to scream for him, someone passed him something and he popped it into his mouth. He swigged it back with sports drink, the translucent yellow liquid swished wildly in the bottle. She froze, she didn't know what he took and negotiated with herself all the things that it could be. Vitamins, ibuprofen. Caffeine. She chewed the inside of her lip. *Don't jump to conclusions. It can be anything.* When the other members of Tres Armadas approached Zazzle, and they argued, her concern surfaced.

"What the hell is this?" she mumbled to herself. She glanced over at Candy.

Her friend clapped her hands and cheered, but grimaced at the sight of the trio in discord. "Maybe an off night?"

Christian Saaks, one of the members, shoved Zazzle and back and forth they went. The third member of the group, Maartin Blas, separated the two and after saying a few words marched angrily to the dials. The crowd cheered when the trio appeared onstage. Zazzle and Christian followed.

The three men clapped their hands above their heads and amped up the sea of fans. They played as a cohesive group. Perhaps all she'd witnessed was a squabble among long-time bandmates. She danced with her friends and when Zazzle jumped up onto the area around the DJ table, and the fans moved with him as he danced from end to end, his otherworldly energy amazed. He continued to dance until he had to get on the dials and play with the other members of Tres Armadas but soon he hopped back up and gave a dance show for the fans. He jumped so close to the edge, and she gasped when he balanced himself back. His chest heaved and sweat poured from him, but he didn't seem to notice.

"We have to go," LED said. "We'll catch up with Zaz at the club."

"Will the other members of the group be there?" Candy asked.

"Nah, just Zaz. He's my surprise guest. It's gonna be lit. Let's be out, kids." LED started his exit.

As Velvet followed him she craned her neck back toward the stage. "It's already lit."

During the helicopter ride to get to the Egyptian, the images of Zazzle, from the backstage altercation to his onstage antics, traipsed through her mind. Her history with her mentor, DJ FeNom, made her susceptible to seeing what might not be there. FeNom loaded up on stimulants and played one too many gigs so high that she didn't know how he'd even gotten through it. Even when they'd argued, and she'd pleaded with him to get help, it fell on deaf ears. One time she had to get onstage and help him like a planned mentor and mentee part of his show. But Zazzle wasn't FeNom.

That fact didn't stop her from skimming through the moments of her time with Zazzle for clues that something might be off. Candy noticed her pensive mood and poked her arm, but their protective earmuffs were off comms for their half-hour trip to LA. Many of her questions wouldn't be answered until she saw Zazzle again. She distracted her mind with music and ran through the tracks she and Candy planned to play tonight.

A few hours after leaving the festival grounds, they rolled up to the Egyptian, the hottest dance music spot in downtown Los Angeles. Velvet glided through the backdoor entrance, still amped from their earlier performance. Candy walked close by, flanked by a combination of security and promoters for their *friendtourage*. Music filled the rooms of the club inside, and the walls vibrated powerful bass.

"You're on, ladies," someone called.

Velvet appreciated that she had little time to overthink things. Candy dragged her toward the stage, and they played for the club. Their performance enlivened her and put her in a better place when she looked out into the faces of club-goers who filled the venue.

"Whoo," Velvet yelled when she got offstage. The adrenaline ran through her and she wiped sweat from her forehead.

"How the hell am I going to follow that?" LED winked at her and Candy.

LED was very popular and could bring the house down with his original trance mixes. "Give them that hypnotic shit, babe." Candy pushed him to the stage before she moved closer and then planted herself in view to watch him perform.

Velvet laughed. "Make us proud, boo." She pressed her middle finger and thumb against her tongue and a whistle cracked through the loud music.

Zazzle arrived a few minutes into LED's performance with a few people and mingled backstage. The group he traveled with entertained themselves with bottle service, and their partying spirit magnified the already hopping nightclub. Their energetic banter and laughs rose above the music.

"Hey." Zazzle darted to Velvet as if he'd drank two cans of Red Bull. He raked a hand through his hair and moved a lot in his personal space.

"Hey." She slowed everything from her speech to her racing heart.

"I missed you today, baby. You look fucking hot. I'm going onstage. You're watching right? I can't wait to get on the dials. We hooking up later?" He sniffled and rubbed his nose. He threw a lot at her and she grappled with pinpointing one thing he said to respond to.

What the shit? The way he jumped topics and struggled to be still concerned her. "You okay?"

"Yeah, baby, yeah," he said and rubbed his hands up and down her arm like he tried to start a fire.

She peered into his eyes and they were so dilated she hardly saw the amber color. "Are you sure?"

He frowned. "What do you mean? I tell you that I miss you and you ask me if I'm okay?"

Velvet bit down on the inside of her lip. His level eight response to her level two question shifted her brain into evaluation mode. "It's just…you seem… I don't know. Restless."

"I'm fine. Let's do a shot." He called one of his friends over. He'd already slung back a few with his entourage.

"I'm good," Velvet said, and worked on not freaking out and justifying his behavior.

"Come on, baby. Do one with me."

She inched away from him. "No, really. I'm Gucci."

"What the fuck?" he cursed.

She glowered at him and checked off her mental list of symptoms she'd used when her mentor had gone on a bender. Reynard's dependency on drugs had turned to abuse, ruined his career and crumpled his dreams. As she watched Zazzle all alarms blared.

"You're high," she stated.

"What if I am?" His grimace softened as if a moment of clarity opened through the cloud of his high. "I—"

His move to touch never quite made it to her skin as LED announced him.

Zazzle approached the stage and one of his friends came up to him and not at all covertly handed him something small and white.

"It's Zazzle time," the man said.

He popped a pill in his mouth and followed it up with two more shots of alcohol. He jumped up and down before running onstage.

"Whoa." Velvet shifted in her stance and her stomach hollowed. Sure, some people in the scene and their fans may have indulged in whatever lifted them off the ground. She and Candy were no saints themselves and drank with their friends, but this screamed old hat and ritualistic.

She couldn't shake the feeling that it was only the beginning. She hugged herself and her heart sank.

"Oh, no. Not again."

Zazzle's performance with LED did indeed tear the roof off the Egyptian. When Zazzle came offstage, his soaked black tee shirt clung to his torso from shoulder to navel. Whatever he ingested before he went onstage made him shakier than if he'd gotten tazed. He made his way over to someone else in his entourage. He took bumps of white powder off his hand and gave the people around him high fives all the while continuing to drink. Velvet's mouth caught flies at the indulgence.

He finally saw her again and staggered over. "You comin' to my place later?"

"Umm… I don't think so. It looks like you already have company." She nodded at his suppliers behind him.

"What? We're just having a little fun."

Velvet had heard that same line so many times it was tattooed on her cranium. She couldn't afford to fall into this kind of chaos again.

"Yeah. Well, that's not my scene, so…" She wanted to take it back and tell him she'd go with him and that they'd fix this together, but how could she? He didn't even know he had a problem. All he knew was that she wasn't interested in his kind of fun.

"So, that's it? You're going to ignore this…between us?"

Don't back down. You know where this road leads. "Something else has your attention and I don't compete with that."

LED bounced over before Zazzle could respond. He separated from her a bit.

"We totally brought the house down." LED turned to Zazzle and hugged him. "Thanks for showing up, man. The crowd wigged when they saw you."

"It was fucking amazing, man." Zazzle swallowed his words and LED eyed him.

"You wasted already, man?" LED asked and handed him a water bottle. "You got all night."

LED looked at her and his features softened with sympathy.

People joined in on the night's excitement.

"Let's party," Zazzle announced, raising an arm to the ceiling.

She staggered back, and gave him room to be "Mr. Here's Where the Party's At."

Disappointment crept into her shoulders, bringing down the joys of the weekend, and all because she fell for a beautiful man with a gorgeous smile and addiction issues.

Candy's belt and bracelets jingled louder the closer she got. "He sure is going hard. I never would have expected..." She stopped and put her arm around Velvet's shoulder. "Uh oh, Velveteen Rabbit. You've already walked down the aisle, had kids and ordered furniture for your white-picket-fenced house with posies on the front lawn."

Velvet leaned her head against her friend's. "This is bad, Candy Cane. Really, really bad."

Chapter Five

Six Months Later

In a few hours Velvet would be officially homeless. The lease on their loner house from their record label, Sticky Sweet Recordings, terminated this month, and so did the time left to complete their album. Despite the simultaneous demands of a heavy travel and performance schedule, she and her bestie, Candy, had managed to lay down all but one track for their forthcoming debut album. They had a final song to work on with their elusive *friendtourage*, but with festival season about to swing into full gear, they'd pleaded with their label for more time, to no avail.

As Velvet pushed the last packed box toward the door, with all the other boxes going to storage, sadness pinched her heart. She and Candy had had fun in the Santa Monica home, celebrating some pivotal moments in their career here. They had become Wallace Entertainment artists in this house, and had dinner with manager Sonny Lopez out on the veranda, vomiting all their dreams and goals at the woman. Soon after Sonny, with her years of experience in the business, became their manager. Velvet and Candy had no doubt she'd work to make their visions a reality.

Now as they headed out on a calendar full of performance dates, Velvet wondered how long it would be before they were finally on their album tour. Planning a tour took months and their team worked hard to organize such a big undertaking, but she longed for solid go dates. For the next three months, Velvet and Candy would be living out of tour busses and hotels, performing their singles and mixing music by other artists. In addition to those worries, she didn't have any new digs to call her own and the feeling of displacement unsettled her bones.

Velvet's younger brother, Trevor, entered the living room and regarded the pile of boxes, assessing the load. He'd rescheduled his bro-cation with some friends to help move her and Candy's stuff into storage until they could figure out their apartment situation. His reward? Trevor and his friends had a free place to stay before they headed to Las Vegas.

Velvet handed the keys over to her brother. "Don't fuck my shit up."

"Chill, sis. I got you and Candy," Trevor said. "Excuse me, I mean, Velvet."

She had been DJing with the stage name since she was seventeen. At twenty-five her brother still mocked her every once in a while. What else was a kid brother good for if not to be annoying?

"Ha ha. Look, you've got one job. Don't jack it up."

Trevor rolled his eyes and kept it moving.

Candy entered with two wheeled suitcases trailing her hunched figure. Beads of sweat wet the blond and pink hair on her temples. "I'm so done with packing, you guys."

"Same." Velvet nodded over to the boxes. Out of the two of them Candy had the most stuff to pack. The Posh Spice of Bedazzled Beats had accumulated quite a bit while in LA. "I see your wardrobe is following us across the pond."

Candy's face had "duh" written all over it. She dropped the suitcases, stood beside her and draped an arm over her shoulder. "Nuts and Blow Pops all packed, Velveteen?"

"Never leave home without 'em." Velvet always packed her travel staples first—her scooter, Nuts, and a wholesale-size box of Charms Blow Pops.

"I'm gonna miss this place. We did good work here. I know we're not done yet but kudos to us for kind of meeting our goal," Candy said.

"Yeah. The single is doing well and I'm so proud of this album. I just hope it gets us the buzz we need to headline Temptation," Velvet responded.

The Temptation Festival wasn't like other festivals. The fans voted for who they wanted to headline. First up was the qualifying round. The artists could be club DJs or the big names. Sixty artists with the highest mentions get on the bill to play. Out of those sixty artists, only the top thirty-three artists move to the final main-stage voting round.

"I want it for us, too," Candy said. "That's why we're getting out there. The qualifying voting round is coming up. We may not have our own tour yet but I know the fans are going to vote us back and I have a good feeling that we're going to be voted as one of the main stage headliners. It's going to happen."

Velvet wasn't so sure. Headlining at the Temptation Festival had been a decade in the making. Playing the main stage consumed her thoughts and every decision they made as a group ended with the question, "Will this help us with Temptation votes?" Now with the power of Wallace Entertainment, one of the most well-known media companies in New York, along with their manager and agent behind them, they had a chance.

"The main stage voting is where it's at. Me and my boys already started talking about who we want to see play."

"You better vote for us, Trevor," Candy warned with a pointed finger.

Trevor flapped his arm. "How do you think you got in last year?"

"Yeah, with your one vote," Velvet smirked.

"Every vote counts."

Every vote did count. The main-stage voting round decided the time slots for the thirty-three artists, resulting from the qualifying round, with the top nine artists taking the most coveted real estate on the main stage—the last three headliner spots of the night during the three-day festival. The artist with the highest overall votes closed out the September event and festival season.

The big names often got the headliner spots, but not always. Sometimes underground DJs with large social media followings got the title instead. If an EDM artist became popular because of the fans' love for the music, then the Temptation Festival was the ultimate popularity contest. Velvet's strategy and measurement for success centered on three things: making Bedazzled Beats more popular on social media, producing music that the fans loved and bringing the house down at every performance.

"I really want it. I don't care if we close out but I want one of those nine spots. I want to headline."

"I know." Candy's tone held reverence. Her bestie knew that headlining Temptation meant more to her than just spinning a two-hour set for their fans.

"All right. Time to bounce. We gotta blow up the business class spot with our presence and rack up some more frequent-flyer miles. We don't want to miss our flight."

"I thought you guys were ballin'. Can't even get a chartered plane to fly privately?" Trevor asked.

"Shut up, you little shit. We only fly privately if it's necessary. It's called budgeting."

Her brother didn't let up. "They're not budgeting for Hardwire, Luke, Tekko, L-ectro, Jan Vanix and Tres Armadas. I'm up on that shit."

"Keep talkin' and see if you ever get invited when we do fly privately," Velvet teased.

The last name her brother mentioned hit a dull nerve. She'd thought of Zazzle over the past six months when one of the sweet memories hit her out of the blue. But like clockwork, the memories brought on the gloom of regret for what might have been. He'd made his choice back then when he'd chosen drugs over her. The day following their night at the Egyptian, she had called him on her way to Chicago for a club gig. When she got his voicemail, she rattled off something about timing, them not wanting the same things and how his focus on partying wasn't a lifestyle she could embrace. She'd had an unabashed cry over it but then armored up because no matter how right they were for each other, he wasn't good for her.

"Our car is rounding the corner." Candy hooked her arm in hers and in mock entitlement said, "Come on, Velveteen. Let's leave the commoner behind."

"Aiight. Remember this commoner and his boys are moving all your crap to storage."

Candy pulled her and they ran to Trevor to smother him with kisses on each of his cheeks.

"Get outta here with all that," Trevor complained but didn't struggle too much.

"Bye, boo," Candy called.

Velvet was right behind her. "Next stop… London."

"Welcome to London," a young man casually called as Velvet and Candy followed their manager. Sonny's black dress hugged an athletic body that at present meant business. The BonBon Fields Festival glowed with neon signs, huge banners and towering stages, covered by white rounded tents to ward off the evening chill. Fans added the color and euphoric energy. They arrived backstage to a low-lit, spacious and slightly heated lounge where artists relaxed on black leather sectional couches, prepped for their set, mingled or networked with industry professionals. Delicate perfumes and spicy body sprays mixed with odorous perspiration, fried food and residual smoke left on the clothes of people filing in from an exit door. Two bartenders tended to the drink demand and a buffet with light appetizers lined a table in addition to snacks piled at the end. Candy grabbed a small white plate and plucked items, with provided tongs, as they moved deeper into the room.

Many of the popular names in dance music were

going to play, including her friends. Velvet didn't have time to study the lineup like she often did, but she was happy to play, focus on meeting her goals and see the performances.

Sonny's voice barked through the thud of music and she ran her hand over her hair. "I just want to make sure my clients are taken care of," she said to someone wearing a headset and gripping a clipboard. Sonny's trademark short dark pixie cut was gelled to sculpted perfection.

Velvet didn't know what she discussed with the young tech, but with Sonny on the case, things were getting done.

"Great, I appreciate it." Sonny finished her conversation and turned to Velvet and Candy. Her floral fragrance mixed with the savory scent of fried food. "You guys go on at eleven. This kind sir will be handling your equipment. There're food, snacks and water over there and another lounge area on the other side at your disposal. If anyone tries to pitch anything to you, send them to me or have them contact Boombox."

"Will do." Velvet gave her the thumbs-up.

Their agent went by one powerful name in the industry. Boombox. He had a short client list but they were on it and Velvet still couldn't believe her luck. They had representatives from Luke Anderson's team. Luke, a fellow DJ, had actually listened to their music when she asked him. He'd later introduced her and Candy to Boombox. They'd always appreciate Luke for the connection because ever since they'd signed with the famous agent, their career had started to take off.

"Thanks, Sonny." A staff person opened the exit door

leading outside and cool air swirled through the space. Velvet welcomed the fresher atmosphere.

"I want to check out the media scene. I'll be back to make sure nothing goes awry between now and showtime. I'm not too worried. This festival runs a tight ship. You guys need anything?"

"Nope, I think we're good," Velvet said.

"Yeah, we're ready," Candy added before moving to sit on a cushy sectional couch. She rummaged through her bag for her equipment.

Sonny motioned Velvet and they huddled close around Candy. "Even though you're not headlining, make them wish you were."

Velvet's smile dimpled her cheeks at Sonny's words. "Always."

"Let me hear the three *F*s." Sonny cocked an ear.

"Fans, followers and fame," both Velvet and Candy recited.

When Velvet and Candy had first told Sonny their goals, their manager created various mantras, affirmations and acronyms to drive home their vision. The three *F*s was one of them and they anchored to it whenever things ebbed and flowed, and to grant them laser focus for Temptation.

"See you after—" Velvet yelped and tried to wiggle her way out of strong arms, lifting her into the air. She craned her neck to see her friend and popular DJ Rob Ready's smiling face.

"Idiot. I was about to give you a lesson in whup-assery." The tension in her body and the spike in her heart rate subsided. She wrapped her arm around his neck and hugged his vibrating shoulders. She once witnessed him doing laundry and recognized the faint smell of spring blossom, from the fabric softener he used, on his shirt that mixed with the sandalwood in his cologne. He put her down and she gave him a proper hug.

"Hey, Sonny," Rob greeted her manager.

"Rob." Sonny adjusted her glasses. "Have a great show, ladies." Sonny left for the press area.

Velvet punched his arm. "When did you get in?"

"Last night. Had a gig at Soundscape. Tekko had a show 'cross town at Ministry. As far as Rob Ready verses Tekko goes? He won hands down. I heard people were still lined up out the door while he played. No worries. I'll get him next time. You guys would have had a blast." Rob's gray, often jovial eyes shined and he scratched his scruffy, more pepper than salt whiskers with the mischief of a prankster. He reminded her of a young version of Taylor Kinney.

"Wish we could have been there but we had to do grown-up type shenanigans and close the house so…" She shrugged.

"There's my tub of sweet jolliness." Rob Ready referred to Candy, who untangled her headphones from some other wire in her bag. A small plate of appetizers she'd snagged from the buffet on their way in sat next to her.

Candy got up and placed the mostly white wires on her seat. She skipped over and gave him a hug as the two exchanged greetings. "Hey, is LED with you?"

"Nah, haven't seen him today, yet."

"But you've seen him?"

"Yeah. He's around." Rob's statement was noncommittal.

Velvet side-eyed Candy. It wasn't altogether unusual

for Rob to give such a response but wholly strange for LED not to have already met up with them.

"I gotta head over to the main stage but wanted to see you guys. 4am eats later?"

"I can fuck with 4am eats," Velvet agreed. By the end of a festival day of dancing and performing, she'd be starving, and backstage appetizers and snacks just wouldn't cut it.

"Mmm," Candy agreed, as she popped a golden brown dumpling into her mouth.

"Bet. Spread the word." Rob disappeared as quickly as he'd appeared.

The area buzzed and cheers from the audience melded with the bass, thudding against the walls, and dance music melodies from outside. Velvet and Candy's equipment was taken care of with the exception of their bedazzled headphones, resting around their necks.

Velvet remembered the times when she'd carried every adaptor compatible for different platforms, and multiple backups of her music because she would be clueless as to what level of tech assistance she'd have. Like most DJs, failure is inevitable and when she had hers in front of a crowd of thousands, she'd learned a valuable lesson. Don't assume anything and take care of your own shit. So she prepared for them all. The most annoying times were when techs didn't think she knew how to set up her own equipment. The struggles of being a woman in an industry dominated by men. Now with their management advocating for them and their riders listing their preferences, things ran more smoothly.

A combination of pre-stage nerves and neuroticism came over her and she turned to Candy. "Let's go over our set once more."

"I thought you were taking Nuts out to see what it's like out there. I want to see who's playing."

"I will once we go over our set."

Candy groaned.

"Humor me, please. I don't know what's up with me but I'm mad nervous and we don't go on for two more hours." Velvet dug into one of her pockets and fished out a lollipop. She quickly unwrapped it and slid it into her mouth. The tart watermelon flavor exploded on her tongue.

"Okay. Lead the way." Candy followed her.

Candy grabbed her bag and food, and they set out to find a quieter space.

Comments and chatter around her muddled together until one penetrated the white noise. "I can't wait to see Tres Armadas perform. Zazzle is back and from what I heard still gives a great show."

Velvet had never slid into a puddle of rubber cement, but as her body folded forward in place and her arms flailed to keep her from falling, she thought it might have the same effect. Her lollipop almost fell out, but due to the desert in her mouth, stuck to her cheek.

Zazzle is here?

She hadn't seen him since the night at the Egyptian months ago. Scratch that last remark. The images of his viral video flashed in her mind. The rumor mill had it that he'd cleaned up his act, which accounted for his recent absence from Tres Armadas. The resonance of his laughter pulsated in her muscle fibers. She shivered at how much she wanted any part of his body against her to feel it, even if it were to her detriment. Whether or not he was clean and sober, Velvet could see him derailing her smooth running train right off the tracks. Do not pass go.

Chapter Six

Zazzle gripped his meditation beads in one hand and a to-go cup of tea in the other. His serene corner of backstage, by the main stage, was quiet and the scent of lavender from the essence he dropped around the room surrounded him. Tres Armadas wasn't on until 1:30 am. They'd finished a shit load of pre-show press but more questions, photographs and videos awaited them at the main stage. The other two members of Tres Armadas were off doing their thing. Maartin Blas no doubt penned music somewhere or checked out the acts at the festival. Christian likely interviewed for his solo project and networked. Christian's solo project still rippled under Zazzle's skin like poison. Zazzle's relationship with his best friend had deteriorated to shit. It was the last thing on his recovery list left to address and the one he wanted to distance himself from with a ten-foot pole.

The music vibrated around him, as did the seductive pull of his old life. Against the advice of his licensed clinician and therapist, he was back with Tres Armadas and ready to take the stage again. He'd felt the call to the dials months ago, but between the doubts of his bandmates, and the suggestion of Tres Armadas's manager, Maggie

Swanson, to take the time he needed, Zazzle had stayed far away at a rehabilitation center in New Zealand.

Overseas, he'd worked with medical professionals to be consistent with his therapy and develop a routine he could fall back on to not only manage the stress of his substance dependency, but also his depression. When he'd been diagnosed, it wasn't news to him, but when his doctor had worked with him to prescribe the right dosage of medication, he felt like himself again and able to cope with the reality of his illness.

Over the last six months of rehabilitation and recovery, his doctors had grown a little more comfortable with the idea of him returning to the stage, but had warned him about the pitfalls of going back to a life where drugs and alcohol circulated freely. As a result, he and his doctors agreed on monthly check-ins with his clinician in New Zealand and weekly sessions with his therapist in LA, who he saw in person when he could, and virtually for extra support.

Nearly overdosing had been rough, but admitting he had a problem was the hardest thing he'd ever had to do. During his three months at the center the combination of cognitive behavioral therapy, a secular 12-Step approach, meditation and physical therapy helped him recover. For the past three months he'd worked to manage his depression and maintain all that he'd learned at the center with his daily routine that helped him stay clean. He'd exposed himself to the scene little by little with interviews when he and Tres Armadas had decided on his return at BonBon and worked on a few mixes with artists he trusted. Now he was ready for his UK return.

BonBon Fields was too huge a festival to make such a comeback, but that used to be his style. Go big or go the fuck home. The members of the trio, though skeptical about his return, were finally on board with him coming back. His onstage persona couldn't be replaced or matched. Not only did the fans want him back but a big part of him still wanted the stage. Above all else, he was anxious to right his wrongs and finish out their current tour schedule. Tonight he was going big.

Backstage, he stuck with his EMETAH—Exercise, Meditation, Eating healthy meals, Tea with CBD oil, Affirmations and Hydration—recovery routine, even in the busy festival atmosphere. Joseph, his therapist, had suggested the CBD oil in conjunction with his depression meds to combat his post-detox anxiety. The non-psychoactive addition proved to be another weapon in his arsenal to his recovery plan.

His friends and artists he admired were playing at BonBon and he wanted to check out some of the performances. If he avoided the denser areas and the press he might be able to see some of the new kids perform. He donned a cap and left his makeshift sanctuary. He ducked into a corridor and passed a lounge where people were chillin' either before or after their set. That's when he saw her. She straddled a scooter and the white stick of a lolly penetrated her lips.

He hadn't seen Velvet since that night at the Egyptian, but the night before he'd let the drugs completely ruin his life... He could only describe that night he'd had with her and their potent connection as magical. She made him laugh easier than anyone he knew, and her passion for dance music knocked his boxer-briefs off. He'd never forget the way she melted in his arms when he made love to her. He'd spent many torturous nights over the past six months thinking about her.

Loss seized his stomach like sour milk. He remembered how he'd spoken to her when he flew high on bumps of coke, MDMA and alcohol. He clutched his chest. He'd made a choice that night at the club. With all that had happened, clearly, he'd chosen wrong. Did she remember him? He took a step in her direction and stalled his advance. It was one step too many toward the lounge where drugs and alcohol circulated. This wasn't who he was anymore.

Someone bumped into him. "Sorry, man."

"It's cool," he muttered.

"Zaz. It's me."

Zazzle did a double take. "Holy shit. What's going on, dude?" They hugged. Seeing LED brought back memories from the night at the Egyptian. LED had suggested he call it a night when he was barely able to stand up. Candy and Velvet had left the club by then.

"I'm headed to the stage to play. I heard you were back with TA. I'm really glad to see you, man. After all that went down…did you get my email?"

"Yeah. Thanks for the supportive words, man. I really appreciated it." Zazzle had gotten a few well wishes. LED had been one of the firsts. The girls wish you the best, the email had read, though he'd never mentioned Bedazzled Beats by name.

"You must be pumped. Ready to give the fans a blowout show. They've been waiting for you, man."

Zazzle had read the headlines leading up to Bon-Bon. *Zazzle Returns to a Broken Fleet*, *The Showman of Tres Armadas Is Back*, *Will TA Fans Forgive Zazzle for Leaving?* The pressure of the current titles weighed him down but also fueled his motivation and determination to turn things around. He'd never please the press, but he could please the fans and slowly regain respect. He had to admit that the current headlines were better than the ones when he left for New Zealand. *The Demise of Tres Armadas*, *Drugs Destroy EDM Royalty Tres Armadas*, and *Is Zazzle Dead?*

"As ready as jumping back on a galloping horse."

LED laughed and his eyes darted to the lounge. Zazzle's gaze followed to where Velvet laughed with Candy and some other DJs. The sound enticed him. She'd laughed with him that way once.

"Zaz?" LED questioned.

Clueless as to what his friend asked, Zazzle answered. "Yeah, man."

LED's thumb pointed backward. "I should get going, but I'll check you later."

Zazzle arched a brow. "You gonna chill with your girl?"

"Yeah. Later." LED had little more to say, which was rare. Without prompting he often gushed about Candy. "Break a leg, man."

"You, too." Zazzle gave him a pound before LED split.

Zazzle peered into the lounge again but this time the group was gone.

Tres Armadas traveled to the stage. Maartin and Christian led their path and greeted industry people lining the corridor, but all eyes were on Zazzle. Full smiles accompanied doubtful eyes and even garnered a few whispers. Though they scrutinized him, Zazzle found the overall response to be positive. No one threw rotten tomatoes or eggs.

"This way, guys," someone said, and they followed.

Camera lights flashed furiously and cheers like "Welcome back, Zazzle" and "Go get 'em, guys" punctured through the thudding music and cheering fans ahead.

Zazzle inflated his chest and focused on steadying his lungs. His nerves fired like his skin and perspiration dotted his black short-sleeved shirt. He drained a bottle of water. He'd always get butterflies before going onstage but the expectations of this performance were magnified by his absence and his return. He reminded himself why he'd come back. He wanted to remove any doubts that Tres Armadas was back on top and show the fans and industry that he loved this music as much as they did.

The usual entourage that once flocked around him backstage, offering him liquor and coke, were nowhere in sight. Many of them had dropped off the face of the earth when he was in rehab. None of them had sent encouraging emails and texts, or gift packages letting him know they wished him the best.

One of them, Willem Graf, had shown up as soon as news about him being out of rehab surfaced. When the first thing he did was offer drugs, Isaak used his newfound strength and resources to keep Willem away from him. He communicated his wishes to Christian and Maartin, whose broken trust was still on the mend, and both men supported him, at least in this. Willem was an adult who could use drugs, share them and influence anyone he wanted. Isaak would no longer be one of them.

"Ready, Zaz?" Maartin asked.

"He better be. There's no turning back." Christian flipped his hair and rattled off set details like Zazzle was some newbie that just got onto the scene. "The third fader is tricky and the mixer might stick due to the moisture here so really listen in the headphones—"

"I got it, Christian. I've been doing this as long as you." That may have been the most Christian had said to him since they'd first seen each other again a month ago. "It's my music, too. I'm ready."

"Yeah." Christian again embraced silence but his "don't fuck up" tone spoke volumes.

Before they went on they huddled quickly. *"Laten we gaan rock en rollen!"* they all shouted. It was time to rock and roll.

Zazzle shuddered at the pre-performance ritual. Over the last year when his substance dependency had gotten out of control, he'd been too high and drunk to remember these small things. Almost having lost it all, he cherished them.

They were announced and the stage vibrated from the deafening roars of the fans. They walked into darkness and scattered lights highlighted their arrival. The thunderous cheers nearly blew out Zazzle's eardrums.

I really need to invest in earplugs. He'd missed this.

The first note of one of their chart-topping songs played and the place trembled. Zazzle beheld out into a field of never-ending fans whose adoration he thought he'd lost. Anticipation shot through him and the thrill of being onstage had its own addictive pull.

When the fans saw them emerge from the shadows they screamed so loud that Zazzle swore the world itself shook. He stretched out his arm and their cries washed over him. Maartin passed him a mic.

"What's happening, London?" Zazzle sang into the mic.

More deafening roars hit him.

"Wow," Zazzle mouthed to Christian and Maartin who pretended to plug their ears. Zazzle laughed. "It's good to be back. You look beautiful tonight." How did they still have voices? "Let's party."

Sandwiched between Maartin and Christian, they played for the ripe crowd at BonBon. Zazzle's body kept time to the beat of the music as if it were coming out of him and he felt every enhancement in the song, down to the tiny element deep in the background of the melody Maartin played. He turned the dial from a belly-heavy bass to a hollowed-out bass that sounded as if air breathed into it, opening the hearts of those who listened.

The fans jumped up and down in appreciation. Zazzle looked over at Christian, whose mix teased to enter into his song, and he increased the volume while Zazzle faded out his tune. The mix blended together flawlessly, coming together as one cohesive song. The trio continued this dance, thrilling the fans with their favorite songs and intergalactic lighting.

Zazzle listened and watched Christian, as did Maartin, as they both moved and danced to the music. They jumped up and down to get the crowd even more amped up as Christian tickled them with musical ingenuity and dropped beats at interesting moments to surprise his listeners at just the right moment.

The tribal and Caribbean beats that Zazzle was known for mixed through and the crowd went wild. They recognized his signature and called for the Zazzle of old, the juiced-up hype man of the group. He wasn't about to disappoint them.

Sweat dripped from Zazzle's shirt as he climbed on top of the DJ table and gyrated his hips. The crowd devoured every move and each instruction to wave their hands from side to side. Their phones lit the audience and recorded the moment. The other members of his DJ trio continued to rev up the beat in a coordinated attack on the senses. He wiped sweat off his face and dashed back and forth in time to the music. Labored breathing accompanied his moves, but it felt good to be onstage again.

Zazzle was sure this shit was easier when he did coke. This was the most energy he'd exerted in months even with his workout schedule. Rehab may have been three months, but recovery exhausted him like a rock climber scaling a mountain at high altitude. If it hadn't been for his meticulous schedule, relapsing might have been a real option. Who was he fooling? Relapsing was always a real option. He valued success. This mentality kept him looking ahead for one simple reason. Staying sober meant his life, and the stakes were higher than money or fame.

He'd failed his bandmates and desecrated his character and their reputation as a group when he'd missed shows, acted out and made headline news. Maggie had worked to cancel shows and reschedule their tour dates while he was in rehab, but there were many shows that couldn't be changed and Christian and Maartin had had no choice but to perform without him, the showman, who was a signature element of their shows.

He pointed at the crowd and they cheered. "Miss me?" He hollered into a mic, egging them on. They lost their heads with screams that bowled him over. "I've missed you, too."

Zazzle felt a tap on his leg. Christian's face glistened and the light show behind him glowed in bright colors, but his scowl commanded Zazzle to climb down, take over the dials, and move on to the next track. Maartin engaged the fans, dancing with his hands up in the air.

Zazzle sang to the light vocals of the song Christian mixed in and now played at full volume. His job was done. Their closing song pounded through the speakers. Though they were all great at closing out a set, Christian's mastery left a crowd so emotionally spent and exhausted they could talk of nothing else.

As a group they hadn't yet decided if their current tour would be their last, but with his antics and absence, he'd lost the trust of the DJ brothers he'd grown up with. He'd do the arduous work to earn back their trust, regain their spot as EDM royalty, and with any hope redeem himself. He left an item off the list. Christian, his best friend who had abandoned him when he needed him most. Zazzle had to settle things with Christian if Tres Armadas had any hope of staying together.

They'd had a good show, the fans were happy, and he was about to pass out. He needed to get his stamina back. Since he came back, words like *classic* and phrases like *vintage Zazzle* swam around him. At thirty-five and the youngest member in his group, he battled against the mature labels. Backstage, he almost fell over his slow shuffling feet. He and his bandmates had barely wiped sweat from their brows when the cameras and lights were in their faces. People wanting a piece of them mobbed them. They answered questions, smiled for photos, dried themselves off with towels provided to them and replenished their fluids.

"Zazzle? How is it being back?"

"Guys, Tres Armadas is a trio again. How does it feel?"

Other versions followed and they answered each one with smiles on their face. Some of those smiles strained. "Great," was always the reply. Internally as a group they were close to imploding and all because of him. The guilt strained his jaw but he remembered what his goals were. He'd take the doubts, be on time for gigs and be the last in their trio standing under the lights and scrutiny of the press. His bandmates had done as much during his absence. He owed them.

The questions started to die down and eventually the press funneled out and on to find other artists. The old entourage of people came through asking about late-night parties and bottle service at the clubs in town. That was his cue.

"I'm going to head back," Zazzle proclaimed. "I need to stay on schedule with my routine."

Christian's tension traveled to seize his own muscles. Whether Zazzle did the right thing or not, these days, Christian only held him in contempt, even more so if it had anything to do with his recovery.

Maartin's voice of reason always made an appearance. "Do what you have to do, man. We'll see you in the morning."

He nodded and headed to the floral-scented confines of his makeshift sanctuary where he sat in silence for a bit before he prepared a bushel of wheatgrass to juice.

Chapter Seven

Thousands of fans held up their phones to capture the moment. These last few minutes at the end of an hour-long set were Velvet's favorite. The crowd was exhausted, they knew the end drew near, and screamed their appreciation the loudest, singing the words to Bedazzled Beats' hot new single.

Velvet descended from the stage, her clothes and hair a sweaty mess. She had little time before she and Candy answered a few questions for the press and posed for pictures in their now-famous face-to-face pose.

They noshed on post-performance treats, and after getting props from their manager, they settled into participant mode. Now that their set was done, Velvet and Candy planned to meet fans and to check out some of the other acts attending BonBon Fields.

"I'm going to meet up with LED."

"You spoke to him? Is he gonna come through?"

Candy held up her phone. "Text."

"Cool. I'm going to take Nuts out. Sonny's meeting us at the hotel before we head to Belgium. So the night is ours. We're doing 4am eats with Tekko and Rob so you guys can meet up with us."

Candy clapped her hands cheerleader style. “Be there with Tinkerbelles.”

“All right.” Velvet threw up two fingers. “Peace, love and Blow Pops.”

Stimulated by the sights and sounds of the festival, Velvet checked out the lineup to see where her friends played. Her shoulders slumped when she found their slots only to see that they were on different stages and playing around the same time. The schedule may have been planned by design to split up the tens of thousands of fans attending daily, but it was no less maddening. She drove her scooter and darted around people, vending and other decorative obstacles. The masses flocked to the main stage. From afar, she saw Tres Armadas’s laser light show and the crowd thickened like ants around a cookie crumble. All of them wanting to witness the return of their lost icon. Zazzle.

The music played and Velvet gripped her handlebars. Her practical mind mapped a clear path for her to exit to another stage, but her gut clenched, her heart beat faster and curiosity got the better of her.

“There he is,” a girl passing her cried as she bounced with her group of friends. Velvet’s eyes scanned the crowd. Patriots held up their country flags and other props. People in bright-colored swimwear sat atop the shoulders of their friends and significant others. The loud cheers, as the members of Tres Armadas waved into the crowd, deafened.

There, dancing across the stage to an up-tempo tribal beat, was Zazzle. He mixed the latest dance moves with sexier ones, and humped the stage in time to the slap of each drum. Three large screens broadcasted it all and bombarded her with images of him. His body rolled to the ground and then he jumped back up in celebration, while waving his hands back and forth. With the skills of a shepherd, he led his flock of sheep, who slung their arms to and fro in time to the music.

Nothing had changed. He was still an exhibitionist. A sexy, hypnotic exhibitionist whose melodic banter bewitched the crowd. Months ago, when Velvet finally had the stomach to watch a whole thirty seconds of Zazzle's viral video from that fateful night at the Egyptian, LED had mentioned that he was in rehab. The headlines were brutal, and she boycotted press about him for her own sanity. She'd offered Zazzle well wishes via LED but nothing more. When she'd walked away from him, she'd chosen her well-being over getting sucked into a codependent relationship. He was out of rehab now, but by his presence onstage, she couldn't tell if he was sober or had lapsed back into his drug circle.

"Why am I watching this?" She sucked harder on her cherry-flavored Blow Pop. Her mind protested, but as the bass rounded out the beats, her body shimmied. She continued to drink in the entire scene. She blamed her genetics for catching the beat and her heart for wanting a different scenario. She grabbed Nuts and scooted away.

Thirty minutes later, she hung off to the side of the stage with a group of other DJs who watched Joe "Tekko" Kim on the dials. He slung back his long, sweaty jet-black hair, the contrast against his Korean features requiring Superzoom slow-mo on Instagram. He was exciting to watch and she crammed on his skills like it was her own personal training session. She remembered her apprehension when he'd first wanted to be friends. A parkour practitioner, Tekko had side jumped off some massive beam in the middle of their conversation. Initially convinced that he had to be on something or an extreme thrill seeker, Velvet had kept her distance until she realized that amped-up was Tekko's baseline.

Candy likely smooched with LED someplace and Rob was onstage, elsewhere. When Tekko spotted her after his set, he made his way over.

"You were quintessential as usual."

"The word choice though..." Tekko kissed his fingertips.

She smirked. "I worked hard on that one."

"Let me hit press and then we can bounce."

"Cool."

Velvet observed the promoters and press clamoring around Tekko. Bedazzled Beats got their fair share but she and Candy had a lot more hurdles to jump and fan base to grow. She practiced her footwork on Nuts. In her younger years, she used to skateboard until one wipeout made her cry so hard she laid off the rails and focused on shit with handlebars.

"Velvet, right?"

"Yes." She looked up right into the green eyes of Alexi. One of the best house DJs playing at BonBon Fields. "Holy...hi."

"I saw your set earlier. It was tight."

"Thanks. That means a lot."

"You here with Tekko?"

"No... I mean...yes. Just waiting for him so we can check out the rest of the festival."

"I'm having a party later. You guys should stop by."

Tekko returned to her side. "Ready, boo."

Velvet's eyes widened so much they dried in their sockets. "Yeah."

Alexi arched an eyebrow. "Great show, man. You killed it."

"Thanks." Tekko clasped Alexi's hand and pulled him into a shoulder bump. "You wanna come with us? We're gonna check out the rest of BonBon."

"I'm having a small party over at Helm. Stop by." Helm was one of the most exclusive clubs in London, complete with indoor Jacuzzi, and the place housed one of the most enormous bars Velvet had ever seen. Online.

"We're meeting up with some friends but we might come through," Tekko said.

"I hope so." Alexi's lips twitched at her and he said his goodbyes.

"Thanks." Velvet shoved Tekko by the shoulder.

"What?" Tekko hunkered.

"Nothing. I'm not about to explain the birds and the bees to you."

"He was mackin' on you? I didn't catch that vibe. My bad, Asha." Tekko hugged her shoulders. "I can't believe I missed Tres Armadas's set. I have to go see them guys and congratulate them. You down?"

Her sockets were parched again. "You know, that sounds like it'll be cool but I don't think that's a good idea."

"Because you still mackin' on Zazzle?"

"Keep your voice down," she hissed. "I'm not nothing on Zazzle."

"Then come with me. Probably lots of promoters and press around. More exposure for Bedazzled Beats?"

Tekko knew the dreams of her heart and how to mobilize her. She would never call herself overly ambitious but she saw her career in her mind's eye so clearly that she could taste it.

"I don't know, Joe."

"Just come on. It'll be good for you to mingle with the greats."

She'd already mingled with one of the greats, six months ago at his rental in San Bernardino.

Tekko persisted. "I won't let you cross over to the dark side with Zazzle. Though I got to tell you. I don't see a dark side. More like green."

"What do you mean? You've seen him?"

"Sure." Tekko shrugged. "I'm amazed at how he's changed."

"Changed? I saw him onstage, giving it to the fans. He doesn't look like he's changed at all."

"It's been a long time since he's been up there. I bet his performance was lit."

"Exactly." She dragged Nuts as they walked.

Tekko's mouth twisted to the side. He obviously itched to say something.

"What?"

"Just come with me." He shrugged again. "What you find might surprise you."

Velvet mushed her hand into her face. "I can't believe I'm doing this."

She didn't know what to expect backstage. *Why'd I let Joe talk me into this?* The Zazzle she knew sniffed bumps before he went onstage. Furthermore, she wondered if she still had the same attraction to him that she'd had so many months ago. Based on the erratic beating of her heart it was clear her body remembered what her mind had tried to forget.

"You good, Velvet?" Tekko asked.

"Huh?" Velvet pushed back her colored strands. "I guess."

She checked her phone. Candy had finally tracked down LED and Rob Ready was at his club gig. They'd all meet up later at Tekko's club performance for their ritual 4am eats.

They passed through a busy intersection of people. Excited fans and promoters swarmed the area. Some mingled loudly with drinks in their hands, and others with headsets over their heads and walkies on their hips. Videographers seemed to be placed everywhere to capture festival moments and interviewers practiced and waited patiently for their turn with the artists.

"Just through here." Tekko pulled the black curtain back and she ducked through. The scent of lavender filled her nostrils, followed by a complaint about said diffused essential oil from none other than Christian Saaks from Tres Armadas.

"Hey, Christian." Tekko slapped hands with Christian before dragging him into a brief embrace.

"What's up, man?" Christian's eyes fell to her. "Candy, right?"

"Velvet." She gave him a sheepish smile and shook his hand. "It's an honor to meet you."

"Sorry. I'm a bit distracted but I know you and your friend Candy are buzzing right now. The fans are wild about you."

"Thanks. It was great to see you guys take the main stage," Velvet replied.

"Yeah." A touch of sadness flattened his smile. "Maartin is around and…well… Zazzle, too."

"Cool. Do your thing, man. We just wanted to say

awesome show." Tekko, always a bundle of positivity, patted Christian on the shoulder before he departed.

"I can't believe I just met Christian Saaks." As far as popularity went, Christian had that in abundance. Maartin held the title of intellectual, and Zazzle the bad boy showman. Yet another reason her mind projected a biohazard sign in front of any image of him.

"There's Maartin." Tekko pulled her along and called after the second member of Tres Armadas.

"What's up, dude? I thought you were playing at the club tonight?" Maartin inquired.

"Yeah. I'm heading over in a bit. Great show. You guys must be psyched to have Zazzle back."

"It's weird, but yeah."

Between Christian's seemingly emotional response to Tekko's question and Maartin's statement, a bitter-sweet elephant filled the room. At Temptation last year when Tres Armadas closed out the festival, Velvet had witnessed some discord between the members before they performed. Surely, Zazzle's absence, stint in rehab and subsequent return had affected the dynamics.

"This is Velvet," Tekko presented.

"Bedazzled Beats, yes?" Maartin asked.

Velvet shook his hand. "Yes."

"I've seen an old vinyl set of yours. Impressive. We should talk music sometime."

Velvet's mouth opened to speak but she fumbled for words. She rarely spun solo in public since she and Candy had formed. "That'd be cool."

Maartin's warm smile made her relax or maybe it was the increasing smell of the bluish-purple flower.

"I wanted to welcome Zazzle back and then I have to skedaddle," Tekko said with a full-body wiggle dance.

Maartin laughed. "He'll be happy to see you. He's just through there." He turned to her with a tip of a fake hat. "Velvet."

She returned the gesture. "Maartin."

Tekko dragged her again until they ducked through another set of curtains. Once they passed through the black barrier, the potent floral fragrance stopped her like a solid wall. What was it protecting? And from what? Scorpions?

A machine blared and she witnessed Zazzle hunched over a juicer as green liquid shat out of the spout. "What the—"

"Zaz!" Tekko tried to call over the noise but Zazzle, engrossed in his current juicing activity, didn't hear a thing.

Zazzle turned off the machine and handled the moving parts like he stockpiled an abundance of time. His vibrant skin glowed against rich dark brown hair that had grown to his shoulders, and the soft muscles of his torso now showed strong definition through his fitted black shirt. Her palm tingled with recollection.

He shot back the green liquid. By the grimace that accompanied an emphatic "Blech," the juice didn't appear to be at all appetizing.

Tekko called to him again. "Bruh. What is that shit?"

Zazzle's joy at seeing Tekko resounded, and then he saw her and staggered forward. Zazzle hugged Tekko. "I, um…juice… It's wheatgrass."

"I know you made some changes but…damn." Tekko pointed to the juicer.

"It's a little…overwhelming for some…but sticking to a healthy routine is important, you know?" Zazzle's eyes slid to her and stayed there. His chest filled with air and she shared a shaky breath with him. "Good to see you again, Velvet."

That accent. How could she forget that beautiful mix of the melodic and formal, that rolled into a phonetic ball? The other members of Tres Armadas spoke in similar accents but Zazzle's was compatible with the blood in her veins.

"You, too." She swallowed so hard, the taste of lavender coated her throat.

"I heard your show was fire!" Tekko cheered.

Zazzle blew out air as if winded. "It took a lot out of me but I'm getting there, energy wise."

Velvet checked his body from head to toe for both visible and invisible scars, and ran down her checklist of signs he might be using. Relief eased through her when his amber eyes weren't dilated, a vision that had haunted her for weeks after LA.

"Velvet said you looked like your old self up there?"

It wasn't a compliment. What the actual fuck, Tekko? She choked her friend with superpowers she didn't possess.

"You said that?" Zazzle questioned.

Velvet remembered many things about Zazzle but the softness on his face and the way his eyes searched hers offered glimpses of the man she'd danced with that night at the festival. The man she'd kissed and held as they waited for the sun to come up. She tried to pull back, to not get wrapped up in him as easily as she did on day one, but the herbaceous perennial did its job and chilled her all the way out.

"Yeah." She was in trouble.

Chapter Eight

Velvet still commanded his attention even when the fibers of her judgment tangled him like overgrown ivy.

"Would you like a green smoothie?" he asked. Those weren't the words he'd envisioned saying to her when they reunited. He owed her an apology. More than an apology, his sincerest regrets about what happened. About ruining the connection most people only dreamed about. He'd had a shot of wheatgrass when she and Tekko arrived, and his Dutch hospitality won out.

"Uhh…no? Thank—"

"Sure, man." Tekko's enthusiasm, in stark contrast to Velvet's uncertainty.

"I have to head back to the hotel in a few." He was wiped and had to get some rest but seeing her again let air into the stifling but necessary barricade to the outside world he'd sequestered himself behind.

"You're not coming out, man? It's London. There're so many hot spots around town. Almost everyone has another gig after to either attend or perform."

"I think they'll be fine without my presence. Right now, I'm limiting my routine to Tres Armadas performances."

"Your PO making you do that?" Tekko frowned. "C'mon, man?"

Tekko was harmless and a friend to his group, but like everyone else, Tekko wondered why he didn't go out. "I don't have a PO. I wasn't arrested. I was in rehab." He eyed Velvet who sported a permanent purse on her lips. He had stayed sober. A feat in and of itself, but doubt came at him from every angle. The current chilly weather came from Velvet's brown eyes.

"Do your thing, man," Tekko said. "It's a shame to waste your talent so I'm stoked you're back onstage."

"The crowd, they were..." Zazzle puffed out air. "I'm temporarily deaf, man. So much love." He patted his heart.

"They were really loud. I don't think I've ever been anywhere and heard that level of applause," Velvet added, her eyes bright. "They were really happy to see you and you guys gave them a great show."

He hadn't realized his shoulders slumped until he pulled them back. That she'd seen his first show back infused him with pride.

Tekko groaned. "Freakin' festival management scheduled us at overlapping times or I would've been there."

"It's cool. Glad you stopped by." Zazzle prepped some wheatgrass and the juicer blared to life again. He handed Tekko a serving of green juice and turned to Velvet. She scrutinized his every move. "Where's Candy? I heard you guys played tonight."

"Yeah, we did." She cleared her throat. "She's with LED. We're meeting up later."

"Sweet girl. Please let her know I said hi." Zazzle ushered them over to a small couch. "You guys wanna sit?"

"Sure," said Tekko.

Velvet. "We should get going. We don't want to disrupt your routine. It's important to you. If you're keeping up with it, you should keep on doing that."

"I'm keeping to it. I appreciate your concern." He couldn't keep the bite of resentment from his voice. As Zen as he was, he still didn't like being monitored. Plenty of people, including his medical team, had him covered.

"That's great. Like Joe said. Do your thing," Velvet repeated.

"Where are you guys playing next?" Zazzle's question expelled from him as if he held his breath.

"Candy and I will be in Belgium."

"Nice," Zazzle encouraged. "I expected you guys would be on the main stage, given your popularity last year."

"Not yet." Velvet shifted her weight to her opposite hip and her scooter tilted toward the same direction.

Zazzle was unsure what part of what he said agitated her but something obviously did.

"Velvet's tunnel vision is focused on Temptation's main stage." Tekko's features contorted like he still tasted his juice.

"Temptation voting will be coming up in the next few months. Still willing to give up an eyeball for it?" Zazzle asked, unable to filter the mischief out of the question.

Velvet lost her fight to smother her smile. "Yeah, but we're working for it, too."

"And your album? I remember you and Candy were getting ready to work on it when we first met."

"You remember that?" she asked.

"I remember everything about that night, Asha," he

said. The slight lax in her scowl gave him hope. Perhaps she couldn't keep her shields up forever. There was still, however, a long time between now and then.

Tekko arched an eyebrow at him.

Velvet cleared her throat. "We're wrapping up the album this month. It'll be out soon."

"Looking forward to hearing how your sound is evolving." Zazzle's hands went to his hips then he crossed his arms.

Her smile knocked him back.

"If you need anything, I'd be happy to help. I'd just have to work around my schedule and routine so—"

"I think we're good, but I'll let you know. Thanks." She gripped the handlebars on her scooter a little tighter and he didn't know if that was a good sign or a bad one.

"No problem." He tried to get a read on where their connection stood. In addition to choosing drugs over Velvet, he'd been away for months. The night they met, their relationship had soared so fast that some of the initial activities never happened. He never got her number or wined and dined her at a fancy restaurant, unless beer, cheese, crackers and fruit counted. And though every inch of her body, from her lips to the soft skin of her inner thighs, haunted his memory, he missed laughing with her, arguing with her about music and holding her against him.

Everything fell apart the night at the Egyptian. Then he went to rehab and was now in lifelong recovery. He could only imagine what she thought of him. Would he ever get even a smidge of that magical night with her back?

He sat with the disappointment of missed opportunity and exhaled to move the stagnant air in his chest.

He'd done it all to himself but now had to breathe through the guilt and shame of what he'd done. He wanted forgiveness but he hadn't earned it back yet.

"You guys playing Inferno Fest?" Tekko interrupted his thoughts.

"If things work out. Apparently, Maggie's not getting a good vibe from it."

"I heard it's supposed to be the festival of the century but there's too much chatter about it," Tekko said. "I'm undecided."

"Boombox pulled us out," Velvet offered.

"That's something to consider. Boombox normally has his finger on the pulse of it all. Ultimately, it's up to Maggie and the other members of Tres Armadas." Zazzle's vote in the group counted for very little these days but he'd relay the information he got from Tekko and Velvet about the festival. The last thing they needed was to be a part of something that might not be what it seemed.

Velvet pulled her phone out of her back pocket and then muttered something inaudible to Tekko.

"We're gonna head out, man," Tekko said and gave him a handshake and hug. "Check you at the next one."

"Take care, Zazzle. I'm glad to see you're doing well."

Velvet's parting words coasted on grim undertones that savored of finality. As she walked her scooter out, he didn't want to believe that to be the case. Before she ducked out of the area, and with a purse still fixed upon her lips, she looked back.

Alone at the hotel, Zazzle showered and packed his bags. They'd be flying out tomorrow and headed for

Spain. With Maartin and Christian partying with their friends on the last night of the festival, he longed to be out and see people he hadn't seen in months, but at what cost?

He quelled the impulse to go out and rub shoulders with the drug crowd he'd, so far, successfully avoided. He'd worked too hard to jeopardize his progress. The fight to keep with his new lifestyle and routine, as the opinions and feelings of others came into play, was a fight worth winning.

The day had gone as well as could be expected. There were no scuffles to break up between him and Christian, and he wasn't being scraped off the floor of some club because he'd sniffed, popped or pounded back too much fun. Being exhausted took some getting used to without coke to liven him up and anytime he got anxious he sipped his tea. Not bad for his first real day back on the performance track.

He jotted down his day in a journal and focused on the feelings he experienced and when. When he met with his therapists and clinician, he'd share the contents with them. His recovery was another full-time job on top of being a DJ/producer with Tres Armadas. The fluffy hotel bed called his name.

He was about to lie down when a knock sounded on his door. He opened it and Maartin stood before him.

Zazzle swung the door open to allow Maartin to come in. "Checking up on me?" Zazzle asked in Dutch.

"Yes." Maartin strolled in and closed the door behind him.

Zazzle may have been annoyed by Maartin's forthright response but the human contact made him feel less alien in an environment where he'd once dominated.

Zazzle spun in a slow circle. "See? No drugs, alcohol or women."

"I didn't think so. I just wanted to know how you were doing, emotionally. You've been alone most of the time since you've been back."

"I'm fine."

Maartin raised a brow.

"Okay, so I don't like being alone. I don't have much of a choice right now."

"People are glad you're here, Isaak. That must count for something." Maartin sat in a desk chair.

"Most people are waiting for me to fuck up again. My old suppliers are hovering in the wings and hoping I'll join the party again."

"Not all."

"There's you and Maggie. At least you both have been encouraging." Maggie had cleaned up a lot of his messes in the past, yet she supported his recovery and since he'd come back tried to bridge some of the distance between the three of them.

Maartin frowned. "I thought they taught you to have a positive outlook in rehab."

"They did, among other things. I'm just skeptical. I'm not quite willing to let down my guard." Zazzle's predictions for the future didn't include him ever completely letting down his defenses, especially if it saved him from himself.

"Let's see what you got in here." Maartin moseyed over to the minibar and opened it to find juice, sparkling water and sports drinks. He pulled sparkling water from the fridge. "Want one?"

Zazzle referenced his teacup. "Are you checking to see if I'm harboring booze?"

Maartin shrugged.

"I wasn't dependent on alcohol. I drank because of the drugs."

"But wouldn't that then create a dependency on alcohol?"

Maartin's genuine curiosity allowed him to be honest. "Touché, but my doctors don't think I'm at risk for alcoholism," Zazzle said. "I'm not willing to test that theory yet and no one needs to know or else they'll just shove booze at me."

"True," Maartin agreed. "Hey, speaking of Maggie. She wants to meet with us tomorrow. She says it's important."

"Yes, I got her message."

"I thought you were no-tech?"

"Only when I'm meditating, the rest of the time I'm low tech," Zazzle clarified.

"I can't keep up with this EMET regimen you have going on."

"It's EMETAH," Zazzle corrected and reminded Maartin of its meaning.

"Yeah, that stuff."

"Thanks for the support." For all of Zazzle's fuck-ups, Maartin still took the time to learn about the routine he strictly adhered to.

"Want to watch a movie?" Maartin asked.

"And braid each other's hair?" Zazzle smirked. "No thanks. Maybe another time."

Maartin chuckled. "How does it feel being back?"

Everything from the time he got on the plane from his home in the Netherlands to landing in the UK moved so fast. He hadn't even really had time to let the performance sink in and settle. "I'm not sure I've really wrapped my mind around it. People weren't complete dicks to me. Some were even pleasant to reconnect with, like LED and Tekko." *And Velvet.* "The fans… They were amazing tonight."

"They make it all worth it, don't they?"

"Yeah." Zazzle loved the fans but he'd lost so much time. He had so much to make up for.

"But?"

"There's a lot for me to fix."

"Fix?" Maartin wrinkled his nose.

"I left you guys to handle a lot of my shit. Questions from the media about my whereabouts. Money left on the table with canceled performances. Disappointed fans. Rumors. I can go on."

"Yeah, you did. But you can't expect to fix everything. Not everything is in your control. Just be the best DJ and business partner we need you to be, Isaak. That's your only requirement. The rest will take care of itself."

"Do you think Christian would agree with you?"

"You know, you don't only have me and Maggie. There's also Christian."

"The same Christian who neither came to visit me or called when I was in rehab?" Zazzle scoffed. "You've always been a good friend, Maartin, but no, I don't have support from Christian."

"You're wrong, Isaak."

"Am I?" Zazzle pressed. Christian had all but abandoned him over the last year when his addiction had reached an all-time high. It wasn't Christian's job to save him, but he'd fought with him instead of being the one thing he needed. A friend. Instead Christian chose his ambition.

"Yes. He's your friend. The sooner you both remember that the better off we'll all be."

"I know what's going on. Christian can no longer hide what he wants and you've seemed to resign yourself to the outcome."

"And what outcome is that?"

"That Tres Armadas is done. You want to go home to your family and Christian wants a solo career." Before Zazzle had almost overdosed a few months ago, Christian had thrown more than enough hints that he'd outgrown the group. They'd been best friends growing up in the Netherlands but Christian's betrayal was like a disease that got worse every day with nothing to heal it—or him.

Maartin sat back and crossed his arms. "Is it any surprise to you? You better than anyone should know that Christian was destined to evolve and move on from Tres Armadas. I'm surprised we've been together this long, to be honest."

Zazzle's behavior and jealousy had only added vinegar to the wound between them, and accelerated Christian's need to distance himself from the trio. "I know I've done damage and now that I'm back we can get back to being the Tres Armadas we used to be. I can help us quiet the naysayers."

"Zazzle—"

"Are you really ready to pack it in? To turn down the music and leave during our biggest moment?" he asked Maartin.

"If we disband it doesn't mean that we can't still make music and be popular in a different way."

"Yeah, well, Christian already has that covered."

"Get off it, man. Don't forget your contribution. You let drugs into your life and addiction run you."

Zazzle sat on the bed. "I did and I've paid the price. Haven't I? I've lost so much time. Missed so many amazing things and now you guys want to end it before I get a chance to reclaim our spot."

"You keep talking about reclaiming our spot. Zazzle, we're the most popular DJ trio and the highest paid. What more do you want?" Maartin asked.

He wanted to experience it. "To be present for it and not high out of my mind."

"Time is the one thing you can't get back," Maartin stressed. "Look, nothing has been decided. You're back now and better. Take things one day at a time." Maartin sighed.

Zazzle nodded.

"This routine of yours is quite strict. How long do you think you can manage it?"

"As long as I need to in order to stay sober."

"The diffuser is a little much at times." Maartin stood up.

"I'll lower the setting," he said.

"And the meditation pillow?"

Zazzle clutched the sandalwood meditation beads that hung around his neck and prayed for patience with his bandmate. "The meditation grounds me. I can sit in a chair but I prefer the floor."

"And the juicer?"

Zazzle hung his head. "What? You're pulling my leg now. You don't like my smoothies and wheatgrass shots. They're good for you."

"I'll pass," Maartin said.

"It'll make you last longer." Zazzle pointed to his

dick. He laughed at the intrigue on Maartin's face. The man had enough kids and though Zazzle didn't want to think about it too much, sex was the least of Maartin's problems.

"How would you know? Have you been fucking around?"

He frowned. "Not lately." The truth was, he was scared shitless of replacing one addiction with another and sex was high on the list of possibilities. He didn't want to fuck his way out of drugs and alcohol only to have to go back in to rehab to get his dick to behave. For now, he abstained.

"That's unhealthy, man. Get laid, will you?"

"I'm good for now." Zazzle lifted his left hand.

Maartin laughed. "I saw Velvet with Tekko. Them two an item now?"

"They're friends. I think." Zazzle had been so involved in his routine he hadn't even considered that Velvet and Tekko might be together. He'd have to dig a little deeper.

"You liked her very much before everything happened. Before you started using the night at Temptation, you couldn't stop carrying on about this magical fairy you met and how she changed your life and how brilliant and amazing she was, not to mention how unearthly sex felt between you two."

"I said all that?" Zazzle blushed so hard he swore steam vapors floated from his skin. He still liked Velvet much more than very much.

"Yeah, you did."

Zazzle's head hung. "I've ruined my chances with her by the way."

"Helaas Pindakaas!" Maartin's curse translated to

too bad. "Are you sure about that? I think she's fucking cool and her music knowledge rivals mine for someone so young."

"No, but after seeing her today? Pretty sure." Zazzle thought about how Velvet's flat tone and scrutinizing gaze had all but slammed the door on reconnecting to what they shared months ago. Yet there were hints that maybe the slightest possibility existed. "I don't know. I have to get to bed."

Maartin shook his head. "Running from your one true love, are you? You're in recovery, Isaak—not in hiding."

"Hiding will keep me out of trouble."

"Not all trouble is bad." Maartin flickered his eyebrow.

Zazzle pondered Maartin's words. "If it is, I don't want to find out the hard way."

Chapter Nine

The next day, in their Brussels hotel room, Velvet patted Candy's back as her grief-stricken friend lay sprawled across the bed with her head buried into a pillow. "4am eats" with their friends never happened, and the time necessary for Velvet to download her interaction with Zazzle had fled as the proverbial shit had hit the fan.

Last night when Velvet had received LED's cryptic text, all kinds of alarms had gone off.

Come get Candy.

When Velvet had received the message, she'd been with Zazzle and working on keeping her own emotions in check by cranking up her judgment to the highest setting. LED had ghosted them most of the festival, and though Velvet had had her suspicions, she'd never expected this.

When Velvet had arrived at LED's hotel room in London to get Candy, her friend had paced while LED sat motionless on the bed. Before she could ask questions, Candy had snatched her to leave. The next morning they flew to Brussels.

Now as Candy shook with sobs, still in her travel clothes, Velvet sat next to her on the bed rubbing her back with one hand and scrolling through her phone with the other. The red dot notification on the green message app read in double digits. Texts inquiring about Candy from Tekko and Rob Ready were among the messages and Velvet tried to respond quickly, even though she had no light to shed.

"You gonna tell me what happened, Candy Cane? You don't have to tell me everything but between this morning and our travels, it's been hours. We're in another country now." Velvet waited long minutes before Candy responded.

"We broke up." Candy rolled to her back and sniffled. "I don't want to talk about it."

"I'm so sorry, girl." Velvet felt her brows knit like crochet loops. LED had been a close friend and though Velvet wasn't privy to everything in his and Candy's relationship, the breakup felt sudden and catastrophic. Candy would never break up with LED any more than LED would break up with Candy. So who was it? Velvet went with the person she knew best and speculated about why LED ended the relationship. "You're sure? It might make you feel better."

Candy rested her forearm over her eyes and shook her head.

Velvet wanted to help, but she didn't push. "I'm here when you do, okay?"

Candy swallowed audibly and nodded.

"Can I get you anything? Some water, something to eat, a charmed spell book to put a curse on Bernard?"

Candy's laugh didn't quite form. "No, thanks," she sniffled.

They had a show in a few hours and Velvet worried that Candy might not be up for the performance. Velvet wouldn't want to perform if she'd just been dumped. With the qualifying round for the Temptation Festival opening in a few months, they needed to win over as many fans as possible each time they played. They needed to talk to as many people as possible, sign merchandise and saturate the media, boost their following and leave the fans wanting more. The three *F*s had to stay top of mind for them. A bad performance could weaken their chances of even being one of the top sixty performers. The pressure to be as perfect as possible stayed at an all-time high, but Candy was in turmoil and Velvet was torn.

"Want me to call Sonny to see if she can cancel our gig? We can try to do that or try to change some things up?"

"You're really going to ask me that, right now?"

Velvet rubbernecked. "I'm asking because you're upset."

"This is my career, too, Asha. Of course I'm going to be okay to play tonight."

Velvet folded her lips inward, her teeth biting down to refrain from unloading. They'd had their squabbles in the past due to fatigue or misunderstandings. Candy's response was in direct relation to her breakup and Velvet would just have to deal with Bonnie the Bitch for a little while.

Velvet went to her luggage and pulled out her outfit for the performance tonight. The white sparkly top and purple leather pants complemented Candy's who would wear a similar outfit in reverse. Velvet unzipped Candy's garment bag and hung her outfit next to hers on the door. They didn't always match but rather tried to attain group cohesiveness.

"I'm sorry," Candy called to her back.

"About what?" Velvet met the tear-stained face and red eyes of her friend over her shoulder and batted her lashes.

A hint of a smile touched Candy's lips. "I don't mean to be a bitch. I'm just—"

"Sad?" Velvet asked.

"And mad," Candy added.

"You don't have to go through this alone and keep it all bottled in. You can talk to me."

"I know." Candy lowered her eyes. "I will."

She and Candy didn't have many secrets and maybe Velvet expected Candy to open up too soon. "You don't have to apologize, Candy. I know you're hurting. Shit, I feel like I'm broken up with LED."

Candy laughed this time. "You don't have to be mad at him, you know."

"Oh, yes I do. Sisters before misters and all that."

Candy flopped back down on the bed.

"How about we go out and see a little bit of the town before our show tonight?"

Candy groaned. "I don't wanna."

Velvet didn't give up. On the heels of a super fresh breakup, the last thing Candy needed to be was inside alone with her feelings. She'd have plenty of time to do that with their day off on their way to Germany. "We can get a coffee and some speculoos for a little comfort? A bit of fresh air and a nice walk?"

Candy propped up on her elbows. "You had me at speculoos. Those spiced cookies sound divine right now."

Velvet abandoned her unpacking task and grabbed her bag. "Let's bounce."

Their show at the Ribaucourt castle—complete with moat—was just what the doctor ordered for Bedazzled

Beats. The diversity among the partygoers as well as the artists had her ears perked for new music. For Candy, the genuine positive vibe, coupled with overdosing on espresso and speculoos, had to lift her spirits, even if only a little.

The festival had a modest lineup but it wasn't until night fell and the crowd amassed that Velvet understood why Boombox and Sonny had agreed to book them there. The sheer number of attendees could garner them massive fans.

"Genius," Velvet muttered to herself before showtime. With not a lot of huge names, she and Velvet were big fish in a little pond. Velvet wanted to go up against the big names and so long as she and Candy were in the conversation, they were headed in the right direction.

"Everyone's so happy." Candy's comment came with a tinge of sadness from the recently unboo-ed.

Zazzle popped into Velvet's head. Being adjacent to the Netherlands she was somewhat close to his home country. She hadn't gotten to know him well enough to get all the deets about where he lived, but during their night together he did speak about living in both LA and the Netherlands. Again, the feeling of loss seized her chest.

"We're going to make them so much happier, Candy Cane. We're going to make them so happy they shit Skittles and fart rainbows."

Candy giggled. "Let's get 'em."

Mission accomplished.

They only had a couple of hours at the Fairyland Festival but Velvet met people from all over including America, United Arab Emirates, Belgium, both French and Dutch sides, UK and Spain to name a few. The philosophy of green living and sustainable futures had Velvet ready to take up the cause.

The castle itself was impressive with its expansive grounds. Attendees were even able to put their feet in the water. Spring was on its way but the temperatures were still winterish. The two-hundred-room castle guarded over the Fairyland participants with its massive curving corner towers and arching ramparts.

Once they performed, spoke to the press, and did some promotional pictures and videos for the festival, Sonny had to get them back to their hotel to pack for Germany. They were racking up the frequent-flyer miles but Velvet kept her eye on the prize and looked forward to the two-day travel breather.

At the hotel, and in the wee hours of the morning, she and Candy packed to travel later that day. Candy went to bed but Velvet could hear her cry in a restless sleep.

As Velvet lay in bed she texted LED. She knew he was still in Europe for gigs and would likely be awake. She hesitated with a traitorous heart but she had to at least attempt to get to the bottom of the situation.

Velvet: How are you?

LED: …

He took a long time to respond and just when Velvet was about to put her phone down he responded.

LED: good

"Hmm… I bet as good as Candy Cane," she whispered and eyed Candy. She was just going to get right to it.

LED: How is she?

Velvet: You mean the girlfriend you dumped?

"Maybe that was too much," she mouthed to the glare coming from her smartphone.

LED: Do you need something?

Velvet: We're friends, right?

LED: With accusations like that? Sure.

"Eewl." Velvet scoffed at the warm-less response. She thumbed back.

Velvet: What happened with you two?

LED: Ask Bonnie. It's not my place. I gotta go.

"Not his place? What the fuck is that supposed to mean?" Candy rustled at her hushed toned and Velvet silenced any further complaint.

The two of them were maddening. Between Candy and LED's tight-lipped explanation she got nowhere. She'd just have to wait until one of them cracked.

Velvet: KK. Talk soon.

LED: For the record, Bonnie broke up with me.

Velvet stared at the message for a long time. *What the fuck?*

Chapter Ten

"What do you mean, Chemistry pulled out?" Christian asked Maggie.

Zazzle puffed air as a countermeasure to the stress level in the room. Tres Armadas had spent a lot of time with their management organizing opening acts by country, by sound and by popularity. Each location sometimes featured a home-country DJ or someone who could help them balance their attendance numbers. Now, they had to make adjustments and no one took it well.

Their manager responded. "It appears they got a deal to tour in Asia for the next few months. They're more than happy to come back toward the end of the tour, but are also willing to break contract and forfeit the remainder of their funds."

"Okay, so where does that leave us?" Zazzle sipped on his tea, the slight hint of grass and earth from the CBD oil mixed with hibiscus and mint. His own special tea blend.

"We need to find a new opening act," Maggie said.

"I can name at least ten acts to replace them," Christian boasted.

"It's festival season," Zazzle noted. Christian ignored

him, his go-to status for dealing with him these days, and rattled off some names.

Maartin interrupted. "To Zazzle's comment, most of those DJs are booked."

"Let's face it, guys. You're not going to get the top-tier performers. We need hungry young talent who are popular and can draw a crowd. Someone fresh, but known," Maggie suggested.

A vision of a woman with punked-out blue hair popped into his head. Bedazzled Beats might be a perfect fit if their schedules worked out. They'd had some success and were backed by friends-to-the-group Tekko and Luke "The Musical Prophet" Anderson, but Zazzle didn't utter a word. Though he and the members of Tres Armadas still played together on tour, he didn't fool himself to believe this was a democracy where he had any say. He'd forfeited those rights the night of the Egyptian.

He placed his tea on the table and listened as Maggie and his bandmates brainstormed. Then Maartin gave him the opening he needed.

"What about that group LED is always with. The name slips my tongue. The Beats or something like that. The two girls."

"Bedazzled Beats," Zazzle offered.

"The two girls?" Christian questioned.

"Yes, that's right," Maartin confirmed. "They're up-and-coming and their skills move the crowd. Velvet really studies the landscape. She's known for her vinyl sets."

"I don't know. Plus, he has the hots for one of them." Christian jutted his head at Zazzle. "We don't need another incident."

"Another incident? When have I ever dated one of our opening acts?"

"You know what I mean, Zazzle."

"Spell it out for me, Christian." Even though he took deep breaths, anger swirled like a mini tornado about to break out of him and do damage. He'd been managing his recovery, silencing his vote in the group and hadn't complained about a single thing since his return. None of it was punishment enough for Christian.

"Okay, guys. Everyone just chill out." Maggie offered Zazzle a sympathetic look. "Bedazzled Beats are a duo so they can be in line with your brand. They're handling themselves well in an industry that continues to cater to the men. Adding women to your tour may expand your fan base and speak to inclusivity."

Maartin jumped in. "I think it's a good business decision. If the only objection is that Zazzle has the hots for one of them, it's a weak one, Christian. You forget how you met your wife?"

"Lotte wasn't a DJ."

"No. She was a fan." Zazzle couldn't help himself. His intention in coming back had been to start to rebuild the bridges he'd incinerated. He still hadn't gotten the courage to have an overdue conversation with Christian and the tension continued to mount. He had to do it soon or they'd implode.

"Klootzak!" Christian fumed at him, ready to pounce.

"I'm the asshole? Have a mirror handy?" Zazzle antagonized.

"Can we just get through this without a fight?" Maartin rubbed his temples.

"Look, Bedazzled Beats are good," Maggie announced. "I can reach out to their agent and see if it's even possible. If it's not, then this is all moot and you two wasted a bunch of testosterone for no reason at all. We need options and they're one of them. How about..."

Zazzle didn't listen to the rest of Maggie's options because he only thought of the possibility of having Velvet on tour with them. He'd be able to show her how he'd changed since the Egyptian. He'd hurt her and betrayed her, and chipped away at their amazing night together every time he'd opened his mouth. They'd once joked about redemption, but now it was something he needed. Despite the internal fighting he would stay the course with Tres Armadas and be consistent as a bandmate and business partner. With the possibility of Velvet on tour with him, maybe he'd be able to right the wrongs of that night months ago.

Velvet's fingers glided over the equipment and she layered effects over the song she and Candy worked on. The give-and-take of creativity between them flowed from years of experience. In the studio, they worked with vocalists and musicians to add depth to their tracks and samples. Their album, like the first draft of a manuscript, told a story. That story, however, needed to be edited, colored, cut and repositioned.

Sonny entered and waited for them to finish working on their current track. Velvet flashed all ten fingers at Sonny to communicate the time they needed and Sonny made herself comfortable on a gray couch at the far end of the room. Five minutes later Tommy Boombox entered.

Velvet's lids lifted. Tommy smiled, like he'd pulled off a gag. Enthralled by the music, Candy bobbed to the beat with closed eyes. Velvet nudged her and pointed to Tommy. The grin that spread across Candy's face was better than if she'd just been invited to a ball. If Candy still suffered in silence, at least seeing Tommy gave her a little shot of joy.

They finished and rested their headphones on their equipment to join their manager and agent.

"This is a nice surprise." Candy hugged Tommy. Velvet followed.

"I had business out this way. I figured it would be nice to have this conversation with you ladies in person since it'll be a while before you're back in the States."

"What's up?" Velvet asked. "Sonny's been hinting at something since we were in Belgium."

"When we discussed your goals, playing the Temptation Festival was high on your wish list," Tommy began, and Velvet's heart raced. Were they a candidate? With voting for the qualifying round starting in a few months, surely it was too early to know.

He continued. "I lead with this because you ladies have been building your fan base steadily, but we need a boost if we're going to have any chance of getting you on the main stage."

They weren't officially on a tour for their album but they had a slew of scheduled club dates and festival spots. Velvet didn't know what more she and Candy could do except perform more. "Do you guys think we're behind? Voting hasn't even started yet. But I'm sure there's talk. Is there talk?"

"No—" Tommy adjusted his glasses "—but momentum can shift unexpectedly and we want you ladies to jump into Temptation with solid footing."

"What do you suggest?" Velvet scoured her brain.

She and Candy had discussed strategy with her team and she couldn't figure out an option she may have missed.

"Something has come up that could be the magic bullet we need, if you're willing."

"If it will help us land Temptation then I'm all for it." Velvet was on the edge of her seat.

"Tres Armadas is touring right now and they have the biggest fan base in all of dance music."

As in Zazzle's Tres Armadas?

"Their shows sell out arenas and house tens of thousands," Sonny added. "Some festivals don't even bring in their numbers. They normally have opening acts but their main act has pulled out due to a solo opportunity to tour Asia. You with me, Velvet?"

Velvet closed her mouth and blinked a few times from dry eye. "Yeah. Yes, of course." The dial on her brain stayed stuck on Zazzle more so than Tres Armadas as the power entity in EDM.

Tommy continued. "They're looking for a DJ to fill the spot. Their manager, Maggie Swanson, reached out to me to see if you ladies might be interested. You have a bunch of obligations that we'll have to work around, but this could be that golden ticket we need for more fan exposure."

Velvet and Candy were putting the final touches on their album and their solo tour was at least eight months away. They wanted to shop some of the songs at a few venues and festivals before their album dropped. The tease of new music might not be enough to get them noticed by the fans to pull in votes. Were things on the back end so grim that they moved from headliner caliber to opening act?

"We want to be the main act for the main stage. Tell us honestly. If we take this gig, are we potentially taking a step back?" Velvet scratched her head. "I mean, I can see how being aligned with a big name like Tres Armadas could be a good thing, but they've had some challenges with some of their members over the last six months." She hated that she had to bring up Zazzle this way, but she had to do right by Bedazzled Beats. If something happened with Zazzle would they be forever associated with Tres Armadas in a negative way?

"Let's lay it all out. Is your major concern about going on tour with Tres Armada due to Zazzle and his…challenges?"

"Not my only one. First, me and Candy really have tried to forge a path on our own. I get that this tour with Tres Armadas will offer us great exposure and we definitely want to connect with their fans. If we open for them, what does that say about us? That we can't hold the main act spot? Second, something like Zazzle's viral video could derail us if it were to happen again. We're already going to be associated with…"

"With this new version of the trio. I'm highly in favor of this deal." Tommy adjusted his glasses on his face. "From my personal experience, Zazzle has been doing all he can to change the narrative around his behavior from exhaustive press to lifestyle changes that I've witnessed firsthand. He deserves a second chance. Do you believe in second chances, Velvet?"

She was torn. She'd met the new version of Zazzle and she could definitely deal with him, but was it going to last? If she answered yes to Tommy's question, she'd be opening herself up to much more than just Zazzle and his recovery. Her heart had been working on tricking her into hoping that second chances might extend to her, too. "Yes, I do."

"To your second point. Many DJs on their way up have taken opening acts spots for exposure. So you're in good company. No one in the industry got where they are alone. I believe it's a good move for you both," Tommy said.

"Let me ask you guys a question." Velvet tapped her chin.

"Shoot," Sonny said.

"What if we don't do it?"

"Well, for Bedazzled Beats we'd have to search for another source for fan access. You're already doing as many festivals as Tommy can book you for in addition to the club spots. Your publicist is working overtime to get you as many lucrative media contributions as you have time for. We'd have to explore other opportunities, but I have to tell you that there aren't many with this much bang for the buck."

"How about Tres Armadas? How does this affect them?"

"Tickets have already been purchased, but they'd have to continue their search for other available artists of your caliber and frankly, with festival season in full swing, there are not many. Zazzle's comeback is a draw but their former opening act, Chemistry, are very popular. It's a bad look and as you both know, the group needs as much stability as possible right now."

Their industry wasn't the most solid ground for a returning artist struggling with substance dependency, and the thought of Zazzle's environment being unstable made her uneasy. Granted, it wasn't her responsibility to think of his situation and she had to consider Bedazzled Beats above all else, but it wasn't like her duo wouldn't benefit from the arrangement.

"Hey, I think we should do it," Candy expressed, then quieted her voice. "You asked for a miracle, Velveteen. Something that would get us in front of millions more fans. This is it. What's that saying…about gift horses?"

"Never smack a gift horse in the face?" Sonny offered.

"Yeah, something like that." Velvet smirked.

"Plus, I could use the change of scenery." Candy slapped down the breakup card. "We have each other but you know how lonely being on the road can be. It might do us good to be around a popular group like TA."

"Are you sure about this?" Velvet asked.

"Can you guys just give us a minute?" Candy pulled her to the side. "You're good with Zazzle, right?"

Velvet wasn't sure. The last thing she needed to do was stress Candy out. Her friend didn't even know she'd met Zazzle with Tekko at BonBon. "Yeah."

Based on Candy's slightly red eyes, she still struggled with her breakup from LED.

"Then let's at least think about doing it." The desperation in Candy's voice almost made her agree on the spot.

They went back to Sonny and Tommy.

"Can we just have a night to think about it?"

"Of course. We work for you guys," Tommy said.

"This is a big decision," Sonny said. "I would expect you to need some time to really think about this."

"Thanks."

"Let us know in the morning. I do have a little something to add." Tommy rubbed his hands together.

"Maggie has set up a mixer with you and Tres Armadas before your show tonight."

"A mixer?" Velvet dragged out.

"Yes, to just see how you guys get along. Granted, when you're on tour with them you'll have your own space and all the other protocols specified in your rider, but this might help you make a more informed decision."

Velvet had already met Tres Armadas. This time she wouldn't be tagging along with her popular friend. "Will you guys be there?"

"Absolutely," Sonny responded. "We won't be watching you or anything, but it's a nice thing that they've put together for us. It's something to enjoy."

Velvet sighed. "Okay."

"Can I grab you for a second?" Tommy asked.

"Yes, of course."

"I can sense your resistance to this. Is there anything I need to know? Because I'd never want to put you in a position that didn't benefit you."

Velvet had a list of why this wasn't good for her. Ever since her incident with Zazzle months ago, her mentor Reynard West, who spun as DJ FeNom, floated in her head. Zazzle reminded her of what she'd given up, what she'd lost, and why she'd sought redemption via the most elusive festival on the scene.

"I'm okay." Velvet trusted Tommy, but this new offer gave her a lot to ingest, most of which she preferred to keep under lock and key.

Tommy arched an eyebrow so high she thought it might actually reach his hairline.

"It's all good."

"Okay, but you can tell me anything if you think it

will help me navigate your career and your opportunities better. We're still getting to know each other in this relationship."

"I will let you know if something is up. Just like I did when I expressed my concerns earlier."

"Good." Tommy addressed the room. "Well, I suggest you ladies finish up your session and get ready for the mixer this evening."

They returned to their hotel room. While Candy showered to get ready for their evening, Velvet sat on the edge of the bed, her arms steadying her on each side. She stared at the door.

"What just happened?"

Chapter Eleven

Zazzle was still finer than a piece of antique jewelry from Cartier, tempting her to steal. As she and Candy perused the light appetizers at the mixer, Velvet was impressed that the drinks didn't include alcohol. The room was in view of, but closed off from, the rest of the Geneva Nightclub, making temptation harder to reach. Zazzle had really gotten his act together and from the current spread, the rest of the group had boarded the sobriety train.

Maartin was the first of the men to approach them. "Nice to see you again, Velvet."

"Same, Maartin."

"Again?" Candy asked.

"Yes. We saw each other at BonBon."

Candy stared at her for a moment. "You didn't tell me that."

Velvet shrugged. Now wasn't the moment to bring up Candy's self-centeredness. Candy was going through a rocky breakup and spent a lot of her energy trying not to be sad. It only made sense that she'd have little time to worry about Velvet's woes.

"I didn't know that you guys were staying in Europe this long," Velvet said to Maartin.

"We've been in Germany since BonBon. My family has come to visit since our shows in the Netherlands are weeks away. Sonny told us you had a great show at Fairyland."

"Yes, it's really conscience-driven. We had a blast playing for that crowd. Right, Candy?"

"Yeah." Candy's voice sounded far off. She blinked as if rooting herself to the room again. "Our set was supposed to be ninety minutes but we ended up playing for an hour longer."

"You won't be able to do that on tour with us." Christian strolled over and ran a hand through his hair.

"We're good at adhering to our time slot. At Fairyland, the festival management asked us to extend our set given the demand of the fans when we tried to leave the stage." Velvet didn't want to toot her own horn but Christian restated the obvious without saying. Tres Armadas was the headliner and Bedazzled Beats would be their lowly opening act, and she and Candy would do well to remember that.

"We're excited at the prospect of having you on tour with us," Maartin said with cheer to cover Christian's portion.

"Is that right?" Velvet challenged Christian but he didn't get a chance to speak before Zazzle's baritone sweetened the air like a speculoos biscuit.

"Yes, we are. You two joining our tour would be mutually beneficial."

"Hey," she croaked.

"We know you're busy with your performance tonight, so thanks for coming."

She nodded. "I'm all about the surprise mixer."

His light chuckle hummed its way right into the pit

of her stomach. He still charmed her without even saying a word.

Christian's eyes bounced between them as he and Maartin chatted nearby.

"You have a sound our fans will appreciate and we like to introduce them to new artists. I think it could be a good marriage."

"Marriage?" She sounded alarmed even in her own ears.

His humor hummed again. "Marriage between our groups on tour."

"Oh, yeah, thanks." Her dark skin hid the heat on her cheeks. She had to get out of his spell. She pulled her shoulders back. "It all sounds good."

"But?" Zazzle asked. He steeped a tea bag in a glass of lemon wedges and ice water. Without the tea bag, it would have gone unnoticed as an alcoholic beverage.

"Candy and I don't want to rush into anything. So, we're thinking it over."

Candy and Maartin moved over to the appetizers and Candy fixed herself a glass of strawberry syrup with a key lime seltzer.

"Anything I can help clarify for you?" Zazzle asked. "I'd like you to feel at ease."

Velvet didn't want to be mean or trigger him but she had a burning question. "I've seen a bit of your routine with Joe. How's that going?"

"It's going well. This environment is less controlled than…where I was in New Zealand, but I have a handle on things."

"Oh." Her mouth twisted and she wished she had a glass of something wet and bubbly in her hand to distract her because his golden, honey brown eyes unabashedly searched hers.

Zazzle straightened. "Do you have reservations about me?" he asked as if ramming the words through his teeth.

She sighed. "You… I've been… I just don't… I can't…" She stopped to see if anyone else witnessed her scattered brain activity. "Yes. I do. I'm happy you've gotten yourself together but I've seen well-intentioned recovering addicts relapse. People I trusted and gave a lot of time and energy to."

He took a long swig of the tea in his hand. "I see."

A young man rushed up to him. "Here you go, Mr. Van Sandt." The man handed him a tiny squeeze bottle with a thick liquid that almost matched the color of Zazzle's eyes.

"Thanks," Zazzle said and squeezed a few drops of the liquid in his tea.

"What's that?" Velvet asked.

"CBD oil," Zazzle responded as nonchalantly as if he'd told her he squeezed simple syrup into his glass.

She felt like the biggest fool. Here she tried to extend an olive branch and he was drinking an edible form of marijuana. "I believed you, and you're using right in front of me."

"Using?" He glanced down at his tea. "No, I can explain."

Her change in disposition caught the attention of others in the room. Maartin, Tommy and Sonny came over.

"What's going on, you guys?"

"A bit of a misunderstanding," Zazzle offered tightly.

Velvet's forehead ached from frowning. "What am I misunderstanding exactly?"

"The oil. It was recommended by my doctors in rehab and is medicinal. It's non-psychoactive."

"That's big in LA," Tommy stated. "Seems to be helping a lot of people medically. You don't get high from it."

"Zazzle explained some of this to us when he came back because we had questions, too," Maggie said.

"So you're not..." Velvet wanted to crawl under dark weighted covers and turn the lights out.

Zazzle's jaw tensed.

Maggie spoke for him. "He hasn't fallen back into old ways. This is part of his new routine."

Velvet's goal wasn't to have the mixer revolve around Zazzle's rehabilitation. Her questions alone might have been hard for him to answer one-on-one, but had to be even worse with the crowd that now formed. She wanted to kick herself for the assumptions but how could she have known that weed therapy was part of his routine.

"I'm sorr—"

"Excuse me." Zazzle's polite but curt word wall stopped her from saying anything further. He left the room.

She didn't know where he went and begged her mind not to make any more assumptions, but she couldn't help herself. She'd been through enough to understand how fragile recovery was and how small a trigger it took to relapse.

"I didn't know." Velvet sat in a stew of her own making, one filled with the ickiness of judgment.

"Don't worry, he'll be back," Maartin offered. "You're allowed to be concerned, Velvet, but he is trying."

Velvet nodded.

Lighter conversation with the group followed. Christian seemed to be more amiable with Zazzle out of the room and also joined in with where they were heading next.

With her bubbly drink in hand, Candy had been chatting with Maartin, Sonny and Tommy. But as Velvet scanned the room she noticed that the other half of Bedazzled Beats had gone missing.

"Where's Candy?"

"She stepped out a few minutes ago," Maartin said.

Velvet peered out into the greater club and though it took her a few minutes she located Candy. She spoke to a fair man with dirty blond hair. Candy threw her head back and laughed as the man continued to engage her.

Candy and LED had only been broken up for a short time. Velvet was concerned that Candy might be in rebound mode, but when the man handed Candy a card, Velvet relaxed a bit. If the two were talking business, Candy would debrief with her later. Velvet backed away from the window and into Zazzle's warm solid frame.

"Oh. I'm sorry," she stammered. Magnet and steel had nothing on them. Velvet forced her body away from his.

"You okay?" he asked.

"Yeah." She swallowed. "I was just looking for Candy. She's out there networking."

The scowl on Zazzle's face was cause for concern. "Zazzle? Hey, listen, about the oil..."

"It's fine."

"You don't seem fine."

He gave her a thin smile. "I need to go. Have a good show tonight." He mumbled something about his routine.

"But—" Velvet didn't get a chance to finish her statement before Zazzle was gone again.

She'd given Zazzle plenty of reasons to be done with her tonight, from accusing him of using and drawing attention to his recovery, to bumping into him and probably pissing him off more in some way. *Take your pick.*

During the mixer, she could actually talk to him, reason with him, and despite the shield of doubt she led with, share a laugh with him. His complete one-eighty disarmed her but she couldn't afford to fall hook, line and sinker into his vibe. He was in recovery and she wondered what version of him was real. The wonderful spirit she'd spent the night of the festival with six months ago, the pre-stage party guy, the drugged out of his mind character, or this healthy, meditating, yet somewhat strict version of him. Would this version of Zazzle remain or would yet another emerge?

Candy wanted them to go on tour with Tres Armadas, as did her management team. Any reason not to that Velvet thought of was flimsy at best in the grand scheme of things. She'd asked for a miracle to help get them to Temptation. How could she say no?

Candy bounced back in. "Hey, girl, hey."

Velvet frowned inside. On a scale from upbeat to thrilled, Candy's status rested somewhere in the middle on a daily basis. Though her personality didn't quite do a one-eighty, something had shifted. "Hey."

"So, are we going on this tour with them or what?" Candy asked.

"Let's sleep on it." Velvet arched an eyebrow at Candy.

"Well, my fifty percent of this group says we do it."

"I hear you." Velvet wanted to go in with eyes wide-open. Right now, there wasn't much steering her away from the deal. She wasn't deliberately trying to frustrate her manager and agent, but this was her career and Candy's. She refused to rush her decision and if her fifty percent ultimately felt differently in the morning, then her team would have to figure out another plan.

"The vibe outside is lit. I'm stoked to perform."

"Hmm." Velvet still couldn't figure out Candy's energy.

"What? Why are you hawking me?"

"Are you okay? I know you've been quiet about, well…you know…the breakup."

"Jeez, Velvet. Why does everything have to come back to that? Let me live." Candy's attitude pinched Velvet's heart.

"It doesn't. You're just mad hyped right now. You don't have to fake your feelings. It's okay to be upset but you have to let it out. Bottling it up isn't healthy."

"And walking around like a sad sap is better?" Candy asked. "I'm cool. If I want your help I'll ask."

Velvet took her hand off an imaginary steering wheel. "No problem. Do you."

"I will." Candy approached the others and started to give her salutations.

What the actual fuck?

Their performance went well under the circumstances. They'd played in the middle of minor tiffs before, but Velvet couldn't get over the feeling that more was going on with her friend than was obvious. Velvet was notorious for digging too deep sometimes. Maybe she perceived more out of Candy's coping strategies than actually existed.

As she laid her head to rest that night, visions of

Zazzle in his hugging black tee shirt with CBD oil tea danced in her head. She'd been unfair. *I have to protect myself*, the familiar loop played in her head. Her thoughts shifted to Candy and one nagging question remained. Why didn't Candy tell her about the guy she spoke to at the Geneva Nightclub?

Chapter Twelve

Zazzle did a body scan from the crown of his head to his toes. What the hell was Willem Graf doing in Germany? Last night, when he'd seen him with Candy, the danger signs flared and flashed. Willem made the rounds and when he did, he sprinkled nothing but empty promises and gateways to mind-altering escapes—all under the guise of publicity.

Zazzle wanted to believe that the other half of Bedazzled Beats was smart enough to see through Willem's charm. He should have said something to Velvet, but between her accusations and her putting his problems on display, he'd had enough for one night. If she doubted his recovery and the changes he'd made, why would she listen to him about someone he used to run with?

Now, as he sat on the floor, grounding himself in meditation, his ass ached. He peeked at the time. Velvet glided through his mind with ice skates and engaged him with verbal double and triple axels. He may have wanted her effect on him to savor of sweet reunion, but he wanted too much. Velvet had made it clear that she would not soon lay down her defenses and believe in him. Maybe he'd misjudged what was possible between them.

The timer sounded. A half hour to get his chakras back in line. He lifted off the floor mat and stretched his limbs. He had only slightly been able to focus but the mindful time was enough for him to regain the control that had begun slipping through his fingers when he'd seen Willem.

He jumped on a scheduled Skype call with his therapist, Dr. Joseph Cooper, to check in. Zazzle had chosen Joseph due to his twenty years of expertise with substance dependency and his location in LA. Though Zazzle spent much of his time after rehab in the Netherlands, Joseph's Skype sessions had been invaluable in reconnecting to the breakthroughs Zazzle had attained in both group and private sessions at the center in New Zealand.

"*Hallo*, Joseph." Zazzle waved to Joseph's tanned and aged image on screen.

"Good evening, Isaak. It's good to see you." A colorful backdrop of books framed the doctor and the sun streamed through one of the windows in his office.

"Same to you, Doctor." From the beginning, Zazzle had liked Joseph. The man had made the long trip from LA to New Zealand to test their compatibility before taking Zazzle on as a client, and then stayed at the facility during his last month to help him transition out. Joseph could have easily done everything virtually but felt the initial connection between therapist and client should be handled with the utmost care.

They went through their regular set of questions, ranging from his desire to use, to how he fared with his recovery plan, before transitioning into deeper investigation on his life outside of the facility.

"Congratulations. This week marks the fourth month you've been out of the facility."

"Wow, I can't believe how quickly time has passed."

When Zazzle had arrived at the center, his doubts started to pick away at his well-intentioned declaration to get himself clean. He'd chosen the New Zealand center because of its twenty-hour plus flight away from his triggers, but when it had been go time he had panicked. Had it not been for his brother Jan, who'd traveled with Zazzle from his home in the Netherlands to the doors of the facility in New Zealand, Zazzle might not have made it. Detox followed and he had wanted to bag in the whole thing and head home, but he had made it through and was determined to work on himself and address his needs.

"Well, don't keep me in suspense. How do you feel?"

"Better." Zazzle stayed away from his automatic "good" response. "I'm maintaining as best I can. I think people are trying to adjust to the new me."

"How are *you* adjusting to the new you?"

"What can I say… I'm in the best shape of my life, I'm eating well… I got the whole mind-body thing down pat…" Joseph offered him the silence he needed to get all his surface ramblings out before going deeper. "I still get overwhelmed by the reactions I get. I think some people actually thought I was dead."

"How does that make you feel?"

Zazzle squirmed in his seat and wanted to change topics. "I don't like it."

More silence from Joseph followed.

"It hurts." Zazzle patted his heart and his lungs inflated.

"You're touching your chest, is that where you're still feeling it?"

His head dipped. "Ever since that night at the Egyptian."

"Sometimes when we experience traumatic events, it leaves its mark on us."

"I know that nothing is physically wrong with me, Doc. I've been checked out. It's just…sometimes it's like my heart relives that moment."

"Would you agree that the residual pain of your experience, as well as the anxiety around it, is still there?"

"Yeah, I would."

Joseph's image grew larger as he moved in close. "You're doing well, Isaak. Give it time, okay?"

Considering where he came from, Zazzle's present state was a gigantic improvement, but he had never done recovery before and sometimes doubted if he made progress where it counted.

"How has it been being back and onstage?"

His limbs electrified and he scooted to the edge of his seat. "Performing has been amazing, Doc. The thrill of being back onstage? The fans? It was the ultimate rush." Zazzle flipped through his notebook to recall the things he wanted to share with Joseph. "The times when I'm not performing are a bit lonely, but I've had support here and there."

"Let's go back to the thrill of performing…"

Joseph worked with him to communicate the rush of performing and address any hazards there with addiction replacement.

Zazzle hesitated to explain, but grew a stronger set of balls. "I feel pressure to be 'the show' and get wild with the fans."

"When you decided to go back to work, these were some of your top concerns. How are things going so far?"

Zazzle felt the skin on his forehead tighten. "Right now I need to do what I have to do for Tres Armadas. You know, right the ship."

Joseph nodded. "Okay, but ask yourself. Does the ship need to be righted by you alone or does its inner working need repair by you and your fellow DJs?"

Zazzle's pen paused mid-sentence and he looked up at the screen. "I'll need to think that over." He continued his note taking.

Joseph nodded, speckles of gray in his brown hair more visible on the top of his head as he penned a few notes. "You've only been back a little while so keep jotting things down and expressing your wishes. It's okay to draw hard lines but we want long-term success.

"What else are you noticing?"

"I gotta tell you, Doc, I knew that coming back would bring a level of judgment with it, but I didn't expect it to come at me from so many different directions. Sometimes it feels like I'm being hijacked from it. I do what I can to not let the stress overwhelm me but it doesn't always go so smoothly."

"Renewing relationships and rebuilding trust is a marathon, Isaak. It won't come quickly."

"Tell me about it." Zazzle's shoulder slumped slightly but then he straightened when he delivered better news to Joseph. "Just to follow up from our last session about the medication. I'm not as drowsy as when I first started and I'm really comfortable with the dosage now."

"That's great. I'm glad to hear it. Are you taking the

recommended dosage of CBD oil to combat your anxiety and depression?"

"That got me into a bit of hot water, but yes." Zazzle explained what happened.

"Take a breath," Joseph instructed. "I can see your shoulders tensing up from here." Zazzle did as instructed before Joseph continued. "You've mentioned Velvet several times in our sessions. Now that you are back, a good thing to note is whether or not the relationship with her is a point of stress or comfort."

At present, Zazzle wasn't sure. What he did know was that he looked forward to seeing her again, and again.

"It's okay if you can't answer that yet, Isaak, but if the relationship is of importance to you then you should explore which it is."

"Got it, Doc."

"If people have questions, feel free to answer them. They are likely just curious. You may also point them to the research. There is still a lot of misinformation about treating addiction, so some confusion is to be expected."

"My threshold for explaining is getting low."

"That's understandable," Joseph explained. "And Christian? Have you two had a chance to talk yet?"

They had not. "I'm working on it." The muscles Zazzle had just worked on relaxing seized up again and no amount of meditation would help.

"The benefits of approaching him make you vulnerable to whatever reaction he might have."

"So you keep telling me, Doc," Zazzle mumbled.

Joseph smirked but didn't let him lose focus. "Your feelings surrounding this issue are like a cancer that will not cease to spread unless addressed. Look at it from the perspective of closure. Trust yourself, Isaak. You've overcome so much so far."

"I will in my own time, Doc." Zazzle sighed.

"That's fair." He'd heard it plenty of times during his sessions with Joseph. Something as small as confronting Christian loomed over his head like his own personal rain cloud.

"Anything else you'd like to discuss?"

Zazzle didn't know if he should mention Willem so he did. "I can't ban him from public places, and if things work out regarding some of our recent business deals, then he may latch onto fellow performers on our tour."

"You may be able to avoid him at times but you can also expose him and use your security detail to keep him at a distance. Any desire to reconnect? He is, after all, your old supplier."

"There's always desire, Doc, but not as strong as before. I can try to ban him but I might get resistance from other artists who appreciate his services."

"A pickle for sure. Stick to your routine. I know you're traveling overseas but get to a meeting if you can. We can strategically schedule our meetings to combat the obstacles coming your way. There is also the hotline."

Joseph went through all the options available, like he'd done when Zazzle resided at the facility. The reinforcement made him feel more in control and supported. Sure, Maartin seemed to be invested in him and Maggie was on board, but there were many days when he felt alone with no one to understand what he was really going through.

"Thanks, Doc."

"Take care, Isaak."

Zazzle ended his call with Joseph. His stomach growled. The desire for food a good sign that he'd leveled out.

He would figure out the best way to deal with Willem. For all he knew, Willem's presence in Germany could be a one-off thing. He couldn't afford to take the chance, so he'd prepare himself to shed some light on who Willem really was, and the danger he posed to not only him but other unsuspecting parties. He just wasn't sure how or when.

The two members of Bedazzled Beats popped in his head, but it was Velvet whose image lingered.

A soft knock on his room door sounded but it was so light he waited for it to happen again to make sure he'd actually heard it. He opened the door and Velvet stood before him in jeans and a silver bubble jacket. Her floral fragrance followed the air produced by the door.

"Hey," she said.

Once over his initial surprise, he greeted her. "Come in."

His hotel room was meticulous but he still searched for anything out of place.

She parked herself on the arm of a couch and crossed her legs.

"Can I get you anything? Something to drink?"

"No, thank you."

He was unsure as to the reason for her visit so he waited for her to start but based on the wrinkle between her eyebrows, she concentrated on whatever it was she wanted to say.

"I just… I wanted…" She sighed. "I'm sorry about last night. I jumped to conclusions and that wasn't fair."

He rubbed his hands against the rough material of his jeans.

"I appreciate you saying that." Her apology meant more than she knew, especially since he'd owed her several, none of which had passed his lips yet.

"Recovery isn't easy and assuming the worst, well… sucks."

"You speak from personal experience?" Zazzle didn't know what to make of her delayed response but her features relaxed.

"Someone I cared about struggled with their dependency on drugs. He'd get clean but…"

"He relapsed?"

She nodded. "I've seen things get pretty bad and nominated myself part of the cleanup crew."

"That couldn't have been easy." He stayed in the moment with her because the small admission helped him check his ego and realize that perhaps her reactions weren't only about him.

"No." She stared at a focal point as if the events played out before her. "The stress did damage, but nothing compared to the damage the drugs did." She jolted back into her body. "I guess I worry about you—"

"You worry about me?"

"No, I mean…yes, I worry if things will stay as leveled as they appear right now with your routine, lifestyle changes and being back here with all this." She shoved her hand into her pockets and her jacket couldn't get any tighter if she tried. "How are things going for you?"

"Good. The facility I stayed at in New Zealand really takes a holistic approach to recovery and developed an individualized plan for me. It had to be tweaked quite a few times because of this environment."

"Did your..."

"Clinician at the facility and therapist in LA." He offered more information than she requested in the hopes that she'd be kinder to her taut jacket.

"Both, huh?"

"Yeah, I video conference with both regularly." He wanted her to be confident in him and his seriousness about his recovery plan.

"Did they think it was a good idea for you to come back?"

"No, but I didn't come back until I was ready and felt strong enough."

"That's good." Her bubble jacket took on a more normal form. "Was it hard for you...being there?"

"In the beginning, yes, but then I finally understood that the addiction was a chronic disease, not some character flaw. Things are getting better. That took a long time." He spared her the physical and psychological effects of detox and how he'd once labeled himself a moral failure for not being able to handle drugs responsibly.

"I thought about what it might have been like for you there and coming back. I'm glad things clicked for you despite my assumptions last night at the mixer."

That she'd thought of him lifted his spirits but that she'd worried about him made him anxious in the same instance. "I'm handling it, Asha. You don't have to worry about me."

"Yeah, but see, I can't help that, and going on tour with you...with Tres Armadas..." She expressed apprehension about his recovery, but by the way her leg flicked, more words rested on her tongue. "I also have to think about the group and our goals. We want to be headliners on the main stage at Temptation."

His brows knitted. "And you don't think you can do that if you come on tour with us?"

She shrugged.

"Do you remember when we first met?" he asked.

"You mean when you got tanked on God knows what at the Egyptian?"

"No, before that."

"Yes, of course, I remember." The emotions played over her face like she relived each moment they were together all over again. He focused on the point he wanted to make over the images of her dancing, bouncing through the festival grounds, and sprawled across the white cushioned daybed.

"We talked about Temptation. Do you remember what I told you?"

She nodded.

"You'll be able to show exponentially more fans how much you love the music." Beyond his desires were her goals. His years in the business helped him see opportunities, and he knew that this opportunity was good for her, even if she believed that he wasn't. "If you do decide to come on tour with us, I'd challenge you to make them want Bedazzled Beats more than Tres Armadas."

He could see the wheels turning in her head.

"Can I ask you something?" he blurted.

"Sure."

"Do you ever think about that night of the festival and what would have happened if things hadn't gone so sideways?" His cheeks warmed and he lowered his eyes, swallowing before he spoke.

Her shaking leg stilled. "You're just going to ask me straight up like that?"

"It's in my nature to be direct."

"Maybe sometimes." She shrugged but the way she licked her lips spoke volumes.

"Well, I do," he confessed. "I don't know if you'll agree to go on this tour with us so if this is my only chance, I'm going to tell you that there's nothing I regret more than choosing drugs over you that night at the Egyptian."

Her eyebrows knit so tightly they formed one line across her forehead and she jolted to her feet. "Why would you say that?"

"This connection between us doesn't happen every day."

"How could you know? You were high." Her eyes went everywhere except to meet his.

"That night of the festival? The night I made love to you? I wasn't high. You know that, don't you?"

Her glistening eyes met his and confirmed to him that she didn't believe a word she'd said. "I let you in, Isaak, without a second thought and..." Her breathing hitched in her throat. "The next day it was like the man I...the man I knew was gone. You were so different. I know the drugs affected you but it changed everything. I couldn't go through that again and I had to choose."

"I'm the same man you had that connection with, Asha."

"How do you know that what we felt wasn't just some random thing that happened?"

He took a slow step closer to her. "The same way that you know. Because I still feel it now." He didn't know what he was doing. He was alone with her and ever since he first saw her again he wanted to tell her that he still thought about her, still wanted her, but how could he ask anything of her after the shit he'd done?

The questions scrolling through his mind didn't stop his hands from resting on her shoulders. "Don't you?"

The rise and fall of her chest pushed against the puffiness of her coat.

"Isaak." His name on her lips made him heady. She made it clear she saw him as one big gamble. Then why did he lay a hand on her face and stroke her cheek?

Her fingers cuffed his wrist and he expected her to pull his hand away, but when she caressed his skin he knew that whatever this thing was between them, she felt it, too.

"Asha." He leaned in, his gaze transfixed on her plump lips and their inviting opening.

She lifted to her toes and tilted her head to kiss his cheek. "I can't, Isaak," she whispered so close to his lips he prayed they'd land. She hugged him and he wasn't sure if it was his heart he felt beating or hers.

He nodded against her head. The last thing he wanted to do was release her but he did. "Thank you for coming by…to talk."

"Yeah, sure. I gotta get going." She sped to the door, opened it and slid through it before he could catch his breath.

Velvet sat at a coffee shop with views of the Berlin TV tower in the distance. Her nervous system only now started to settle down. Zazzle disrupted her to her core. She still felt the ghostly presence of his touch on her cheek, and the scent of the cedar in his cologne, mixed with lavender essence, still lingered in her nostrils. How could she ever forget the electricity between them? As soon as they'd met up again in London she knew. More reasons to not go on tour with Tres Armadas piled on.

She needed a distraction from the dangerous path her imagination traveled. She pulled out her journal.

She had ideas about a vinyl set and scribbled down some notes. Scratching records and mixing music in its purest form brought her back to her roots when she'd become a staple in the clubs. Later when Candy had seen her play, she'd fan-girled her hard. Soon after Candy had admitted her crush on Velvet but the power of their friendship overruled any romance, and the two of them came up with the idea of DJing dance music together.

Maybe being creative would help her reconcile the decision she had to make about the Tres Armadas tour. When she set out for the coffee shop that morning, she'd needed a little space from Candy. They were together so much that sometimes letting a little air out of the balloon and allowing distance to hang between them was the therapeutic mini vacation they both needed.

"Headliner or opening act? Appetizer or main course? Foreplay or sexercise?" Velvet immediately regretted the poor choice of her last comparison when an image of Zazzle hovering above her flashed like high beams on a dark road. She erased the image like an Etch A Sketch and reevaluated her decision from the fan perspective. "Exposure or exposure times ten?"

She wrote *Temptation Festival* in her journal and drew circles around it. She took a drink from her small espresso cup and added a few hearts and stars to the page.

She sighed. This wasn't how this was supposed to happen. She and Candy were supposed to work hard, put out amazing music, connect with fans they loved, and the road to Temptation would be paved in gold—yellow-brick style.

Tommy had emailed a copy of the tour schedule and she looked at it on her phone. Three months of international dates, including the US and Canada. On top of the clubs and major festivals they were already booked for, their scheduled was packed. She was no stranger to hard work, but they had to get their album out. New music only boosted their fans.

Tommy, Sonny and Candy wanted this. Could she want this, too?

Her phone buzzed and *Knucklehead* popped up on her screen.

"Whaddup, fam?" Her brother Trevor's normally annoying voice was better than a home-cooked meal.

"Don't take this the wrong way, Trevor, but it's really good to hear your voice."

"Secretly, you love me."

"Not so secretly. You are my brother after all."

"Germany must be treating you shitty if you're thrilled to hear from me. What's good?"

"Germany's fine. The gigs have gone well. Boombox came out and…new opportunities are coming our way."

"You make the new opportunities sound like a prison sentence."

"It's not." She left her statement open-ended.

"Step into my office, young one—"

"I'm older than you." She cut him off as she always did when he treated her like *his* baby sister.

"Like I was saying. Step into my office. I'm a fix this shit up for you right quick."

She frowned so hard her head hurt. "Okay, big shot. Candy and I have a chance to tour with Tres Armadas."

"Whoa. That's huge."

"As their supporting act."

"Umm…still huge."

"Most agree with you. We're trying to be headliners ourselves. I don't know. It just keeps making me feel like we're taking a step back."

"Chill on that for a second. As far as I know, you want to play at the Temptation Festival. So what does it matter if you are a supporting act. The exposure can help you get there, right?"

"I hear what you're saying but…"

Trevor moaned. "I have the hots for your manager."

"What?" Velvet was so confused she laughed. "That's mad random. And honestly, I don't need to know your dirty thoughts."

"You told me something she said to you and Candy once. I can't remember exactly but you said it made you hungry to attack your dream. What was it? Something about regret, maybe?"

"Not exactly."

"But you know what I'm talking about, right?"

"Yeah." Velvet then recited Sonny's words. "'Even though you're not headlining, make them wish you were.'"

"That's it. She is legit a boss and everything I want in a woman." Trevor's groan made Velvet want to leave the room and give him some privacy.

"Trevor!"

"Anyway, it'd be a shame to have access to that big-ass platform and not light it up."

Velvet's throat tightened.

Her brother-turned-motivational-speaker made the blurry vision of her current situation crystal clear. "That was pretty good, Trev."

"Facts, facts, facts. I'm in awe of my own self."

Velvet rolled her eyes and scoffed. "How are you?"

"Me? I'm Gucci. I feel like I hit my flow doing this freelance work. My skills with social are on point."

Trevor had found work with a tech start-up doing social media. He was freelance, which gave a young party boy money to live with a bunch of roommates in the heart of New York City, save some funds and still give him the flexibility to entertain himself.

"How's your other half? She still sprinkling fairy dust as she skips through life?" When Trevor asked about her "other half" he should have referenced Velvet's boyfriend, but like recently un-booed Candy, Velvet, too, was boo-less.

"Candy's okay under the circumstances." Velvet informed her brother of what all went down with LED in the UK.

"That's rough. I saw them two settling down, you know, in a soccer mom life kind of way."

"Same. I keep trying to dig on both sides but I need to mind my own business and let them live. They know where to find me if they need my help."

Trevor busted into laughter. "Nice try. You can't not care. Sorry, sis, but you're not built that way. Don't set yourself up for failure by ever making that statement in public."

"Shuddup." The truth of Trevor's words didn't set her free, more like bound her in a curse from an evil stepmother somewhere.

"Yo, me and my boys want to come through, but you're a moving target. I can't keep up with your schedule."

"Well, when we're on tour with Tres Armadas we'll be in Ibiza in June. That will give you some time to actually work. You knuckleheads should come out then."

"Where are you heading first?"

"Florianopolis, Brazil, at the end of this month."

"Burn. I would have loved to hit up that spot. Anyway, I gotta catch the game. March Madness is almost over." Trevor's excitement mixed with the sorrow of college basketball season's end.

"That's right. I forgot it was that time of year already. It seems like yesterday Candy and I were playing New Year's Eve in Dallas."

"Hold up. Does that mean you're gonna do that shit? You're going on tour with TA?"

"Looks like it, Trev. Looks like it," Velvet said. Going on tour with Tres Armadas aligned with her three *F*s doctrine of gaining more followers, fans and fame. She may not want to be an opening act and she still had concerns about Zazzle but she reminded herself about the ultimate goal, to play a headliner spot at the Temptation Festival, not only for her but for fallen mentor DJ Reynard "FeNom" West.

"Yes! I'm so good." Trevor celebrated himself more than her decision.

"Whatever."

"Don't forget to give Granny a call. She hasn't heard from you since you left LA."

"I will." Velvet's grandmother had raised her and Trevor since their mother died when they were in kindergarten. Velvet's memory of her mother was hazy with only pictures to root them, and all Trevor knew was Granny. Their musician father lived in a different city regularly. Neither she nor Trevor connected with him much anymore. They had each other, Granny and their friends.

"How is she?"

"According to her? Killing it in her Zumba class."

Velvet busted out and silenced her mirth for the patrons in the café.

"I gotta go but I'll be in touch. Love you."

"Yeah, yeah."

Velvet scoffed. "Bye."

"Peace."

She hung up with her brother and walked back to the hotel, where she found Candy mixing music.

"Hey. I was looking for you earlier." Candy shut her computer.

Velvet laid her bag on a dresser by the door. "I thought you could use some space."

"About last night. I haven't felt like myself and…"

"I shouldn't have pushed. I'm sorry."

"Me, too."

"I have some good news, I think." Velvet plopped down next to her. "We should go on tour with TA."

"Really?" Candy bounced on the bed. The effect rippled out to Velvet and her body moved on the mattress. "This is the best news ever. I really needed this. I know it wasn't an easy decision and you want what's best for us but I think this is a good thing."

"Yeah, we'll have a bigger platform going with them. We have to really use it. That'll take work."

"We can do this, Velveteen."

When she and Candy were on the same page, she didn't doubt it. "We still have three weeks and seven shows before we're on the same bill but yeah…we're doing this."

Velvet tabled her concerns about Candy's emotional state for now. Breakups were hard and she needed to be a better friend.

"Let's tell Sonny and Boombox," Velvet said.

Candy raised her arms to the ceiling. "Floripa, Floripa!"

Chapter Thirteen

Zazzle knocked his knuckles against Christian's hotel room door. The rehearsed lines ran through Zazzle's head like a looping teleprompter. Joseph's words rang in his ear. His therapist had encouraged him to make amends with Christian, but Joseph didn't know Christian or his short fuse. Something Zazzle and Christian both shared.

Christian whipped open the door with his mobile held against his ear, and the smile on his face evaporated. "Things are good, love. We'll be home in a few weeks but once the kids are out of school I'd like you all to come out for a few locations."

"Is that Lotte?" Zazzle's hushed question was only audible to Christian.

Christian nodded and listened to his wife on the other end.

Zazzle gave him a Boy Scout salute.

"Isaak says hello," Christian muttered. His lips flubbed after listening for a few seconds. "What is that supposed to mean?"

Zazzle had met Lotte at a party almost a decade ago. She'd been a fan of his, but when she met Christian, she became his biggest fan. She'd always been sympathetic to Zazzle's struggles with substances over the years and encouraged his healing. Zazzle would bet money that Lotte gave Christian a tongue lashing about behaving himself.

"I am being patient." Christian reddened.

Zazzle stifled a smile.

"I must go, love. I'll call you tomorrow. Kisses to you and the kids." Christian hung up.

"Everyone doing well?" Zazzle slid a chair out from its nestled position under the desk and sat. The chair hissed under his weight. He figured the furniture sensed the additional weight of his burden in having this conversation.

Christian hung up the phone. "What do you need? Our photo shoot with Bedazzled Beats isn't until later and I have to take care of some things beforehand."

Each time Zazzle attempted to communicate, Christian hurried the conversation along as if en route to his next appointment. Over the past few weeks, Zazzle had used Christian's avoidance as an excuse, but now they were back on the performance route together and Zazzle finally had the courage to pin him down.

"Do you need to be somewhere? I wanted to—"

"Yeah, I'm conferencing with Maggie and Wallace Entertainment to go over some things."

Zazzle adjusted himself in his seat and his body temperature rose. Wallace Entertainment handled solo Christian, but as a member of Tres Armadas Maggie needed to represent the group Christian.

He again considered abandoning this subject, but Christian had given him a segue.

"How's that going?"

Christian scoffed. "Good."

Zazzle's cheeks tightened and he stretched his jaw to release the pressure.

"Not the answer you wanted to hear?" Christian challenged. "I know you're hoping I'll fail, Isaak. Let's not pretend otherwise."

Did he want him to fail? The green eyes of jealousy had possessed him a few times but regardless, he still wished Christian the best. Didn't he? "I want you to do what you feel is right."

"And doing my own thing, instead of only focusing on Tres Armadas, isn't the right thing?"

"I'm trying to talk to you about the group we both care about, Christian. Ever since we were young kids fucking around with instruments and equipment, having this kind of success has been our dream. You want to go solo, that's fine, but as a member of Tres Armadas, I'm having trouble understanding why you didn't communicate your interests to us. It all felt sudden." Zazzle used the words he'd rehearsed.

"It felt sudden only to you. I *communicated with* Maartin and Maggie because they weren't high all the time. When I did try to talk to you, you were shit-faced. Do you even remember?"

Zazzle remembered some things while others remained fuzzy. For much of his last year with Tres Armadas, he had been high. Zazzle freed the air in his lungs. "I fucked up, Christian. I've apologized countless times and I'm doing my best to bring back our credibility. You need blood?"

"I'm sure you're sorry. Sorry that your actions have directly caused this dynamic within the group and because of that we're toast. Let's face it, Isaak, we're not what we once were and I don't want to fight about it anymore. It's time to put Tres Armadas to rest."

"Why does pursuing your solo project mean the end of Tres Armadas?"

"Because I don't want to do both anymore. You want the stage? Well, it's yours. We all know you need to be the one everyone is watching."

Zazzle's defenses jolted up. "So, I like the stage and performing? What does it matter?"

"You don't need us any more than we need you to be successful, Zazzle. I know you want to pretend that the only reason you're coming back is for the group but be honest with yourself. The stage is as much a drug for you as the ones you sniffed."

When Joseph had mentioned Zazzle's exuberance for performing, Zazzle had received the information as something to evaluate and investigate further. However, Christian weaponized his weakness and even if he was right, it ticked him off.

"That's it, then. I don't get a say or have a chance to make things right?"

"You spoke loud and clear when you missed interviews, when I'd rush to your hotel room to see if you were alive. Let's not forget all the questions Maartin, Maggie and I had to answer about your viral video while you were in rehab."

Zazzle tempered his response and kept the responsibility on his side, even as his blood bubbled. "All true, and I can never repay you all for taking the heat for me."

"But?"

"But what about you?"

Christian straightened and squared toward him. "What about me?"

"I did my part onstage. I was the Zazzle everyone needed me to be. While you communicated with your muse behind the scenes and Maartin studied. I paid for it. Have you ever taken a minute to think about what I was going through? Why the drugs?"

Their rise to fame had been swift and unrelenting. Zazzle often loved to fool around and dance, and though he, Christian and Maartin worked on music together, Christian was the one with loads of unreleased tracks that piled up when he let his creativity flow. When the demand for his antics onstage grew, Zazzle struggled to turn off after gigs. His recreational drug use wasn't an issue as a Dutch youth, but when the stage followed him to after-parties, clubs and hotel soirees, his dependency on drugs had snowballed.

"We had plans. To live the dream and be famous—"

"We are famous. We are the only DJs to headline cities and venues and draw record crowd numbers that are normally reserved for traditional artists or multi-artist festivals. We've done it. You just missed the best part of it all. The last part. We can't go back in time. I'm ready to move on. Maartin is, too."

Zazzle's hands fisted and his knuckles cracked under the pressure. "We used to talk about our plans and make these decisions as a group."

"When the three of us were partners…friends."

Zazzle had never been bitch slapped but assumed it felt something like the blow Christian dealt him. Why did he expect a different result? "I thought we still were, but I guess you made that clear by your absence when I was in rehab."

"I'd seen enough." The guilt on Christian's face left as briefly as it came. "I've done my part, too."

"That's not a fucking answer. I was dead. Right there on screen in the video," Zazzle yelled. "You called me brother once. It might have been nice to hear from you. Just one time."

Zazzle expected a physical retort, but instead Christian stammered as if a conversation with himself took place between his ears. Zazzle longed to be privy to that repartee. "You're trying to get back, Isaak, but things have changed. I'm tolerating the adjustments you've made with this routine because it's helpful to you but I'm out of gas."

For Zazzle's part he wanted to say more but thought it best to table any further conversation on the matter for a later date. Christian was right. He'd just come back. He couldn't recover in a month what took years to lose.

"Understood. Enjoy your meeting." Zazzle rose to his feet. "For the record, I don't want you to fail." He just didn't want to be the only one left behind without any idea about what lay beyond the retired fleet.

The realization that Bedazzled Beats would be heading on tour with Tres Armadas hit Velvet like a brick wall when she and Candy touched down on hot Brazilian soil. Velvet didn't know whether to cheer or cry. Either or both may have been appropriate. One part of her envisioned exposure to more fans than she could imagine and the other part conjured up scenarios of what could go wrong.

Back at BonBon in the UK, when she'd first heard Zazzle had returned, her goal was to stay away from him, not join his tour. In the situations when she tried to avoid him, she kept finding herself in his space, chatting with him. When she almost kissed him in his hotel suite in Germany, it was obvious her control waned.

With the new addition to their schedule, Tommy capitalized on their location and booked them for a club in Rio. Now she and Candy were on a short jaunt in a private plane, courtesy of Tres Armadas, heading to Florianopolis.

Velvet had been to Rio and Sao Paulo but when the blue waters and sandy beaches of Florianopolis, with the city as a scenic backdrop, came into view, it stole her breath. Hercilio Luz Bridge in the city center was reminiscent of San Francisco's Golden Gate Bridge and the warm summer temperatures commanded less clothing.

After hours in air, Velvet and Candy finally touched down in Florianopolis.

"*Bem vindo ao* Magic Island," their driver said, stuffing their luggage into the trunk.

"Obrigado," both she and Candy sang. Their antics garnered amusement from the man.

Bedazzled Beats didn't yet warrant security, but Sonny traveled with them. A small media team accompanied them as well to capture highlights, pictures and interviews to share with fans on their vlogs and other social media.

Unpacking was kind of a joke because they were only in Brazil for two nights. Candy and Sonny headed to the beach with their crew while Velvet had to change her clothes. During the rest of their European performances, the chill of winter mixed in with warm days. Unlike Candy, Velvet refused to travel in anything less than her silver three-quarter bubble jacket.

Once changed into her crochet bikini, Velvet headed toward the aquamarine waters of the Atlantic to meet up with Candy and their team. Tourists filled the hotel and Velvet spotted the groups of friends decked out in colorful beachwear, psychedelic headbands, neon face paints and body art. Velvet admired them and nostalgia about her early festival days had her daydreaming back to when she'd lie out on the grass letting the beats and bass warm her body like the overhead sun. Close to the venue, their hotel housed many of the fans that'd come to see Tres Armadas play live.

On her way to the exit, Velvet passed the gym. Through the wide window, she saw a man huffing on a treadmill. By the speed at which Zazzle's legs flew on the large black rotating band, she had little doubt the machine was on high, if not at full speed. Anyone with that kind of pent-up energy was either running away from something or burning off steam. Her curiosity piqued.

"Jeezus, this is exhausting to watch, even." She couldn't pull her eyes away from the magenta sports top clinging to the sweat along his chest and abdomen. She hadn't seen him in weeks but his impact on her was no less powerful.

His head rotated her way. He did a double take and nearly wiped out on the machine. Her heart clenched and her hands pressed against the cool glass of the window as if to stop his fall with unearthly powers.

Zazzle stumbled back and off the machine, but the momentum threw him and he landed on his rear.

Her cheeks warmed and she ditched her plan to duck and hide. Instead, her nature kicked in and she rushed inside at the thought that Zazzle might be hurt.

"Are you okay?"

"Yes. Fine." Zazzle rolled over onto his hands and

knees, and then pressed his hands on one leg to get up safely.

"I'm sorry," she blurted.

Zazzle tilted his head. "Why are you sorry?"

"I distracted you." She ignored his grumpy mood. Had she just flown off a treadmill and landed on her ass, she'd be grumpy, too.

"Not your fault." He winced and rubbed his butt.

"You were going hard. Is this part of your routine?" She inhaled eau de workout mixed with the orange-scented hotel soap she, too, was familiar with.

"Yes." He stretched. "I was going to just take a walk but I needed to blow off some steam, you know?"

"Sure." Though she'd been right about what caused his stationary marathon, more questions about the cause popped up.

"Plus I didn't want to have to double back for a shower before I met up with everyone for our photo shoot. Is that where you're headed?"

Images of him in a shower with and without clothes danced in her mind's eye. "Promo photos on the beach. Candy and I are doing some solo stuff and then I think you guys are meeting up with us."

He slow-scanned her lime green, Carolina blue and navy crocheted bikini top and white cut-off jean shorts. Velvet became aware of the scarcity of her perfectly put together ensemble.

She swallowed. "Are you feeling better? Now that you've blown off a little steam?"

"You don't have to check up on me."

"I wasn't checking up on you. I was just asking because you're grumpy as fuck. What is it with everyone anyway?" Her hands rested on her hips. "I ask a question and all of a sudden my concern is a bad thing."

"Hmm…not sure if you noticed but it's often iced with judgment."

"No it's not." She shifted in her stance and crossed her arms. She may have a way of doing things and a lot of times she hoped people shared her outlook. How did that make her judgmental? "How the hell does that make me judgmental?"

He scoffed. "Okay." He grabbed his towel and his water bottle.

"Wow. Here I was running to help you." She spun on her heels and stormed to the exit, betrayal and a bruised ego the wind beneath her wings.

"Thank you, I appreciate it," he muttered.

"Bye." She didn't need his shit. He'd been kind to her since they'd met. When they almost kissed in his hotel room, their attraction was undeniable. Now he was snapping at her?

He cursed in his native tongue. She recognized it from his altercations with his bandmates, and the thought that he used it anywhere around her ruffled her feathers even more. "Hey, wait up," he called, but his time was up.

She navigated her way through the pool area. It wasn't until her feet hit the sand that she realized he followed her. He touched her shoulder and she spun around. "What?"

"Easy." He put his hands up. "I should apologize. I got into it with Christian earlier and… I'm sorry."

"For what? Snapping at me? Cursing at me? Being fucking ungrateful?" She kept walking, her back to him.

"Yes, for all, and for the record, I didn't curse at you. That was self-directed."

His admission improved her mood by an unnoticeable amount. "Everyone's been up my ass lately, I'll just add you to the list."

"Everyone?"

"Yeah. Candy, you."

"That's two."

She turned on him and a boyish smile was on his lips. If her anger was the cliff she hung on to then Zazzle was the pressure removing one finger at a time. She softened like a roasted marshmallow in a s'more.

"I'm only trying to help."

"I'm sorry I snapped at you and for being fucking ungrateful." He touched her arm and his smile worked on her like a gust of unexpected wind.

"Accepted." She lingered like she didn't have plans.

"What's going on with you and Christian?" His directness must be rubbing off on her.

"We have some things to sort out between us. Things are in flux and I… I don't feel like I have much control. It's frustrating at times, especially when your personal relationships suffer."

Cryptic but she understood. She and Candy's squabbles may not be as intense as Zazzle's and Christian's, but it came with its personal and business trials. "I'm sorry to hear that."

"And I'm sorry to hear you're having issues with Candy."

She nodded. "Thanks."

"Want to talk about it?"

She rocked on her heels. "She's being weird. Maybe I need to be more patient and empathize with her a bit more but we have a lot on our plate. I need her with me. You know? It's nothing."

He hit her with the half smile. "Well, if you ever do, I'll listen."

"You have your own problems to deal with, but thanks."

"That doesn't stop me from helping you if I can. Whatever you need." The wind tousled his hair and his light brown eyes mesmerized.

"You need a haircut." His mostly straight hair carried a natural flip at the ends, even with the slight waves caused by workout sweat.

"I'm letting it grow for now." He lived out the dreams of her fingers and raked his hands through his near shoulder-length strands.

"Rock a half ponytail. Like in the front." She wrangled his hair together to show him. "That'd look ho… cu…nice." She released his strands like their temperature shot to piping hot and wiped wetness off her hands and onto her shorts.

"Yeah?"

"Yup." She folded her lips inward. The more time she spent with him, the more he infiltrated her armed ranks. "I…um… I have to get to the photo shoot and you need to shower for me… I mean before…well… whatever it is you have to do." Velvet split before her mouth further betrayed her trust.

His light chuckle followed her and she bit back a smile.

As she and Candy pranced on the beach and posed for pictures, they could see the metal structure erected for the concert tonight. The magnitude of their first show on Tres Armadas's tour took on a life of its own.

"A stage to play some music," Velvet declared in an attempt to keep the moment in perspective.

Candy put her arm around her shoulder. "Initiation night, girl."

The harsh lines of the stage were in direct juxtaposition to the sands of the island. There were a few festivals coming through Brazil for the summer but that Tres Armadas could command their own weekend spoke to their demand.

Velvet smiled. "You nervous?"

"Nah…so long as we're up there on the decks together, it'll be fun."

Velvet only half believed her friend. Candy's emotions were like shaking a Magic 8 Ball. All Velvet could do was be there for her friend in the hopes that she'd level out eventually and talk about what had happened.

"Here they come," Sonny called, and the three men of Tres Armadas strutted toward them as if the sand they trudged through was their own personal runway. Two big hulking men hung in the distance to secure the trio.

"They really are hot." Candy's contagious giggle followed. "Especially Zazzle."

Velvet's head darted to the amusement crinkling the corners of Candy's pink-shadowed lids.

"Gotcha!" Candy pointed at her and shimmied her shoulder, doing her glee dance.

Velvet sucked her teeth. "Stop. That's not even on the radar."

"Yeah. Sure," was Candy's mirthful response.

The men of Tres Armadas greeted them.

"Good afternoon, ladies." The wind whipped through Maartin's curly dark hair. "Welcome to Florianopolis."

"Thanks. This island is absolutely gorgeous." Candy waved her hand at her immediate surroundings.

"Is everything to your liking?" Christian asked.

"Yeah, thanks. If it wasn't, Sonny would make sure everyone was aware." Velvet nodded toward their manager, who chatted with a photographer.

"Sounds like Maggie," Christian said, his mood as relaxed as his white tee shirt flapping against his body. His demeanor gave no outward sign that he, like Zazzle, needed to blow off steam.

Velvet couldn't help but notice that Zazzle hovered close to the group, but visually wasn't quite part of it.

"I heard your recent single on satellite during our layover. It's pretty cool," Velvet said.

"Thanks. Of the ones I put out in the past year, it's my favorite." Christian's less abrasive approach was night and day from their last interaction.

"Will you be playing any of your solo stuff tonight?"

"We don't mix Tres Armadas and our solo projects. At least, not right now," Zazzle said.

Christian's buoyant energy sank.

"That's a shame. I'm sure the fans would love it." Velvet eyed the impact of her comment. Both Christian and Zazzle returned tight smiles.

Maartin, however, offered a brilliant one. "Let's take some photos, shall we?" He hooked them both on one arm.

"Are they okay?" Velvet inquired to Maartin. Zazzle expressed him and Christian's personal tug-of-war but Maartin presented as neutral. Perhaps he had more light to shed so that she could stop wasting time guessing at what she already knew.

"They'll be fine if they want to be. Soon as they get over their shit, they will be okay."

"What shit is that?" Candy asked.

"Making amends with the end."

Chapter Fourteen

Bedazzled Beats barely had time to get warm in Brazil before they sprinted through a few shows in the sweltering heat of Manila, Jakarta and Kallang to Asia before heading back to Europe for a few weeks. Velvet marveled at the size of the Stockholm, Sweden, crowd. She and Candy weren't even the headliners for the tour, yet they played to a pre-show crowd of thirty and forty thousand. With Tres Armadas scheduled to go on only thirty minutes after them, the stadium already neared capacity.

"Holy shit."

Some of the fans booed when they came on and Velvet chalked it up to them not knowing who they were. That or they were disgruntled Chemistry fans. Velvet's sixty-minute objective? Romance the fans. By the time they were done, Bedazzled Beats would be the dance music artists the fans chatted, texted and posted about.

Onstage, she and Candy did what they did best and moved the crowd with their bass-pounding remixes, uplifting melodies and unique choices. They bopped across the stage and amped up the crowd through their mic and with their music. The show helpers and volunteers shot tee shirts and flung glow sticks, with their bedazzled logo and connect signatures, into the audience.

"That was great. Did you see that crowd out there? I almost crapped my pants in the beginning," Candy said.

Velvet laughed. "That was unbelievable." She thought back to Zazzle's words about making the most out of this opportunity. "All we do is have a good time, show them how much we love the music and win their fans over one show at a time."

"I'm with you." Candy grabbed her bag. "I'll be back."

Velvet hung around as techies moved their equipment and roadies prepped for Tres Armadas. The stage morphed into an even bigger, more elaborate, strobe light and LED masterpiece with moving parts.

Velvet sipped on some water. She could go backstage but she enjoyed Tres Armadas's entry and the fans' excitement gave her motivation to be better and to one day command the same level of fandom.

Tres Armadas had a few minutes before they took the stage. As they mingled with a small group, Velvet's eyes targeted Zazzle and she absorbed his image, from his dark brown hair down to his black leather and white-soled kicks. His loose zebra print shirt with red design on the front complemented the black jeans form-fitted against his thighs. She appreciated his fashion sense but his confidence made him irresistible.

"Hey," she greeted him.

"Awesome set." His half smile weakened her knees and she leaned on a speaker.

"Thanks."

"Where's Candy?"

"She's off doing Candy things. She'll be back."

"Cool." He scratched his head, and a mix of earthy scents emitted from his clothes.

"I don't normally see you until just before you guys go on."

"I sometimes sit in a bit of silence backstage. I guess you can say I'm taking baby steps to smooth the hard edges of my day to day."

"Adjusting to life on the outside, huh?"

He chuckled. "Something like that."

Someone came and handed him a to-go cup with a tea bag paper dangling out the top.

"Your weed tea?" she asked.

"If that's what you want to call it. I just call it tea." He blew at the steam rising from the opening and sipped.

Velvet still wasn't convinced about the advantages of using the oil but she hadn't researched it yet. "Tell me again why you drink it?"

"It's to help with anxiety and depression. Separating from drugs and alcohol is like losing your best friends. Grief plays a part. So it helps me stabilize those emotions along with medication." Zazzle side-eyed as if he evaluated her reaction to his admission.

She nodded. "It's not easy to share that, Isaak. So thank you." She stroked his arm and the fine hairs there. He exposed details most people kept secret. Even if they weren't together, he felt comfortable enough to be vulnerable. "Do you need it? The oil I mean."

"I wouldn't say I need it, no." He took a longer sip from his tea. "It's helpful, in addition to meditation and therapy."

Reynard used to be neurotic about doing things the right way when he got out of rehab but Velvet had seen the tightrope DJ FeNom walked. Zazzle, on the other hand, kept to his routine but he sure was Zen about it and that knowledge strangely relaxed her.

"Want to taste?" He offered her his tea.

"What's it taste like?"

"Let me think about that for one second…hmm… tea." Humor decorated his face, swirling her around like a bowling pin that refused to fall over. Months ago when she'd crashed into him with Nuts, her scooter, his comedic streak ran down his back then, too. He offered her the cup.

"Will it do something to me?" She read the cup like tarot cards.

"As opposed to doing something to me?" He again blew on the cup to cool the liquid and then handed it to her.

"I can't believe I'm doing this. You promise it won't do anything to me?"

"I promise." His baritone was too heavy and if the tea didn't make her high being this close to him did.

She took a sip of the hot liquid. She tasted lemon and green tea leaves with grassy, earthy notes. She smacked her lips.

"It's tart but minty and it doesn't really taste too much like anything other than tea."

He smirked. "See, you can trust me."

"I don't know about all that," she mumbled. Part of her did trust him. Glimpses of the man she'd gallivanted with at the festival shined through and if she wasn't careful, she'd fall headfirst again, but this time she feared she'd smother him with critical evaluation and caretaker behaviors.

The MC announced that Tres Armadas would be onstage in a few minutes and the thunderous roar echoed around them.

"That's for you guys." She pointed in the general direction of the audience. "Do you ever get tired of it?"

He peeked out at the packed crowd. "Never. If I did, I should retire."

She nudged him and shivered at the slight touch between them.

"What I'm trying to do now is leave Zazzle on the stage and live my life as Isaak."

She related to what he spoke of. Going after her dream, her grind was nonstop. "I get it. I feel like I have to be on all the time. The fans have almost a cult following for your onstage persona. Has that been hard for you?"

"A bit, but my routine supports the separation. The transition from one to the other after performances is almost…ritualistic? It's not a clear line but I've come to understand myself better so I prepare and plan as best I can." He shifted gears. "There isn't much we can know before voting opens but do you feel like you're making progress? I heard the boos earlier but the audience cheered for you by the end of your set."

"Yeah. I've been checking our numbers and our hope is to drop an early single or two from our album but it has to be fire, you know. If it doesn't hit, it could do more harm than good. I love what we have so far but Candy and I still have work to do."

"Your stuff is great. Trust it. I'm sure it'll work out," he said.

"Thanks." Doubts continued to cloud her creativity but his faith in her gave her new energy. Her time with him was sectioned into two phases: before and after the Egyptian. For the first time since their reunion, warning signs about his recovery didn't flash about him. The warning signs around her heart, however, roared to life. All she'd done was taste his tea. She blushed at the puns tickering above her head.

Candy approached and Velvet welcomed her arrival until she saw who accompanied her. The same man Velvet saw when they were at the mixer in Germany. That this guy was in Stockholm had her instincts up.

"Coincidences, my ass. Who is this buster?" Velvet glowered in the man's direction.

"Hey, you okay?" Zazzle asked.

"I saw this guy in Germany. I guess he's part of the scene but it feels like he's following us."

Candy's stalker dude walked in line with her and Velvet decided it was time to get to the bottom of this.

"Hey," Velvet delivered in cool tones. "Didn't I see you in Germany?"

"Good memory," the man said then turned to Zazzle. "Isaak. Long time no see."

Zazzle gripped his tea tighter and Velvet feared he'd squeeze out the hot contents.

"We weren't introduced," Velvet noted.

Candy must have recognized her not-so-friendly disposition and turned up the cheer dial. "This is Willem Graf. He's a publicist of many talents and we've been talking."

"Talking?" Velvet leaned in. What conversations about business did Candy discuss with Willem that didn't include her or Sonny?

"He's been giving me a few pointers about style and stuff. Like how to be an individual even when you're part of a group."

"I'm good." Velvet squared to Willem. "We're good."

"Well, I think we should hear what he has to say. He wants to help us with getting Temptation votes," Candy said.

Someone in the stage area called Zazzle and waved

him over to where Christian and Maartin gathered with grips and roadies to get ready for their stage entrance.

Zazzle leaned down and whispered against her ear. “Don’t believe anything he says.”

“Umm… O-kay.”

His hesitancy to leave unsettled her stomach. “I have to go.” Zazzle left, giving Willem a lingering glance that made her cringe.

What was that about?

“Mind if I watch the show with you two? Candy says you like the opening.”

Candy sure gave this guy a lot of information about her. “Yeah, I only stay for the opening.” *Then I take my scooter out into the crowd while sucking on a Blow Pop, which is entirely none of your business.*

Velvet watched Zazzle with the members of Tres Armadas, and their agitated body language lifted her eyebrows. Whatever triggered them was directed toward her, Candy and Willem. If she were a betting woman, she’d put it all on Willem. Who was this guy?

The artists disappeared and everything went dark. The cheers deafened and goose bumps prickled Velvet’s arm like they did the last few times she’d seen their opening number. The stage, equipped with a false bottom, housed an elevator, and as Maartin, Zazzle and Christian emerged from below, lights flashed and darted over the blackened arena. The crowd exploded and their cheers vibrated every inch of the venue.

“This never gets old.” Velvet’s hushed tone was only audible to her. This was where they aspired to be and no matter how long it took them, converting one fan at a time, Velvet was invested in their future. Witnessing Tres Armadas on tour, and how their team handled their shows and their media, was education worth its weight in emeralds, and Velvet studied hard.

"That's going to be us, Velveteen," Candy whispered. "We should hear what Willem has to say. Anything helps, right?"

The show continued and Candy, Willem and Velvet moved further backstage. Velvet still heard the music, but its muffled sound allowed them to carry on a conversation.

"So Candy tells me you guys are really excited to be on tour with Tres Armadas." Willem moved closer to her. "I can help with that. Put you in front of the right people."

"I'm pretty sure that's what our agent and manager do for us."

"Not that cookie-cutter shit they do for all their clients, but just for you. Just for Temptation."

"Hmm." Boombox's short list of clients allowed him time to develop a unique vision with them based on her and Candy's goals. Leona Sable, one of the best managers in the business, had recommended Sonny when they considered Wallace Entertainment to handle their management. The "right people" already worked for her.

"I can also help with things like your image and wardrobe. Not for nothing, but you could use a sexier look. Candy's almost there and I've given her some pointers. I wouldn't mind helping you out, too."

"Yeah?" So that's what he'd been chattering in Candy's ear? Promising her more exposure, updating her look?

"Yeah. I can get you into some elite parties. Extremely exclusive. Places that the regular Joe would mortgage his house to attend."

"You mean exclusive like that festival that was well advertised by that con artist that never happened? Exclusive like that?" She arched a brow.

Willem frowned. "I know you may want to do things on the straight and narrow but I suggest you loosen up a bit and let someone who knows the landscape help you ladies out."

Obviously, Willem didn't know anything about her because her path had been far from straight and narrow. She wasn't a phenomenon signed at age fifteen, and her history housed good and bad stories. She worked hard to be here, studied music and networked one gig and party at a time.

"Tell you what, Willem. I'll think about it and talk it over with Candy because that's what we do in a group. We'll let you know." Velvet's condescending tone couldn't be missed but since when was Candy okay with someone telling her about her wardrobe?

"I hope you'll do more than think about it. You guys are big enough that you should be headlining by now." Willem used the passive-aggressive arts to manipulate her.

Velvet didn't have time to answer her own internal questions when two security guards flanked Willem.

"We're going to have to escort you from the venue."

"Excuse me?" Willem's flustered inquiry accompanied the redness that darkened his face.

"What's happening? Why does he have to leave?" Candy seemed more frantic than Velvet thought the situation warranted.

"Hey, calm down," Velvet encouraged. "I'm sure there's an explanation."

"Sir, you must come with us. This way." The Swedish guards didn't put their hands on Willem but referenced the path they expected him to travel.

"This is ridiculous." Willem huffed.

"The artists and their management have revoked any previous backstage access."

"But why would they do that? He's with us," Candy explained.

"Not exactly," Velvet mumbled.

"Velvet?"

Velvet shrugged. "I don't know what's happening. I just met him."

Candy flapped her arms.

Velvet didn't know what shit storm she stepped into but if Tres Armadas and their team revoked Willem's backstage access, as a publicist, that meant he was blacklisted. Being blacklisted was never a good thing.

"Okay, I'll go." Willem turned to Candy, gave her a lengthy kiss on the cheek and whispered a few words before he was escorted away.

Candy had started to give chase when Velvet stopped her in her tracks.

"Whoa! What's going on with you? You barely take fashion advice from me. Now you're taking it from this guy?" Velvet asked when Willem was barely out of ear-shot.

"It's called change and I'm allowed to do it," Candy said.

"We change all the time, but it's because we're creatively expressing ourselves. Not because some dude suggested it. Not to mention the same dude that was just escorted out of here. Doesn't that bother you?"

"He wants to help me."

That Candy no longer referred to them as a group punched her ego.

"What about Bedazzled Beats?"

"Sometimes it's okay for us to express ourselves artistically as individuals."

Velvet studied Candy. Her friend's lack of eye contact was so obvious her head bobbled like a doll.

"We still talking about fashion?"

"Willem thinks it would be good for me to be featured on some other tracks. Get my name out there."

"I've never held you back from doing that. I've always had my vinyl projects since before we met and were learning together. You talked about doing some creative things, too. We used to talk with LED about doing that all the time."

"Fuck! You bring him up now, Asha?"

"Hold on." Velvet held up a hand. "When did it become off-limits to even say his name?"

"Since we broke up."

"And I'm supposed to know that how? You won't talk to me about it."

Candy gnashed her teeth. "I don't have to tell you everything."

Velvet scoffed. "We've been best friends for years and you've literally almost told me everything."

"I have to go get ready."

"Willem taking you out somewhere?"

"Yeah. Actually he is."

Velvet ground her teeth and served Candy all the sauce she could muster.

"Maybe—" Candy shifted "—things are changing. You're just going to have to deal with it." She stormed off.

"I'm already dealing with it." Velvet stared at her friend's back.

Chapter Fifteen

Zazzle kicked himself in the ass for not broaching the Willem subject with Velvet and Candy. The way Candy had clung to Willem made it obvious he'd already gotten to one half of the duo. He wasn't about to let Willem get his claws into Velvet. When Zazzle, Maartin and Christian had identified Willem, they did something they hadn't done since the months leading up to his UK return to their tour. Agreed.

"Get his ass out of here." Christian had called security over. "That man over there is banned from backstage access for all Tres Armadas concerts."

"Yes, remove him, immediately." Maartin texted Maggie to make her aware.

For a brief moment, he and his bandmates weren't at odds and made a decision together without argument. For the first time since he'd been back, their interactions felt like the partners and the united friends they once were.

"Do the girls know who he is and what he's capable of? What he's done?" Maartin asked.

"No. I haven't told them. He was in Germany at the club."

"And you didn't say anything to them then?" Christian scolded.

"Isaak." Maartin winced. "You have to tell them. You may not want to relive your drug days but they have no idea who Willem is."

"You're on, guys," a stagehand directed.

"I will. We have to get onstage."

They didn't see security take care of Willem but if Maartin texted Maggie she'd make sure that Willem was off the premises as soon as possible.

In the past, Willem had been a friend. One who supplied him with drugs when he needed them. In his dazed-out memory he couldn't quite remember if it was always at his own behest or if Willem kept him high and making bad business decisions to keep his drug income steady. Either way, Zazzle had a bad feeling about how Willem hung around Bedazzled Beats. Velvet seemed immune, as opposed to Candy's intrigue. They traveled together as a team and for his own sake and the sake of the tour he'd keep Willem at a distance.

He concentrated on their show, and the fans that they played to, for the next few hours.

After the show, Maartin and Christian attended an after-party downtown and he went back to his hotel room. The hotel still crawled with concertgoers who weren't ready to let the night come to an end. He tightened the black leather jacket he donned to ward off the chill evening temperatures of Stockholm in late May. Since his sobriety he felt the cold down to his bones a bit more and shivered. A security escort walked with him though the vacant pool area, where the sound of splashing water caught his attention. A woman, sitting on the edge of the pool, dangled her feet in the water.

Her jeans were rolled up to her knees, and her high-top boots and a scooter lay behind her. If it weren't for the silver bubble jacket she wore, he might not have been able to make out Velvet's figure.

"Wait here, please," Zazzle said to his security, and then went to her as if she called him. "Velvet?"

"Oh. Hey."

"What's going on? Shouldn't you be out partying somewhere? It's Stockholm in the spring after all."

"I got into a fight with Candy," she confessed. "So I took Nuts out for a bit and then I came back here. Don't much feel like partying."

"Oh." A type of heaviness came over him from the sadness in her quiet response. He referenced the space next to her. "May I?"

"Sure."

He sat down. "I'm sorry you had a falling out with Candy. Did it have anything to do with Willem?"

"You know him, right?" Her eyes searched his for answers.

"I thought you might have remembered him from that night at the Egyptian."

She tilted her head. "He was there?"

"Yes. He partied with me before my set with LED."

She squinted her lids and her eyes darted as if scouring her brain for a connection. "He *was* there. I remember now. He gave you drugs."

"Yes. In Germany, I should have said something to you when I saw him with Candy." Guilt took up familiar residence in his heart and his neck tightened.

"Wait, you knew who he was? Why didn't you say anything?"

"I didn't know if it was my place to say anything. I'm not the most credible source."

"For this you are. He was your supplier." She huffed.

If she smacked him it would have stung less. Velvet's passion spread across all areas of her life and though he suspected her response came from worry and concern for those she cared about, it didn't hurt any less.

Her jaw relaxed and her shoulders pulled from her ears. "I didn't mean—"

"Why? It's the truth." He stared ahead.

"Isaak, I'm sorry. That was unfair and—"

"We had him removed." He plowed on. "So he can't come backstage at our shows. It's the most we can do. If he wants to see Candy elsewhere, we can't bar him."

"What's he want with Candy?"

"I'm not sure. He's fronting as a publicist but he's bad news. He'll get her into exclusive parties and drugs will be a heavy part of it. It's what he's known for. Some people, myself included, sought out that life. I don't know Candy well enough to assume that's what she wants or doesn't want." Candy was the epitome of her namesake, but he didn't know her like he did Velvet. He didn't think she belonged in Willem's crowd but that wasn't his choice to make.

She scrambled to her feet. "She's probably out with him now. He wants a new client and probably not just as a publicist. She doesn't know. I have to find her and tell her." Candy could hold her own but if she was intentionally being misled, Velvet needed to be a good friend and shine some light on this Willem guy.

"I'll come with you. I know the clubs Willem would likely frequent."

"What? No, you can't."

"I feel responsible and—"

"There is so much temptation out there. It's not a good idea. Actually, you coming with me is the worst idea."

He half smiled. "I'll be okay."

"Isaak, please—"

"I can't hide forever."

"Yes, you can. All you have to do is go to your room and go to bed. Just follow those steps." She rubbed the shaved side of her head.

He'd gladly go to bed, if she'd join him there and let him hold her. He took her hand in his. "I'm coming with you. I should have warned you about him. Let me help."

She picked up her scooter. Her fingers choked the brakes on her handlebars. "I can't stop you from going, can I?"

"No." He smiled. "I'll be fine."

Indecision racked her movements. "Okay."

She put Nuts in her room, he released his security detail, and then the two of them hit the Stockholm nightclubs.

Velvet and Zazzle were patrons at their third club of the night in search of two people who probably didn't care to be found. Zazzle had had plans to meditate, drink his tea and go to bed. Instead, blaring music, gyrating bodies and glasses filled with alcohol all taunting him to his old ways surrounded him. Despite her guilt, Velvet was relieved to not be a solo foreigner asking questions about Candy and Willem.

A man with a Caesar haircut, dressed in a snug steel blue shirt and black pants, shook Zazzle's hand and greeted him in a language she didn't understand but assumed was Swedish.

The only words she got out of their conversation were *Zazzle, man* and *English* before the men changed languages and she could understand.

"I heard you and Tres Armadas were in town and kicked ass tonight. I was wondering when you were going to come by and see us."

"Nice to see you, Sigge." Zazzle unzipped the leather jacket he wore.

"Glad to see you're back. After that video of you at the Egyptian, I didn't know if you were alive, man." She stood slightly behind Zazzle and Sigge tilted his upper body to get a full view of her. "This your lady?"

"Velvet, from Bedazzled Beats." She introduced herself but fought with the surge she got from Sigge's mention of Zazzle's viral video. She'd only seen a small portion of it and by Sigge's description she was glad. It didn't stop curiosity from budding.

"Nice to meet you, Velvet." Sigge's Swedish accent didn't impact his command of English.

"Nice to meet you, too."

"What can I get you guys?"

"Velvet?" Zazzle asked.

She could use a drink right now but traveling with her recovering companion, she opted to keep things virgin. "Ginger ale."

"Same for me."

"For real?" Sigge asked. "I have Svedka Citron. If I remember, you take it with bitters, yes?"

"I'm not drinking."

Sigge studied Zazzle like a newfound relic. "You sure, man?"

"He's good." It would have been quieter if she'd used a megaphone.

Zazzle raised a brow and she shrugged. "Ginger ale is fine."

"All right, man."

"We're not staying long, but we're looking for someone. Have you seen Willem around?" Zazzle rested an arm on the bar in a habitual gesture and then quickly stepped away. Even more than before she acknowledged that he should not be here.

Sigge on the other hand looked like a permanent fixture. "He passed through earlier but I think he's gone. Had some girl with him. His client, I think."

"Yeah? What did she look like?"

"She's dressed kind of like your lady friend here. Except she was white. No offense," Sigge said to her.

"None taken?" She wasn't sure what she was supposed to take offense to. Candy being white? Her being black? That Candy looked like her? This particular mystery didn't warrant further investigation. "That's Candy."

"Yeah, that's the name."

Zazzle adjusted his weight from one foot to the other. His eyes rested squarely on the bottles racked on a neon blue shelf. "How long ago did they leave?"

"Oh, about a half hour ago. Everything's closing up soon, so maybe they called it a night." Sigge winked.

Nausea crept into her stomach. It hadn't been a month yet since Candy and LED broke up. She could be rebounding with Willem, but that wasn't Candy's style. Velvet's certainty wavered.

"Thanks." Zazzle shook Sigge's hand.

"We should head back."

Velvet punched in a text to Candy and then dialed her number again, but Candy remained unresponsive. "She's so annoying right now. Pick up your phone, beeeetch!" Velvet yelled to a nonexistent receiver.

"Take it easy. That's not going to get her to respond."

"I'm going to strangle her." For Velvet, drugs had their recreational place but her mentor struggled with addiction, so did Zazzle. She didn't know for sure if Candy used anything but the combination of Willem's profile and Candy's current emotional state made Velvet uneasy enough to hunt her down in not one, but three clubs.

The place reeked of alcohol and though Velvet liked to drink, this had to be a little bit painful for Zazzle. He took this ride into the belly of the beast with her to find her friend. She was still pissed that he knew about Willem and didn't tell her or Candy, but his help had already proved to be invaluable.

Her phone buzzed.

Candy: I'm at the hotel.

Relief relaxed her shoulders. "She's back at the hotel." Zazzle didn't respond and she found him ogling VIP like a disrobing lover.

"Hey. Let's go. We don't even need to be around this anymore." She pulled at him and he snapped out of whatever trance had entrapped him.

"Yeah. Let's go."

"Do you mind, Sigge?" She pointed to containers of bottled water.

"Anything for my guy." He instructed one of the bartenders to hand him the bottles before he handed them to her. “On the house.”

“Thanks.” She had already assumed they were free.

Sigge arranged a taxi for them and they headed back to the hotel. Velvet shivered in the back seat of the car and overlapped her unzipped coat around her middle. “Come through, spring.”

Zazzle chuckled and blew warm air into his fisted hands.

“These might actually be warmer.” She pulled the bottled water from inside her bubble jacket.

“I appreciate it.” He opened the bottle and took a gulp. “Ahh.”

A short bout of silence followed until Zazzle’s rich voice filled the small area.

“Candy say anything more in her text?”

“No, but I’ll talk to her at some point.”

“Listen, if you want to help Candy you gotta lay off a bit. Crowding her will only make her pull away.”

Her defenses rose into position but slacked enough for her to hear him. “So that’s a no to waking her up for a chat?”

“Yes.” He hummed and she wanted to kiss the grin off his face.

“Well, how the hell am I supposed to do that, knowing she’s hanging out with someone who might be pushing drugs on her. She’s sad, susceptible. If I don’t wake her ass up, who will?”

He touched her arm. “Just take my advice on this. Even if she is taking something, it doesn’t make her an addict.”

Her head swirled with all she’d learned in the past few hours.

She gave Zazzle a once-over.

"You okay?" She angled her body toward him. "Being in there? Meeting old friends from your past life?"

"That's been happening since I've been out of rehab. People know. Some care and go overboard on accommodating me. Others don't give a shit and try to get me to party."

"And that's okay with you?"

"I'm handling it. I'm only responsible for controlling one person."

She nodded. "You did good in there. Not that my opinion matters—"

"It matters." His eyes lingered on her and for more than a split second she forgot she handled a Candy crisis. His hand touched her cheek. His thumb caressed her jawbone and slid forward to stroke the underside of her trembling bottom lip. His touch did more to her than any foreplay she could remember with well…anyone.

His fingers moved to cup the back of her neck, the action tickled the short hair hanging there. The city lights glimmered though the back seat. He made no move toward her, but with his eyes smoldering as if she were the sole cause of the desire within them, he didn't have to.

She fell onto his lips, one hand framed his head and the other pressed against the taxi door window. The aroma of leather and botanicals intoxicated as it lessened the impact of the poor choice she was about to make. When Zazzle's free hand glided up her side and she arched into his touch, she yielded.

What am I doing? She pulled back. "I'm sorry. Did you want… I—"

He parted her jacket to reveal the sheer black tank she wore and cool air entered the warm barrier. His hand moved to the front of her shirt and his palm moved over her breasts until he gathered the material into a fist. "I've dreamed of tasting you again, Asha." He pulled her to once again meet his lips and whispered, "It's not enough."

She'd craved this since before that night in his hotel room, since their last kiss months ago. Now as his mouth massaged hers and their tongues played, she knew with all certainty she hopped into trouble with both feet. Her steady hands gave his freedom to seek warmth under her shirt and she flinched from his cool fingertips but leaned into his touch nonetheless. His one arm encircled her waist, and the other stroked over her chest, molding to her breast. They both moaned at the new touch.

"Isaak." Her whisper was barely audible over the hum of the car.

The car. The driver. "Oh, shit." She leapt away from him.

Zazzle reached for her and her eyes oscillated from him to the driver. Zazzle scrubbed his face and his chest rose and fell with speed that competed with hers. She pinched her bottom lip in an effort to quell its longing for more.

Did off-limits *suddenly develop a new definition?* The car jerked to a stop at the hotel entrance. She'd opened Pandora's box when she'd kissed him. Maybe she'd wanted to distract him from reminiscing about the various bottles he could be throwing back or the bumps of snow he could be sharing in VIP. Maybe it was her nerves about the pin she was about to poke in

Candy's balloon about Willem. Whatever the reason, she'd wanted to kiss him and by the way her heart continued to race, she wanted to do it again.

They exited the car and entered the vacant lobby. As they waited for the elevator Velvet jumped at the featherlight graze of Zazzle's hand on hers. If she wanted to avoid his bed tonight she needed to leave tumbleweeds in her stead.

"You know what? I'm going to take the stairs."

"Asha." Her own name seduced her like dulce de leche swirled in ice cream.

"Thank you for coming with me tonight. I really, really appreciate it."

"So." His tongue rested on his upper lip. "We're pretending what happened in the car didn't?"

As if she'd open a can of unruly worms by answering his question. "Goodnight, Isaak." She all but ran in search of the alleged staircase.

Six flights later, breathless and sweat-drenched, Velvet finally arrived at the hotel room she shared with Candy. Her friend snored in a deep sleep with a bunch of water bottles around her. Against her better judgment, Velvet opted to not wake her up.

As she snuggled under the sheet and toasty duvet, she wondered if Candy had tripped on Ecstasy that night or if she was just really thirsty.

Chapter Sixteen

The next morning Velvet was up and packed for their travel day before Candy rolled out of bed. It took all of Velvet's willpower not to jump into a rant about the previous night. She jostled her friend a little harder than normal to wake her.

"What time is it?" Candy stretched.

"We leave in two hours. Thought you might want to get packed and maybe eat something."

"Yeah." Candy tossed under the covers until she snuggled back into the pillows.

"How was your night?" Velvet bit out.

"Fun. Willem took me all over and we met some cool people."

"Did you get my texts? My messages?"

"Some, yeah. Reception was wonky." Candy yawned.

I bet! "You're going to love them when you hear them," Velvet mumbled. She didn't flat out believe Candy lied but history had proven that Candy stayed glued to her phone.

"Huh?"

"Nothing." Velvet sat on the edge of her bed. "I might sound…tight when you do listen to the messages. I went looking for you because I found out some stuff last night and needed to talk to you."

Candy sat up slower than a Sunday afternoon. "What stuff?"

"Stuff about Willem." Velvet's body wanted to explode with a tantrum to end all tantrums but Zazzle's words echoed in her head. "I'm not sure he's legit."

"Why? Because he's interested in me?"

"What? Of course not." Velvet balked. The tip of her tongue weighted heavy with perspective. "People have experience with him, Candy. Do you remember when we first met Zazzle? Willem was there. He was the one offering Zazzle drugs."

The lack of animation in her friend meant only one thing. "You know?"

"Willem mentioned it."

Velvet's next question stuck in her throat as if she'd swallowed a wad of peanut butter. "And you're still hanging out with him?"

Candy fiddled with her hands.

"What's with all this?" Velvet's finger flicked like a conductor's baton to the various water bottles. "Did you take something?"

Candy leapt out of bed, snatching clothes and toiletries about the room for her suitcase.

"Are you?" Velvet demanded.

"Maybe I just want to feel good."

"Even after all that happened with FeNom?"

"I'm not an addict." Candy let out her exasperation. "See? I knew you'd freak out. It's just fun. I need that right now."

"Fun?" Velvet crossed her arms.

"Yeah, fun."

"I thought we had fun when we played together."

"We do. I need something different. Everything feels different now. I don't know." Candy rubbed her eyes.

Velvet wanted to bring up LED but Candy bit her head off every time she did. Things felt different without him and Velvet only guessed at how much that affected Candy.

"What about all the things Willem is promising you? If he knows you're in a...rough place. Don't you think you should be a little bit cautious?" Velvet sweat from the amount of word plucking she did, but if it kept Candy talking, she'd pluck away.

"Look, if you don't want to work with him, that's fine. Don't make him out to be shady."

"Your words, not mine." Filter gone.

Candy growled like a caged cub.

Velvet prayed for patience.

"Okay." Velvet clapped her hands together. "You're smart and responsible and wouldn't let anyone take advantage of you. I just wanted to bring it to your attention." She tossed each word as casually as she tumbled back onto the seat on the couch. Her feet dangled over the armrest.

"I am," Candy stated.

"Uh-huh. I'm sure you can handle yourself." Velvet pressed her lips together and stared at the ceiling.

Candy continued packing. "I heard some positive buzz when we were out last night. The fans really liked our set. Some even asked us about new music."

The feedback helped take the sting out of everything that happened. They'd only been on the road with Tres Armadas for a little while and had already gotten some praise. They needed to light up their next big show with something memorable for the fans.

"We need to use our next stint of club gigs and appearances to build it up. It's risky because we haven't decided on a track yet, but the pressure will help us shit a diamond."

Candy giggled. "We can totally shit a diamond."

"We have one more track to send and we're done. Joe and Rob are going to work with us when we're in Spain next week. Maybe we could debut one of the tracks for the festival show."

"That'd be delicious." A glimpse of the old Candy emerged.

"I honestly can't wait to see them guys. Trevor and his boys are coming out, too." Velvet loved Candy but during festival season she saw her friends much more than she did being on tour with Tres Armadas. The good news was that on occasion their tour and festival dates put them in the same cities.

"Now that's a party." Candy's glee filled their hotel room.

"It's going to be bananas."

Candy threw her clothes up in the air and danced around. "Spain doesn't know what's coming, Velveteen. Temptation puts out the qualifying acts in a few weeks. We'll be in Vegas. I know we're going to be on the list. Our next few shows are really going to help. I feel it."

Velvet hoped it wasn't the drugs Candy felt.

She sat up and fluffed her hair. Candy smiled and hummed one of their songs as she packed. Her demeanor was less heavy than the days in Europe, when Candy's puffy eyes and sniffles were staples in their room. Velvet wanted to talk to her friend about her breakup but Candy was still so sensitive about it. If Velvet missed having LED around, then Candy sure as hell did.

Before she got on the plane she thumbed a text. A month had passed and maybe the answers would be different. She hoped that Spain would lend answers to so many questions she still had about Candy and LED's breakup. They'd be in Spain for a long weekend. Perhaps the new exciting location would give her and Candy time to reconnect and find the heart of their friendship again. Most of all she prayed that Willem didn't follow.

Zazzle let the water fall over him for as long as time allowed. If there was a day he needed his routine it was today. Though he didn't drink or take any drugs, he nursed a hangover from the resistance alone.

Last night he took a chance going to the club. He'd experienced the fragility of his recovery before and come out clean but he thought it best not to make dabbling in those waters a habit. He definitely missed the nightlife.

As the hot streams poured over him, he flashed back to Velvet. He had a hard-on that wouldn't quit. It wasn't the first time thoughts of her drove him to grip the rigid flesh between his legs. This time, the feel of her lips, and his hands on her soft skin and flesh were palpable, and seared into his mind. The hotel lotion emitted notes of a light fragrance he couldn't place, but it didn't matter. The slick layer it provided allowed his hand to glide as he squeezed up and down. The buildup was quick as his need and fulfillment collided. He pressed his head into the tempered, natural-colored ceramic in the shower, his release squirting out with impressive distance. He lasted only seconds and promised that if he was ever fortunate enough to be buried in between Velvet's legs again, he would damn sure last longer.

He needed a nap but finished his shower and dressed to check out. He rolled his luggage to meet up with Tres Armadas. When he arrived at the lounge, breakfast was set up for them and the crew. He found Maartin and Christian and both men scrutinized him as if a list of charges designed his navy tee shirt instead of yellow headphones.

"Goedemorgen," Zazzle greeted in Dutch.

"Something you want to tell us?" Maartin asked when Christian continued to clank his silverware against a porcelain plate.

"No?" Based on their demeanor he wasn't sure any answer would be correct.

"We heard you were at the club last night?" Christian inquired in between chews.

He plopped into a chair across from the two men. "I was."

Maartin sighed. "I thought you were off clubs for now."

"Or were you reconnecting with old friends like Willem?" Christian stated more than asked.

Zazzle folded his hands on the table. "You forget, I was the one who suggested we ban him from our shows."

"Then what were you doing there, Isaak?" Maartin rooted for him and the last thing Zazzle wanted to do was cause him concern.

"Helping a friend." Zazzle didn't know how much of Candy's situation he should reveal. Maartin and Christian's tolerance tank ran pretty low. If Willem exerted his influence on Candy, they'd want to know about it. Not that either man didn't smoke the occasional joint or drink but their vexation with Willem was based mostly on how he preyed on a person. Something Zazzle remembered all too well.

"It looks bad. You've just come back. You're one of the most famous DJs in the world. Did you think people didn't see you?" Christian's tone held contempt but the tapping of his foot under the table gave him away.

An assistant to the group brought Zazzle a hot tea. "Thank you." Zazzle dunked the bag several times. "You don't have to worry, I'm fine. Trust me. Do I look like I've been partying all night or tanked on something?"

Well acquainted with seeing him at various levels of fucked up, Christian certified his sobriety. "No."

"Not even one drink?" Maartin persisted.

"No. You may ask Velvet if you don't believe me."

Both Christian and Maartin stopped mid-feed and chew respectively. Maartin regained motion first.

"Velvet, huh?"

Zazzle cursed himself. Now that his DJ brothers knew he'd been out with Velvet, the floodgates were opened.

"Before either of you say another word, yes, I like her and no to everything else."

"So you haven't kissed her yet?" Maartin teased.

Zazzle bit back a response.

"He's kissed her," Christian stated. "Why were you two at the club? She's worse than we are about your recovery."

"Honestly, that's Velvet's business. Between us, all

you need to know is that I was helping her and not partying. Settled?"

"Settled." Christian gulped his coffee and for a moment, Zazzle experienced how he used to interact with his Tres Armadas comrades. He hoped that with each challenge he overcame, Christian and Maartin would come to trust him a little more.

"Settled but..." Maartin pointed his fork at him. "By the look on your face, things with Velvet are just heating up."

Zazzle hung his head and regretted ever mentioning his time with Velvet. Neither Christian nor Maartin would let him forget it. He wouldn't see her again until Spain but things between him and the scooter-riding member of Bedazzled Beats were in full blaze.

Chapter Seventeen

Ibiza's warm June temperatures were an improvement from the still chill of Stockholm. The island's party season had just opened yet already operated at full swing as islanders and tourists flooded the peaceful, rural landscapes. The unique and thriving nightlife drew world-renowned DJs to the Spanish island's stages and clubs and Velvet was ready to play.

With the perfect weather and beating sun, Velvet's first order of business was a dip in the crystal clear Balearic Sea. That was after she and Candy found their friends and worked on their final track on their album. The not so fun perks of working in paradise. The water surrounded her and the sea air filled her nostrils, but it'd be hours, maybe even a day before she'd get to swim.

With little prompting she conjured up an image of her and Zazzle running on the beach, holding hands and splashing in the water like in some cheesy B movie. She hadn't seen him before they left Stockholm. The trio had flown privately to their weeklong calendar of six shows in Greece, Ukraine, Austria and Croatia. The opening acts for those shows were covered. Bedazzled Beats however kept it pedestrian and racked up more frequent-flyer miles for their nine performances at clubs and hotels in four different countries including Denmark, France, Italy and Croatia. Not only did Velvet suffer from exhaustion, she missed Zazzle.

Part of her didn't want to admit that she longed to see him and the other part replayed their kiss over and over. Her skin fired with longing for his lip action all over her body.

"Velvet?" Candy called.

"Huh?"

"Where are you?" Candy waved her hand in front of Velvet's face.

"I'm right here. Why? What'd you say?"

"I asked you about the guys."

Velvet rubbed her eyes in a pinching motion with her index finger and thumb. "I spaced for a sec. I think I'm just tired from last week." She'd also lost herself in the memory of Zazzle's arms in the back seat of a Stockholm taxi.

"Must have been a good space. You kind of sighed. Like this."

Velvet's eyes widened at Candy's impersonation. "That's pornographic." She laughed.

Candy waited for more explanation but Velvet kept her trap shut.

She hadn't told Candy about her night with Zazzle. Perhaps it wasn't only Candy who had changed since they'd left their house in LA.

"The guys are already here," Velvet responded to Candy as she thumbed a response to Rob. Tekko traveled with him, and they were both ready to lay down the last track on Bedazzled Beats' album.

"Where are we meeting them?" Candy weighed her shoulders with a backpack.

"Their hotel this afternoon. They set up a space for us. Coolest friends ever." Velvet smirked and showed Candy her phone displaying Rob's text.

Rob: We got snacks!!

"Yuuuuusss." Candy snapped her finger a few times.

Velvet laughed at her bestie. Candy's mood shift since leaving Stockholm was a delight. Velvet didn't know if their packed schedule or the work they'd been putting in on their album was to blame, but something had changed. The new location and shot of vitamin D didn't hurt either. Whatever the cause, Velvet was thrilled.

Sonny met them at the hotel. Their manager traveled a day ahead of them to conduct some business in Madrid. After a brief greeting, Sonny reminded them about their press circuit.

"I'll grab you both for your performance at the day club tomorrow. I've checked the setup. Where you'll be performing is somewhat shaded, but the sun is strong so be mindful of your hydration."

"I'm in need of a tan," Candy chirped.

Sonny continued. "Then you have the Sol de Soul Festival the following day. Tres Armadas is headlining the show on Saturday. Given that you're also not opening for them here, you do have a little more downtime even with your nightclub performance at Narnaja before we head for Amsterdam."

"Anything we need to know?" Velvet double-timed her steps to keep with Sonny's speed.

"Your New York residency starts in the fall but Tommy and I are considering negotiating an additional one here for next year's summer season, so keep that in mind. If you like the vibe here we'll do it. If not we'll find another international spot."

"We'll like it all right." Candy waved her hand at the endless expanse of blue waters. "This place is paradise."

"I like it, too. The history of this place for dance music makes it really special. I mean… Alfredo Fiorito, the 'Father of the Balearic beat,' played here. It's special. We'll definitely consider it." Velvet couldn't wait to tour the island and the historic hot spots and the thought of having a residency here would allow Bedazzled Beats to be in a pot and stirred with an elite group of DJs. "And Vegas?" Velvet ambled through a door that Sonny held open.

"We have to be strategic here. Let's see how Temptation goes and then we'll talk Vegas."

Velvet would have appreciated a different response but, so far, Sonny hadn't let them down. They had played a lot of the big festivals even on the smaller stages and their club circuit schedule was jammed with venues that wanted them to play. Not to mention, they were on tour with icons in dance music.

"This is an exhausting four days but you do have slivers of downtime here and there so when you're not performing or hanging with all who'll be here, I highly recommend naps."

"My brother is coming into town with his friends so…"

Sonny squared to both her and Candy. "Get some rest or sleep will find you in the most awkward of places. I've seen it happen."

Velvet didn't take the words lightly, she'd once woken up on a moving baggage claim carousel. Pre-Sonny,

Velvet and Candy had sixteen shows in ten days. She remembered sitting on the edge to rest her eyes and wait for her luggage. The next thing she had felt were hands under her arms, yanking her off like the luggage around her.

"Got it." Velvet gave Sonny a thumbs-up.

"I'll leave you to it. Tell Rob I said hello." Sonny ducked her head but Velvet saw the crimson stain on her tan cheeks.

"Oh, really?" Velvet crossed her arms. "I have questions."

"I wasn't sure about your energy in the UK but this is oh so telling," Candy chimed in.

Sonny mumbled something in Spanish, waved her off and kept going. "Later, guys."

"Let's get to work. There are bikinis with our names on them wantin' some of this Ibiza sun." Candy dragged Velvet with her.

Velvet's stomach lurched as Rob threw her into the air. "No more," she cried and laughed at the same time. "I'm legit gonna hurl."

Rob's lips smacked her cheek. His suntanned face reddened like an emoji from exercise. "My favorites are finally here."

Candy, still recovering from her round with Rob, chuckled.

"Stop fucking around, Rob," Tekko scolded with zero authority, and which Rob ignored.

When she and Candy arrived, Tekko locked them into a group hug. Now settled back into his seat, he placed some DJ equipment on his lap. A dark monitor pulsed with colorful lines, circles and bars.

"How have you guys been?" Velvet asked as Rob slid her to her feet. "I've seen most everything on social but anything new?"

"Like everyone this time of year, we're vying for Temptation votes. Performing like mad. A few DJs incorporated meet and greets into their pre-show repertoire for the fans. I'm going to get in on that," Rob responded.

"We have a few of those set up. It helps if we have our own tour, but we're working with what we got," Velvet said.

"Ticket sales open in like a few weeks. Time freakin' flies. It'll be sold out in a few days because the fans want to make sure they can vote in the qualifying round for who they want there. You can't vote if you don't have a ticket," Rob crooned.

"You sound like a modified version of the lotto slogan." Candy grinned.

"I do kinda, right?" Rob gave a brief nod to Candy. "There are so many more gigs between now and Temptation. Those are important. Lest we forget, there is at least one fan at each of our shows that has never seen us. We tear the roof off for them."

"You're cute, Rob." Velvet hugged his shoulders. She thought of her goals and though she did think of the fans in terms of votes, she still loved the music she played and wanted them to, too.

"Man, I'm happy to be enjoying summer in Ibiza. There's nothing like it. You guys are gonna fucking love it."

Velvet and Candy played in Spain a few times but their schedule had never brought them to Ibiza before.

Now their team made sure they were present where every major event happened.

"Whatcha been up to, Joe?" Candy toddled over to him.

"My schedule is packed this year. Eddie is just too motivated. He's crAsian."

"Crazy and Asian," Rob clarified.

Velvet laughed. Tekko's brother and manager squeezed out dollars wherever he could. As a result, Tekko, who Velvet thought should change his name to some version of the Energizer Bunny, was overworked.

She'd once viewed a media package for Tekko that chronicled his life over three days. He played ten shows in six countries. His only sleep happened on planes, he crafted new songs in his hotel before and after gigs, he changed clothes during his run to the stage, grabbed an energy drink or food after press or before he slept, and kept it moving. The next time Velvet had seen him, she'd hugged him and suggested they do absolutely nothing. That lasted about five minutes before they both needed to do something.

Tekko continued. "I had to have my agent cut some shit. I wanted to actually enjoy some of the countries I'm visiting instead of jumping in and out all the time."

"Facts," Velvet related. "Our Asia shows were crammed tighter than anchovies in a jar. All we did was perform and sleep."

There was glam to their life for sure but when they weren't traveling or performing, they tried to catch up on sleep. For solo artists like Rob and Tekko it was even worse. After being juiced from a performance or getting loads of attention at clubs and parties, they'd go back to the solitary confinement of their hotel rooms.

Sometimes with company, but most DJs worked or slept. Velvet at least had Candy to share things with. It was one of the reasons they always shared a room. Her mind wandered to Zazzle. He was part of a trio but with his EMETAH routine, she hoped the isolation helped him and that he didn't drown in loneliness.

"I like my schedule this year. It's tight but there's some wiggle room baked in," Rob said. "How have things been with Tres Armadas? The tour is all anyone is talking about. And peep this. There's some chatter about this bangin' DJ duo called Bedazzled Beats that's bringing the house down and making it hard for TA to follow."

"We wish. We've just been doing our best to give the fans a good show, win them over, and pray they vote for us for Temptation. They make us feel good and chant for us. It's been really cool." She loved the support her friends gave her and Candy but Bedazzled Beats still had work yet to do before Temptation voting started.

"The modesty is killing me." Tekko stabbed at his heart with an invisible knife.

"What? What am I missing?" Velvet's eyes ping-ponged between the two men.

"This." Rob pulled out his phone and showed her an article in *EDMworld*, an online publication, about her and Candy. Velvet scanned the article. Words like *showstoppers*, *uplifting*, *hypnotic*, and *best show in town* jumped off the page.

Candy came over and read over her shoulder. "When did this drop?"

"This morning."

"I don't think Sonny saw this or she would have told us," Velvet said. "By the way she says hi."

"Yeah?" Rob grinned and scratched his beanie-covered head.

"Did she say hi to me, too?" Tekko asked.

"Nah. Sorry, boo. I think Rob finally wore her down."

Rob beamed and his chest puffed. He truly was the cutest thing on two feet.

"This article really pumped up our Ibiza shows." Candy continued to read.

"If it has the desired effect, your shows are going to be outstanding." Rob threw his head back for emphasis.

"I think with some of the in-fighting with TA that's been reported, they're focusing on the positive. I'm down with that." Tekko pulled his long black hair into a man bun.

Velvet served him duck lips. "Talk to me some more about this in-fighting."

Tekko arched an eyebrow. "Intrigued?"

"Thoroughly," Velvet answered.

"It's mostly between Zaz and Christian. I don't know all the details but there's some jealousy about Christian going solo." Rob grabbed his iced coffee from a side table and offered her and Candy some.

Velvet shook her head.

"No, thanks." Candy looked from Rob to Tekko waiting for one of them to continue.

"And of course, there's some contention since Zaz's drug days," Tekko added.

"Recovery is tough. Zazzle works really hard at staying sober. Support is such a big part of it." Velvet didn't know all the details but everything in her body barked that there was more to this story.

"He's definitely come a long way. You guys remember that video? Scary stuff."

How could she forget? The video of Zazzle, the chaos, the women, his rant, all caught on tape. "I saw like five seconds of it. That shit was straight awful."

"The media often ask him about it." Tekko punched some buttons and then shifted to his computer. A mad scientist in his laboratory came to mind. "You know, they love to pump you up when things are good and kick you when you're down."

Bedazzled Beats hadn't shared much press space with Tres Armadas. As the main act the trio were the meat and potatoes, and Bedazzled Beats the appetizer kept on a separate plate. In addition she and Candy were their own artists. They may have traveled with the trio, but they were an act on the rise and vying for a spot at Temptation. However, the questions Velvet often heard asked of Zazzle were about being back and how he was "doing."

"I've noticed some stuff but they still perform really well together and Zazzle is still entertaining onstage. He needs to give me dance lessons." Candy tapped her chin. "You never know what's happening in people's walk-in closets."

"Well, we should get started," Rob announced. "You ladies sure you don't want anything?"

"I shall partake in snacks as advertised." Velvet pretended to wave her hands to her underlings.

"Yes, thanks." Candy pulled her computer out of her backpack and Velvet did the same.

"You guys can plug in here." Tekko pointed to the ports on his equipment. "We've laid down some stuff for you ladies to check out and see how it vibes with what you sent us. If you like it, then we can edit and play with it, but this is your track. Whatever you want, just let us know."

"We just want you to bring that fiyah," Velvet exaggerated.

Candy plopped into a chair. "Nice. Let's hear it."

The four of them labored over the track for about two hours until they got a product they liked. Velvet and Candy's original house sample with their vocals drove Rob's drum and bass bars into a creative dubstep break. Tekko's electro house tied-in. It was a lovely mess of genres melding together.

"Something's missing," Candy announced.

"I concur. It's good but I keep wanting to hear something tribal, maybe even dancehall," Velvet agreed.

Tekko nodded. "If you ladies are cool with it, I want to bring in one more heavy hitter."

Velvet and Candy deadpanned to each other. "Yeah."

"I'm phoning a friend." Tekko thumbed a message and when it alerted, he smiled. "He'll be here in an hour. Just enough time for us to have dinner, and let the music breathe."

Rob already waited at the door. "Yeah, we'll come back with fresh ears. Let's chow."

"Wait, who'd you call?" Velvet asked.

Tekko rubbernecked. "Zazzle, who else?"

Chapter Eighteen

The thought of seeing Zazzle lit Velvet up like a smartphone flashlight. She, Candy, Tekko and Rob shared Sofrit Pagés and Zarzuela de Mariscos at a small Ibizan restaurant in town. Unlike most people who ate less when their nerves hit, she ate more. Candy noticed as she attacked the traditional dishes.

"Hey. You okay?"

"Yup." Velvet shoved a roasted piece of sausage from her Sofrit Pagés into her mouth. "This is so good."

"Anything to do with Zazzle coming to work on the song with us?"

"Nope."

"If you don't want him to come, just tell the guys. It's our track, they'll understand."

"That's the thing, Candy. I do want him to come."

Candy's smile widened as she prepped a mussel from her Zarzuela de Mariscos. "You want to see him?"

"I see him all the time." Velvet tried to dismiss the question, even though she'd already admitted her feelings.

"Yeah, but something had to happen for you to want him to come. Deets, sister, now."

Velvet gave Candy the quick and dirty about the

kiss, but conveniently omitted the parts where she and Zazzle searched for her in three clubs.

"He's better now. Why not give it another chance?"

"Nope." She sounded like a toddler.

"Velveteen?"

"Candy Cane?"

"I'm just sayin'... You put up this wall of judgment sometimes and it's okay to let it down. I know being with someone in recovery is tricky for you after Reynard, but maybe things could work if you give it a try. You know what not to do now."

"Knowing and living are two different things." Velvet already saw her obsession with his routine and her interest in his mood. Now that she wanted to be closer to him, all signaled to past behaviors that were bound to get out of her control. But how could she keep denying the way they plugged into each other like headphones into a jack.

"Don't rule it out. You fell for him from the start. But right now, the guys think he's the key to unlock this track. This will be interesting." Candy twirled her fork before she gathered food on it.

Velvet let the words sink in. When she and Zazzle kissed there was nowhere else Velvet wanted to be. Their attraction from the start never left her, like someone had surgically opened her heart and put Zazzle in there. Similar to healing tissue, all her experiences grew around him, making him part of her and she couldn't get rid of that feeling.

Two hours later, they arrived back at their makeshift studio at the hotel. Velvet smelled lavender and upon entering the room, the visual of him lounging in a chair with a to-go cup of tea resting on his belly greeted her. He had a day of scruff on his cheeks and chin and though Velvet liked him clean-shaven, she could get used to this look, too. He climbed to his feet when their group piled into the room.

"I hear you have a track you think I might be able to help with."

"Hey, man." Tekko gave him a hug.

Rob followed. "Lookin' good, man."

"Ladies, glad to see you arrived in Ibiza okay." Zazzle addressed both her and Candy.

"Thanks." Candy waved and grabbed her computer.

Zazzle moved over to Velvet. "How are you?"

His fragrance worked magic on her, like it had countless times. "I'm good. You?"

"Happy to be useful." He scratched his chin. "You okay with me being here? I would have texted you but I still don't have your number."

She handed him her phone. He punched in his number and called himself.

"Problem solved," she said. "And yes. I'm okay with you being here."

"Let's play the track and get to work," Tekko interrupted with his plans for the session.

She planted herself down next to Candy and played the track. They were all in view of each other's screens.

Velvet and Candy were at the helm behind the digital audio workstation Tekko had set up for them and evaluated the song with more discerning ears. She noted areas they could do a bit more but the hole of a lost element remained.

Zazzle listened to the track from beginning to end. "Play it again, please." He opened up some mixing software and worked on a pad controller and created beats as he listened. He moved quickly.

"You know the drop, here? Stop there."

Velvet paused the track.

"Let me do this." Zazzle layered in a Caribbean beat that was quick like soca but dynamic as calypso. "Rewind it back to just before Rob's dubstep break and fade it in."

Velvet did as he asked and then gradually sped it up to match the electro tempo of Tekko's section. Candy layered an effect to meld the two.

They continued with the rest of the track to signal Zazzle's grounding beats and hinted at the motifs in other parts of the track to make it more cohesive. They listened, nodded and smiled.

Zazzle danced off to the side. "That's really nice. It makes the drop more interesting. Unexpected."

"That's fucking spectacular." Tekko jumped out of his seat, his long hair flying out of its bun and about his shoulders and back.

"That's so cool." Candy grinned.

"I love it!" Velvet cheered as she listened.

"Your label might have a sound engineer make some final changes but this track is straight fire," Tekko said.

"Exceptional track, ladies." Coming from Zazzle, the compliment meant more than she admitted.

Velvet tipped her hat and Candy bowed several times.

Rob slapped Zazzle on the back. "Nice job, bro."

The idea she came up with in Stockholm popped up like a dialogue box by her head. "We should test it out tomorrow night at the festival."

"I'm into it." Rob raised his hand.

"We can surprise the fans, come on for that track, and do it live," Zazzle suggested and Tekko agreed.

Velvet blinked so quickly even she noticed. "You'd do that for us?"

Tekko rubbernecked and then pointed to her while frowning at Rob. "Of course." Tekko's *obviously* tone made her regret even asking the question.

"It'll be a fun ride," Zazzle offered.

"You guys should totally play with us." Candy clasped her hands in prayer and only clapped her finger.

Rob pumped a fist. "The crowd is going to go ape shit."

Velvet, Rob and Candy all started reciting the words to The Carters' "Apeshit." Zazzle wasn't an insider to their friend group and missed the cue, watching in fascination.

"Okay, okay. 'Be You' is our final song so I say, let's do it two or three songs before the finale. The middle will be expected and we want to really surprise them." Velvet couldn't sit still.

"Perfection," Candy sang, moving tracks around on her computer. They'd have to mix into their set to see where exactly the song fit but Candy did the work while the ideas flowed.

"We're geniuses," Rob said, his gray eyes shining.

"This guy." Tekko smirked.

"What are you guys gonna call it?" Zazzle asked.

Velvet thought of their songs and the positive vibes they wanted to send out. The summer was here and they wanted the track and the title to grab their fans. "'Love Me Love You'?"

"I love it," Candy concurred.

"Bong!" Tekko slapped an imaginary something.

"That's not on brand at all." Rob stretched and winked so hard Velvet thought he may have hurt himself. "Now that's all sorted. Any suggestions on how I get Sonny to go out with me?"

Crickets.

"O-kay."

"You're on your own. I think we've done our part there. The ball is one hundred percent in your court. So… Good luck." Velvet grinned at Rob.

Candy sent the final downloaded track to the record label and copied Sonny and Boombox.

Velvet sauntered over to Zazzle. "Thanks for your help tonight."

"My pleasure." He smiled as he packed up his computer.

"Christian is the one who is forging a solo career, but you're really good at this. You have skills, too. Maybe you should think about doing more production outside of TA."

"I've done a few features. I've thought about it before. Maybe I'll do more. We'll see how this one's received."

"I'd like to hear more and I know the fans would." His onstage performance couldn't be matched, but he had offstage skills, too. If no one reminded him of that, then she would.

"Thanks." He cupped her shoulder and his smile warmed her heart.

"We're going to catch the sunset at Cala Escondida. One of the locals put me onto it the last time I visited. It's a little harder to get to but less populated," Rob presented to Zazzle more than to the rest of the group who already knew the post-session plan.

"I'm in," Zazzle responded.

Velvet turned her back to her friends. "I know you have your own schedule so it's cool if you don't want to interrupt that."

"I can see you're surprised." Zazzle smiled. "I don't want to intrude."

"No, no. I think it's great."

"Great, huh?"

"It's great for all of us…not only for me… I mean me, too." She ran out of steam in her attempt to qualify anything else that came out of her mouth. "I'm just going to put my stuff away." Her sharp movements must have been as dizzying to watch as they were for her to experience.

The sound of his humor haunted her steps.

Half an hour later, Velvet and her crew were at Cala Escondida watching the sun disappear below the endless waters of the Mediterranean Sea. The spot was popular with nudists, which she and her friends found out with plenty of supportive visuals.

"I respect the clothing optional situation," Velvet said as she walked through.

However initially surprising, their global travel and cultural exposure left them curious yet unfazed.

They were only about fifteen minutes out from San Antonio but the seclusion and expanse of the water made the location its own little planet. Far away from the inner chaos, the parties and the dense population that descended on Ibiza summers, peace settled over her.

"Is this cool, man?" Rob asked displaying an Isleña beer bottle.

Tekko, Rob and Candy shared the popular Spanish beer.

"Yeah, do your thing," Zazzle responded, giving them the all clear to drink.

Velvet drank water and sat next to him on the rocky surface.

"You want one, Asha?" Rob asked.

"Nah, I'm still dehydrated from the plane ride today. Maybe later," she responded, but deep down she wanted Zazzle to kiss her again. If he did, she didn't want to inadvertently give him a taste of alcohol.

He nudged her shoulder. "You can drink, it's okay. I have my tea."

"I'm cool." She waved it off.

"You're very supportive."

"I've had a lot of practice." She'd spent days cooking to make sure Reynard ate something and cleaned him up when he'd return after going on a bender with whatever he could get his hands on. He'd promised over and over that he was ready to change. Each time she'd believed him. Countless nights she'd lain awake stressed about the day he didn't make it back. One night he didn't.

"Is that why you're so…curious about my treatment and my routine?"

"I guess old habits surface when I'm around you."

"Who did you know that was in recovery?"

The high perch and calming sunset gave the illusion of a safe space.

"My mentor, Reynard West. A lot of people know him as DJ FeNom."

"Yeah, I've heard of him. Known for his 'iron beats.' A vinyl master, I think they call him. Right?"

Velvet smiled at the tag. Reynard's vinyl skills were world renowned. "Yes. That's him."

"He's your mentor?"

She affirmed. "He worked with Candy, too. That's how she and I met."

"Wow. I did hear about his overdose a couple years back. I'm sorry. They said when he came back, he was never the same."

"So many times before that night he tried to get clean but he kept getting pulled in. I'd always want to help and take care of him, and make sure he was doing things right. I thought I could single-handedly help him kick his habit. What an ego."

"What happened?"

"He'd go back and each time it killed me. The week he overdosed he found out that the fans had voted him into Temptation. Main stage. We celebrated the accomplishment but..." She finally braved to look at him. "He never made it to the festival. Instead he landed himself at county hospital."

Zazzle's posture erected. "Did he make it out?"

"Yeah, but it changed him. Left the scene. Candy and I didn't completely sever ties but we haven't seen or spoken to him in years so..."

His arm moved against hers and the touch soothed her. "Is that why playing the main stage at Temptation means so much to you?"

She gave him a sheepish smile. "Reynard always hyped it up. It would have been the highlight of his career. For Candy and me it became our dream for him, too. Now—"

"It's your dream."

She sipped her water. Sentiment blocked her throat. No matter how many years passed, thinking about DJ FeNom still elicited sadness and raw pain. "I don't mean to be so nosy about your recovery, Zazzle, or doubtful sometimes. It's just that I've seen someone get lax with their recovery, and relapse, only to end up in the hospital with a grim prognosis."

"And you think that's going to be me?"

"I don't know but I see myself falling into my role as a caretaker and trying to be responsible for things that are not my responsibility."

"All I can do is take things day by day." He scratched his chin, his scruff crackled.

"I know, but us being attracted to each other makes that problematic."

"So you're attracted to me?" She didn't have to see him to know he smiled.

"Like that's some surprise to you?" Their conversation lightened up a bit and she ingested a cleansing breath. A sense of spaciousness, like the endless sky above, once again found her.

"No, it's not."

"Okay, well…"

"So you don't want to get involved with me because you think you'll want to take care of me?"

"You're supposed to take care of each other in a relationship. I just don't know if I can do it in a healthy way, a non-mothering, non-sponsor way. And if you ever relapsed—"

Her fingers tossed the water bottle acrobatically in her lap. He stayed her hands with his.

"I don't plan to relapse. I want to live a happy and healthy life."

"But you can't promise you won't."

He sighed. "No. I can't. I don't think anyone in recovery can. This is a forever illness that requires forever recovery."

"It takes a lot to admit that, Isaak." She covered her hand over his. "Thank you for being honest."

"So that's it?" He scoffed. "Where do we go from here?"

"I don't know." If she let her guard down she feared what she'd become. With everything from her well-being to her career goals at stake, she had to protect herself, even though their connection haunted her. What she needed to do and wanted to do weren't lining up.

"We've tried to stay away from each other before, Asha, and we've ended up on tour together. We deny our attraction to each other and you end up kissing me in the back of a taxi. Those aren't just coincidences and they'll keep happening."

Her body temperature flared at his truth and she swallowed hard. "You're right. I wish I had all the answers, but I don't." She unraveled her crossed legs to stand. "We should go join the others."

He reached for her hand and pulled her into his arms. "I think about that night months ago when I chose to party. I never should have left you."

He kissed her, right there in view of her friends. His kiss was light to the touch but no less mesmerizing and she stumbled over the unsteady surface when he released her.

She cleared her throat. "We should, um..." She pointed to her friends and despite the seriousness of their previous conversation Zazzle chuckled. When they rejoined their friends and watched the last embers of the sun dim to darkness, Velvet was glad she'd chosen to drink water over beer.

Chapter Nineteen

The dangerous outside world overflowed with temptation. His biggest one wasn't alcohol or drugs. Those kept him inside. Velvet on the other hand lured him to seek her out. If boredom didn't kill him, being left with his own thoughts if he stayed inside would.

He and his bandmates hadn't yet confronted the state of Tres Armadas past the end of their tour next month. What would he do if they decided to split? Where would he go? Would he sell his LA property and move full time to the Netherlands? Without an occupation to drive him he was dead in the water.

He peered out the window. The beach views teased him like children sticking their tongue out at him and singing "na-na-ni-boo-boo." Last night, Cala Escondida offered him a glimpse into the kind of fun he could manage. Where respect and support for his recovery was ever present. He wondered if he'd developed the muscles to take another step.

Their show wasn't until tonight and different acts were playing all over Ibiza. Christian was playing a day club at one of the hotels. Maartin hopped around town and wanted to check out some of the other DJs at the festival. He had friends there, too. People who would want to see him now that he was out. People like Velvet. His desire to share Ibiza with her hit an all-time high around noon.

Zazzle had never seen Christian play a solo gig. With things between them a bit more cordial, he received the idea with less angst. He threw on a cap and his sunglasses, and decided to stop by.

Zazzle ducked and slunk through the hotel and into the club with incognito skills only acquired through years of practice. He slipped backstage and immediately regretted his choice. People recognized him and offered him everything under the sun. He declined and pulled down the bill on his cap, inhaling the lavender essence he sprinkled inside. Still, the alcohol flowed around him. The temperature was comfortable yet he dripped sweat under the constant decision-making. Inebriated giggles and chatter swirled with the beats of Christian Saaks, who faced a poolside crowd.

Someone offered Christian a shot and he slung it back with laughter and chiding. Zazzle couldn't remember the last time he saw Christian so free. Here at the day club, Christian didn't have to babysit him or worry about him using. He didn't have to think about his choices around alcohol or drugs. Christian hadn't lost his alcohol and drug use card. Zazzle had.

Christian spun around, cheering to those backstage, and spotted him. He didn't quite scowl but the brimming happiness on his face lessened.

Zazzle tipped his hat to him and moved to leave. The feedback from a microphone cracked through the music.

"I got a treat for you, Ibiza. You'll be seeing this guy tomorrow night when Tres Armadas closes out Sol de Soul Fest. Give it up for Zazzle!"

Zazzle froze in his tracks.

"That's you, man," a guy with a tall tropical drink said to him and jiggered his shoulder. Someone else pushed him toward the stage. Thanks to autopilot, he made it to Christian and waved to the crowd. He did a few dance moves and the cheers grew louder. Christian squeezed his shoulder.

"You're great, man." Zazzle slapped hands with Christian and they bumped shoulders before leaving the stage. Zazzle wanted to stay and chill but this moment belonged to Christian and he should enjoy it without him there.

On his way out the club LED caught his eye. His face brightened as he waved. They weaved through the small crowd toward each other.

"That was great. Seeing you and Christian up there. You should have jumped on the dials," LED rattled.

"Nah. This is all Christian. How have you been, man? I thought I'd be seeing more of you now that your girl is touring with us."

LED's facials dropped and his cheeks reddened through his tan. "Oh, we're not together."

"You guys taking a break?" Zazzle must have looked perplexed because LED rushed on.

"That's a nice way to put it but we're pretty broken up. I thought you would have known by now. My girl… I mean, Candy doesn't really hold things back. So I assumed it was old news."

"Why'd you guys break up?" Zazzle bit his tongue. He was often direct but not meddlesome. "You don't have to answer that, man."

"It's cool. We had to make some choices. You know?

She just didn't choose me. She hasn't said anything about it?"

"No, she hasn't said much about it, but..." Zazzle's mind shot to Candy and Willem. He didn't want to alarm LED or insert himself in the middle of a lovers' quarrel.

"But what...?"

Zazzle rummaged through his brain for a sentence-ending response. "Any chance you guys can be friends? She's been working hard and is here on the island." Not his best work but it was hard for him not to shoot straight.

"She has Velvet." Zazzle couldn't miss the bite in LED's tone. "She'll reach out if she wants."

"You playing tomorrow?" Zazzle's change of subject was not at all smooth but he needed to extricate himself from divulging information about Candy that wasn't his to share.

"Nah. I'm playing tonight on the Trance Beats stage. Come through if you're up to it."

"We close out tomorrow night. It would be great to have our friends there," Zazzle said.

"Yeah, Christian mentioned it. I'll try. If not, I'll catch you guys in Amsterdam. I'm heading there, too."

"Cool."

"Where are you off to now? The island is madness."

"I'm actually looking for Velvet." Hunting for Velvet wasn't something he'd planned to admit, but he tested LED's reaction.

When LED's brows knitted briefly, Zazzle confirmed that whatever had happened with his girl, Velvet had something to do with it.

"Candy and Velvet love Bliss. They wouldn't miss her play. She's on this evening."

"Thanks, man."

"Hey. I have no business asking but look out for them, okay?"

"Both of them?" Zazzle raised a brow and LED caught his unspoken meaning.

"Yeah. They're family."

"Will do. I'll check you later, man." Zazzle had new insight into Velvet's concern for Candy but another level of curiosity roused from speaking to LED. Not that a breakup would cause Candy to become dependent on drugs but the heartbroken were sometimes susceptible to poor decision-making. Something he could attest to with Tres Armadas. He didn't know how else he could help but for both members of Bedazzled Beats, he'd try.

He left to find a woman with punk'd out purple hair.

"Whaddup, fam?" Trevor rolled four boys deep. "You changed your hair color again? It was blue on social like a week ago."

"The ends are still blond. I like to keep you on your toes." Velvet fluffed her purple strands and hugged her brother, his bare chest partially covered by an open Hawaiian shirt that paired with his Bermuda shorts. She kissed his cheek and was happy to see him. "Where're the rest of the guys?"

"Ahh. They couldn't make it. Two big trips in two months? Nah. They want to come through for Temptation. That's the ultimate. So you better get there. No pressure."

"Right," Velvet mumbled. "Then you better get your ticket when they go on sale so you can vote."

"Bet. This crowd is massive. Who else is playing?" Trevor asked.

"Just us." Velvet frowned at her brother and turned to Candy. "Should we be insulted?"

"Trevor is a walking insult." Candy placed an elbow on her shoulder.

"I'm just sayin'. The buzz is out."

The day club overflowed with patrons in beachwear, but this was Ibiza, everywhere was packed. Fans called her and Candy by name even though they weren't on-stage yet. "Yeah, I guess it is." She rolled her shoulders and tried to keep it all in perspective.

"Thanks for the VIP passes."

"Thank Sonny. I was gonna let you chill in GA."

"Kill that noise." He cut under his neck and a bunch of admission bracelets and other beaded jewelry decorated his wrist.

"Did they give you any trouble?" Though Trevor was a little shit, he was her little shit and she asked to make sure that her brother got the friends and family treatment.

"What? They treated us like royalty. It's good to be king."

"King of what?" Velvet tossed her brother a quizzical look.

Trevor ignored her. "Hey, girl, hey," Trevor teased Candy and gave her a hug.

"Welcome to Ibiza." Candy punched his arm. "I see you brought part of the knucklehead squad with you."

Trevor's friends already lost interest in Bedazzled Beats and squirrel-chased pretty girls in string bikinis.

"Dude." Trevor gave Rob Ready a shoulder bump and pat.

"What's up, man? Glad you could come out," Rob said.

Trevor greeted Tekko in similar fashion.

"We're on in a few. I don't have to tell you to have fun." Velvet referred to the drink he already had in hand.

"Nah. I got this, sis. Do your thing and uhh—" Trevor ogled some ladies nearby "—we'll do ours."

"This kid." Rob laughed. "We have to head out in a bit. We're all playing at different places tonight if you wanna hang. You definitely have to check us out at the festival tomorrow. We have a little surprise during Velvet's set."

"Bet," Trevor said.

Velvet hugged her friends before they shot off.

"I'm gonna go plug in," Candy said.

"All right. I'll be right there," Velvet called after her.

Trevor watched Candy's departing figure. "She doesn't look too heartbroken."

"She's been better since we've been here, thank goodness." Velvet didn't know the shelf life on Candy's present positive disposition, but she hoped it lasted. Willem hadn't shown up and that was more than a blessing.

"Do we get to meet Tres Armadas after the festival tomorrow?"

"Maybe." Velvet side-eyed her brother.

"Come on, sis. Me and the fellas came all this way."

"And here I thought you were coming to see me."

Her brother's shoulders slumped. "That's how you're going to do me?"

"Fine. I'll get you backstage." She winked.

"Yes. That's what I'm talking about."

Zazzle ran through her mind like a marathoner on a treadmill and she wondered if he thought about her at all. Several times she itched to text him, but each time she refrained from making a complicated situation worse. She'd opened up about her feelings and why their relationship was doomed. His kiss made her want to believe otherwise.

"Okay, we gotta go and I doubt I'll see you again until tomorrow. Since everyone is together we're doing 4am eats before they head out after the festival."

"I'm down. I'll tell my boys." Trevor's friends had already melded into the crowd. "Kill it."

"Thanks," she said and left to meet up with Candy for their performance.

Velvet and Candy mingled after their set. Sonny introduced them to a few influencers and promoters. The positive response to the *EDMworld* article was the main topic of conversation.

"We couldn't ask for better timing." Sonny spoke to a reporter. "Ibiza is a small island but its impact on the greater dance music community is very relevant. This is a great place to attract new fans."

Velvet was over the moon by the attention for Bedazzled Beats. Along with their planned surprise for the fans, she radiated like a ball of ecstatic energy.

Candy low-fived her as they interviewed with another vlogger.

"Your spot on the Tres Armadas tour sounds like it has been a positive experience. Any truth to the rumors about discord in the group?"

"The guys have welcomed us and they bring the house down every night for their fans." Velvet's strategy in all her interviews? Tell her truth and stay positive.

"They're great," Candy said.

"Have you seen their opening?" Velvet swooned,

leading her interviewer down another path. "If you haven't you should check it out but come to see us, too."

She spoke into the camera and soon Sonny led them out and they huddled up.

"Nice finish, ladies. It's not easy but you're handling both the new attention and the inquiries like the pros you are. Gear up for the festival tomorrow but have a little fun, too."

They were hot and sweaty and headed back to the hotel for a quick shower and change before they donned their swimwear and shorts and headed to the festival. Not only did they need to mingle but they wanted to take in some of the highlight performances and get an idea of the layout for when Bedazzled Beats performed tomorrow.

Velvet dragged Nuts while Candy hopped alongside her through the barricaded section where VIP and artists socialized under the evening Ibizan sun. Velvet longed to mingle with the fans but she and Candy waited for their friends. What good was a festival in Ibiza without witnesses? Trevor was with his boys and sent her Instagram-worthy texts.

"Knucklehead," she mumbled, laughing at a picture on her phone of her brother, sucking on a large colored drink with too many floral accessories. She showed Candy.

"He's doing Ibiza all right," Candy giggled.

They linked back up with Tekko and Rob who rolled up in a golf cart.

"Come on!" Rob hung on to one of the rails and waved them over. "We got big things to do."

Candy sprinted beside the whirring vehicle and jumped in while Velvet pumped her scooter. Nuts couldn't keep up as she ran, and she almost choked on her Blow Pop. Her friends took pity on her and stopped, so she could jump in.

"Get in already." Rob abandoned his beanie and his short, messy, gelled strands barely moved.

They drove the cart through a less crowded beachside path, surprising unsuspecting fans. Festival attendees rushed the golf cart for a picture. Tekko wore a tee shirt with "free hugs" splashed across the front and his loose hair flailed in the wind. As usual Tekko performed a flip, high jump or something parkour-ish to give them something for "the 'gram."

"Drop me off here, I want to check on the vendors," Candy said. "I'll meet up with you guys at Bliss's set. I'll text you."

Candy disappeared into the festival.

"And then there were three." Velvet slapped the side of the cart. "Giddyup."

Tekko drove on.

Her upbeat mood conflicted with her thoughts of Zazzle. She wondered how his day went and if she crossed his mind the way he'd been ping-ponging through hers all day. She may not have sent a text but her phone wasn't blowing up with one from him either. She stretched her thumbs but again, talked herself out of communicating. If he wanted to have some peace from the lively island, she didn't want to be the one to disturb him.

They abandoned the cart with security and Velvet arranged for someone to get Nuts back to the hotel before they headed deeper into the festival.

"Do you guys think I'm judgmental?" Velvet blurted.

Tekko raised an eyebrow.

"I don't know. Let's check." Rob pulled out his phone. "Am I judgmental..." he said as he thumbed the screen.

She moved the lollipop to the inside of one of her cheeks. "I could have done that."

Rob read on. "'15 Signs You're Overly Judgmental.'"

She rolled her eyes. "No one said overly."

"If you're asking the question you're probably next-level judgmental. Why are you asking anyway?"

"It's been mentioned," she confessed.

"Well, from personal experience I think you can be a little judge-y, but we love you anyway. Plus I think it's because you care and not because you think you're better than anyone." Tekko scratched his chin. "You can be a bit of a know-it-all, though."

"I didn't ask for extra insight," Velvet said.

"Let's just get it all out. It's obviously on your mind."

Rob's head tilted back slightly with his lifting brows. "Zazzle one of them? You know? Who mentioned it?"

Her eyes narrowed and she regretted asking the question. "That's presumptuous."

"Is it, though?" Rob studied her.

"Yes. Why do you say that?" she asked as if her friends didn't know she and Zazzle hooked up.

"Just asking." Rob never just asked anything.

"Maybe you two smacking lips last night might have something to do with it?" Tekko stated more than asked.

"I warned you guys to never speak about that. Like ever," she warned, but she'd known that was a losing battle from the first moment.

"As if that was a real thing." Tekko's frown intensified. "Candy may have said something, too."

"Ooooh! Burn," Rob bellowed.

Her friends had a laugh at her expense, which she took like a champ. "You guys are the worst."

"What's up with you and Zazzle anyway?" Rob asked.

"It's nothing." Her cheeks were hotter than the sun they recently sought shade from. "I guess we like each other," she mumbled.

"I'm sure. You both think no one notices but we do," Tekko added. "I'm a guy. He's tryin' to hit that. It's obvious. No game, whatsoever."

"Oh my God. Stop." She ducked. Zazzle had already hit that last year at Temptation. Her time with him was one of the best experiences in her life. Even if she wanted to deny her feelings, her heart and soul were forever marked by him.

"Candy says you crushed him from jump."

"No, really. You can stop now, Rob."

"All right, all right," Rob chimed.

Velvet checked her phone. No Zazzle but even worse, no LED. She'd texted him about Ibiza before they flew to Spain but he hadn't responded. "Has either of you guys heard from LED? I thought he'd for sure be playing here."

Neither Rob nor Tekko responded, which was in and of itself weird.

"What?" Velvet's outstretched hands welcomed more information.

"He's here," Tekko said.

Her eyes bulged. "He is?"

Rob nodded. "Does no one check the lineup anymore?"

"When do we have time? I only know that Bliss is

performing because it literally gets texted to me whenever she plays."

"Bernard's been sort of staying to that side of the island. I don't think Candy knows."

"Anyone know when he plays?"

"I think his set should be finishing up soon."

Velvet had a feeling that not only did Candy know LED was here but that she wasn't checking out vending. Perhaps seeing LED had contributed to Candy's raised spirits. Velvet hoped that if her friend sought out LED it equaled reunion. If not she had no idea what to expect.

"She knows."

Chapter Twenty

A combination of rose, lilies and suntan lotion smothered Velvet.

"What the f—"

"Finally!" Throaty laughter rang in her ear.

"Bliss!" Velvet wiggled out of the embrace and focused on Evie Turner's cheery face. Her bronze skin was tanned and golden from the sun.

"Trance is definitely in the building." Velvet yanked Bliss back into a hug and jumped like a kid who'd been told they were going to Disneyland. "It's so good to see you, Kiwi. I can't believe your ass wasn't at BonBon."

Bliss, an Australian native and trance aficionado, had been one of her crew since they met four years ago. With Bliss so far away in Australia, Velvet rarely saw her. When Bliss came to this side of the world, her extended stays lasted, at minimum, one month to take advantage of the festivals. Her massive following came out in full force to see her play, and included Velvet, Candy, Tekko and Rob.

"My sister delivered her first baby girl. I had to be there." Her silver tank top, black three-quarter leggings and black sequined sneakers gave Candy a run for her money with the posh-ness.

"I saw on IG." Velvet gushed. "She's super cute. You have to show me more pics later."

Bliss's big energy encapsulated their surroundings. "I will. She's a couple months old now and I just want to gobble her up. I want one, but not really. Maybe one day."

"That's how they get you." Velvet's maternal urges were kept well at bay for the present but she knew she wanted to fulfill her genetic legacy in the future. She and Candy once thought it would be cool if they were pregs at the same time.

Bliss's long dark brown hair was tied into a ponytail and Velvet stuck one of her Blow Pops inside. "It's customary."

"I miss these." Bliss's laugh carried. A man Velvet remembered meeting earlier that year entered their space. "This is Alexi."

"We've met. Nice to see you again," Alexi said.

"Yeah. At BonBon." Velvet waved at Alexi and took in his tall figure. His black hair gave off angsty boy band in a new wave kind of way. "Are you enjoying Ibiza?"

"I am now."

They were still in the greetings portion of their conversation yet Alexi already put his flirt game in play. Bliss regarded the natural splendor of the festival and didn't seem to notice.

Velvet linked arms with Bliss. "I'm so glad you're here. The male energy is cool but we need a chick booster shot."

Most of the female DJs were kind and an unspoken level of camaraderie and competition existed between them. As women they fought for stage spots, time slots, pay and press equivalent to their male counterparts. They greeted each other with huge energy, excitement and support at the festivals. Velvet made it a point to know each and every one. Some had arrived on the scene through hard work and grind while others slid in through contests or more manufactured and contrived ways. A dance music history and culture savant, Velvet embraced anyone who loved and respected the music. Anyone who missed the heart of why dance music united the masses rarely lasted a year. Those with proven longevity were successful like the Miss Kittins, Cassys, Nervos, Honey Dijons, Annie Macs and countless others on the scene.

"Candy Cane is going to freak when she sees you," Velvet said to Bliss.

"Where is she?"

Velvet didn't know. Candy had gone vendin' but Velvet suspected she'd gone fishin' for LED. "She had to take care of something but she'll be here soon."

"Oh my God! Is that Zazzle from Tres Armadas?" Bliss's deep-set eyes widened. "I heard you were on tour with them. I'm so proud of you by the way. Sorry I haven't emailed to congratulate you guys but I have to meet him. Our schedules hardly ever line up. I mean I've met him, in passing, but not like this," Bliss rambled and Velvet's brain worked to keep up.

"Zazzle?" Her Zazzle? Zazzle was here? And out? Velvet found Zazzle choppin' it up with Rob and Tekko. *What is he doing out of his room?*

Before Velvet comprehended the new scenario, Bliss pulled her over to Zazzle.

"Hi." Bliss's throaty voice turned shrill.

"Okay." Velvet still tried to catch up.

Zazzle's eyes landed on her. "Hey."

Bliss nudged her, and Velvet peered up at her. Though from Aboriginal descent, the rosacea from her German-English heritage splotched her cheeks.

"Hey. Bliss." The introduction couldn't get more awkward. "I mean, this is my friend Bliss. Zazzle, this is Bliss. Bliss, Zazzle." *WTF?*

Zazzle eyed her as if the top of her head had opened and an alien had popped out and started flossing. Rob and Tekko's foreign appraisal followed.

"I know who you are." Zazzle's charm snared both Velvet and Bliss. "I think we met some years back."

"You remember me?" Velvet almost heard Bliss's "oh my God" precursor to her question and smiled.

"Oh, yeah. They call you the Kiwi Trance Princess in the media. Like we don't have enough aliases." Zazzle flashed Bliss that adorable smile. "You're great."

"Thanks. I was hoping you'd be back with Tres Armadas by the time this festival came around. It'll be a treat to see you guys play tonight. I love to watch you dance." Bliss's exhilaration continued to rise.

Velvet's head whipped to her friend's flirtatious tone. Velvet didn't know Bliss had a crush on him, nor did she have any idea how deep that crush went. Her pulse raced as the tendrils of jealousy vined around her heart.

Zazzle studied Velvet and bit his lip to stifle his amusement.

Velvet opened her mouth to say something, but what? *I'm into Zazzle.*

We've hooked up?

He's off-limits? Anything she said would reveal more about her than she wanted to broadcast. She snapped her mouth closed.

Alexi came over and settled next to Velvet and whispered in her ear. "Take a walk with me?" His seductive smile gave her an instant brow lift.

Zazzle straightened, his amber orbs cut on Alexi.

"Go." Bliss winked at her and tilted her head toward Alexi. "We'll catch up after my set."

Velvet sought answers in Tekko and Rob whose eyes slid back and forth as if they watched the final match at Wimbledon.

Her eyes met Zazzle's. His visage a blank canvas that neither claimed nor dismissed.

"Sure." Velvet followed Alexi and all but ignored Zazzle's eye daggers that now shot at her.

Zazzle's body stiffened and no matter how many different ways he stretched, relaxation was elusive. He doubted all the moves he made that day. He had hoped to spend time with Velvet, and when he finally met up with her, she passed him off to her friend and ditched him for Alexi? He took some deep breaths. He hadn't had his tea since the day club when Christian played.

He talked with the beautiful Australian for a few minutes until it was obvious his attentions lay elsewhere.

"I didn't know you and Asha were a thing. I'm going to strangle that girl."

Zazzle chuckled despite his cramped shoulders. "I don't think Asha knows we're a thing." His humor was tinged with frustration.

"Well, I'm on. You're lovely." She pinched his cheek too hard for it to be mistaken for anything other than friendly. "Enjoy."

Tekko and Rob kept him company as they listened to Bliss's set.

"Fret not, man. She'll be back," Tekko said.

Zazzle worried. When he saw Velvet next, he had every intention of confronting her.

"Bliss!" Candy stretched her arms out to her friend. The other half of Bedazzled Beats arrived a half hour into the set. "Hey, guys. Where's Velvet?" she asked, over the hypnotic sounds of the music.

"Ummm...she's with Alexi." Tekko's eyes darted to him.

"O-kay..." Candy scratched her head and exchanged glances with Rob, who shrugged, and Tekko, whose lips pursed.

Zazzle had a thought to leave but not before he spoke to Velvet.

A few minutes later, Velvet returned with Alexi, whose flat features were encouraging. Had something happened between them, he was confident that he would have picked up on it.

Bliss's set ended and the Aussie chatted with the press, then they all decided to abandon the festival and head into town.

"Let's grab Evie and get some food before we split up to play our club gigs tonight," Tekko suggested.

"Free time is over," Rob announced. "It was fun while it lasted, but I'm hyped to play tonight."

"You guys should come out if you're not busy." Tekko winked at Velvet who returned a combination of a frown and eye roll.

"I'm going to walk back to the hotel and chill there for a bit. Text me where you guys are and I'll try to meet up."

"You good, Velveteen?" Candy asked.

"Yeah..." She sighed. "You? What did you get at vending? Anything good?"

"I...umm...nope. Nothing."

"You're sure?" Velvet persisted but Candy ducked responding. Velvet held up her hands. "Okay."

Zazzle arched an eyebrow at their exchange. They said a lot but nothing at all.

"I'll walk with you." Zazzle gave a few departing words to the group and trailed Velvet, who already headed for the hotel. His patience waned but he kept it in check for the fifteen minutes it took for them to get out of the festival and on a town road to the hotel.

"Did you have fun tonight?" He attempted interest.

"Yeah, thanks." The last time he saw Velvet so restless was at the club in Stockholm. He assumed many things but despite his irritation, he wanted her to talk to him.

"You okay?" he asked.

"I'm Gucci." She marched toward the hotel but he was on her heels.

"What's up with you and Alexi?" The question weighed like lead in his mouth. He trusted their connection but he tensed, waiting for her answer.

"How about you and Bliss?"

Annoyed that she didn't answer his question, he responded. "She's your friend. I was being polite."

"Yeah, polite." She drew brakes and faced him, her scowl deadly. "Why are you out of your room?"

His fists clenched at his sides. "Am I not allowed out anymore?" He hadn't been sentenced to house arrest.

"You're supposed to be EMETAH-ing and all. Remember? Exercise, Meditation—"

"I'm an adult man, not a child. I don't need to be reminded, Asha."

"Clearly you do." Her eyes challenged.

Frustration traveled through his veins and he inflated his chest with air. "Why not just say what's really bugging you."

"Nothing's bugging me. I'm Gucci." She pounded a fist in her palm.

He chuckled wickedly. "You keep saying that but you can't see yourself and all you're doing." He mimicked her.

Her eyes glowered at him. "What is that supposed to be? Some 'angry black girl' reference?"

He cocked his head. "You'd really ask me that?" The night they spent together they talked about so many things including race until the sun came up. He believed she knew his heart and that their heightened state led to miscommunication and stirred feelings he was not privy to. When she didn't answer he swallowed his pride and his privilege and continued. "No. It's an 'Asha is obviously agitated and upset' observation. So what is it?"

"Nothing!"

He raked his hands through his hair. "This is exhausting. You can't say it, can you? You can't tell me that you're pissed off because your friend flirted with me?"

"I don't care about that," her voice quivered.

"Right. Then what do you care about, Asha?"

"I care that I don't know what this is or how to speak to it," she yelled. "What was I supposed to say? That we kissed? That I don't know what to do about it because getting involved with you is dangerous for me? That ever since we met there's this thing that exists between us? That something's inside of me that I can't get out?"

He closed the space between them and he held her face on either side. "Let's get it out of you, then." He captured her lips, his arms encircling her against him.

"Isaak." The heat from her mouth stung his lips and he welcomed the sweet burn. Her taste controlled him and he lost his senses.

"I hated seeing you leave with him," he said between shaky breaths against her mouth. He quelled the heat of jealousy at the image of her and Alexi.

Her hands grabbed either side of his face with cool, shaky fingertips. "Why didn't you stop me?"

"The same reason you left me with Bliss." His mouth sought hers, desperate for closeness and forgiveness, but her inquisition continued.

"Why did you come out?" Her eyes, reading him for what, he was unsure.

"Because this is Ibiza and I wanted to spend some of my time here with you—"

Her mouth smothered anything else he planned to say. He matched her frantic need and devoured her. Her tongue breached his mouth, and the secure lock on his emotions fractured. He wanted her to be his, needed her, and if she wasn't ready to hear the words, showing her was well overdue.

"That thing that is inside you, Asha, is inside me, too."

They weren't going to make it to the hotel. She didn't want to hear any more. He'd won. He cracked her heart open and she surrendered to him as they kissed. All she wanted was him.

She wasn't jealous of Bliss. She loved her friend. Velvet's envy targeted something altogether different. Bliss had fearlessly showed her interest in Zazzle while Velvet hid her feelings, judged him, worried about him, and ultimately allowed someone else to claim him. So many things could go wrong if she opened herself fully. But what if they didn't?

He sucked her bottom lip, moaning with her, months of controlled desire now set free. Even if she wanted to, there was no turning back.

She didn't know where he'd dragged her, but a stone stairway protected them from view. The combination of high-perched street lamps provided enough light for her to see the desire on his face. She drew his face to hers again before they were fully concealed. His hand roved her body, lifting her shirt and bra to her neck. His lips abandoned hers to kiss the skin around her dark brown nipples. He lavished brief licks to her tightening areola before he lapped her nipple, drawing it into his mouth.

"Isaak," she moaned and stumbled backward. Her naked spine hit the rough tepid stone of the stairs. Her fingers messed his hair and she pressed him harder to her. With one breast thoroughly suckled, he tended to the other.

She pulled at his shoulders. "Kiss me. Isaak. Please kiss me." This was different from their first time on the daybed in San Bernardino. Back then, she'd found him and lost him in less than forty-eight hours. They'd both undergone massive changes in just over half a year. Now as they reunited she welcomed the new experience of being with him again.

He obliged her and as his hands worked on her shorts, his mouth found hers again. Within seconds he yanked the material of her jeans and panties to her knees. She wiggled them down to the floor and barely stepped out of them before his hand was buried between them, playing with her.

He said something in Dutch and she had no idea what it meant but it felt good in and against her mouth. Almost as good as his fingers inside her canal and the growing sensations swelling her clit. Her breath caught in her windpipe as he continued to massage, and the scent of the sea further intensified her arousal.

Again he spoke in Dutch, this time to her. "What?" She could barely speak.

"Can I kiss you?" His glazed eyes peered down between her legs and his hand patted her pussy.

She gulped. "Yes."

He dropped to his knees and draped one of her legs over his shoulder. She arched her back and thrust her hips until they lined up perfectly with his face. His head bobbed like music and his tongue played her like a delicate instrument.

"I love the way you taste, Asha." She squirmed under the vibration of his mouth.

"Holy fucking shit." Velvet was pretty sure she'd never said that combination of words in her life. "Don't ever stop, Isaak."

He didn't. He only pleasured her with an expertise she couldn't comprehend. One of her hands clawed at the stone holding her up and the other pressed his head into her center. The pressure built in her like hot bubbly water left in a car trunk. Her limbs trembled as she tried to hold on to each stroke of divine pleasure he gave.

"Isaak," she hissed through clenched teeth. Her body exploded, jerking and shaking. His arms cradled her hips and he sealed his mouth to her, continuing his assault on her clit.

She groaned in ecstasy, the intensity brutal and liberating. Her hips fought for freedom as hard as her leg squeezed him even tighter to her pussy. She squealed with each shock wave rippling through her. He relaxed his grip on her hips, delivering last licks.

He lifted to his feet and she was in full view of his body. His freed cock angled at her. Her desire for him smoldered. "I want that." She pointed to him.

He agreed with a rumbling moan from deep in his chest. "You can have that and so much more, baby." He slid a condom from his back pocket and she recognized the festival logo. He tore open the wrapper, and fitted himself with speed.

She further exposed her neck as he traced kisses along her collarbone. She pressed her palm to her forehead at the delicate touch.

Zazzle's mouth left her neck and his eyes met her. "I can't believe I get to touch you tonight—"

She silenced him with a kiss and her arm hooked his neck. "Stop talking, Isaak, and fuck me."

His tongue slid across her bottom lip. *"Ja, schatje."*

She repeated his words, pushing her hips against his hard-on. "You said that to me back then, too. Didn't you?"

"Yes, my little treasure," he translated for her.

The restraints fell away and she wrapped one leg around his. Isaak ducked to lift her and she hung on to him as her lower limbs trapped his waist. He worked below until she felt the tip of his cock at her entrance. Still wet from their previous session, he glided in effortlessly and filled her.

She fisted his hair as he pinned her to the stone wall. Her insides rejoiced as each hard thrust tingled the bundle of nerves building with pressure. His mouth captured hers and his tongue darted in similar fashion to his cock. She met each hard thrust. His panting clued her in to one simple fact. He was going to come before her.

She reached between her legs to assist her own orgasm. Zazzle's eyes shot open at the feel of her hand.

"Let me?" he asked. "I want to."

She nodded and embraced his shoulders. His hand replaced hers and he held her with the other, driving into her. His blissful touches sent her soaring. She was wrong. Her orgasm ripped through her body again and her insides clamped his muscle. Wave after glorious wave electrified every cell that existed within her.

"Hang on, baby," he whispered. His movements increased as he readjusted his arms around her middle. He howled his climax into her neck, shaking with labored breaths. She stroked his hair and neck. Her heaving chest restricted by his.

Seconds passed and though uncomfortable she stroked him and he kept her trapped in his arms. She felt his member soften before he simultaneously set her down and pulled out. He tied the saturated latex in a knot before finding the discarded wrapper and slipping the condom inside. Even the way he handled the prophylactic turned her on.

"I'll trash it later." He slid the wrapper into his back pocket.

"Don't sit on it," she teased.

His laugh sang to her heart. "That'd be awkward."

The back of her wrist rested on her forehead to meet the beads of sweat from her rounds with him.

She breathed in cooler more humid air from the surrounding stone.

Velvet's senses returned as did her responsibilities. "Oh, shit!"

"What?"

"We're supposed to meet everyone for food before they play their club shows later."

She stuffed her boobs back into her bra and pulled down her shirt. He found her bottoms and handed them to her before buttoning his shorts.

"I—" What does one say after being ravished under a stone staircase?

He ran his fingers through his hair. "So…umm…" He spun around himself and looked for nothing in particular.

She folded her lips to keep her laughter at bay. "You're invited to eat with us. You comin'?"

"Yeah." His eyes brightened a bit but he dawdled as if questioning his next move.

"Nah-uh. You can't go all weird on me now." She dragged him with her. "Come on, let's get outta here."

There was no going back. She knew it and she was sure he did, too. Where they headed and whether or not she'd be strong enough to love him, body and soul, without turning into his caretaker was the real mystery. All she could do was hope because the more time they spent together, the more intertwined they became, and the last thing she ever wanted to do was let him go.

Chapter Twenty-One

Tres Armadas met with Maggie in a small conference room early the next morning. Zazzle coasted on cloud nine and replayed the events of last night. He enjoyed their effects in his shower, his bed, even the couch in his suite. He was scheduled to show up at Bedazzled Beats' DJ set and surprise the fans. He longed to see her. He sent her a text to let her know he thought about her and received a you too back, which further elevated his mood.

Nothing lasted forever, though. He should have expected the bottom to fall out from somewhere.

As he sat with Maggie and Tres Armadas, statements like "it feels right," or "we've gone as far as we can go together" and "the machine is no longer content, there's no more challenge" floated around him. The day when they stopped talking around the issues in their group had finally come and they had to make a decision.

"I hate to see you guys end, but both Maartin and Christian have made it clear that they are okay with dissolving Tres Armadas as a group," Maggie said. "And you, Zazzle? What have you to say? What are you thinking?"

He didn't have the words to express himself but as

Christian shifted in his seat, and Maartin twiddled his thumbs, they both needed him to answer.

"If this is what everyone wants," he delivered between tight lips.

"What do you want, Isaak?" Maartin encouraged through his impatient movements.

"I'm not ready to say goodbye to Tres Armadas, to us as a group. When I came back, I wanted…no, I needed to make things right. I wanted to help bring back the credibility to the group, so that we weren't a joke or labeled 'a has-been drug trio.' Most of the burden is mine but I wanted us to come through the fire together, stronger, like we once were."

Zazzle hung on to the fun they had, the music, the records they broke and the adoring fans. He'd experienced it with Maartin and Christian for most of their careers. Christian was right. He'd missed the last part—their best years. He wanted that time back with his DJ brothers, but as he looked into their faces, he could see he was the only one.

"That's understandable, Isaak. You're back and sober and you want one last run and to redeem yourself. Here's the reality." Maggie crossed her legs. "This is the end. In a group of three, two want to disband. The question is no longer if, it's when."

Outvoted, Zazzle's shoulders slumped. He poured his heart out to them and it didn't matter. It was over. The group he'd been part of for almost sixteen years was ending.

Maggie patted his shoulder. "So this is what I propose. You finish out the rest of this tour next month. Sometime between now and then, we send out a press release. Let's face it, everyone is already speculating about TA and the alleged in-fighting."

"I'm not in-fighting," Maartin offered.

Maggie frowned at Maartin's ill-timed humor.

She continued. "This will give you time to decide if you want to do a farewell tour next year. Take a breather…pursue your solo endeavors. Then you may come back one last time to give the fans, who have followed you for all these years, a proper send-off. You guys are stinking rich and don't need the money, but there's that to be made, as well. I don't expect you to make this decision overnight so think about it and let me know."

"I like the idea. We can document it, as well," Maartin said. "We can incorporate our families and friends and create some special experiences for our fans. We can even have a bigger, more elaborate stage, if that's possible."

"Excellent contribution, Maartin," Maggie praised.

Christian, like him, had been silent during Maggie's proclamation.

"I'm ready to follow my creativity and be challenged in a different way than with TA."

"Are you saying no to one last tour?" Maggie asked Christian.

"No." Christian's voice was reverent to the magnitude of the moment. "But I'm not saying yes either."

"Neither am I." Zazzle surprised himself. "The thrill of the stage and entertaining the fans is addictive and something I've been working on. Trying to turn off Zazzle once I leave the stage and just being Isaak is a battle sometimes. It might be time for me to think about more behind-the-scenes projects. I don't want TA to end but if it is ending, then prolonging it may not be in the best interest for any of us."

"Zaz," Maartin called.

"I failed you guys," Zazzle choked. "Maybe this was inevitable but my addiction played a role. I wish things had turned out differently." Zazzle rubbed his eyes and a heavy hand rested on his shoulder. He assumed Maartin comforted him but found Christian instead.

"You had a problem, man, and we weren't great at dealing with it." Christian's response released the tension in his body. Maartin joined them and the ball that lodged in his chest shrunk in intensity.

"You guys." Maggie sniffled.

Zazzle received the blow better than expected and though he shared a moment with Christian and Maartin, the idea that Tres Armadas was over no less broke him. "Was there anything else, Maggie?" Zazzle asked.

"Not on my agenda. Guys?" Maggie opened it to the room.

Maartin and Christian both shook their heads.

"Will you at least think about it, Isaak? This is no longer only about Tres Armadas, but your fans, too," Maggie reiterated.

"I will." He barely got the words out. He gave her a curt nod and left.

Zazzle needed to digest what just happened. Tres Armadas was no more. The end had finally come. He expected his heart to be broken, but surprisingly it wasn't.

Velvet grinned like a lovesick puppy. Her screen stared at her instead of the other way around. Candy's giggle jolted her back from visions of stone stairwells and Zazzle's head between her legs.

"Wow," Candy gasped.

Velvet moistened her drying mouth.

"Don't," Velvet warned.

Candy's body shook from suppressing her laughter. "I didn't even say anything."

"I texted the guys. They know when to be here."

According to social media, Rob and Tekko's late night hadn't ended until daybreak. Velvet, on the other hand, had tapped out. Between their travels, their performances, her emotions and the sexercise she and Zazzle shared, she'd called it a night at three in the morning.

"Cool." They were debuting "Love Me Love You" toward the end of their set at Ibiza Fest and Velvet's nerves got the better of her. She hoped the fans loved the song like she and her friends but it was always hit or miss. All she could do was her best. If this went well, it might help them with Temptation and keep them top of mind when voting opened.

She and Candy were ready and made their way to the stage. On their way she saw Zazzle and her mouth dried like a dish towel on a clothesline on a hot day.

"Hey," she greeted him.

"Hallo." She wanted to kiss his smile right off his face.

"Hey, Zazzle," Candy cheesed. "See you at the stage, Velveteen."

Zazzle pulled her to a spot with less people, which was no easy feat. Between the stagehands, artists, entourages and promoters, all eyes were curious about a pair of popular DJs searching for solace.

He pinned her against a false wall. "Open your mouth."

Her heartbeat quickened as she did as he asked. Surprisingly, she didn't question why.

Zazzle produced a pink Blow Pop and placed it on her tongue.

"Suck," he instructed.

She complied and he studied each bob of her head, and every pucker, lick and seal her mouth performed on the confectionary.

Holy fuck. Her heartbeat thudded in her inner ear and her center was a wet, hot pocket of desire. She identified the flavor—*watermelon*—and moaned as he rolled the wet candy against her lips. He kissed her around the hard, tart sweetness and rested his hand on her cheek. His scent mixed with the fruity flavor and her senses went wild. Her body moved closer to him as he withdrew the lollipop. His tongue ran over her lower lip before he caught it in his teeth and then sucked gently. The exhilarating caresses made everything, except him, vanish. She opened wider to welcome his seeking tongue.

The passion in his kiss increased and something felt different. Her hand framed his face and though she hated to do it, she pulled him away and caught her galloping breath.

"You okay?" She longed for more closeness, but when her eyes searched his, she was sure of it. Something bothered him. Her arm craned his neck like an anchor.

He ran his hand over her chest until he settled on one breast. The tenderness in his touch made her as gooey as chocolate on a warm range.

"Asha," he called her name and he pressed his head into her chest.

"What's wrong?" She stroked his hair and tried not to fall into doomsday thinking.

He shook his head. He kissed her lips, again. "You have to go onstage. We'll talk later."

"The stage can wait." Her own words startled her.

"No it can't."

She straightened. She wanted him to get whatever ailed him off his chest but her performance time encroached on his disclosure. "No it can't."

He tapped her chin. "I'll see you onstage for the song."

"Promise you'll talk to me later, okay?"

"I promise."

Reluctant to leave him, she left to meet up with Candy.

The sun lowered, bringing on the bright night, and Bedazzled Beats started to play. The crowd cheered. Huge displays surrounded the raised platform. The lights were either designs or parts of video clips of the group on tour. And the fans ate it up. The duo got on the dials and the cries of the attendees swelled. Their signature headlined above in LED lights. A never-ending sea of smartphones captured them onstage. The higher they took the crowd the more energy the fans poured out to them just to feel them and maybe even to mystically touch them. Velvet and Candy fed off the energy in a mind-blowing sphere encapsulating the moment.

The time had come for them to debut "Love Me Love You."

"Ibiza! We have a new one we're debuting here for you tonight. Do you mind if we bring on some friends?"

The crowd cheered.

"Welcome to the stage, Tekko, Rob Ready and Zazzle!"

Candy bopped to the beat and faded in their new song. The three men came onstage and not even the sky could contain the noise.

"Oh my God." Velvet awed as the screams vibrated though her and reverberated in her inner ear to the point where she had no choice but to press them shut.

"Wow." Candy mouthed and bounced to the beat as her friends came to the stage. Velvet was sure her friend said the words but they barely heard the music.

They all played, jumping on and off the dials for their parts, sharing musical space. When the beat dropped Velvet encouraged them to lose control.

"Everybody. Jump! Jump!" Velvet screamed into the mic and the thunder of their feet rattled the foundation of the stage.

Tekko pointed out into the crowd and Rob swung his arm around him. Zazzle climbed up on the DJ table and danced. Velvet was flying high and wanted this feeling to last forever. She didn't think the crowd could thicken any more but during the song it swelled to the point of capacity and the crowd mimicked a pin art impression box.

"Ape shit," Tekko mouthed to her and she laughed, working the dials.

Eventually they moved into another song and played until they ended their set with "Be You" and they literally brought the house down.

When they got offstage, they were greeted with praise.

"Best set of the night."

"'Love Me Love You' is an instant hit."

"This summer's new anthem."

"Ibiza loves you."

The crowd continued to cheer for them. Velvet hugged Candy and they jumped up and down.

"I can't even believe how awesome that went." Sonny materialized. "You ladies killed this festival." Sonny normally kept her excitement within manager limits but she dribbled out of bounds.

Tekko, Rob and Zazzle squeezed her and Candy into a group hug.

"Outstanding," Rob howled.

"I'd say they liked it."

They continued to celebrate as they chatted with media.

"Fam?"

Velvet's eyes located Trevor and his friends who gave her air high fives.

When the press finally released her and Candy, Velvet hugged Trevor.

"You're my sis and all but I have never seen anything like that. You and Bonnie demolished that shit."

"Thanks," Velvet gushed. She then introduced Trevor to Zazzle.

"Man, it's an honor." Velvet rarely saw Trevor humbled and he'd only met one-third of Tres Armadas. His boys gushed, as well.

"It's a pleasure to meet Velvet's family. Have you been enjoying Ibiza?"

"Hell yeah," Trevor responded. "Me and my boys have been all over this island."

Zazzle smiled. "Will you be at our closeout set tonight?"

"For sure." Trevor affirmed with his whole body.

"Cool. You can meet the rest of the guys."

"Oh, man." Trevor crumbled and Velvet fought back rolls of laughter.

The press dragged Zazzle away for commentary. She wanted to talk to him but with so many people around she didn't know if they'd get their chance. Tekko and Rob were playing their festival sets soon and they'd all bounced around to catch parts of their performances. Zazzle had to leave to meet up with Tres Armadas for pre-show press.

"We're doing 4am eats to send everyone off before we split up again. You and Tres Armadas should join us."

"I'll tell them," Zazzle said.

"I'm sorry we didn't get a chance to talk."

"We will." He planted a brief kiss on her lips.

"See you at your set later."

"Have fun with your friends, *schatje*."

She blushed so hard. The last time he'd called her that, his hard-on had poked against her belly and he'd been about to fuck her in public.

He tapped her chin and left.

"Come through, romance," Trevor teased. "And with an Armada no less."

That her brother had witnessed her and Zazzle mortified her. "Mind your business."

Later they gathered at the Tres Armadas set. As the crowd cheered for the men who stood behind the DJ table and started on the dials, Christian, of all people, collected Zazzle and Maartin into a hug. The fans gasped and awed and the emotion spread through the festival. Backstage they'd huddle but she'd never seen them hug before.

Velvet couldn't shake the feeling that the unceremonious tender moment between the men had something to do with the low spirits she picked up in Zazzle earlier, before she'd performed. Tres Armadas played their set and Velvet danced off the excess energy with her friends. Before their final song, Christian picked up the mic.

"Thank you, Ibiza! We love you." And hell if Christian wasn't choked up.

In the wee hours of the morning, their group of thirteen, including Bliss and Alexi, made it to 4am eats. Velvet enjoyed the time with her family and friends, sharing food and laughs with recounts of the night.

Zazzle sat next to her, and Maartin and Christian chatted with their group. Velvet looked over at Candy and thought they were missing one. LED.

Zazzle touched her thigh underneath the table and while her friends and brother carried on she leaned into him.

"I enjoy seeing you happy like this. It reminds me of our night at Temptation last September. When we watched the performances with Candy and LED, like fans without responsibility."

"Yeah, we did." She smiled but the sadness in his tone alarmed her.

"Unlike these hard business decisions." His voice was far off but he glanced at Christian and Maartin who fooled around with Tekko, Candy and Bliss.

She grabbed hold of his hand, the gesture out of view of unwanted attention. "Hey. What's happening with you? What did you want to tell me?" she asked him.

"It's official. Tres Armadas is breaking up."

She peered into the sadness in his eyes and her face crumpled.

Chapter Twenty-Two

Amsterdam's pleasant but cooler temperatures reflected the change in her heart. Her friends were off to different festivals, clubs and residencies, and like always she missed them. She'd see them soon enough but the initial separation brought with it a case of the blues.

Bedazzled Beats played two clubs in Barcelona before meeting up with Tres Armadas in the Netherlands. Between the early morning gigs and travel, Sandman sprinkled her head with his sleep dust and Velvet spent much of her first day in the Netherlands undercover.

Zazzle had dropped a bomb on her about Tres Armadas and she wondered how the news affected him beyond 4am eats. Onstage, the trio rocked a crowd and were united in music but if they were breaking up then what kind of relationship did they really have? She thought about Bedazzled Beats. She and Candy had always been a cohesive unit, but with some of their recent squabbles Velvet wondered if that would always be. Could they end up like Zazzle, Maartin and Christian?

When Velvet woke up, Candy was gone. Her friend's mood lived somewhere in the area of amped Candy and thrilled Candy, which seemed unusual, as well. Velvet scolded herself. What did she want—a sad, lethargic Candy, or a happy, energetic one? With all the happenings in Ibiza, and snappy travel, Velvet put her inquisition on hold as to whether or not Candy reconnected with LED. He one hundred percent ghosted her. Ibiza wasn't a big island and yet LED had managed to avoid her completely.

"How did I become someone he doesn't want to talk to?" Maybe he still stewed over her accusations.

Her friends complained she never looked at the lineup or searched where people would be playing. That was about to change. She connected to the hotel Wi-Fi and typed in LED's website. She clicked on events and scrolled through.

"Ibiza…pshh…seriously?"

She continued to scroll and there it was. Amsterdam, the Netherlands.

"Oh, you're going to see me this time, buster. I got you." She snuggled under the covers and the sun rays filled the room. She stretched, her body cracking awake. She took in the small moment of peace until her phone buzzed.

She connected to her message app.

Zazzle: Come to my house for a coffee.

Velvet read his text from the confines of her duvet. She'd forgotten that they were in Tres Armadas's home country. The trio lived full or part-time in homes near or close to Amsterdam.

Velvet: Is that code for something else? :)

Visions of him naked swirled like cinnamon buns in her cranium.

Zazzle: Are you asking about smoke shops?

She fumbled with her phone and made a mess of her bedding.

Velvet: No! I meant...

She smacked her forehead and stared at the message. "Oh, what the hell." She typed sex and pressed send.

Zazzle: lol

Zazzle: It's code for a coffee but that can change.

She bagged a response to his statement. "Way to go, Asha." Granted, Zazzle had grown up with marijuana smoke shops and coke had been his drug of choice, but it didn't seem like the conversation to have with someone in recovery.

Velvet: Okay. Trading in Nuts for a bicycle.

Zazzle: See you then

His address followed.

Velvet: See you in an hour or two

Zazzle: An hour, please

Velvet texted a dark brown thumb-up emoji to end their conversation. She should be running in the other direction, but instead her toes wiggled. Being intimate with him opened the floodgates and an avalanche of conflicting feelings tumbled out of her. She'd hoped sex with him would satiate her attraction and cut the ties thickening around her heart but it only made it harder for her to regain control.

She hopped out of bed and showered. With only herself for company she freely expressed her anticipation, singing "You Want This" into her deodorant, and jiggling her hips in the mirror as she giggled and dressed. She longed to see Zazzle, wanted him, and speculated about whether she possessed the strength to be his. Her feelings for him overruled her urge to flee at the thought of who she might become in this relationship. That fact scared her more than she could measure, yet she prepared to leave.

She didn't bother to text Candy but instead scribbled a note and placed it on the dresser. Velvet had visited Amsterdam a few times for gigs and had some idea of the layout so she followed a map to his place and blended with the locals on a bicycle. She arrived at his apartment in fifteen minutes.

Zazzle's yellow home sat nestled within a quaint row of colorful houses on the swan-speckled Herengracht canal. The structures, more tall than wide, were almost identical. Velvet parked her bicycle, approached the entrance and rang the bell.

Footsteps above grew louder and closer. Zazzle swung open the door and Velvet's heart raced. Her eyes widened at the white powder that dusted his nose and part of his cheek. Some even painted his shirt.

In Ibiza, Zazzle had been out quite a bit but didn't appear to indulge in the alcohol or drugs floating around the scene. So what the fuck was on his face? He was either a messy, wasteful user or the white powder was something else.

"Hallo." The divine smile he greeted her with faded. "Asha?"

She pointed to his face. "What's that? You have white powder everywhere."

For a moment he stared at her as if she were the one with unexplainable white powder on her face. Then his expression softened and his brows leveled.

"I'm making pannenkoeken."

"What?" She hurried him along to get a clearer understanding before she overreacted more than her current status.

"Please come in." He ushered her inside.

She climbed a steep narrow staircase, each step heavy with the weight of Zazzle's pending explanation. *And what the hell is pannenkoeken?*

The higher she climbed the more potent the thick smell of hot oil and something fried penetrated her nostrils. When she reached the top, the space opened into a larger dining and living space with a connected kitchen. The scent, akin to a funnel cake cart, filled the room.

"You're cooking?"

He nodded. "I'm making pannenkoeken for Christian's daughter. She only likes mine. They are her favorite. She'll be here shortly to pick them up so I have to make them fresh. I made some to share with you, as well."

"Oh." Heady from the mini adrenaline shot, she rolled and shrugged the tension from her shoulder. A more sensible list of what the dusting of white on his clothing could be scrolled through her head. "Flour?" She pointed to various parts of him.

Zazzle slapped white powder off his shirt. "*Poedersuiker.* Eh...sweet." Zazzle snapped his finger to find the right words. "Powdered sugar... Confectioners' sugar?"

"Yeah...umm...both are correct." Within her, a category four level of berating commenced.

"Taste." Before she could object, his powdered finger touched her lip and the tip of her tongue. The sweetness, a bitter medicine to take for her assumptions. "What did you think it was?"

Her eyes landed on the couch, the kitchen and the window. She crossed her arms over her middle. "Something bad. I was surprised. It's stupid."

The tension in his body reached hers and she wished she could take everything spoken and unspoken back. *What's wrong with me?*

He touched her chin, forcing her to look at him. "You may greet me better now," he said. His eyes scanned her face and rested on her lips.

Her heart cried for how her insolence must have made him feel.

She hooked her arm around his neck and brought his face to hers. She licked the sugar off his cheek, then planted a kiss in its place. She repeated the action several times until her mouth joined with his in a sweet kiss.

"Better?" She rubbed her nose against his.

"Yes." He pecked her nose and she squeezed him tight.

"I'm sorry."

"I know." He smacked her lips with one last kiss.

"And the coffee shop thing…"

"A misunderstanding." He dismissed it with a wave of the hand and she prayed she didn't insult him again. She hadn't even been in his house five minutes.

"What's pannenkoeken?" she asked.

"Pancakes. Similar to a French crepe."

"Oh." She'd enjoyed both the savory and sweet crepes from the street vendors in France.

"Come enjoy some." If what Zazzle offered her was anything close to those delicious treats, she was all in. She followed him to the kitchen.

He poured the thick batter into a hot pan, moving the handle to spread the contents around.

"Look at you. I didn't think you cooked."

"I don't. This is all I'm good at, really."

He flipped it in the pan and then onto a plate for her and grabbed the powdered sugar. "And a little cocaine for you."

Velvet gasped but her smile tightened her cheeks. "Not funny."

He pushed chopped berries and a jar of honey her way.

"Show me how to do it," she demanded, and scooted onto a high dining stool.

He obliged. "First the berries." He sprinkled them over the golden brown pancake and drizzled a smidge of honey on top. "For flavor. It's already sweet." He folded it and cut a piece before feeding her.

She opened her mouth and gobbled the soft, warm, doughy forkful. "Mmm…that's really good. Umm… *Dank u wel.*"

"Graag gedaan." His face shined. "You're learning?"

"I may have picked up a bit here and there on tour with you guys."

He turned off the stove and covered a large stack of pancakes in foil. He did the same with two smaller stacks before he changed stations.

"I can help you learn more, if you like."

"That'd be great." She savored her food.

"They say the best way to learn the language is to take a Dutch lover." He winked at her and an espresso machine blared or else he would have heard her choke on her pancake. His shoulders bounced with laughter as he fixed her a coffee, and one for himself.

"You're so silly." She cleared the dough from her throat. "You're not having your tea?"

"No, I wanted to have a coffee with you."

"That's a lot of caffeine, no?"

"I'm trying out some things I used to enjoy to see how I do." He fixed himself a pancake and took a healthy bite.

"That's great." All she saw were addictive stimulants. "Did you do your exercise and meditate today? The schedule's been all over the place."

"Our press has been nonstop and there were some sponsor things we had to take care of so I slept quite a bit late today. I hope to get to the rest of it later. I meditated and this is breakfast."

"Sugar?"

He sighed and she folded her lips to quiet her mothering. She raised her espresso cup to him. "Cheers."

"Proost." They both drank.

She lifted another bite of food to her mouth. "So how are you doing? You know, with the whole Tres Armadas thing?"

"I guess it's what must happen. I thought I had more time but I wasted it."

"Man, you guys are so good together. It's a shame. The fans will be heartbroken. Is there any way you can work it out?"

"Don't you think I've tried? It's over," he snapped.

She dished him a lengthy glare. "I'm not your enemy." She poked at her food with her fork. She struggled with letting go, too. DJ FeNom? Candy? The situations weren't entirely applicable but they all boiled down to one thing, getting over herself. A lesson she still learned and one Zazzle might learn from, as well.

"Forgive me. I don't mean to—"

"No, I get it. This is hard stuff. You're losing something, right now. All I can do is listen."

He ran his fingers through his hair. "I still want to play with them but I'm outvoted. There is a possibility of one more tour but it's torture to think about right now." He leaned on the table.

"But you guys are still friends, right?"

He didn't answer right away. She'd witnessed him and Christian bicker and Maartin had commented on the state of things on a few occasions.

Another heavy sigh escaped him. "We're trying, I think."

She treaded carefully with her next inquiry. "You and Christian?"

He nodded. "Things began to unravel with us before my addiction got out of control. We'd always been in this music thing together, but Christian often sought to expand creatively with others. When it was clear he longed for a solo career, I did not take it well."

"Is that why you turned to drugs?"

"No. Have you ever realized that I'm the only one in the group with an alias?"

"Huh? You are. How did I not realize that?"

"Well, when we first got noticed fame really did happen for us quickly. My stage presence got labeled as 'Zazzle time,' and yes, it's a nod to MC Hammer."

She smiled. "Glad you noticed that."

"Anyway. Everywhere I went, people expected me to be that person. Over the years, I had a hard time turning off. I partied harder, used coke to keep the euphoria and energy up, you know."

"And the drinking?"

"I thought I had a drinking problem but when I went into rehab, they diagnosed me with depression and when I explained how I drank more with the drugs they saw the connection."

"So you can drink?"

"Probably."

"But you don't."

"Correct. I prefer it that way for now."

She stroked his cheek. "I'm so proud of you."

He held her and continued.

"Anyway, I also like to party and had successfully cultivated an entourage of enablers. By the time I realized I had a problem it was well out of control, but I needed something to blame, so…"

"You blamed Christian."

"My habit just made things in the group worse. No one could communicate with me and I cruised in full-on asshole mode."

"Have you said this to Maartin and Christian?"

"Yes. Maartin has been a good friend and supportive, but trust has been broken and is not so easily regained."

She rubbed his back. "Do you know what you're going to do?"

He shrugged. "I'm thinking about what you suggested. Go behind the scenes, I don't know."

"You're a great artist, Isaak. Maybe now is a good time to change things up. Reinvent yourself."

"Maybe so." He nuzzled her hand. "Thank you."

"You're welcome." She continued to feed her face and thought of her brother and friends. Her real and found family. Who did Isaak confide in about these things?

"Do you have family here?" she asked, distracted by the soft wet kisses he now placed on her skin.

"My brother, Jan, in Breda."

"Where are your folks?"

"They're retired in Curaçao but come back here annually to see me and my brother."

"That sounds heavenly." She added "retired life on a Dutch Caribbean island" to her bucket list.

"When my grandparents were alive they lived there, as well. I spent all my summers there. I think that's where my love of African and Caribbean music started." His lips traced up her forearm and then guided her hand back down on the table.

"No doubt influenced those dance moves, too." She willed her pulse to simmer down to no avail.

"I'm sure it did."

"Will you see Jan while you're here?"

"No, but he'll be in LA for our final shows," he delivered nonchalantly but the significance of "final shows" wasn't lost on her. "I'm in rehab because of him." Zazzle explained how his brother had intervened and flown with him to New Zealand.

"I love him already. I mean…maybe I can meet him someday."

Zazzle straightened from his bent position and grinned. "I'd like you to meet him, too."

She lifted another bite of food to her mouth and Zazzle lowered it back down to the plate. "I'm eating. Where are you taking me?" she asked as he pulled her with him.

"Upstairs."

"What's up there?"

"Coffee."

"Coffee? But…oh…" She climbed the stairs with a bit more pep to her step. She had a few seconds to take in the cool red and dark gray colors, popping off cream-colored walls in the large master suite before he was pulling on her shirt.

"Is this okay?" His hand slid underneath and she flinched at the cool touch.

"Now you ask?"

"I want to be sure."

"Yes. It's okay." She unbuckled his jeans. He peeled her shirt off and once freed she worked on his. "Arms up," she instructed, and yanked his shirt over his head. Her hand ran over the lean muscle in his chest.

They toddled to the bed and while Zazzle addressed his jeans, she disrobed, tossing her leggings and underwear to the side. The last time they were together had been intense, amazing and with no clear leader. This time as she climbed on top of him, she claimed the title.

"Condom," she commanded.

He extended his arm to the dresser, rocking her body, but he was unable to reach.

"Let me help you out." With feline agility she stretched

and found one in the drawer. Inside, she found a colorful array of foil and plastic wrappers, with different event and festival logos. "Ahh…the collection."

She pulled out a few and sprinkled them like confetti over his chest. She moved against him in her straddled position and asked, "Which one?"

"Asha." His husky warning thrilled her.

"Pick," she teased.

He hastily plucked one off the bed and called her name again. She was about to tear into the wrapper when his doorbell sounded.

His native language tumbled out of him and he rubbed his face.

"They've come for pannenkoeken."

"What? Who?" Velvet's heart raced and she scrambled off him.

"I made them for Christian's daughter. She is here to get them with her mother. I wanted you…this… I forgot." He dressed with haste.

Velvet jumped back into her clothes and smoothed her hair, sure that her face and body screamed, *I want sex now.*

Zazzle's hard-on formed a lump against his jeans.

"You really need to do something about that." She twirled her finger at the area between his legs.

He marched to a window and slid it open. He called out to his visitors below. All she understood was "hello" and "minutes." She really needed to learn more Dutch.

He returned to her and his hands cupped her face. "I'm sorry, *schatje*. Our loving will have to wait."

"Slow down. It's okay." Velvet observed him with fascination as he bolted to the bathroom, and laughter bubbled out of her.

"You're laughing at me?" The ring of humor circled his question, echoing from the bathroom.

"Yeah. You have to admit it's kind of funny." She leaned against the doorframe.

"Funny that my balls will be blue."

"You'll live." She chuckled.

He entered the bedroom. "I'm sorry."

"Me, too."

Zazzle ran down the stairs to open the door while she settled at the table where her food waited.

Velvet heard a lot of Dutch and a male voice she didn't expect but recognized. Christian. As they all piled up the stairs, Velvet stood to greet them. The conversation turned to English when they saw her and she was grateful to not be a complete outsider.

"Hey, Christian." Her cheeks warmed as Christian's eyes slid back and forth between her and Zazzle. She awaited distaste to etch his features, but instead he smiled with an arched brow.

"Sorry to interrupt." Christian winked.

Her cheeks burned.

Zazzle dove into introductions. "Asha, this is Christian's wife, Lotte, and daughter, Mila."

"Nice to meet you." Velvet shook Lotte's hand. The woman's light brown hair framed her face.

"Yes, Velvet? You are on tour with the guys."

Velvet nodded.

"I like your songs. Very positive."

Surprised, Velvet's gratitude was delayed. "Thank you." She addressed Christian's daughter, as well. "It's a pleasure to meet you, Mila." The girl was a perfect combination of Christian and Lotte.

"Cool hair," Mila complimented.

"Thanks. The color changes often," Velvet noted.

"We know," both Christian and Zazzle said at the same time.

An unspoken understanding passed between the two men.

Velvet rolled her eyes. "Whatever."

"You two used to do that all the time," Lotte mentioned.

Velvet strangely felt good to hear Lotte's memory. Maybe things were getting better between them despite the Tres Armadas breakup.

"How old are you, Mila?" Velvet asked.

"Eleven," she responded, then whispered to her mother. "Mom, can I get purple?"

Her mother tapped her lips. "Hmm… If you want it after a week, we'll see about a little bit here." Lotte touched the back of her daughter's head.

"You must stay for a coffee," Zazzle said, and went to the machine.

"No, no," Lotte said, but somehow the decline wasn't firm enough to stick.

"We can't stay long, as we are on our way to see the grandparents and collect Bram," Christian added.

"My son," Lotte clarified for Velvet.

"Oh."

The espresso machine revved and Zazzle shared shots of the aromatic coffee. Velvet chalked up the exchange to Dutch hospitality.

Zazzle handed the huge stack of foiled pancakes to Mila. He said something to her in their language and the girl smiled.

"Hartelijk bedankt, peetvader." Mila kissed his cheek. The sweet exchange was a crowd pleaser.

"His goddaughter," Lotte said. "He's very good to her."

"Yeah, she's got a huge stack of loving pancakes to prove it," Velvet laughed. "How'd you all meet?"

"I was a fan at one of their shows. I actually came to the shows to see Isaak."

"Oh, is this a scandalous story? Do tell."

"Not at all." Lotte laughed. "When I met Isaak he was kind, but very uninterested in me. We became good scene friends over a year's time. Then he invited me to Christian's birthday party. Christian says it was love at first sight but I don't know."

"It was," Christian confirmed.

Lotte scoffed. "He saw me a few times before but he said I looked different dressed up. That's when he really saw me. Not in shorts and face paint."

"Face paint." Mila did the equivalent of a more respectful New York eye roll.

She and Zazzle exchanged glances. "It's definitely not Isaak's thing."

"No, it's not," Zazzle confirmed.

Their face painting conversation at the carnival hadn't been anything spectacular but it spoke to the details that they both collected and cherished.

"Do you like your dad's music, Mila?"

"Yes. He is very good. You, too." She pointed to Zazzle.

"Well, thank you," he teased.

"You look well, Isaak. It is good to see you like this. You come have dinner with us next time. Bram would love to see you, as well. Christian?"

"Yes. That sounds good," Christian agreed.

The moment felt huge and good. Velvet peered over

at Lotte and the beaming woman confirmed that a bridge had been made.

"We really do have to run, Isaak. Thank you for the coffee."

Kisses were shared before they departed.

"I'll be back. I'm just going to let them out," he said.

As Velvet waited, she was glad she met Lotte and Mila. It gave her a little more insight into both Zazzle and Christian. She started to clear the table when her phone buzzed against her butt cheek.

Candy: Can you come back?

A sad face emoji with teardrop popped up next.

Zazzle thumped up the stairs. He pressed his body against hers and placed his hands on her waist. "Now, where were we?"

"I gotta go, I think. I just got a message from Candy. I have a bad feeling she saw LED."

"I know he's here so maybe."

"You knew he was going to be here?"

"Yeah, I saw him in Ibiza and he told me he'd be here."

"You saw him?" Her volume went from three to six. "Why didn't you tell me?"

"I didn't know I was supposed to."

She sighed. "I've been trying to connect with him to get to the bottom of this thing that's happening with him and Candy."

"And you're upset with me for not telling you something I had no idea about?" He parked his rear on a stool. "LED told me that they broke up. You might have mentioned that."

He had a point, but she was still frustrated that she'd missed her opportunity with LED.

"Are we quarreling over something that has nothing to do with us?" His accent made his statement sexier than it ought to have been.

"I don't know? Maybe?"

He sighed and eased off the stool. He grabbed a small stack of the foiled pancakes and handed it to her. "Go to her. You'll feel better once you two talk."

Velvet wasn't so sure. "Thank you. This was nice." *While it lasted.*

Chapter Twenty-Three

Velvet returned to the hotel to find Candy in disarray, pulling at her clothes and rubbing her face as she paced the room.

"What is going on?" Velvet asked.

"I saw Bernard and he's such an asshole! He just keeps pressuring me!" Candy's sentences jumbled together and Velvet grasped at them like puzzle pieces.

"Tell me what happened. Do I need to call someone?"

Candy halted and stared at her. "Call someone?"

"Like the authorities. If he put a hand on you I'll kill him myself."

"No, no, no."

Velvet took a breath. "Candy, please tell me what's happening. What is he pressuring you to do?"

"To be with him."

Velvet struggled like she was learning a new language. "And you don't want to be with him anymore?"

"I do," she blubbered.

Velvet's shoulders inched to her ears and her head was about to explode. "Then what's the problem? Why'd you break up with him?"

Candy looked about ready to jump out of her skin.

"Speak to me," Velvet yelled, an alternative to slapping Candy out of her tailspinning.

"You!"

Velvet backed up. *Me?* She looked around for another version of Asha Kendall. "Me?"

"He wants me to leave LA and move to Vancouver. To get more serious, but I can't leave you."

Velvet swallowed. "Leave me?"

"We're family. I take care of you and you take care of me. How are we Bedazzled Beats if we're apart? We've been together since we decided to be a group. We live together, travel together, play music. How's that work if I'm in Canada? It doesn't," Candy cried. "He made me choose between you and him."

"So you broke up with him? But you love him."

"No shit."

"I don't even understand what's happening. You could have worked it out."

"What?"

"You heard me."

"How can you say that? I did it for you. For our career together."

Velvet vented through her nose. "Because it's true. I don't know his side because he's not talking to me and—" She put two and two together. "That's why he's not talking to me? He blames me, too?"

"I broke up with him to save us and you tell me I should have worked it out?"

"Yes. You and Bernard could have worked it out. Instead you ran away from him like some scaredy-cat, and have been flat-out mean to me. You made me pay for your decision when all I've done is be a good friend to both of you."

"So you don't care about Bedazzled Beats?"

"Of course I care. We could have made a plan, discussed options with Sonny and Tommy. We always figure things out, compromise, lead and follow, talk. Why? Because that's what friends do. But you stopped talking to me. It's been months and now you're telling me that I'm the reason you and LED broke up? That's bullshit and you know it."

Candy rubbed her face. "It's not."

"And Willem? Don't you think I know what went on when he was around? Your mood, your ups and downs? I can't take the drugs out of your hand but I supported you and this breakup because I said to myself, Candy's gonna talk to me. She'll tell me what's up, eventually."

"Willem was right. You think you know everything. He said you'd turn this on me," Candy said.

"You've been seeing Willem?" Velvet recalled the times in Ibiza when Candy would disappear. Apparently LED wasn't the only one who knew the island well enough to stay out of view.

"You were sneaking around with Willem in Ibiza?"

"You didn't want him around so..."

Velvet sunk to the bed. "Who are you? It's literally like I don't know anymore."

"You're right. You don't." Candy grabbed her bag and stuffed some clothes inside.

"Where are you going?"

"Anywhere but here."

Velvet wore a hole into the tarp flooring backstage. Nail biting was never her thing. Neither was rubbing her knuckles on a metal grater, but the notion of doing that was far more appealing than her current situation.

"Well, someone has to perform." Maggie Swanson voiced the concerns of her clients.

Bedazzled Beats were twenty minutes away from being in breach of contract. Like a ballot box with a gaping hole in the bottom, Velvet saw the Temptation Festival votes slipping away. Tickets went on sale in a week, which also opened voting. Candy had never returned to the hotel to get picked up for their performance. Even with their ugly interaction earlier, Velvet had assumed Candy would show. She wanted to add *irresponsible* to the list of growing characteristics that were unlike Candy, but more importantly, Velvet didn't know where Candy was, who she was with or what state she was in.

"We're working on it." Sonny held a phone to her ear. The epitome of calm Sonny strolled further and further away as she talked and listened.

Informing Sonny had been no picnic and when her manager phoned Boombox, Velvet felt worse than a kid who'd been found out for sneaking to a party. Velvet called LED and when the message went to voicemail, she angry-thumbed him a text and also emailed the events.

"I noticed some things with you guys but I thought it to be minor squabbles," Sonny admitted. "You should have told me you were having business disagreements. Perhaps I could have mediated."

Velvet had honored Candy by not disclosing the Willem situation and just gave a blanket explanation that they were having business disagreements before Candy stormed out.

Though concerned, the other members of Tres Armadas had pre-show press to attend. Zazzle, however, remained close by but gave her flailing arms, pacing and face rubbing a wide berth. She'd given him the rundown and though working through his own schedule, he'd come to her aid.

"You should go, too. We've done enough damage. You don't have to bail on your responsibilities for me."

"I'm not bailing. The guys will cover for me 'til I get there."

She rolled her neck. "This is the worst nightmare ever."

"It'll be okay, Asha."

"How?" she pleaded, truly and deeply wanting an answer.

He didn't have time to answer before Sonny rushed over to them, Velvet hoped with good news. "We're out of time. You'll have to do it."

"What?" Nausea crept up her throat and her body wobbled.

Velvet wasn't sure if she was up to performing, much less performing alone. It wasn't that she couldn't figure out what music to play or how to entertain a crowd. Candy was missing and was dark on her technology. How could she concentrate, be upbeat, give the fans what they came for, and be an appetizer for Tres Armadas with Candy missing and dark on her tech?

Sonny scratched the back of her head. "There's no sign of her. You'll have to go on alone."

"I can't do it. It's not right." Velvet's heart beat so fast.

Zazzle inserted himself and held her by the shoulders. "You can do it."

"Velvet," Sonny began. "You're successful, not only because you have Candy by your side but because you are talented. You love music and want to share that love with your fans."

"I can't—"

"Won't." Zazzle angled her to him.

"What?" She saw him through a lens that grew blurrier by the second.

"Replace *can't* with *won't.* Right now and say it out loud," he commanded.

His request drew a skeptical expression from Sonny.

"Isaak, this is stupid—"

He clasped her shaky hands with his steady ones. "Humor me for a minute. Say it."

"I won't do it," Velvet recited. The statement echoed in her head and she repeated the words.

"You have a choice, Asha," Zazzle continued. "You have a really good excuse not to go out there. No one would blame you for it. But you can also decide to play a set that will bring the house down, and be the powerful artist we all know you are."

"But Candy—"

"Candy is fucking up right now. That's harsh, I know, but let's be clear. *She* left. I've been there. She made the choice. You're a good friend. Going up there and playing doesn't change that."

Sonny jumped in. "She'll show up eventually, Velvet, but you both committed to this tour and have an obligation to play for these fans. Only one of you is down."

"It's time to rise, Asha." Zazzle's words breathed life into her.

Velvet hopped from one foot to the next. "Okay, I'll do it."

The last time she'd performed on her own was at a party in Brooklyn. DJ FeNom had come out to rep her as his protégé. Candy'd been in the crowd, excited that they'd be moving forward as DJ duo and the future was bright. Velvet recalled the words Reynard had said to her that night.

"The privileged may not want to open the doors and give you access, but they can't fuck with your sound. Bonnie might make the idea of you more palatable but your music is going to transcend all that bullshit. Trust."

Two days later Reynard was found, unconscious, after going on a bender at a known drug house. This last relapse almost did him in and that was when Velvet cut the cord, unable to continue to be a caretaker and cheerleader only to have her heart broken every time he went back. She'd been to one intervention too many and suffered more broken promises than she could count. Candy followed and soon, they'd both moved out of their mentor's congested shadow.

Now, as she climbed the ramp to the stage, she fought to keep the memories and tears at bay. She summoned the courage to bounce to the beat that played and level out her shaking hands. She picked up the microphone.

"How you doing, Amsterdam?"

The crowd replied with resounding cheers.

"Candy couldn't be here tonight..."

Awws and *boos* seeped through the crowd and up to the stage.

"But I know she'd want to be with each and every one of you." The lie burned her throat worse than acid reflux.

Cheers and whistles bubbled in waves. The headphones, only half on her head, played a song in her ear that linked with the one thumping through the speakers.

"So let's party so loud and hard she hears us! Let's go!" Velvet dropped the mic and mixed in the song with flawless skill. As she freed the beat and it rippled over the forty thousand fans, the music took from her the anger, contempt and negativity that had been darkening her heart, even if only for this solo set. Each time she mixed in a new song that would normally be Candy's entrance, Velvet cursed her friend out, and then followed her mini rant with a prayer for her safety. Velvet loved Candy but hated that she'd put her in this position. Where did it all go wrong? Why had Candy let her breakup with LED change her into this Hyde of a person Velvet barely recognized?

The cool mist hissed out into the crowd and the lights flashed. The end of her set approached. *Bedazzled Beats* flashed overhead and Velvet pointed up to it as she danced across the stage to amp up the fans for the finale.

When her set was done the fans cheered so loud her ears rang. She went backstage and Sonny hugged her.

"You did great. I knew you would."

"Thanks." Velvet took the towel Sonny offered her and dabbed her face. She guzzled water from a water bottle, the plastic crinkled like the current situation. "Any word?"

Sonny shook her head. "She's going to show up, Velvet."

She scanned the faces nearby for Zazzle. "Is Isaak around?"

"They had a pre-press thing and they're popping up from below stage so they're getting set up."

"Right." For a moment she forgot she wasn't the show and that the headliners performed next. Velvet fanned her neck. She felt her phone buzz in her back pocket. She yanked it out.

Zazzle: You were great.

The message wasn't from Candy and through her disappointment she received Zazzle's words. He helped ground her and get her through this.

"Do you hear that?"

Velvet looked into Sonny's beaming face. It was only then that Velvet made out what the Amsterdam fans chanted.

Velvet!

Velvet!

Velvet!

Zazzle heard the cheers and his heart warmed for the appreciation the fans gave Velvet. She needed to know that no matter what happened, she would be okay. She'd told him about her mentor and her apprehension around addiction. He dared to hope that through all she'd experienced, she wouldn't run on him.

Maartin slapped his back. "Under the circumstances, your girl did well, Isaak."

"Yes." Pride filled his lungs. "I knew she'd be great. Going it alone like that isn't easy."

"She shouldn't have had to," Christian noted. "We contracted with Bedazzled Beats."

"Christian is right," Maartin said. "Velvet did great but what about the next show? Velvet can only cover for so long before she's a solo act."

"I'm aware." Zazzle's stress level elevated. Without tea he relied solely on his breathing to stay mellow.

"I'd never expect this kind of flakiness from either of them. Do you think they're splitting up?" Christian asked.

"No. I'm sure she'll turn up. Maggie and Sonny will sort it out." Zazzle itched to color in the lines but Candy's business was her own. He'd help Velvet, but he left the business decision to their respective managers. "Right now, the temporary situation might be the only option. I know it's a lot to ask but can you guys just support Velvet while she handles things with Candy?"

"Of course." Maartin slapped his back.

"Yeah," Christian also agreed.

Zazzle remembered Velvet mowing down club after club in Stockholm, the night she had initially found out about Willem, looking for Candy. It was a wonder she'd been able to perform tonight. Was that who she thought she'd become with him? Was that what it had been like for Christian and Maartin?

"We'll check in with Maggie after the show," Maartin said.

Zazzle wanted to be there with Velvet, cheering for her and comforting her through this, but like her, he had to put his game face on. The home crowd came out in droves to see them and he needed to give them his best, maybe his last show in the Netherlands as part of Tres Armadas.

As they huddled as a trio, and among the chaos of Bedazzled Beats, the support from Maartin and Christian united them. Zazzle thought it apropos that the decision to end Tres Armadas lit a spark for a new beginning.

Zazzle rushed to Velvet's hotel after all their post-show itinerary. According to the media, Candy had had an emergency. Zazzle didn't know how long that story would hold up. Someone had to see Candy. Not to mention *who* she was with. If Willem played any role, then real chaos had not yet been unleashed.

He knocked on the door to her hotel room.

She opened the door dressed in pajama bottoms and tank top, her eyes red and face puffy. He'd never seen her like this. She ripped his heart apart. He stepped inside and enveloped her like a special telegram to be kept safe and cherished.

"You okay?" he whispered against her ear.

She nodded and separated from him.

"Any updates on Candy?"

"She came back to the hotel while we performed to get the rest of her stuff. She reached out to Sonny. She's on a plane to Las Vegas for our show there at the festival, then we'll be in LA for your final shows. I'll play the Holland and France shows alone again like I did tonight and then meet up with her in Vegas. Perhaps the space will help us."

"That's over two weeks."

"Want even better news? Temptation tickets go on sale tomorrow, which means—"

"Voting opens."

"Bingo. Perfect timing, don't you think?"

He scratched his head and blew out a puff of air. "Has she been in touch with you, at all?"

"No. She won't talk to me." She fiddled with her hands. "But she did tell Sonny she's with her 'publicist.'" Velvet air quoted.

"Have you heard from LED?" At the stadium, Velvet had given Zazzle some splotchy details about Candy blaming her for the breakup with LED. By the way Velvet's lip quivered, the accusation had wounded her.

"He emailed. He's on his way to Montreal. I let him know she showed up. I couldn't attest to whether or not she's okay."

"I should have known that Willem would be in Ibiza."

"You're not responsible for either of them, Isaak. She confides in him. 'Willem says…'" she mimicked. "I have no idea what they talk about because, again, Candy hasn't told me shit. I mean…who am I dealing with anymore? This one thing happened and this is her response to it?"

"It's irrational." He chose the word purposely. At some point Velvet had to realize that her friend behaved differently, and approaching her the same way as she'd done in the past was insanity. "Not to mention unprofessional."

"That's not Candy. At least it wasn't."

Zazzle had heard the same things recanted to him about his behaviors that had abruptly changed, and his unpredictable responses. Tempted to recoil from the sensation in his chest and shoulders brought on by his memories, he instead focused on being present for Velvet. Candy's change in behavior and unprofessionalism didn't mean she had a problem, but he couldn't help but see the similarities.

He rubbed her back. "Candy's making some bad choices right now. She called Sonny and that's a good sign. When you see her in LA, you guys can talk then. Give her some space."

"It doesn't seem I have a choice," she said.

He kissed her temple.

"How was your show?" Velvet asked.

"Awesome. Home cooking from the crowd. They didn't disappoint." Despite all that had happened during the pre-show, the fans had welcomed them home with loud cheers that hugged him and his bandmates.

"I missed the opening." She wrinkled her nose.

"You love that part, don't you?"

"I really do." She sank into a small loveseat by the window. "What do you think about all this? You know Willem. Does Candy stand a chance?"

He sat next to her. "It's not as catastrophic as you might think."

"What do you mean?"

"It depends. Right now, I don't know if the moves Candy is making are Willem's, or hers. She says he's her publicist, so he could be suggesting things to her that normally might not be a good choice but under the influence of something might. Or…"

"Or what?"

"Or, if she's using she could be tired when she comes down and just loses track of time. There is such a huge spectrum, baby."

"In Ibiza Candy laughed and joked like her old self. I guess I wanted to believe that she was feeling better. She could be addicted to anything by now."

Zazzle wished he could dispute the fact but it was all true. Willem knew a lot of people and at this point, and unchecked, he could be offering Candy a cocktail of things. Candy may or may not be taking them.

"Let's hope for the best and focus on the positives," he said.

"Like what?"

"The fans loved it when you played. They chanted for you."

"Fans, followers and fame," Velvet recited.

"Your three *F*s." She didn't give him a full smile but he'd take it.

"We've worked so hard and come too far for it all to unravel now."

"Don't worry. They'll vote you in. You have two things going for you. A great performance last year that fans can access in the highlights, and your success this year. I know it's anyone's game but I'd be more surprised if you weren't voted in."

She leaned on him. "Thanks." Her body fit against him like the puzzle piece he'd been missing all day.

"You're welcome." They snuggled for a bit and he never wanted to let her go.

"You should get back. I'm sure all this drug talk isn't part of your routine."

"I can stay."

"You don't even have your tea and—"

His mouth silenced her. His hand captured her face, pressing her to him.

"Isaak." Her call for him gave his tongue entry and he slipped inside. He missed her taste and when her tongue played with his, she unleashed the restraint he'd had since they were interrupted at his house.

He stood with her and tugged down her pajama bottoms. She was topless seconds later. He worked on his clothes with her help. Still clutched in an embrace, they staggered over to the bed. They landed with a soft bounce and his mouth left hers to deliver kisses down her body. He spread her quickly and settled between her thighs like the space between them had been carved for him. As his hand fondled her breasts, his head dove to her center.

Now in the light he could see the dark patch of hair covering her and her brown folds, glistening with her growing desire. Her hips rocked up to him, longing for his touch. His hands left her breasts and he opened her, the delicate pink of her clit called to him, taking the choice from him.

His mouth covered her and the soft moan of surrender escaped her lips. It had been too long since he tasted this part of her. His passion rumbled in his chest and he slipped his fingers inside her. Her hips bucked and he wanted his dick to share the experience his fingers enjoyed. He pulled out of her.

"No," she whined. "Don't stop."

"Forgive me, love." He scrambled to his jeans for a condom, and then fitted himself with unsteady hands. He returned to her outstretched arms and her face was splashed with unveiled lust; a vision he'd not soon forget. She pulled him down to her so hard her bones dug into his muscles.

"Now, please." Her breathless plea brought his dick closer to explosion.

He didn't hesitate and filled her in a single motion. She cried out and all her limbs tightened around him. He groaned as he surrendered to the sensation of her body inside and out. As his hips pumped, her nails dug into his back and her body begged him for harder strokes.

"Harder, Isaak. Don't stop, please harder," she begged.

They both needed this and he obliged her with pumping hips. The bed creaked and knocked under their weight. Their panting swelled and echoed through the room. Her cries signaled her peak. He wanted to come with her, needed to come with her.

His mouth found hers. "Tell me. Asha. Tell me you're coming." He withdrew for a moment, rose to his knees, and flipped her over. He entered her from behind, pounded into her as she backed into his thrusting pelvis.

"I need you, Asha. Need to hear you. Tell me," he delivered between breaths.

Her high-pitched sighs quickened and she fisted the pillows. Her back arched and folded. "Isaak! I'm coming. I'm coming."

His fast movements slapped against her shaking ass and the pressure in his lower abdomen released and flowed through his dick. Heaven descended on him as he shouted his orgasm.

She screamed into a pillow and he collapsed onto her back, his arms wrapping around her torso.

She flattened to the bed. He slipped off his rubber and trashed it before returning to her side. He fought the urge to nap, not only because he'd just come but because they'd had a long eventful day. He stroked the smile on her face, and then smoothed her messed hair.

"Okay?"

"Better than okay," she cooed.

He kissed her and pulled her into his arms. "Let me stay with you, tonight."

She eased gently out of his arms and sat up. His stomach dropped at the distance she put between them.

"Did I say something wrong?" he asked.

"No." Her hand stroked his arm. "I just think you should go. It's been a supercharged day. If you get back to your routine it will ground you. You said so yourself."

He rubbed his face. "I'm grounded. This being with you, here."

"You know what I mean." She got up and started to dress. "I can't be worried about you, too."

"Worried about me? You don't have to worry about me."

"Did you exercise today? Have you said your affirmations and eaten anything other than those pancakes?"

He had not, but one day wouldn't kill him. Obviously she'd been keeping score. He inched off the bed and grabbed his jeans, yanking them on one leg at a time. "I don't need you to monitor my routine. Like I mentioned earlier, I'm trying out some things."

"Like completely abandoning what's been getting you through recovery?" She crossed her arms.

"No." He pulled on his shirt. "My recovery isn't my routine. It's about managing my urges, my feelings and my emotions in an everyday setting. It's not a fix-it-all. There are other things involved like talking, trusting people and myself, knowing that they have some confidence in me."

She chewed the inside of her lip.

"Look, you're upset about Candy. Maybe you're a bit sensitive to what's happening with me."

"I'm not sensitive, Isaak. I'm worried that you keep skipping things that help you. I can't keep up."

"I don't need you to keep up. I need you with me."

Her brows knit. "It only takes one slipup and you're back to square one."

"Are you waiting for me to do that? To slip up?"

"Of course not."

"It sounds like you are. From the beginning you've kept tabs on me, evaluating me against some points system. I understand your concerns, and what you've been through. I've tried to bend with them because of my feelings for you, but I'm not FeNom or Candy."

"That's not fair, Isaak."

"So you haven't been checking on me?"

"Yes… I mean…not like that. I just want you to be okay. Is that a bad thing?"

"No, but it can be…sometimes—"

"What?" she demanded.

"It's stifling, Asha. All I can do is the best for my life." Winded, he stilled himself to slow his heart rate. "Before people labeled me an addict I was a regular person. I liked to enjoy things like drinking a coffee and eating pannenkoeken. I rode ATVs in the desert and spent time with Christian and his family and my brother. I studied music and hunted for vintage albums. I traveled, hiked, and the list goes on. I'm not abandoning anything. I'm trying to take small steps to being me. Not the addict and not the addict in recovery. Just me. I need someone to trust me, not doubt me."

"You're right." Her words trembled with regret but he couldn't pinpoint the cause.

He drew her to him. "You've had a hard night and a lot on your plate. I don't want to add to it."

He wanted to keep her in his arms for the rest of the night and wake up to her the next morning. To put her at ease about Candy and assure her that everything would work out. But the heightened activities messed with them both. "We'll talk soon, okay?"

"Okay." She squeezed his middle tighter than he expected and a lump formed in his throat.

He had a bad feeling that despite her words, nothing was okay.

Chapter Twenty-Four

"What the actual fuck?" Velvet tiptoed through an empty hotel suite on the Vegas strip. She texted Sonny, who confirmed that Candy had requested her own room. Candy had sent a clear sign that she was no closer to speaking to her than she had been that afternoon in Amsterdam. They hadn't had any contact in over two weeks, which Velvet was certain hit some record.

She dropped her luggage on the floor and plopped to the bed. She and Candy had always roomed together, even when LED had been in town. Candy would just stay in his room or at his place. Her bestie's absence gave her too much time to think. If Candy's goal was to hurt her, she'd succeeded.

Velvet and Tres Armadas played their scheduled shows and she interacted with the trio. However, she hadn't seen or spent any time with Zazzle outside of their public engagements. She'd dated enough to appreciate his avoidance tactics. Maybe they needed a little space from the cyclone of events, but she yearned for his arms. The growing distance she felt between them further altered her mood, and felt too far for her to ask him to hold her. Every move she made to help, protect or be present for those she loved backfired.

She sat more erect on the bed. "What? Oh, no." In the quiet space the pounding of her heartbeat sounded in her ears. She didn't know if it was that she missed her friend or the fact that she just admitted to herself that she loved Zazzle but the threat of a meltdown swelled inside her. She had to hold her nerve. Temptation announcements were at midnight and she'd find out if Bedazzled Beats were chosen to perform. They were a few weeks from knowing which of the artists announced tonight would get to play the main stage. Two months ago, she and Candy had been flying high. Their careers were in full bloom, and everything was grand. Currently, she didn't know if she was even still part of a DJ duo.

She scrambled for a Blow Pop in the hopes that the sweet cherry flavor would ward off her pain, but silent tears rolled down her face. She swiped them away and tended to her luggage. She had a show with Candy tonight. She emailed her set list and hoped Candy got it. Velvet was out of options and steam.

Her phone sounded and she wanted to ignore it because, recently, all it did was deliver bad news. She checked it nonetheless.

LED: In Vegas on my way to Reno. Meet up and talk?

She rolled her eyes and wiped her tears away. "Now you want to talk? In the middle of this shit show?"

Velvet: Sure

LED: Strip House at 4 ok?

Velvet: ok

LED: kk

Velvet freshened up from her travel and made her way to the other end of the Vegas strip to meet LED.

LED sat at a table waiting for her. He chugged water and fatigue showed on his face. By the way he moved in his seat, Velvet thought he was either nervous, stressed or some combination of the two. He spotted her and stood. The formal gesture irritated her but they hadn't seen or spoken to each other in months.

"Hey, Velvet," LED greeted her and made an awkward gesture to hug her before finally capturing her in a bear hug. "How have you been?"

"I've been better," she responded.

"How's Candy?" he asked.

"How the fuck should I know? I haven't seen her in two weeks. She's not talking to me. Got her own room and all. I don't know what she's sniffing or swallowing these days. Maybe she's done being part of a duo." Velvet must have picked up Zazzle's directness because her words gunned through a nonexistent filter.

LED's face reddened like the cherry Blow Pop she had earlier. "I've been trying to reach her since you guys were in the Netherlands."

"How about before that?"

"She told me to stay away."

"How about talking to me? I mean, are we even friends?"

"We're friends, Velvet. I'm sorry I've been off the grid but breaking up with Bonnie…it took its toll on me, too. She's loyal to you in a way I can't compete with. Maybe I felt some way about that."

"So, she blames me and you blame me but no one ever asked me about anything. I want her to be happy and I want you to be happy but no one stopped to think…hey? Is Velvet happy? Instead you both have been the biggest assholes."

"Don't hold back."

"Do you understand what I've been through trying to support Candy, and bust my ass for Temptation? I've been performing solo. Now, I'm trying to figure out if rehab's her next vacation spot?"

Velvet gave him the story about Willem.

"Is she with him?" LED took in a shaky breath.

"Like romantically?" Velvet asked.

"Yeah."

"I don't think so."

LED appeared to relax but only slightly. "What do you need me to do?"

"I don't know. You realize we have zero control over this situation. She's an adult. She may be doing stupid adult things but it has literally taken me up to now to realize that. I've said all I can say, especially now that she doesn't even want to room with me."

"I know, Asha, but we have to do something," LED said.

"Why couldn't you guys just work it out?" Velvet whined.

"Well, when you ask your girlfriend of two years to marry you and she breaks up with you because she says she can't leave her best friend, there's not much left to discuss."

Velvet's mouth caught flies. "Did you say *marry*?"

"I did."

"I had no idea." Velvet felt more distant from Candy

than ever. How could she not have told her about something as major as a marriage proposal?

"I figured she hadn't told you."

A waiter arrived with a dessert and two glasses of scotch.

"You remembered." Her shoulders slumped and tears threatened again but this time she sucked it up.

At least once a year Velvet, LED and Candy came to Strip House to enjoy their famous 24-layer chocolate cake and a glass of buttery scotch. It was one of several little traditions they shared.

"I thought it might help you to forgive me but it doesn't look like that's going to happen anytime soon."

"You fucking proposed to her?" She still couldn't believe it.

He nodded. "I knew it was a long shot but now that I think back, only part of it had anything to do with you. I think I scared her…no…petrified her when I proposed."

"But she loves you."

"I know she does." He handed her a fork.

She cut a chunk of the cake and gobbled it up. The delicious bitter sweetness of the chocolate cake and creamy frosting was a signature treat.

"I'll always love Bonnie. I wanted to work it out but she told me to stay away. When I saw her in Amsterdam, she was different. I thought maybe she wanted to get back together. I begged her to come back to me and she kept saying, 'you're pressuring me' over and over. It gutted me, so I left. I had a panic attack in the air when I got your email." LED gave her a tight smile. "Fun."

"My bad." Velvet only half felt bad for delivering the news about Candy to him, mid-long-flight to Montreal. But maybe had he responded to her, they might have been able to contain this shit storm.

He lifted his glass and clinked it with hers. "You look like you need this more than I do."

She took a big swig of her scotch and coughed.

"When's the last time you had a drink?"

"It's been a while. With Zazzle around, I guess I've been drinking less. You know, in solidarity, and all?"

LED gave her the eyebrow. "You two a thing now?"

She shrugged. "I don't know."

"I saw him at the day club when Christian played in Ibiza. He looks good. He was on his way to see you."

"He was at the club?" Zazzle had told her he was trying out some things, and in Ibiza she thought he only came out to the festival to link up with her and her friends. She didn't know he'd hit the clubs.

"Yeah, we chatted a bit."

"Oh." She nodded.

"Everything okay?" LED asked.

"Yeah."

They shared the rest of the dessert.

"I have a performance in Reno tonight, then I'm back here and then in LA for some other gigs." LED struggled with what to say next. "If Candy needs my help I'll always be there for her. You gotta know I'm worried about her, too."

"I know," she said. "Stay in touch, okay, and don't ghost on me again."

He gave a light chuckle. "I won't."

They left the restaurant and Velvet got ready for the show.

When Velvet arrived to perform, she was relieved to see Candy in one piece. Velvet envisioned them seeing each other, diving into a hug and squashing everything that happened. She instinctively went to hug Candy, but when she got the cold shoulder, her hopes of a family reunion were obliterated.

"Hey," was all Candy had to offer.

"Hey." Velvet swallowed. "Did you get our set list?"

"Yeah, it's fine."

They were on in a few minutes and Velvet summoned up all her acting ability to deliver for the fans. It saddened her that being onstage with Candy was worse than being onstage alone. When their song "Love Me Love You" played, Velvet remembered their time in Ibiza and the fun they had but when she looked over at Candy, her friend worked the dials like she waited for software to download.

Velvet's sadness morphed into anger. If Candy couldn't sum up energy for her, she could at least try to do it for the fans. Velvet picked up the mic.

"Come on, girl. Let's go!"

The crowd cheered and Candy lazily waved her hand. Velvet couldn't wait to get offstage.

Sonny greeted them when they descended the short black iron staircase. Willem waited for Candy several feet away, and before Sonny could even get her words out, Candy was heading out with him.

"She's not doing press today," Willem announced.

"Who the fuck do you think you are telling anyone what they will and won't do?"

"I'm communicating what Candy wants."

"She's part of a group that is under contract," Sonny informed.

"We're working on changing that." Willem turned to Candy. "Ready, love?"

Candy's eyes were cast down and she nodded.

"Candy?" Velvet approached her but Sonny stopped her. "We hear if we qualified for Temptation tonight. You're just going to leave?"

Nothing.

"Is this what you want, Candy?" Sonny asked.

"Yeah."

Willem smiled. "We'll see you in LA."

Sonny and Velvet exchanged concerned looks. It took all of Velvet's will not to trample Willem.

"Can you stop them?" Velvet asked Sonny.

"No." Sonny folded her arms. "This is worse than I expected."

Velvet pulled at her short hair. "This is insane. So that's it? I don't see her again until LA?"

"If she shows." Sonny patted her back. "I need to communicate with our legal teams. Based on Willem's threat, it's a good idea to get it on the radar."

Velvet went back to the hotel with her tail tucked between her legs. She packed for LA. She got a big dose of on-the-road loneliness, with no roommate to gab with. How had her friends done it all these years? Guilt seeped into her heart. She texted LED what happened and he texted back that they'd link up in LA.

Tomorrow couldn't come fast enough. She wanted to be in LA where Tres Armadas were building up their final shows and prepping for the big press release about ending as a group. More than anything she wanted to hear Zazzle's humming laugh, to kiss him and stare into his light brown eyes. Since their tiff in the Netherlands, he had been friendly to her around other people but made no attempt to be alone with her. She'd catch him working out and his tea was more or less glued to his palm. She couldn't have been happier to see him following his routine, but her obsession with his recovery had cost her intimacy with him. What else was it going to cost her?

She readied for bed and slid into the sheets. With hours spent surrounded by the busy town and festivals filled with loud music, the silence in the room was deafening. She turned on the TV, scrolled through the channels, and settled on a rerun of *The Golden Girls*. The theme song was weighted with meaning and her mind flipped through memories—of Candy, of her friends, of Zazzle. She wrestled to her back and stared at the ceiling. A stream of tears leaked back against the pillow.

A knock on her hotel room door jolted her upright. She dabbed at her waterworks with the back of her hand.

Maybe Candy had come to her senses. Maybe Sonny had some news. She squinted through the peephole and flung open the door, uncaring of the sleep bonnet she wore or her disheveled pajamas. The homecoming smell of lavender uplifted and invigorated her.

"What are you doing here?"

Zazzle leaned against the frame. "Care to take a road trip with me to LA?"

"Yes!" She jumped into his arms, and wrapped her limbs around him. His humming laugh was music to her ears and she refused to let him go.

"Congratulations." His rhythmic strokes up and down her back hypnotized her.

"Thank you but for what?" She breathed his scent, kissing his neck.

"Bedazzled Beats were voted onto the Temptation Festival lineup. Now the real voting begins. Did you not get the announcement?"

With everything that happened, she'd completely forgotten to check.

Chapter Twenty-Five

Daylight had just started to break when Velvet opened her eyes. Her road trip with Isaak had turned out to be a long four-hour car ride in the wee hours of the morning from Las Vegas to Los Angeles. After a few naked rounds in bed at her hotel room, she'd checked out and they were on their way. The taste of the thick savory sweetness when she'd taken him into her mouth and how hard he'd come as she sucked him to fulfillment still enchanted her to seek his dick. The memory of him imprinting her against his body afterward was one she'd never forget.

Velvet didn't care about the hour or the logistics around her flight and hotel or that Sonny was still in Vegas. She allowed herself to snuggle up to Isaak in the back seat and have one happy moment in a sea of unhappy ones.

When they arrived in LA, he took her to her hotel and helped get her settled.

"Thank you again for coming to get me."

"Thank you for not shutting the door in my face, and for coming with me." His brilliant smile made her giddy.

"I have to take care of some things on my property

since my brother is coming in. But we have one last free day. Can I take you to dinner?"

"Like a real date kind of thing?"

He laughed. "Yes."

"I'd like that." She kissed him.

"It'll be a late one."

"How late?"

"Not 4am eats late but…hmm, about eleven? That okay?"

"Yes."

"Good. *Tots straks.*" *See you later.*

"*Tots straks*, boo," she teased.

He rubbed his face. At least she still made him laugh.

She communicated her whereabouts to Sonny. Her manager understood and even relayed that she thought Zazzle driving Velvet to LA very sweet.

"I'm getting on a flight now. Boombox wants to touch base and just make sure that we are still okay contractually. No alarms yet so don't worry."

"Sounds good."

"And, Velvet? Congratulations on landing a Temptation spot. You worked hard for it. Both of you."

"Thanks, Sonny."

"I know things have been wild but Bedazzled Beats are still in the running for the main stage."

"That's if Bedazzled Beats even still exists."

"I'm hopeful this situation with Candy is temporary."

"I'll stay positive but… I miss her. I don't know what else to do."

"Don't give up," Sonny said. "My flight is boarding. We'll talk soon."

As Velvet unpacked for the five-hundredth time this year, she wanted to believe Sonny, but unless Candy was ready to see the light and wanted things to change, they'd all just have to wait or fear losing her for good.

Velvet was tired from the little sleep she got earlier in the day and passed out scrolling through the Temptation Festival announcements. She dreamed of Bedazzled Beats in lights. She still wanted to play the main stage but she'd give it all up to have Candy back and okay. LED was on his way to LA and she prayed he'd be able to do what she could not. Connect with Candy.

The cheer fairy gave her a boost when she thought of seeing Zazzle. She took a quick shower to wash off the cloudiness of her nap and got ready for dinner.

She chose a black romper and thought Zazzle would appreciate the plunging neckline. She wanted to wear her sneakers but instead dug a pair of strappy sandals from the bottom of her luggage. She had a few of these outfits for the very rare formal occasion. Dinner with Zazzle felt special, so she dusted off the relics in her wardrobe.

As she combed through her hair, her phone chimed and an unknown number popped up.

"Who even calls anymore?" She frowned at the screen. The number called again. She picked up and started talking.

"You have the wrong number—"

"Asha?" Candy's whispering voice came through the line.

"Bonnie?" Velvet's excited nerves fired.

Candy's muffled voice, a garble of indecipherable words.

"What? Bonnie? I can hardly hear you. It's so loud."

The phone went dead.

Velvet's excitement deflated. Perhaps Candy had butt-dialed her by accident, but then why did she say her name?

The hairs on Velvet's arms rose. Something was off. She tried to call the unknown number back, but it just rang. She tried to call and text Candy's cell number, but she got no response.

Velvet tapped the phone on her chin. When Candy didn't try to call her back she continued to dress but the phone call unsettled her. Velvet felt like she was the one on drugs, with these high and low moments that strung her life together over the past few months.

She wanted to look nice for Zazzle tonight. After all, it was their first real date. She added a few more makeup touches and fluffed her hair.

Her phone rang and the unknown number popped up again. Velvet picked up. "Bonnie?"

"I think I'm in trouble, Asha. I took too much. I want to leave but I can't. There are these guys around. Can you come get me?"

Candy didn't sound quite lucid, but she didn't sound totally high either. She did sound scared. "Where are you?"

"I'm at the Egyptian."

"Is this your new phone?"

"No, I borrowed this girl's phone in the bathroom."

"Where's your phone?"

"In my bag at the table. Don't call it."

"I already did."

Candy groaned.

"Are you afraid of Willem, Candy?"

The long silence spoke volumes. "No, not really. I don't think so." Candy sighed. "I don't know."

That meant yes in Velvet's book. "I'm comin'."

"Thank you."

Velvet requested a Lyft to the Egyptian. She messaged LED the scenario. He was on his way to LA but she wasn't sure if he'd arrived yet. She didn't want to go to the Egyptian alone. She had to text Zazzle. She hated cancelling their dinner plans but given the situation with Candy, Velvet was sure he'd understand. Maybe he could go with her…

Her body went rigid and the viral video of him at the Egyptian popped into her head. All the reasons why she shouldn't ask him to go with her swirled around her. She went through a list of people she trusted to help her and none of them were in town yet. The only person available was about to have his date with her cancelled, was in recovery and had had his drug and alcohol bender recorded.

Her shaky hands typed and deleted her text to him several times. She spun around with her hands on her hips before she tried again. She had to ask him. Candy was scared so she should be at least cautious to walk into the situation solo.

Velvet: Hey sorry. Have to cancel dinner

Velvet: I think Candy's in trouble at Egyptian

Velvet: Heading there now. Don't want to go in alone…

She closed her eyes. "Please." He'd helped her in Stockholm and she prayed he'd do the same this time.

Velvet: Can you meet me there?

When he didn't respond immediately, she figured he was on his way to her, but her lift would arrive in a few minutes. She was caught between two stools, waiting for him or leaving to get Candy.

There are these guys around... Candy's words haunted.

Velvet grabbed a small pink Swiss Army Knife and maneuvered it into her bra. She slid the strap on her clutch over her wrist, and took the elevator down. When her car arrived she folded inside.

In the back seat of the car, she checked her phone again. Still no word from Zazzle or LED. The ride was long with nighttime traffic and partygoers heading to the same general area of downtown LA.

A long line greeted Velvet at the Egyptian. If she waited behind the endless row of people, she'd be there all night. She didn't know if Candy had that kind of time. Velvet had no insight into what lay inside the Egyptian's walls. She decided to give VIP a shot.

"Yo, you're that chick from Bedazzled Beats." A bouncer greeted her before she even announced herself.

"Yup, that's me."

"I hardly recognized you but the hair. Lookin' good." He winked.

"Thanks."

"You come to hook up with your girl? She's here with a group of characters?"

"Yeah." She plastered a smile on her face.

"Go 'head in."

What did he mean by a group of characters?

She went inside the massive venue. With the different rooms and the span of VIP circling the club she didn't even know where to start. The black light of the bar and pops of illuminated color drew the eye. The last time she was here was as an artist backstage with LED and Zazzle. Now, as a patron, the heavy feeling of the club was in contrast to the vibrant energy she'd known back then.

Velvet's phone vibrated and she checked to see if it was Candy, LED or Zazzle. She read the text and stared at it for a long time. An avalanche of emotions tumbled through her. Her heart sank and she'd never felt more alone than she did reading his words.

Zazzle: I can't go there

Chapter Twenty-Six

Zazzle's hands twitched as he pressed send. Velvet needed him and it killed him to let her down. He paced in his LA beach house. The view of the ocean did nothing to ease his guilt. His heart rate bullied him, but to what end? To help her? To protect his recovery and stay away? If the thought alone made him feel this uneasy, what would happen if he stepped foot inside?

He messaged her with one line and no explanation because he'd need endless text boxes to convey the fear and shame lashing at him like a whip. He sipped his tea and sat in a chair. He tried to be mindful, to count, to relax, but the same thought continued to wave like a banner behind his eyelids.

Don't want to go in alone.

This was a test he didn't want to take. As it related to recovery, he knew that one day, his salt would be tested. He wasn't putting himself on the line for something trivial. The woman he loved needed him. Who would he be if he didn't show up? No matter what happened between them, how would he feel knowing that in her darkest moment, he'd failed her?

He requested a car, grabbed a hoodie and hoped he wasn't too late.

* * *

Zazzle had vowed never to set foot in the Egyptian again, and yet here he stood at the VIP entrance. The bouncer recognized him and let him in without making a big fuss as if the hoodie he wore didn't scream, "I'm incognito." His pulse pounded harder and faster than the beat thumping against the walls of the club. As he walked down the dark corridor, sweat started to wet his pits and his forehead. He remembered everything: the bumps of coke, the alcohol he threw back by the liter, the Ecstasy.

When he flashed back to that night, he wondered if he was trying to kill himself. That's what the doctor ultimately asked when he was sober enough to put a decent sentence together. Now here he was. Back in the VIP section circling the club. Familiar bartenders tossed out drinks. The black light bar illuminated the dark space, and aerial dancers in point shoes floated from the ceiling. The thick, fragrant smoke swirling the atmosphere from the hookah pipes choked him.

His breath grew shallow and he leaned against the wall to slow his heart rate. He focused on why he was here. Velvet needed him. He had to get himself together. He continued deeper into the belly of the club and saw LED's blond mop of hair before he saw Velvet standing next to him. He beelined toward them.

When he got close enough, Zazzle dropped a hand on Velvet's shoulder.

"Isaak? What are you doing here?" She put her arm around his waist.

"You can't be here, man. This place is not for you anymore," LED warned.

"I wanted to help you. You needed me."

Velvet evaluated him. "You don't look so good."

"It's a little..." The words wouldn't come and he tried to use his hands to communicate. As far as helping went, he would soon become a burden. He heaved in air. "Don't worry about me. Let's find your friend."

LED and Velvet exchanged glances. Zazzle's clothes clung to him in a mess of sweat, but he'd promised to always be there for Velvet and he wasn't going to go back on the promise. Not now when she needed him most.

Velvet's hands fidgeted with her clutch. "Okay, but as soon as we find her I'm getting you out of here."

The shot men and women were relentless, and every few feet they offered one free starter shot. There were dealers camouflaging as partygoers muttering the name of the various drugs they had.

Snow.

Molly.

X.

California Sunshine.

His palate watered like a meal had been placed before him after a three-day fast.

"No, thanks." Velvet pushed them back with her body. She cleared a path for them to walk as they continued to scan the club for Candy, when two men flanked him on either side. He balled his fists and readied to protect himself.

"Take it easy, Isaak." Maartin's deep but melodic Dutch penetrated his left ear.

Zazzle turned to his right and Christian stood next to him.

"How?"

"Velvet told LED that she was coming here and that

she texted you. So he called us. We knew you wouldn't let her do this alone."

"She doesn't know." He responded to his friends in Dutch. "She doesn't know everything that happened here."

"Let's worry about that later. Right now we need to get both you and Candy out of here."

Velvet did a double take when she saw Christian and Maartin. "What are you doing here? Are you guys out of your mind? You're Tres Armadas?"

"Don't worry. We brought extra muscle." Christian pointed to their bodyguards.

"Let's go," Maartin said.

Fifteen minutes later, as they circled the extensive VIP section of the club through a muddle of people, LED made Candy out.

"There she is." He pointed.

"Yeah, that's Willem," Zazzle said when he spotted her.

As they got closer Zazzle dreaded what state Candy would be in but as soon as he was able to see her clearly, he realized she was like a fish out of water.

"I could be wrong but I don't think she wants to be there anymore," Christian said.

"I don't get it. Why didn't she just leave?" Velvet asked.

No one had an answer.

"I'll get her," LED announced.

"Will she go with you? I mean…you guys have been all weird and shit. She might stay to spite you. She called me, maybe I should go," Velvet suggested.

"She'll come with me… Just get Zazzle out. He's been in here way too long."

"We'll go with LED to get Candy."

"Okay, text me when you get her." Velvet manipulated his body toward the exit. "Come on."

"We can help you. You're sure you don't need us to get her away from them?"

"I got this." LED left, and true to his word, when Candy saw him she went willingly with him.

"He's got it. Let's get you home." She pulled on him until they were once again in the cool evening air.

He kept his hoodie on until they were in their Lyft and on the way to his house. He leaned his head against the seat back and closed his eyes.

"You okay? God, you're sweating so much."

He took deep audible breaths, cleansing his lungs of the smoke, the energy and the scents that haunted his memory. "I will be."

She rubbed his leg in long methodic strokes, soothing him. "I can't believe you came."

"Mmm."

"I'm sorry, Zazzle." He opened his eyes and met the worry lines etched on her forehead as the streetlights shined into the car. "That place is the devil's playground. I never should have asked you to help. That was stupid and inconsiderate."

"Stop, Asha." He wrapped his arm around her shoulder and nestled her against him. Her body quaked and he kissed the top of her head.

"Everything's okay. Candy is safe with LED. Christian and Maartin will make sure of it. And the Egyptian is already old news."

He wanted to believe that, but the tension in her body gnawed at him. He still needed to calm down but he had to be strong for her, had to show her that despite his challenges, he could still be the man she needed him to be.

Zazzle showered off the scents and invisible coating left on him from the Egyptian. Velvet had to get him out. He knew going there would have an effect on him, he just didn't know how much until it was too late. He made it through the lion's den but not unscathed. Over the last week he hadn't abandoned his routine altogether, rather had added things that he used to enjoy.

He went into the living area and found her wearing a hole into the carpet. "Asha."

She jumped at his voice. "Hey. How do you feel?"

"Better now that I had a shower. Any word on Candy?"

"LED texted. He said she's okay. They're talking things out and she wants to see me so..."

She crossed her arms tightly to her chest and her mouth twisted with what to say.

"That's good to hear." He continued to evaluate her. "You look lovely in your outfit. Was that for dinner?"

She looked over herself. "Yeah. Yes it was."

"I'll need a rain check."

Her chuckle never quite made it out of her. "Can we talk for a minute?" She pointed to the couch.

"Sure." He didn't like this version of "we need to talk." In his experience, nothing cheery or uplifting followed such a line.

"Thank you so much for everything tonight. You didn't have to show up for me and you did. I couldn't have done it without you. I knew that going back to the club might bring up some party memories and the last thing I wanted was to have you reminisce about the past."

"I did it for you, Asha."

"I know, and that put you in the worst position possible and I'm sorry about that."

"Don't be. It was my choice." He reached for her hand. She patted his knuckles as a parent would before easing out of his grip. "What's happening here?"

"Remember in Amsterdam when you said you needed someone to trust you? You were right. I'm turning into exactly who I didn't want to become and you deserve so much better than that. You deserve someone who has confidence in you. Who isn't always worried that you're going to trip up or fail. But really, I'm the one that's failing you and it's not fair to you."

"What is fair? I want to be with you. If it's something we both want, we can figure it out." He moved closer to her but it was like an invisible force field surrounded her.

"What if something happens and I leave then? Would that be any better?" she asked.

His stomach flipped and nausea crept up his throat. "Something did happen and we're standing right here, together."

Tears rimmed her lids. "Tonight I was so scared for you and for me and I had no control over any of it. I don't think I can do that again. I'm not strong enough."

He'd seen her handle the ever-changing tide in her relationship with Candy, and stay focused on her goals even when things went south. "You're one of the strongest women I've ever met. You may not realize it but you are."

She evaded his eyes and fidgeted with the shorts hem of her romper. "I'm not and one day you'll need me to be and I'll let you down."

"Asha," his voice cracked. "I love you."

Her tears streamed down her face. "I love you, too."

He rubbed his eyes and blinked at the moisture threatening to release. "Don't leave. We can work this out, baby."

She wiped her tears. "I'm no good for you." She stood up and headed for the door. She stopped and turned back to him. She hugged him so tight his breath came out with a whimper.

He rubbed her shoulders as if the action could make her stay. "Take care of yourself, Isaak," she mumbled into his chest. She broke him into pieces.

Before he could respond, she was gone.

Velvet wandered via the scenic route to Candy's suite at the hotel. Ending things with Zazzle had left her in total body shock. *I'm doing the right thing. He's better off without me*, rotated like a music roll on a self-playing organ.

She knocked on the door and LED let her in. Candy sat on the edge of the bed and LED rejoined her there. Their loving embrace spoke of reunion and forgiveness and tore Velvet's already shredded heart to pieces.

Candy jumped up. "I'm sorry, Velveteen. You have every right to be really mad at me and kick me out of Bedazzled Beats. I've messed up so much this whole time and I should have just told you what was going on earlier." Candy rubbed LED's knee. "I pushed him away and blamed you both for it."

Velvet's body was numb even though the storm inside her threatened to break free. She'd spent the better part of her time in LA tracking down her friend and/or stressed about Zazzle's recovery. She was relieved to see Candy healthy and unharmed, and that she and LED were back together, but Velvet had just sent the man she loved packing.

"What happened in the Netherlands?" Velvet asked. She leaned against the door, relying on its support to hold her up. "Why didn't you show up?"

"I took something…crystals… I think Molly, and I had too much. Then I drank and smoked to bring me down and I was out of my head. I couldn't go onstage like that. I tried to sober up but then passed out…"

Velvet's face must have shown horror because Candy quickly clarified.

"Not unconscious. I just fell asleep…like that drunk kind of sleep. When I got up, I realized I missed the show. I was in no shape to perform."

"Why didn't you call me? Like you did tonight?"

"I was embarrassed. I know it sounds stupid but it's the truth. That's why I couldn't look at you in Vegas. I stressed knowing I had to show my face, explain how I did that to you. I got some Valium from Willem and during the show I could barely keep my eyes open or put my hands up. I wanted to disappear." Candy's tears streamed down her face. "I really fucked up. We worked so hard and I just kept fucking it up."

"And tonight? Was someone going to hurt you?"

"Tonight, Willem wanted to introduce me to some people who he said would help me with a solo career, but that's not what I wanted. I wanted to be part of Bedazzled Beats but he kept implying that I couldn't go back. Not like in a direct way… I don't know…it felt controlling."

"Did you take something tonight?" Dark circles rimmed Candy's eyes like she'd been up all night and her sluggish movements supported the theory.

Candy nodded as if her head were too heavy. "I know I've listened to Willem in the past about stuff but I started to see that he was no good for me. When we were at the Egyptian I felt alone so I took more drugs. When I started coming out of it I wanted to leave, but Willem kept telling me to chill out. He didn't tell me I couldn't but again I just felt like I couldn't. I know it doesn't make sense. It seems like I could just leave but he had been there for me in the beginning and though he's not great, he had introduced me to influential people, and took me to places I didn't even know existed. And though some of his advice wasn't good, some of it was. I felt like I should stay and not embarrass him…" Candy wrung her fingers. "I was being…"

"Polite." Candy's biggest strength became her greatest weakness.

"I'll do anything, Velvet. Bernard and I have been talking about me going to talk to someone and I just…" Candy broke down. "I'm so sorry. In the beginning, everything reminded me of the breakup, the proposal and the choices I made—the music, you, the scene, and I couldn't get away from it. I just wanted an escape and to feel good. Willem gave me that in some ways. Then it just got to be too much and I took more, more often and things got out of control."

Candy moved to embrace her and Velvet held up a hand. "I'm glad you're okay."

"I've been such a bitch. I totally deserve that. You've

been so patient and the best friend I could ever ask for and I… I let you down, Velveteen. I know you're mad and I'll do whatever it takes for you to trust me again." Candy cried but Velvet had nothing in the tank to console her or even pretend that her heart hadn't been trampled in a dirty ditch and close to failing to ever beat again.

"You good, Asha?" LED asked.

Her head didn't quite nod.

"And Zaz?"

Her shaky breath vibrated through her limbs.

"Zazzle?" Candy questioned. "What about him?"

Obviously, LED hadn't mentioned that Zazzle had put himself in danger to help get her away from Willem. So Velvet enlightened her friend.

"He was at the Egyptian tonight. He put himself at risk to help me and LED find you. Christian and Maartin came to help him. To make sure he was okay because being back in the club did something really bad to him."

"I thanked them for helping me. I—"

"You're a good person, Bonnie, and I love you but you've made the shittiest decisions. I can appreciate that you felt allegiance to stick with me, and Bedazzled Beats. We're family. That's what makes this so hard. I have always been here for you, been patient and bending with your mood swings, and supporting you the best that I knew how to. You've put me and so many other people in difficult situations and that's so fucking irresponsible."

"I know and I'm sorry—"

"All I hear when you speak is *I* and *me*. What about LED, Zazzle, Rob, Tekko, Tres Armadas? What about me? Do you even really know what you're sorry about? You hurt people, Candy."

"Asha?" LED called to her and her head whipped to him. His hands patted the air downward with a soothing gesture. He'd chosen well because voicing to her to calm down would have had the opposite effect.

"I—" Candy gnawed at her thumbnail. "Is he okay?"

"He was better when I left..." Velvet's lip quivered and she pressed them together. The dam holding back her anguish cracked a little more. Her vision blurred and she went from zero to full bawl in seconds. "I left him."

Candy rushed to her and gathered her in her arms and hugged her. LED wrapped them both in his.

"He needed me and I abandoned him."

Chapter Twenty-Seven

Velvet curled into a fetal position as Candy rocked her shoulders back and forth.

"Wakey, wakey, Velveteeny," Candy sang. Velvet full-body groaned. Not even summer in New York could get her out of bed.

"I don't wanna," she whined.

"We're back in New York, bitch! You're not going to make me go to our old stomping grounds alone are you?"

"You go. I'll chill here."

It had been three weeks since the end of Tres Armadas's tour and almost a month since she'd wrapped her arms around Zazzle for the last time. She and Candy had played a few North American shows but Velvet needed a day's rest and a shot of espresso just to get through one performance. The photographs in the days following her and Zazzle's split weren't kind. Even in the heat of summer, Velvet dotted on concealer to diminish her puffy red eyes, and foundation to brighten her "walking dead" color. She layered on the brightest eye makeup she owned, and for a few hours tried to be her best. Main stage voting for Temptation had closed the week prior and now all they could do was wait, but her energy around the goal had been tainted with heartbreak on two fronts. At performances, Velvet gave her all to fans who deserved one hundred percent, whatever one hundred percent looked like after giving up the man she loved.

She didn't want to do any of that today. "Let me be miserable in peace."

"I did. Now it's time to get your Velvetness back."

Velvet rolled her eyes so hard it hurt her already throbbing sleep hangover. Zazzle's texts had stopped dinging her phone only a week ago and it was as if she were at the start of her mourning process all over again.

"So I guess you don't want to do a Fat Witch brownie run with me at Chelsea Piers?"

Velvet's ears perked. Her energy level didn't quite light up to green, rather hung somewhere in the yellow range. "I didn't say all that."

"Come on. I promise not to say anything about anything. You've been on bed duty for weeks now and it's just not good for you."

Velvet groaned again.

"Please." Candy's soprano accompanied fingers knitted in prayer and batting eyelashes.

"Fine." Velvet gave in but still didn't move.

Candy yanked the bed covers off her.

"Candy," she yelled.

"I'm just making sure you don't change your mind."

A half hour later Velvet found herself on a bike ride through Central Park. Candy had failed to mention that the bike ride around the city was a precursor to their brownie run.

"This is not what you advertised." Velvet huffed as she pedaled up a steep incline in Harlem.

"A little exercise before we play tomorrow is just what we both need." Candy wheezed louder than the clicking gears she changed on her bike to accommodate the hill. "My therapist cosigns and would even be thrilled that we're doing it together."

Candy had completed ten days of intense therapy after the Tres Armadas shows were over three weeks ago. Her therapist stayed in touch with her via Skype while they traveled to perform, and would recommend someone for more long-term treatment when Candy finally settled on a place to live. Velvet had sat in on a few sessions with Candy and thought it would be a good idea for her to reconnect with her old therapist, as well. As soon as Velvet had finished her first session she'd wished she'd reconnected sooner. The road still had its bumps but both she and Candy donned a bit more padding.

By the end of the bike ride, Velvet's chest felt clearer. She strolled to return her rented bike with a bit of pride that she finished the entire route. Her fatigued muscles recycled new blood and her opened pores tingled. For the first time in weeks she breathed full, unconstructed breaths with less anguish and guilt.

They got their brownies after returning to their hotel to shower, and ate them on their way to Wallace Entertainment to meet up with Sonny, Tommy and Abraham Wallace, the owner of their management company, who were all in town. With year-end approaching and their goals looming they needed to status check and firm up the details around next year's tour.

"Ladies," Sonny greeted them. "You both look well."

"Hi, Sonny." Velvet hugged her manager.

Candy followed. "Thanks, Sonny."

"We have a conference room set up for you here." Sonny ushered them down a corridor. Inside, Abe, Tommy and a representative from their label awaited them.

"This feels formal," Velvet mumbled to Candy.

"Yeah," Candy whispered over her shoulder.

Greetings were exchanged and they all gathered around the rectangular table.

"So," Tommy began. "I'm sure you're wondering why we're all gathered here today."

"To discuss our goals and next year's tour?" Candy offered.

Velvet studied everyone at the table. Something was definitely up, but she wasn't sure if it was good or bad. Based on the somewhat stoic faces and lack of too much eye contact her interest piqued.

Tommy continued. "Well, you guys made a lot of sacrifices this year. You had a tough performance schedule and really solidified your connection with the fans."

"The experience we gained will only help us for our tour next year," Velvet stated in the affirmative. If for any reason their tour wasn't happening or postponed, the blow would devastate her already devastated sensibilities.

"I agree," Sonny said. "You put ego aside and went on tour with Tres Armadas to focus on the goal to gain votes to qualify for your big goal this year—the Temptation Festival."

"And all while continuing your own already heavy club and festival performance schedule," Tommy said. "I know because my team booked all ninety-three gigs."

Velvet nodded. "It's been exhausting but we love the music and the fans."

"You've suffered some internal challenges as a duo. It's great to see you both working through those hardships and putting things in place for long-term success and group harmony. I hope you never have a situation like what we saw in Amsterdam or Vegas again." Sonny's eyes landed on Candy.

"The liability would be too great and the blemish could possibly be career ending," Abe added.

"I got it," Candy said. "We're working it out and are making some personal changes that will only make us stronger DJs." Candy grabbed her hand. "And friends."

Velvet smiled at her. After the Egyptian she and Candy had discussed how to make things work living separately. Velvet never wanted Candy to feel so tied to her that she couldn't have the life she wanted with LED.

Once Candy cut ties, Willem didn't show up at their performances anymore. Their new security detail didn't hurt and they both felt safer, especially with their growing fame. Willem had tried to contact Candy a few times but with support from her and Bernard, Candy no longer needed to be polite about her wishes.

"Good. So here we are." Tommy brimmed with enthusiasm and Tommy rarely brimmed.

"We have good news."

"Okay." Velvet readied herself and the suspense brewed in the office space.

"We want to welcome you to the Millionaire DJ Club," Abe said.

"I'm sorry, the what?" Velvet asked.

"Yes. With your performances so far this year you've pulled in an annual salary of $3 million. Each."

Candy and Velvet looked at each other. Not quite sure if they understood Abe correctly.

Tommy and Sonny nodded to confirm.

"We still have to compete with the men on the financial side. It's still a struggle but your success this year has been undeniable," Sonny added.

Velvet squealed and linked arms with Candy. "Oh my goodness." As women their challenges were great but their manager found ways to navigate and work around the male dominance of the industry. "I think I'm going to burst." Her skin tingled and she pressed her palm to her lungs.

Hitting the million mark had never been the dream, but the accomplishment filled her with pride. As a woman of color, sometimes the obstacles were even greater but her mentor had given her the gift of knowledge, history and DJ skills. She would never be able to express her gratitude to Reynard. His lessons gave her the freedom to reclaim the culture and educate all while elbowing her way in one gig at a time. Now here she was a bona fide millionaire?

"But wait, there's more." Tommy rubbed his hands together.

"More?" Velvet's eyes widened.

"What?" Candy asked.

"You still have fall and winter performances left and we fully expect that number to increase substantially." Tommy grinned.

Velvet didn't understand what was happening.

Sonny beamed. "They haven't officially announced it yet, but Bedazzled Beats will be playing the main stage at Temptation this year."

"No way!" Velvet leapt out of her seat, dragged Candy up, and nearly unhinged her friend's arm at the shoulder socket in the process.

"Yes," Tommy cheered. "Not only that but you also got one of the nine headliner spots for the weekend. Saturday I believe."

"Is this really happening, Bonnie?"

"We did it, Velveteen," Candy hollered and hugged her.

"I can't believe it. We're playing Temptation's main stage as headliners," Velvet repeated to make it real and tears wet her cheeks. She'd wanted Temptation so much. Part of her had doubts especially over the last weeks when she hadn't known if Bedazzled Beats still existed and if she had Candy as a friend. But she pushed through it, even if some scars remained. Now she and Candy would be headlining the biggest fan event for dance music DJs.

"Bravo, you two," Sonny said.

"I can't even." Candy gulped breath. "We've been through so much this year. So many changes. I know I've personally fucked up. But still the fans heard our music, felt the love and rallied around us."

"There's a bit more," Abe offered.

"What?" Velvet gasped. She didn't think she could take any more.

"Bring it on." Candy's fingers wiggled.

"We're opening early bird sales for your tour at the end of next month. We'll finalize and clear everything with you, creative, media, staffing for promo and marketing, but the train has left the station." Abe offered them his famous Southern smile.

"It's official," Tommy said.

"And your album release date is scheduled for the middle of next month."

Velvet plopped into the office chair, shaking her head in disbelief. Happy tears dripped off her chin and Abe handed both her and Candy a Kleenex. Velvet tried to speak but the constriction in her throat prevented her from verbally expressing the grandeur of the moment.

"We still have some finer details to discuss about next festival season, but you ladies have a lot lined up for the rest of the year. Your performances will jump in attendance and popularity," Sonny said.

"All this gives us an upper hand in future residency discussions," Tommy stated. "This is a good start. Now we can push those negotiation conversations regarding your residencies and gigs a little harder."

"Still here, Velveteen?" Candy asked.

Velvet nodded but she barely heard the rest of the conversation. They were headlining the Temptation Festival. She was happy but the pinch on her heart grew. Zazzle would have liked to know what happened to them. Would have wanted to celebrate her and toast her with a green smoothie or cup of herbal tea. Her fingers twitched to send a text but he'd stopped texting her and no matter her accomplishments she still struggled with her inadequacies to be the person he needed and deserved.

"They make the official announcement next week so don't share, but who are we fooling here. Lead with code of silence if you do."

They ended their meeting and as she and Candy descended in the elevator, Velvet was still digesting the huge meal Sonny, Tommy and Abe had given them.

"DJ FeNom would be proud of us," Candy announced.

"Yeah. He would be." Velvet blinked back tears.

"So would Zazzle." Candy hooked her shoulder. "You should tell them."

Velvet waited for Reynard at Cafe Lalo on the upper West Side. It had been two years since she'd seen him. Bedazzled Beats had played the XO festival on Governors Island. Candy departed to Vancouver to spend her days off with LED, and with her late flight back to the West Coast, Velvet reached out to her old mentor.

She arrived at the café early to settle her nerves. How would he look? Would she recognize him? When the bell on the shop door dinged her head darted toward the sound. Several people she didn't know entered and sat at various tables.

"Calm yourself, girl," she said to herself.

The next ding of the bell she didn't even bother to check.

"Asha?" She heard the familiar deep bass of Reynard's voice.

"Hey." She stared into his light brown face and dark brows. She rose to her feet and hugged him, careful not to knock over the elaborate coffee drinks on the table next to her. Strong muscular arms hugged her back and he smelled like cigarettes and star anise. "So good to see you."

"You look really good. You wear success well." He gave her the up and down perusal.

"Thanks." She laughed. "You, too."

Still handsome, Reynard's upbeat energy reminded her of old times. The area around his eyes was darker than his skin and spoke of fatigue, but this was the best shape she'd seen him in in quite some time.

"How long has it been?" he asked.

"Like two years."

He bobbed his head. "That long, huh?"

"Yeah."

She pushed her guilt aside. "I heard you're playing at the Brooklyn Library on first Fridays."

"Yup. I found my groove with that gig. Low-key, no fuss. People come for the art and the music, plus the dance parties jam." He still had that heart-stopping smile that commanded both men and women to smile back.

"I love it. I wish we were in town long enough to come through."

"Candy stopped by the house on her way to the airport. It was out of her way, so I appreciated it. It was nice to see her. She told me about all that went down. That must have been tough."

"I'm glad she told you. It was a rough time but we're rebuilding and taking it one day at a time." Velvet hoped Candy got some insight from Reynard but that conversation was and should remain private between the two of them.

"Too bad we couldn't all meet together. That would have been a trip." Reynard's animated suggestion made her grin like the teenager she was when she had first met him.

"Yeah, it would have been. She and her boyfriend have plans so..."

"What about you? Where's your boo?"

Velvet shifted in her seat but Reynard called her out.

"I know that move. You're not going to duck and cover. On me?"

"I'm really here to see you and hear about all that's been going on with you, not to discuss my love life."

"So there is one?"

"Was. We broke up. I mean…we weren't really dating, just together. That sounds horrible." Her hand smothered her face.

"What happened? He couldn't handle your success? The jealous type?"

She hadn't met with Reynard to dredge up the past. Like always the past just seemed to find her, no matter how hard she tried to hide from it, or bury it.

She fanned him off. "No, it was none of that."

"What then? Too busy? You gotta make time for that good healin'."

"He was recovering and I couldn't handle it." She ripped the bandage off and tears she thought she'd gotten under control sprang to her eyes. She missed Zazzle more than she could tolerate but she wasn't good for him. Those in recovery needed support and strength, not doubt and hovering.

"How long's he been out of rehab?"

"Eight months."

Reynard nodded. "He's awake now. In the beginning you hold tight to your routine and then when you think you're managing, you let up a bit. Try to live a more balanced life. Some people relapse but others do find that balance. There's no guarantee one way or the other."

"I wanted to take care of him, you know, but I kept doubting him the whole time. Judging him or being a smothering mom."

"You must really love him if you feel all that and still let him go."

She nodded. "I just miss him so much." She told Reynard about Zazzle helping her and LED find Candy at the Egyptian.

"That place has more lives than any cat. No matter how many times it dies someone keeps reviving it and it's worse each time. I had my fun there." Reynard's bitter smile spoke volumes.

"I asked him to help me. I should have never done that." She bit her lip so hard the metallic tinge of blood coated her tongue.

"You did a lot for me back in the day. A lot of which I didn't deserve. My recovery never should have been your cross to bear. But I wasn't strong enough to ever really tell you that. The support I've gotten through groups, therapy, meds…and the support I'm still getting are always helpful but recovery ultimately boils down to how much I want to stay sober. Some days are better than others but each day, I'm fighting myself and every pull to use something but still, it's all on me."

"I know."

"No. You don't, Asha. You have experience with an addict. With me. It's not the same as being an addict and knowing you are living with a chronic illness. Every day. It took me a long time to accept that." Reynard sat more erect in his seat. "This man put himself in danger for you and came out the other side still in recovery. I don't think it's him you have to trust. You have to trust yourself. And the Asha I know? Can do this."

She wiped her eyes. "I didn't come here for all this advice."

"Well, you're getting it anyway." He laughed. "Free of charge."

"Let's eat. I've been getting hungry waiting for you to get here."

They caught up and chatted as if time had never passed—the way old friends do. She told him about

Trevor's work and Granny's move to Florida and he updated her on his family in the Bronx.

"So I heard you got a spot at Temptation again."

"Candy didn't tell you?"

He crinkled his face. "Tell me what?"

"Code of silence because they haven't made the official announcement."

"I swear."

"We got the main stage and one of the nine headliner spots."

"What? Congratulations." Reynard gave her a one-handed high five. "I guess all that rooting for you paid off."

"Would you make the trip?" Asking him to go was a long shot but she still hoped he'd say yes.

He shook his head. "I know my boundaries and that's too much. I'll catch every minute of it on live stream, though."

She smiled. Reynard at any festival was a big ask. "Candy and I worked really hard this year. We toured with Tres Armadas and continued to play our own spots. And our album drops next month. The payoff wasn't guaranteed so this is icings."

"The music did its thing. The fans have spoken. I'm proud of you."

Between Zazzle and Temptation her shoulders stayed pinned to her ears like jewelry. Reynard wasn't only her mentor, but doubled as a father figure. Hearing his words touched her heart and she didn't know how much she needed to hear those words.

"So where are you headed to next?"

"Back to LA. We have a little time off coming up before the festival but I need to find a place to live."

"You staying on the West Coast?"

She'd considered going back to New York but she thought of her future. Being close to Vegas, where she ultimately wanted to have a residency, and be in a hub city where she could fly internationally, made the West Coast ideal.

"I think so, for now. I like it out there. I'll always love New York, though." She patted his hand.

"New York loves you right back."

Chapter Twenty-Eight

For someone who'd just entered the Millionaire DJ Club, she had no business being on her brother's couch and in a rental house full of his boys in East Anaheim, an hour out from LA.

"Who does this?" She needed to find a place stat. Most of her things were still in storage so at least she wasn't lugging a bunch more unnecessary stuff.

The occupants of the house were out doing work things and Velvet did what most people did with too much downtime after being busy for months—trolled social media.

She got caught up on everyone's stories and posts, and checked to see where they played. Rob graced the Manchester stage in the UK and Tekko basked in the Guadalajara sun. They'd cross paths at Temptation soon but seeing their faces gave her joy. She snuffed the urge to visit Tres Armadas's page and mourn over what Zazzle's life looked like without her. She also didn't want the algorithm to list her profile under the "recently visited" title on his feed. He didn't need to see her and be reminded of her any more than she needed to gaze longingly at his photos wishing for a different outcome.

Every day she questioned her decision more and

more. Seeing her mentor and Candy's absence gave her too much time with the ticker tape of her own thoughts. All of them tattooed with images of Zazzle, his touches, and the laughs they'd shared even during the dark times with Candy and Willem.

It was September and she didn't love him any less. The longing for him hadn't diminished and she didn't know what to do. She continued her Internet stalking and read through some of the recent articles, and there it was in black and white.

Tres Armadas calls it quits, leaving fans with a documentary and farewell tour.

She sat up from her lounged position. "What?" Her heart broke for Zazzle over the dismantling of the group, but if they were doing a farewell tour then they must be doing better as friends who wanted one last run. That was great news.

Her fingers itched like she'd swirled them in a mason jar filled with poison ivy. She hesitated for all the reasons she'd been telling herself for the past few weeks.

"Fuck it."

She thumbed a message to his number. According to social, he was back in the Netherlands. *What time was it there?* "Bitch, does it even matter?" she responded rhetorically.

Seconds later she pressed send.

Velvet: Saw the Tres Armadas announcement. One last tour. Great news. Hope you're okay.

She didn't expect a response and went back to her eventless millionaire lifestyle.

Her phone buzzed and she saw an incoming video call from Candy.

"Whatcha doin'?"

"Nothing. Trevor and his roommates are out trying to make millions, meanwhile I've spent two hours on social. I think Netflix is next."

"Then you have no reason to say no."

"No to what?"

"Come out to Vancouver. Me and LED are trying to put a party together. Rob and Joe are flying down close to the weekend. Come with them."

Trolling social was one thing, being social was the complete opposite. A party might be more than she wanted to experience.

"Great. I'll take your silence as a yes," Candy said. "Get your stuff together and secure your ride."

"I didn't say yes," Velvet reminded her.

"I miss you. We've been together almost every day for like the past hundred years. Please come," Candy whined.

How could she say no? "No," Velvet stated.

Candy scoffed. "Seriously?"

"Nah. Just kidding." Velvet giggled. "See you this weekend."

Zazzle felt more like himself, even if that included the pain of wanting a woman he couldn't have. He stayed on the recovery road but also continued to take small steps to enjoy things he used to, before addiction trapped him in its claws.

Under the care of Joseph, his therapist, Zazzle appreciated the occasional decaffeinated coffee and even a bit of sugar without overstimulating. When he'd had espresso in Amsterdam, the jitters had racked his body. He couldn't pinpoint if the restless sleep had resulted from the espresso or his desire for Velvet in his bed.

"I actually prefer tea nowadays but it's nice to change things up a bit here and there." Zazzle sat in Joseph's office. "My limits fluctuate in different settings so I just need to be vigilant and stay aware."

"It's good to see you respecting your boundaries, Isaak. It's a process."

"I'm willing to do the work."

"Anything else on your mind?" Joseph asked.

A list long enough to hit the floor came to Zazzle's mind. "There's always a lot on my mind."

"Anything you want to share?"

"No. The information you gave me on relationship stress was great, Doc. I think it helped give me more closure with Tres Armadas."

"And Asha?" Joseph asked. "The last time we spoke you were still pretty torn up about it. How are you doing?"

He was still wrecked at losing Asha and wasn't ready to forget her, even though she'd shut the door on the special relationship they'd experienced together.

"I'm getting there," Zazzle offered and transferred his weight to one hip and leaned on the armrest. "There's still a large part of me that's unwilling to give up on her."

Zazzle had come clean with Joseph in an emergency session the day after the Egyptian. Coupled with his breakup with Velvet, the urge to placate his pain had gnawed at him. Joseph had provided him with some tools and encouragement to help him through the bumpy road.

"We can explore your feelings about this..."

"Maybe another time, Doc." Zazzle had opened himself to therapy and did his best to express his feelings but his breakup with Velvet continued to be too raw to vocalize.

"Of course. I'll be here when you're ready."

They wrapped up his session shortly after and scheduled his next appointment.

Joseph stood and shook his hand. "You're doing well, Isaak. You should be proud of yourself."

"Thanks."

Zazzle returned to his LA home. He'd be here until Tres Armadas played Temptation. Over the next few weeks, he, Maartin and Christian had a lot of scheduled press and meetings with Maggie about their plans for their documentary and final tour next year.

He'd finally made amends with the end of Tres Armadas, and felt grateful he got to do one more tour with his DJ brothers next year.

His phone sounded and he scrolled through a list of new messages. His eyes bugged out and his pulse soared when a message from Velvet was in the list. He typed and deleted several times. For the first time he didn't know what to write. Nothing he typed seemed an appropriate response for her message. For a long time he stared at the blank text box until he finally typed.

Zazzle: Thanks.

"Laffart," he cursed at himself. Only an asshole texted the woman he loved with a one-liner after a split.

It was the best he had until he could figure out what

to say to her to get her back. She'd given him the opening he'd longed for and he'd squandered it with *thanks*?

"I'll work out. Yes, that's what I'll do." Perhaps if he exercised his body, the blood flow would help his mind create a better response.

A half hour and a high-intensity five-mile run later, he still drew a blank. He wanted Velvet back but she didn't think she possessed the strength to be with him. He spent a lot of time agonizing over the choices he made in the past, but he'd done his time in rehab and managed his recovery. He couldn't change her beliefs any more than she could change his. He put the idea of an additional response to rest.

He headed for the shower when his gate monitor sounded. He checked the camera screen and saw Christian and Maartin's faces displayed.

"Christian?"

"Let us in, man." Zazzle let him in, no questions asked.

A few minutes later Christian and Maartin piled into his home. The energy of old friends lifted the room.

"Pack a bag, you're going with us." Christian waved a hand to encourage his hustle.

"Go where?" Zazzle asked, stuck between packing a bag and listening for an answer.

Maartin also hurried him along. "We're going to Vancouver."

"What's in Vancouver?"

"A party," Maartin answered.

"And the VC Festival," Christian added.

"But really, the party," Maartin emphasized.

Zazzle's head oscillated from Maartin to Christian and back again. "I can't party, you guys know that."

"This one will be okay." Christian leaned against the white archway in his living room. "We've made sure of it."

"What party? Whose party?"

"LED's party by the lake."

"But we have press and engagements, here in LA. Meetings." Zazzle raised a skeptical brow. Christian and Maartin weren't in the habit of blowing off their schedules.

"We don't actually leave until the weekend," Christian clarified.

Zazzle flapped his arms. "Then why are you telling me to pack now?"

"Fair point. We wanted you to get excited." Maartin clapped his hands overhead and did a two-step he normally reserved for the stage.

Zazzle cleared his head of the mind aerobics his friends dragged him through. "I really don't think I should go, but thanks."

"A little bird named Candy heavily alluded to the possibility that Velvet will be there." Maartin's admission focused Zazzle's concentration.

Zazzle shifted his weight.

"You've been moping around like most fools in love." Christian, who'd been leaning against the archway, pushed off his shoulder and stood up straight. "Just go see her."

"She doesn't want to see me." He'd tried to mend things for weeks after the night they broke up, with no luck. How could he expect anything different at this point?

"You really believe that?" Maartin asked.

"I don't know what I believe anymore." Each time

Zazzle made a decision a new opportunity to connect with Velvet came up.

"We're leaving in two days. At the very least we get to see our friends play at a festival we're finally not headlining," Christian said. "Get your shit packed. You're going."

Chapter Twenty-Nine

"Welcome," LED said as more people poured into his Vancouver home. With drink in hand he ushered each one inside.

Velvet hugged him tight before entering the house.

"Why you have us come all the way out here is beyond me. It's straight boonies, man, and colder than everywhere else," Rob said.

"I'm a light-emitting diode. Just partake in my microcosm of positivity," LED said.

"Dafuq?" Rob asked.

Velvet laughed at their interaction. "That's what LED means," she whispered to him.

Rob flipped back his short dark hair that had grown over the summer. The trip with Rob and Tekko was just what the doctor ordered.

"We smuggled this one across the border." Tekko pointed above Velvet's head.

"Quit it." Velvet swatted at him.

"Headlining Temptation Festival has changed you."

"Shuddup, Rob." She laughed.

She was happy to be out of LA and with her friends even though what she needed to find was a place to call home. LA wasn't the same without Candy but they needed healthy separation. Vancouver with LED was Candy's home now.

Candy had only left for Vancouver a week earlier, but Velvet was excited to see her friend. She and Candy had a week or two before they would be meeting with their label. At that time, they hoped to finalize the cover and tracks and get the actual release dates. If Velvet hadn't come out, that might be the next time she saw Candy.

Candy ran in from the back of the house, slammed into Velvet and gathered her into a hug. "I miss you!" Candy yelled.

Velvet couldn't stop laughing. Candy had dyed her hair jet-black but maintained a blond streak. It was the only way Velvet recognized her.

"Wow! That's a big change," Velvet said when Candy released her.

"I know. I debated doing it because black is so tough to change back, but I'm rockin' it, no?"

"I love it." Velvet played in Candy's hair. "It's much more edgy. No more pixie."

"I'm glad *you* like it." She side-eyed LED. "*Bernard* prefers the blond but he knows he has zero say."

Velvet laughed.

"Who's playing first?" LED asked.

"I'm on it." Rob smacked his hands together and rubbed them. "A house full of DJs? Let the 'jonesing' commence."

"Colossal," Tekko cheered.

"Excellent choice, my friend." Velvet pressed her finger to her nose and pointed at Tekko.

"I thought you'd like that particular word varietal."

More people piled into the house and Velvet's ears perked. "Did someone say Luke?" she asked Candy.

"I think they did."

In a moment the two women were bolting to the living area to find Luke "The Musical Prophet" Anderson, with Leona Sable by his side. Velvet smiled when she saw them. Not only did they arrive together, but were holding hands and quite open about their relationship. Velvet wasn't sure she'd ever seen them be this intimate publicly because Leona was so professional.

Luke's green-gray eyes spotted her and Candy. "What's up, ladies?" He extricated himself from the small crowd and came over to both her and Candy. Being a taller man, he bent to give each of them a kiss on the cheek. "I can't stop hearing about you guys. Congratulations on Temptation. I'm proud of you."

Luke always smelled so good and he as usual made her blush.

"Thanks," Candy said. Similar reaction.

"You always believed in us. We'll always be grateful for that," Velvet said. "It's like a dream come true."

"How do you feel about the album? 'Be You' and 'Love Me Love You' are feral tracks."

"We're happy with it. It was hard work but it comes out soon. Thanks again for working with us on one of the album tracks."

"Anytime," he said. "I can't wait to hear the finished product. You guys should talk to Leona about your tour. I'm sure she'll have some insights that can help you out."

Luke departed and Velvet and Candy found their way to Leona. They were here at the party to relax and have fun but they tried never to miss an opportunity.

"Hey, Leo." Velvet jumped in as soon as Leona was released from her conversation.

"Hey, guys." Leona hugged both her and Candy.

Leona, who often rocked a high bun, had her hair out in natural spiral curls. Her dark skin glowed from the sunbeams filling the room. "It's good to see you. Congrats on everything you accomplished. Wow! What a year for you. I'm glad you guys went with our company to represent you. Sonny's great."

"Yeah, she is. We really like her," Candy said.

"She told me that you guys are touring next year."

Velvet nodded. "The album is done and we're really proud of it. We want to come out with the best tour possible, so we were hoping that you'd think about working with us. We do early bird ticket sales starting next month."

Leona was quiet for a moment. "So, I will tell you guys the same thing I told Sonny. I need to think about it and get back to you in a few weeks."

Velvet met Candy's somber pout.

This was not the response Velvet had expected. Velvet tried to keep her shoulders from slumping. She hadn't said no.

"It's just that Luke and some of my other artists keep me pretty busy. I may not be in a position to physically go on tour."

Her and Candy's shoulders slumped some more.

"But it's not a hard no." Leona smiled.

"We'll take it," Candy squawked.

"If I can't do it, I'll make sure you get a legitimate tour manager, not a scam artist." Leona gave them a knowing smile. Everyone had heard about the greatest festival that never happened by this point.

"Thanks, Leo."

Luke made his way back to his girlfriend and wrapped his arms around her waist from behind and kissed her neck. Velvet witnessed Leona as she struggled out of Luke's embrace, but ultimately leaned into his affection.

Velvet remembered when Zazzle had given her a similar caress not too long ago. She craved everything about him from his support and advice, to the way he stroked her back when they lay in bed together. She blushed at the intimacy between Luke and Leona.

"Enjoy the party, you guys."

"Come on. Let me show you the place. We can't stalk them all night. That'd be weird." Candy pulled and started the tour. The gorgeous property sat by the lake. A pathway connected to the dock. The four-bedroom house complete with studio had a homey feel with touches Velvet immediately identified as Candy. In addition to her clothes, there were fresh, bright-colored flowers in the bedrooms, and photos of them with their friends on tour.

"I keep telling Bernard, we have to invite people here next summer. The lake is amazing. People can hang out on the patio and even do some boating and swimming. Everything's been updated and so much light comes in here it's sick."

Velvet watched her friend. Candy sounded like she was talking about their house and the property as if it were hers. Velvet stifled a smile.

"What?"

"Nothing," Velvet said. "This place suits you. You're ready. You know, for all of this with LED."

"Am I that bad?"

Velvet linked arms with her. "Not at all. You feel at home here, with him. That's important."

"He's being so patient with me." Candy fretted.

"As he should."

"But he's my one and only." Candy hugged herself in that "I'm so in love" kind of way.

"I miss having you in LA, but you belong here with him."

"Vancouver is pretty far from Cali."

"It is. But you're a millionaire now," Velvet teased. "You can have an apartment in LA and a home in Vancouver."

Candy's face brightened. "You're right."

"I'm just sayin'," Velvet sang. "But whatever you want to do, we'll work it out."

"And whatever *you* want to do we'll work it out," Candy flipped it on her.

"Yeah, we will." She nodded.

"So…umm…how are you doing with…you know, the Zazzle situation."

Velvet swallowed hard. "I miss him but I screwed up."

"What'd you screw up?" LED parked himself behind Candy. He massaged his girlfriend's shoulders.

"Eavesdropping as usual, I see." Candy waggled a finger at him.

LED had been there that night and had witnessed all the gory details.

"I don't even know if he wants to talk to me." Velvet crossed her arms. She remembered the message he'd sent back when she texted him about Tres Armadas. "Thanks" was all he had to say to her.

LED let out a heavy sigh. "He went to the Egyptian for you…that place—"

"I know that's where Zazzle's bender was caught on video," Velvet recanted. "The partying, the drugs, the girls. That's why he didn't want to go back. Bad memories."

Velvet had seen Zazzle do okay in other situations, but she'd been worried about Candy and made the mistake of asking him to help her.

"Wait. Do you know what happened at the Egyptian that night?" he asked.

"Yeah, I just told you. The video."

LED's expression slacked and he pinched the bridge of his nose. "I don't think you do."

"What are you talking about, babe?" Candy appeared as curious as Velvet felt. Whatever troubled him had to be dreadful.

"His heart stopped. Like people thought he legit died that night," LED delivered with deserved drama.

"What?" Velvet's voice boomed. Her throat went dry and her knees wobbled.

"You didn't know. That's why being there affected him like that. Not just because he partied there or because drugs and booze were around. I've seen him in a club setting in Ibiza and he just chilled with his tea."

Velvet didn't think she could feel any worse, but she was wrong. She should have held Zazzle in her arms that night, kissed him all over, stroked his hair and spoke to him in her shitty Dutch. Instead she'd left.

"Don't, Velvet. You didn't know." Candy put her arm around her shoulder. "You were trying to do what you thought was best for him. For both of you."

"I need to find him." Velvet's shoulders slumped. "I don't even know if he wants to talk to me anymore." She pulled out her phone and her fingers moved with inhuman speed.

"Whatcha gonna say, Velveteen?"

"Probably everything inappropriate to put in a text," she said.

There was some commotion and all Velvet heard was Tekko's loud excitement from the living room.

"Oh, man. I didn't think you guys would make it. This is bananaz!"

She followed Candy and LED to find all three members of Tres Armadas.

"Oh my gosh," she said and held on to Candy. "Did you know?"

Candy grinned. "You don't have to text him. You can go tell him all those things."

"Yeah." She rubbed at the lens of tears covering her eyes.

Christian, Maartin and Zazzle navigated their way through handshakes, hugs and peer fandom in a house full of DJs.

Zazzle's eyes found her and she recognized the softness in his features. It was the same softness she saw when he told her he loved her.

"Velvet," Christian greeted her first with a goofy grin on his chiseled features. He kissed her cheek.

"Hey," she croaked.

Maartin hugged her. "Nice to see you again."

"Yeah, same."

Zazzle made a move toward her but stopped.

Velvet vaguely heard Candy and LED ushering people toward other parts of the house. The room cleared and she heard the inner workings of her own respiratory system. His, too.

His Adam's apple bobbed and he approached her, uncertainty in his steps. "I'm happy to see you, Asha."

"Me, too." Her hoarse voice gave her away. She appraised him. "Have you been okay?"

The closer he got to her the faster her heart raced, as if it would pound right out of her chest and into him.

"Yes, but I'm better now that I see you." He hit her with a half smile and she took it like a bullet. "Congratulations on Temptation. I know that was big for you. Did you get my text?"

"Yes. Thank you."

"I wanted to send something but I don't know where you live." He scratched his head.

"I don't have a place to live, yet," she said. "What were you going to send me?"

"Pannenkoeken," he said softly.

She reached for his hand.

Her body remembered his touch. The way he stroked her hand and kissed her temple. The feel of his warm body against hers and how he pleased her. She wanted to cry from longing and to hold him close and feel protected in his arms again.

But her heart needed him more and sought his forgiveness. In this moment she didn't judge him or mistrust herself to be with him. Every cell in her body objected to being without him.

She wrapped her arms around his waist. "I'm sorry." Her sobs weakened her and she couldn't even squeeze him.

"Why are you sorry, baby?" He separated enough from her to cup her face.

"I left when you needed me most. I didn't know about the Egyptian and what happened there. I never saw all the video because I couldn't watch, not after what I'd been through with Reynard. Seeing you like that would have killed me." She put her hand on his heart and huge droplets fell from her eyes. "Your heart stopped. For a moment you were gone. I didn't know, Isaak."

"Don't cry, *schatje*. It beats now." He kissed her lips. "For you."

She kissed him back and her salty tears wet their lips. His warm tongue played with hers and she consumed his scent. She moaned and smiled against his mouth.

"What was that?"

"I missed the lavender," she said.

"Just the lavender?"

"I missed you so much, Isaak. I never should have left you. I was scared, but being without you scared me more than anything."

"I've been existing these past few weeks. I don't want to be in survival mode anymore. I want to start living again, with you, and be better for you."

"You're perfectly imperfect just the way you are, Zazzle. Rehab, recovery, EMETAH and everything, and I want to be with you."

He wrapped his arms around her and pressed her against him. "I want to be with you, too." He kissed her neck. "All of you."

"Even the judgy, smothering bits? Because you know I'll be that sometimes."

"Yes, even those bits." His laughter vibrated against her breast like the wings of a hummingbird. "And do you think you can be with someone who will be in life-long recovery and will probably make mistakes but loves you and will do everything in his power to do his best?"

Her cheek rubbed against his shirt, signaling she agreed. "We can work at it, right?"

"Yes, *schatje*. Together we can do anything."

"I love you."

"I love you, too."

Epilogue

Velvet sucked the last bit of cherry flavor out of the gum left over from her Blow Pop as she ogled the Temptation Festival's Garden of Life–themed main stage. The aroma of hot grass wafted in through the VIP viewing area. Artists and festival staff funneled in and around but she'd garnered a small quiet space. The massive audience enjoyed the sounds of the current performer. Bedazzled Beats were a few hours away from being on that same stage for the first time. Her arm hurt from pinching it over the past few weeks to triple and quadruple check that she hadn't dreamed all this up.

"Schatje." Hands slinked around her waist and she turned, cocooning her body to Isaak's arms.

"Hi." She peered into shining amber orbs.

"Hallo." He pecked her lips and regarded her clothes. "I like this… Exquisite for your main stage debut."

"This old thing?" Velvet said. She'd dressed up for the occasion in high-waisted, skin-tight black latex leggings and three-quarter-sleeved hot-pink mesh shirt with yellow stitching. Her visible black bra underneath created another level of sexy.

"If this is old then I'm dying to see the new one." He tipped her chin up to his for another kiss. "What are you doing over here all by yourself. Candy said you took Nuts for a ride. It's a wonder I found you."

Her gloss stained his mouth and she thumbed it off. "I just wanted to take it in." Velvet shared this moment with so many people but she had finally made it here and she'd only wanted a few solitary minutes to relish the pre-performance anticipation.

"How are you feeling?"

She flapped her lips. "So much has happened since last year's festival. We met here."

"We did. Our first kiss was right…over…there." He pointed to the field.

"Stop being super cute." She pondered her statement. "No, don't stop."

He laughed. "It's been a wild year."

She scanned all the events, good and bad, like a movie on fast-forward and her emotions swelled with each one. "It's unreal but I wouldn't change any of it."

"Me either."

"I'm so ready and so excited to be on that stage."

"It's going to be fucking amazing, *schatje*."

"Thanks, baby." She hugged his hips.

"By the way, someone wants to say hello to you." He walked with her until they reached a man who stood close to Isaak's height and with his likeness.

"Hi, Asha."

"Jan. It's nice to see you again." She hesitated to embrace him. At the last Tres Armadas show Zazzle had introduced them but given their breakup, it didn't seem right for her to linger past their initial greetings.

"Same here," Jan said.

"Your brother forgot to mention that you were coming." She smacked Zazzle's butt.

"Surprise," Zazzle said.

Jan smiled at their exchange. "We just wanted to wish you a good show for tonight."

"Thank you." Velvet wanted to get to know Isaak's brother especially after all she'd heard about him and how he'd really stood by Isaak when he decided to go to rehab. "Will you be in town long? I'm hoping we can hang out or something."

"I heard of this 4am eats thing…"

Velvet laughed out loud. "Yes! You should come."

Zazzle massaged her shoulders.

"I certainly will."

"Well, I should head back. I have to meet up with Candy and the team for pre-show press."

"We'll walk you back."

Zazzle and Jan walked her back to the main stage where they connected with the team. He had his own press to do with Tres Armadas but would be back for Bedazzled Beats' set.

"Knock 'em dead, baby," he said, giving her a deep and lengthy kiss before he departed.

She couldn't wipe the smile off her face if she tried.

The setting sun shined down on the crowd and the temperature was as perfect as warm fudge brownies out of the oven. The wind that kissed Velvet's dark skin was much cooler than the places they traveled during the year.

"It's showtime, ladies."

"You nervous, Velveteen?"

"Not at all, Candy Cane." The weight of her tears pooled in her lower lids.

"We made it, girl." Candy hugged her shoulders.

"Yeah, we did." Velvet offered Candy a shaky fist bump, which she returned. "Let's get 'em."

They were announced and the thunderous roar of the fans at the Temptation Festival rumbled through Velvet and her heart swelled. On the bumpy road to Temptation, Velvet had almost lost Candy to the dark side and Zazzle to her fear. Though excited to headline, she would trade it all to have the people she loved alive, happy and safe.

Her legs felt like jelly and she and Candy mounted the stairs to the DJ table. In her dreams she imagined Temptation's high and elaborate stage countless times. This year's Garden of Life theme had to be the most elaborate ever. Now as she absorbed the massive structure, bedazzled in their honor, she was speechless. She should have dreamed bigger because what she conjured in her mind didn't compare to her present reality.

The music blared through the speaker as their intro played and she and Candy hid from view of the audience. The fans cheered for them to show themselves and Velvet had to stop herself from jumping before it was time.

The mood of the music changed. She and Candy jumped up and onto the dials. The crowd went wild and Velvet spoke into a mic.

"Whaddup, LA! Are you ready to get loud?"

Ear-splitting cheers were returned.

"Let's go!"

Velvet donned her headphones and played the beginning of their first track, tapping buttons and turning dials for the desired effects. The music approached its crescendo and the crowd soared to new heights of excitement, frantically waiting for the beat to drop. When Velvet brought the beat back, the bass trembled through the crowd. She nodded triumphantly over at Candy and smiled.

The fans appreciated their selection, their arms waving like a horizontal flag in the wind over the festival grounds. The beauty of the San Gabriel Mountains, from perched position, offered an endless venue for them to perform. Velvet's love beamed out to every one of the fans who had come out to hear her and her bestie play. Velvet moved to the beat and her bedazzled headphones, resting on her cheek, sparkled against the lights. She picked up the mic.

"LA! We're thrilled to be here playing for you tonight. Thank you so much for voting for us. You loved us and supported us and we're giving it right back!" Both she and Candy formed their hands into hearts and beamed them out to the crowd.

"Mind if we invite some friends onstage?" Velvet tossed it over to Candy.

The crowd went bonkers.

Candy grabbed her mic. "Let's bring 'em out! Welcome LED, Rob Ready, Tekko, Bliss and Zazzle to the stage!"

The melody to "Love Me Love You" played. Velvet could barely hear the music over the cheers. She swallowed the lump in her throat as she looked to her right, where Candy bounced to the music. Candy, more posh than ever with her black hair, remained the posy-picking pixie Velvet cherished. To her left, the man she loved, who helped her realize she could love without smothering. And sandwiched in between were their friends who always supported them. They all played their parts of the track. Velvet's fans exploded. Zazzle hopped up onto the stage and the fans gobbled up his signature dance moves.

"They're wild'n out!" Rob yelled.

LED and Bliss weren't on the track but crew was crew and they danced with Tekko, Rob and Zazzle.

They played the rest of their set and the past year of

her life flashed before her. The places she'd been, the people she'd met and the experiences she'd had. The emotions welled inside her and she channeled it into the music. The music she loved, the music that transcended generations and transformed and evolved.

"DJ FeNom. I know you're listening. This one's for you," Velvet shouted.

She and Candy dropped into their song "Be You," and the fear that the stage would crumple under them from the vibration of thousands of feet was real.

"Thanks, guys, you've been awesome! We'll see you soon." Velvet danced and jumped around on the stage as Candy closed out their set. The excited cry of the audience echoed through the venue.

She reached her hands out to the swarm of people as if wanting to touch each one and sang the song with them. She bounced over to Candy and hugged her friend. Her eyes found Zazzle dancing on the sidelines and she blew kisses at him.

Velvet had her friends and the man she loved, and life was sweeter than she'd ever imagined.

* * * * *

Acknowledgments

First and foremost, I thank God for His gifts and blessings.

A heart-filled and hearty thank-you goes to the dynamic duo: my agent, Sarah E. Younger, and my editor, Stephanie Doig, for your support of these books, these characters and this world. Thank you to Carina Press and team for always honoring my work with great imagery and content.

To my phenomenal writing partners and beta babes, thank you for all your insights; Tanya, Tere, Maria, Adriana, Anna, Michelle and Tamar. Thank you for your time and support. I am so lucky to have you. Thank you to RWA/NYC, the romance writing community and those within it who continue to honor, share and promote diverse stories.

To my family and friends for your understanding, love and support, as well as for helping me find balance so I can enjoy this journey. You rock and I love you.

Last but not least to the readers and fans, thank you for escaping in these stories with me. I hope, whether in books or in real life, that you are loved.

About the Author

JN Welsh is a native New Yorker and natural storyteller. As a young student in school, she was a voracious reader who stole her older sister's romance novels. She graduated to writing entertaining love stories, in the form of long notes passed in class, for her friends. The writer was born.

She writes entertaining, often humorous, and provocative tales about strong, career-driven, multicultural heroines who are looking for love. Her punchy, flowing dialogue and big-city stories are heartwarming and stick to your ribs. When she's not writing she can be found dancing, wine-ing, rooting for her favorite baseball team and/or indulging in countless guilty pleasures.

Twitter: www.Twitter.com/JN_Welsh

Facebook: www.Facebook.com/JNWelshBooks

Instagram: www.Instagram.com/JN_Welsh

Read on for an excerpt from
In Tune,
the first book in author JN Welsh's
Back on Top series.

If Leona Sable had known how this day was going to turn out, she would have stayed in bed, nestled against her boyfriend pillow with the covers pulled over her head.

How the fuck did I get here? A conversation with her boss and mentor, Abraham Wallace, that started with "The client only wants you" and ended with "Meet me at the Metro Hotel this evening at seven and be dressed for a night out." That's how.

Ever since that conversation a few short hours ago, Leona had been collecting intel on Electronic Dance Music DJ Luke "The Musical Prophet" Anderson.

Had Abe not looked so stressed and hell-bent on acquiring said potential client, she'd still be in hiding, paper-pushing due diligence forms.

Leona sat in the hairdresser's chair in Midtown Manhattan. Her tight corkscrew curls dripped wet onto the towel draped over her shoulders, while she pressed the cell phone to her ear.

"Dale, sweetie, you're telling me that Luke's manager left his tour? Just like that? Why?" Leona strained to hear above the light music playing in the salon.

Dale, her fabulous, long-time source, swam in the know while others simply dipped their toe into the pool.

"Allegedly, there was a mash-up of problems. Money issues and fraternization," he whispered into the phone.

Leona wasn't a gossip but she sometimes had to play the role of one to get the information she needed.

"They were dating? Was it serious?"

"Who knows in this industry? But I will say that hearts were broken. And..."

Leona couldn't believe the next words that came out of Dale's mouth, and neither would Abe when she briefed him. "No!"

"Yes, but you won't find a lick about it in the rags. The family is wealthy and adamant about her privacy. They keep paying out."

"Then why would she do that?"

"I don't know, girl. Money got these people like... whoa!"

"Stop." Leona laughed, assessing her milk chocolate brown image in the mirror. "Thanks, D. You gave me a lot to work with. I appreciate it."

"Listen, love. Please don't ever go underground again. I need my concert tickets."

"I promise." Leona hung up.

Her hairdresser started to work. "Let me get started on your twists."

"Change of plan, Kim. Geisha bun. Sleek and sexy."

Kim stilled with wide-toothed comb in hand. "You haven't had that style in a while. Does this mean you're back?"

Kim's excitement surprised her. "No." Leona's raised voice carried above the music.

"Okay, okay. Just asking." Kim's grin reflected in the mirror.

Leona surveyed the room and tapped her left earlobe. "The last thing I need is that rumor getting out."

Kim readied her tools—complete with blow-dryer and brush—for Leona's hair. "Maybe after tonight it won't be a rumor."

For the past year, Leona had stayed out of the spotlight. Lately, she had to admit that the administrative role Abe allowed her to perform was a snore fest, and she'd thought about waging a comeback and once again doing the work she loved. Though she was an experienced personal manager, with production and tour experience, the entertainment industry was fickle and would make her pay for her absence. More importantly, a nagging question remained.

Am I ready?

Leona checked her messages and returned a call to Tracy Ruiz, one of the resident lawyers at Wallace Entertainment. "Hey, Tracy. Got anything on Mr. Wonderful?"

"He doesn't have any priors, but there have been some disturbances of the peace. Mr. Anderson has had a string of episodes involving angry outbursts, but no one was hurt. Only a couple of scuffles here and there."

"This just gets more interesting by the hour. Okay, Tracy. Thanks."

What the hell did Abe get me into? A client with a shady business past and anger management issues... Seriously? A shiver scuttled up her back and her shoulders shimmied in release. *Just get him in the door, Leo, and you'll be done.*

Kim took a brief break from pulling at Leona's kinky curls. "You cold, girl?"

"Oh, no, I'm good. Just some old ghosts trying to bully me."

Kim patted her shoulders.

Leona was tempted to contact Luke's family members for more information, but her experience with her ex-boyfriend gave her pause. The media craziness had adversely affected the Sable family. And though she only sought information—it was a line she was unwilling to cross.

With her hair completed, Leona thanked Kim and headed home. In her walk-in closet, Leona chose her outfit while she listened to one of Luke's interviews. He mentioned a fondness for animal crackers and she chuckled. "And not just any kind either." She loved researching potential clients. Sometimes their quirks and preferences were predictable, other times quite unexpected.

Her phone rang. She picked up when she saw it was Abe.

"Leo? I'm on my way to the hotel. What'd you find out, darlin'?" he asked. Though from Scottish and Spanish stock, Abe had been born and raised in North Carolina. He used the touch of Southern twang in his voice to sweet-talk anyone into doing his bidding.

"He's very into his fans. In fact, that's why this guy is all over the place and not just in the States." She put Abe on speaker and scrolled through some notes on her phone. "Yeah, Brazil, Australia, United Arab Emirates… Yikes. The list of worldwide appearances goes on for pages. What a treacherous schedule."

"Hard worker. What else?"

"He's passionate about his music and active on all social media outlets. We like passion."

"We?"

"Wallace Entertainment," Leona clarified. "People have nice things to say about him. But, Abe? There's a bit of controversy around his last management. His ex-manager stole some astronomical amount of money from him and—"

"That's an unfounded rumor. We need him, Leo."

There's that desperation again. "I get that you want him, but..."

"No, Leo. The company needs him."

"The company? Okay, Abe. What's really going on here?"

Abe was silent. "I'm in a cab, coming up on 14th Street. We'll talk later. See you in a bit."

"Abe..." she called to a dead line. *Damn it. What the hell?* She breathed deep.

She dressed in snug off-white leather bootleg pants and a fitted black shirt with capped sleeves. Sexy black lace accented the top of the shirt—from above her bust to her neck—and covered her back. It was the perfect day-to-night outfit, yet still professional. Too much time had passed since her life required such attire. The outfit felt foreign at first, until the old familiar part of her began to stir.

A sheer off-white shawl draped over her shoulders allowed the light material to pop off of her brown skin. Black peep-toe booties added four inches to her five-foot-four frame. She quickly evaluated her image in the mirror and extended her arm to the reflection, as if offering a handshake to see how her outfit moved. She hadn't done that in years. *You're nervous.* She wiggled her shoulders. *Shake it off. This is old hat, Leo.*

She didn't know what situation awaited her at the Metro Hotel but she was as ready as she'd ever be.